THE FIVE
SORROWFUL MYSTERIES
OF ANDY AFRICA

Stephen Buoro

BLOOMSBURY CIRCUS

LONDON • OXFORD • NEW YORK • NEW DELHI • SYDNEY

BLOOMSBURY CIRCUS
Bloomsbury Publishing Plc
50 Bedford Square, London, WC1B 3DP, UK
29 Earlsfort Terrace, Dublin 2, Ireland

BLOOMSBURY, BLOOMSBURY CIRCUS and the Bloomsbury Circus logo
are trademarks of Bloomsbury Publishing Plc

First published in Great Britain 2023

A catalogue record for this book is available from the British Library

ISBN: HB: 978-1-5266-3799-4; TPB: 978-1-5266-3802-1;
EBOOK: 978-1-5266-3800-7; EPDF: 978-1-5266-3803-8

2 4 6 8 10 9 7 5 3 1

Typeset by Integra Software Services Pvt. Ltd.

Printed and bound in Great Britain by CPI Group (UK) Ltd, Croydon CR0 4YY

To find out more about our authors and books visit www.bloomsbury.com
and sign up for our newsletters

THE FIVE
SORROWFUL MYSTERIES
OF ANDY AFRICA

for my Mama
her marvellous mysteries

all
africans
have
haloes
circling
around
their
heads
someday these haloes will fuse into a planetary fire
that
HXVX
cannot
stand

I: The Agony in the Garden

Definition: A permutation is a one-to-one correspondence between a set and itself.

1

Dear White People,

I love white girls. Especially blondes. Blondes who wear their hair in ponytails and once a week in pigtails. Is this a fetish? I don't know. I'm just pretty sure I'll marry a white girl, a blonde. Do I think Black girls are ugly? Of course not. That would mean Mama is ugly. And I'm not gonna take that shit from anybody.

The problem is, I don't know what blondes are really like. Yes, I've watched a million Hollywood movies from pirated DVDs. My phone is a database of blonde shades 'cause I can't pass a blonde pic without downloading it. I've got exactly seventy-two blonde friends on Facebook. And at night when everyone has boarded sleep to Mars, I check out Pornhub™ for blonde pubes and use a hand, etc.

In fact, I haven't *seen* a blonde before. Because this is Africa. And there are -0.001 blondes here.

I hate myself for telling you my $64,000 secret. See, my mama is blacker than you can ever believe. Skin as dark as blackberries, hands as rough as sandpaper, but with a kiss as wet and cool as lip gloss. Her stomach was cut open twice: first when Ydna refused to be born, and second when I was born. Her stomach was cut open. So that I could step into this damn world. And say I prefer blondes! I don't know who Papa is. And Mama has been licking me sweet all through my life. Licking my earlobes and my eyelids. And here I am saying I prefer blondes. Blondes who I have never seen!

Epic.

I don't hate myself. But you get the idea.

I'm sure Ydna hates it when I talk about blondes. He came out of Mama two years before I was born. Like a figurine. No sound in his open mouth. No heartbeat in his chest. I know I'm him somehow. That I peeped into this world, saw how shitty it was, and turned back. Every day I feel him around me, in me. His anger pulsing in my blood, his breath foaming under my skin. He must be the reverse of me. Because he tells me stuff about myself that I don't wanna hear.

Still, I love blondes. Each strand of hair like a long, sweet sun. Hair like ripples of water chasing each other. I swear I can see my face reflected clearly on each strand! I go to bed hungry most nights. I sleep on my dead mat in our dead living room with dead electricity. And with my last energies I reach into my shorts and think about blondes. And peace flows down my heart to my stomach and down to my feet. And I'm filled. And I sleep satisfied. Like a boy who's eaten a dozen cheeseburgers, though I don't know the taste of that shit. And I sleep knowing the future is mine.

A fifteen-year-old African genius poet altar boy who loves blondes is not a criminal, not a racist, not a sell-out.

But a sweet, cool, pitiful African boy.

+

God must be testing my love for blondes. Because at this time when I constantly see visions of them, even at Mass, Eileen comes to Kontagora. Isaiah is telling Mama and me about her.

'She didn't come from Ikeja or Obudu Ranch,' he says, as if Mama and I don't know her name sounds foreign. 'She came from the UK. From Father McMahon's country. In fact, she's Father McMahon's oldest niece.'

That's the kind of guy Isaiah is, with his shiny bald skull and eternally red eyes: a donor of useless details. He's Father McMahon's cook. He's always begging Father McMahon for some English crisps, toothpaste, cream. He's always asking Father McMahon about snow: 'Is it sweet like ice cream? Do dogs lick it?'

He's chilling out, legs crossed, in the plastic chair we offer guests. A cup of water stands untouched on the table before him, a fly noising around it, undecided, because the cup doesn't contain Fanta. A faint smell of perspiration separates Mama and me. We're sitting on our sofa pretending not to feel its valleys and gorges or see the ant zigzagging about the arm. At the door-mat a fleet of ants are fooling with a dead cockroach. Pulling and kicking. Cursing, calling for backup. If Mama sees the ants, or worse the cockroach, she'll smack me on the back for not properly sweeping the living room.

It's Sunday. We've just returned from Mass, our necks still fizz-ing from the stings of the yellow sun. Mama hates Sundays. She earns no naira and must padlock her photo studio. 'Cause every-one in our town, even the imams on our streets, expects her to keep the sabbath day holy.

There are churches and mosques in our neighbourhood, and in most neighbourhoods of our town. Some used to be shops, their grilles and shelves still intact; others were warehouses, still dark, still stuffy. We hear the members of Soul of Christ chanting a cappella. They chorus in bass and soprano, crying like almajirai, calling to Archangels Michael and Uriel to open the Gates of Heaven, to send down fire, to shower the Face of God on Africa. They never clap or dance or play musical instruments. Because these lead to Hellfire. Because Christ and His Twelve never clapped or strummed guitars, because God never dances. I wonder whether Christ and His Twelve sang a cappella with such hungry, helpless voices, whether Christ's voice was bass, whether Judas's was falsetto.

We hear the drumrolls and the makossa singing of Apostolic Faith, the lead singer as she spits 'Devil shame on you', like a mother spitting on her wayward son, her cold saliva reclaiming all the love and blood she wasted. We feel the gusto of the back-ups, the stabbing of feedback.

Isaiah fans himself with the Sunday bulletin. 'See, she's very white,' he says, checking and rechecking, for our benefit, the rusty watch Father McMahon gave him. 'White like chalk. So white, unlike Father McMahon, who our evil sun has turned to a red man.'

He smooths the collar of his English polo shirt with the London Eye printed on the front. He uncrosses his legs, leans forward.

'And she's got long hair. It's like white gold. Seriously.' His big eyes sparkle as though he could steal her hair and get rich. 'They call it blonde hair. Or is it platinum? Anyways, she's a good girl. Like all whites, she brought gifts from the UK. Gave my little girl a toy rabbit. Can you believe it? She also gave me this foreign shirt. A good lady, I tell you. Like all whites.'

His gaze darts from me to his Nokia and back to me. Piercing. Eyes redder than ever.

'Why're you looking at me like that, boy?' he cries. 'I'm not her, you see.'

Mama chuckles, flashing her teeth stained with palm oil. 'You don't have to worry, Bro Isaiah,' she says, slapping me on the shoulder. 'Andrew mè will marry a girl as black as me. Isn't that right, Andy?'

She winks.

I force a smile. But I can see in the weak glint of her eyes that her laughter is forced, that she doesn't believe I'll ever marry a girl like her.

My eyes rove: Polished wooden cabinet. TV on top. The three of us mirrored, sitting, diminished. Beside it the desk calendar of Father Achi's priestly ordination – his palms pressed together, like a flame, in holiness, golden chalices hovering around him. Next: the crack on the blue wall, the crucifix of pale Jesus hanging, bright-red blood trickling from His hands and feet and sides.

Many times I feel Mama isn't my *real* mother because there's nothing visibly transferred. Her coal-black skin vs my chocolate. Her charcoal eyes vs my brown eyes. Her dimples vs my high cheekbones. She loves looking in mirrors and taking photos; I turn away from mirrors and hide at the rear in group photographs. She hums songs and I tune her out of my head; I check out blondes in movies and she orders me to eject any movie with even a blonde boy in it.

Maybe I'm like Papa. I really want to know who the hell he is.

his dusty feet
his booming voice
his grip on my shoulder

But Mama always refuses to say even a syllable about him.

Anyhow, I don't give a damn about who she thinks I'll marry. The x of the equation is that there's a blonde here in Kontagora, a platinum blonde if I'll believe Isaiah. A Marilyn Monroe who has never had mosquitoes sing in her ears and suck her blood, leaving red swellings as they fly away. A Princess Diana who has never woken up at midnight with hunger. A Taylor Swift who has never experienced a blackout.

'And the girl is so tall,' Isaiah says. 'Like, so tall. She's far taller than Andy boy here even though they're age-mates. She's even as tall as her uncle. She's like an athlete. Like a model.'

Mama is popping gum noisily like the hos that prowl outside her studio. 'That's the result of all those greens whites eat,' she says, nodding. She taps me on the shoulder. 'Don't worry, Andrew mè. You'll grow as tall as her someday. Even taller.'

I shift slightly in my seat, moving deeper into a valley. I wish she hadn't said that, about the greens whites eat. What greens is she even talking about? Such a comment makes me think of someone else, of Mama 2. Mama 2 wouldn't say such a thing.

'And Father McMahon is throwing her a massive feast this evening. With B-B-Q chicken, Sprite, and so forth. And he wants you to cover it,' Isaiah says to Mama.

She brightens instantly. Although Father McMahon owns a fleet of cameras, like all whites, he still invites her to photograph his events. He doesn't haggle with her like we Blacks do. In fact, she adds like three thousand naira in the receipts she writes for her services, and Father McMahon still pays. 'Things aren't this cheap in his country,' she'll say in Ososo with a laugh. 'Besides, whites are so rich that they can wipe their anuses with money.' She gives me a stern look whenever I don't laugh with her, and I join her with a false chuckle.

Whenever I spot her writing her receipts, I quickly look away. She holds the pen by its stem with utter concentration, her veins jutting out, as though she's performing surgery. Her handwriting, tbh, is like the prints of a hen digging for food, i.e. barely legible. Mama 2, on the other hand, writes as clearly and sweetly as Hillary Clinton. Still, those times I'm forced to confront Mama's writing, there's something amidst the clumsiness that stops my breath, that pierces my chest.

As Isaiah stands to leave, he slaps his shiny skull and calls himself a monkey.

'I always keep forgetting important things,' he says, turning to me. 'Father McMahon is inviting all you starving altar boys to Eileen's party.'

Mama raises her brows at him for calling me starving, but says nothing.

'There will be chicken feet and Cabin biscuits and Super D for you boys. Come in your best, Andy. Preferably in your Sunday wear.'

+

It's just Mama and me mirrored on the TV now. She yawns, her dimples burrowing. She's almost naked, wearing only the wrapper patterned with one thousand green yellow red blocks, tied around her chest, covering her down to her knees. She yawns again. The bump fastening her wrapper loosens. She quickly opens her wrapper – I catch the dark crooked line of her cleavage, the resignation of her fallen, mitten-like breasts – straightens it and ties it again, locking it under her armpit, forming a new bump. The hem of her slip peeks. She tucks it into the wrapper. She hasn't mended her bras this weekend. She often mends her two black bras on weekends, with a needle and white or yellow thread. I don't know why she never uses black thread. Why does she want to notice the stitches?

I always imagine her other self: Mama 2, who she'd be if she'd not been born on this crappy continent. For example, Mama 2 never needs to mend her bras. She has like a thousand in her wardrobe. She also doesn't wear wrappers. She wears flower-patterned pleated dresses, green or peach. Unlike Mama, who reads her Bible with a finger, slowly pronouncing or mispronouncing each word, Mama 2 is a doctor or lawyer, owns a Range Rover, wears glasses, and reads a book a week. She lives in a city in America or Europe, does not believe in ghosts, does not smell of must or perspiration. Her voice is calm and funny, and now and then she uses trisyllabic words or phrases such as 'so to speak'.

Mama finishes with her gum. She leans forward and plants it on the centre table. She sits back, rests her head on the sofa, closes her eyes. Her lips are heavy, pouty, alive, like black petals. Her cornrows are long and full; streaks of grey lean out of the dark mass, drooping, waving like a cornfield in the breeze as she turns and turns her head.

This is my mama:

the goddess
i want to be
and don't want to be

the seed
of my
shame

the twist
of my
fear

I want to say something to her. But I don't know what to say. I feel a strange need to talk to her, a duty to hold her hand. She's so close to me. 30cm away. Veins pushing out to me. Breath whistling in my ear. But she feels so far away.

The older I grow, the less we seem to speak. I remember those yellow days when she and I moulded sandcastles after rainfalls ... leaves smelling, stones glistening ... when she laughed out loud as I tickled her sides, telling me to stop but wanting me to continue. Those speechless moments when she looked in my eyes and smiled knowingly, her dimples sucking me in ... when

9

I found circling round their folds the words she couldn't speak: words without spellings, without sounds.

In times like this, in the epicentre of silences like these, I remember Ydna. And I miss him. And I try to trace time back to the very moment when this silence began. When it appeared suddenly like mushrooms do. Without a seed.

+

When you're younger you're closer to the world of the Unborn, to the world of the Recently Dead. Once, Ydna and I were One and the Same. We were concentric circles by day, fractals by night. He was my buddy, my shadow. This was before I turned eight. He had long, thin dreadlocks. He liked yellow shirts with blue collars and red flowers printed on the front. I felt him everywhere. His breath hissing in my ear when I did the dishes or solved maths, his eyes chasing me when I played football with other kids in the neighbourhood. At night Ydna and I whispered in the dark. We whispered after Mama and I had said Hail Mary and We Fly to Thy Patronage, after she was sure that I'd covered myself from mosquitoes with her old wrapper, that I'd closed my eyes and my chest was rising and falling normally.

Ydna and I talked about trees, the tallest one he dreamt of climbing, the sweets Okey had licked, the little homeless girl he'd seen sitting by the stream alone, with no one to talk to, her hair sandy and tousled. I shared my dreams of birds and my fears of snakes and juju with him. I was always dreaming about birds. Big white ones. With green eyes. Birds that neither sang nor cried. Why didn't I ever dream of sheep or lions or snakes, but only birds, arboreal birds?

Ydna always sat beside me on my mat. We inhaled and exhaled together. His head rested on his palm, unblinking eyes on me. I stared at the rain-stained ceiling, not seeing the dragon-shaped marks in the darkness, but picturing and reanimating them. His fingers and toes were unmoving, his soul absorbing every word I said. His breath smelt of mint or leaves sweating dew; my breath smelt of eba and egusi.

Every night Ydna and I whispered till the cocks crowed.

Everything changed when I turned eight, when I watched *The Matrix* and *Superman* and *Spider-Man* and told Ydna about them. Walls and mountains and black holes grew between us. Obstructing. Shattering. Everything changed when I told Ydna that I wanted to be like Neo. Like Clark Kent, like Peter Parker. That I wanted to be different.

That I wanted to be white.

Because:

only white people
could
freeze time
could
read minds &
stop bullets
could
fly

'Ydna, only white people can fly!'

He was silent. He didn't react. I repeated myself. Over and over, louder and louder. A tear dribbled down my cheek, down my ear. Down, down, until I heard its spatter on my mat. He didn't even look away when I turned to him, when I fingered his toe. I became sure that the mountains had grown between us because he suddenly rose and told me that he was sleepy, that he needed to go, when we hadn't even whispered for an hour.

I didn't see Ydna the next day.

Or the next one.

Or weeks after.

The rains came. Their waters smelt of fish. Looked like fish when they landed on the ground, when they rolled, when they hurried away. And at night, from my mat, through the window, I searched every drop of rain for Ydna.

My brother. His toe prodding my side. The way his front teeth shone in the dark and tore into the bread I'd saved all day for him. I kept saving bread for him even though I knew it would turn to crust by morning. But at least he ate the freshness. My Ydna savoured the freshness.

My dreams of birds stopped.

Several months afterwards, he finally came. It was night. I was on my mat, burning with malaria. He came after Mama had gone to her room, after she'd wailed that I shouldn't die, after she'd babbled prayers to St Michael and St Mulumba and Blessed Tansi. He walked into the room, dimmed the lantern so that I could see him clearer. He didn't say much. He just said, 'How far, Andy?' and sat down on our worn-out sofa (he'd never sat on the sofa before), jiggling his foot, banging the sofa with his heel, worsening my headache. I didn't mind. In fact, I got up. Shooed the malaria.

'What's up, bro?' I said.

'Fine,' he said.

'I really like your dreads. Seriously.'

'Okay.'

'Did you climb that tree?'

'No.'

'Why?'

Silence.

I felt his to–fro struggle to talk to me. His eyes kept beating off the finger of my gaze. His eyes: dark, watery, rippling. In them I spotted the most complicated jigsaw I've ever seen. Each piece of the puzzle was microscopic, shapeless. Each contained fish, birds, mountains, satellites, light speed, light years, an encyclopedia of info.

But I was not in them.

He leant forward, cleared his throat, parted his big lips. Then he got up and left. And I've not seen him since.

I often want to tell Ydna that being alive isn't easy. (Why else did he turn back and refuse to be born?) Death and dying are easy. Even boring. Life is hard. And senseless. Life is lifting a mountain without touching it, quenching a volcano without using even a drop of spittle. Life is waking up and finding hooks in your heart. If you remove any, you die. If you leave any, you die. You end up stuffing more hooks into your heart to stay alive.

But Ydna doesn't want to hear any of this. I know of his refusal to listen to me because I eavesdrop on his thoughts and record them in my diary. He accuses me of living the life he should have lived. He claims to have turned back, in Mama's womb, for a breather, so that he could refresh himself and arm his muscles for this world. But by the time he was ready, by the time he peered into Mama's womb, he saw that it was already full, nine months full. So he tried to push me back, to wherever I'd come from, so that he could slip his soul into my body and be born. But I refused to let that happen. It was this struggle that prevented Mama from bringing me out the normal way, that made the doctors cut her belly and pull out my Cursed self. It was this struggle that made the quack surgeons cut her in the wrong places, ruin her organs, so that she's now neither a woman nor a man.

I'm sure Ydna still cares about me. This is because, since I began to think about sinking my fingers into blonde hair, since I began to think of HXVX, since my maths teacher Zahrah Returned from the Sahara, I've felt him peeping at me several times. He peeps at me through the curtains, pretending to be a light breeze so I don't notice him. His voice filters into my head, repeating poems and phrases, pretending to be earworms. I often want to call him out on it. But I don't. I'm afraid that it would further chase him away from me. From my horizons, from my closed-bounded intervals.

+

I'm in our compound drawing water from the well for Mama. I lower the guga into the well, feel it land on water, and hold the rope for half a minute for the guga to fill. Above: Dancer-shaped cloud pinned to blue sky. No birds. Sunlight like a steam iron on my neck. The evil yellow sun ever blackening us, rather than painting our skin its colour.

'Allahu akbar!' the mosque behind our house calls for prayer. A rooster kukurukus in response. The conical loudspeakers of other surrounding mosques croak to life. Feedback spirals through the quiet. 'Allahu akbar! Allahu akbar. Ash-hadu alla ilaha illallah.'

There are mosques in every corner of our town. In fact, Kontagora is over 70 per cent Muslim, like most of the North.

On our streets are women in flowing chadors, men in jellabi-yas and hulas. Christian girls who wear trousers or short skirts or display their cleavages are chased and whipped by Muslim youths, their trousers or skirts shorn with scissors. Mama and I are from Ososo, in the South, which is mostly Christian, where girls can wear trousers without much hassle.

I pull out the guga and pour the water into a blue bucket with a sticker that says *Chioma wed Isaiah*. When the bucket is full I close the well with a roofing sheet. Place a car tyre on top – the sheet squeaks – and I carry the bucket by its handle to Mama.

She's sitting on a low stool outside our house. A charcoal fire is before her, a pot of egusi on top, a ladle in her hand – she stirs the soup. Although there's no meat in the soup, although there are only egusi and waterleaf and Maggi and onion in the pot, her expertise clouds the air with the pepper soup aroma you'll only smell in Utia and at naming ceremonies. The egusi coagu-lates into yellow patches, like fried egg, as Mama stirs and stirs.

'Fetch the garri, Andrew mè,' she says.

I pick up a plastic bowl beside her foot and march into the house, into her room (mattress, mirrors, lotions), which is also our food store, and untie a sack standing on the floor. I pick a mudu from the floor and use it to transfer garri from the sack to the bowl. Mama is preparing both lunch and supper so that she won't have to cook again when we return from Eileen's party. I fetch a double amount of garri, just enough for us to eat twice. I'm sure Slim or Morocca would've fetched much more so that they'd have extra to eat. But I don't dare provoke Mama.

Sometimes she ignites and explodes for almost no reason. Such as on those few mornings I get so lost in my wilderness of Ydna or blondes or Zahrah that I forget to greet her 'Good morning, Ma.' Or when, on those rare days we have electricity, she catches me watching Angelina Jolie as she raids tombs in supertight catsuits or Richard Gere as he places Julia Roberts on the piano and paws her boob. Mama will force me to sit beside her on the sofa. She'll clutch me by my neck, sometimes even make me sit on her lap. She'll sob. Remind me, again and again, how I stole her life from her, how the caesarean ruined her.

'Andrew mè, I'm empty. Neither here nor there. Nobody wants me.'

Once, years ago, I was so stupid that I replied, 'I want you, Mama.' She slapped me. Threw me off her lap, and I landed headfirst on the sofa.

Did I remind her of her husbands? I know she's been married more than once, but she's refused to tell me how many times. Whenever the thought flits through my head that Mama has been with two perhaps three perhaps four men, I usually don't know what to do with myself. The flashes of their hands on her body make me want to jump Somewhere, into Something, into Everything. To stop myself from jumping I begin to scream at my Cursed neurones to fucking shut up, to remember all Mama has done for me, all the sleepless nights she spends in her studio, the spitting she receives from pissed-off customers.

Whenever I have beef with Mama, I turn to Ydna in my diary. He makes me return to her. He tells me something new and funny about her that I don't know, like how she got the gap in her teeth. Sometimes he even lies to me. He says that most mamas don't dream about their kids, but that Mama often dreams about me. I know he's lying. But I believe him.

I stand and wait for Mama to take the garri from me. Slim or Morocca would've dropped the bowl by their mamas' feet and bounced to the living room, back to their EA mobile games. But I don't dare. Mama rests the ladle on a plate and takes the bowl from me.

'Ògbò, Andrew mè,' she says.

I sometimes pity Mama and wish she'd find someone asap. I've heard her men customers whisper about her 'nice legs' and 'phat booty', but none seems interested in crossing the line. In the past five years, three have shown interest. The first two only lasted a few days and vanished. But during their Super Bowls with Mama, they bought her earrings or panties or undersized shoes. Morning to night she faked smiles, wore eyeshadow and red lipstick and body-hugging dresses, trying to look like a twenty-something girl. But after each of the men disappeared she returned to the sighing make-up-less greying woman that she is.

But Mr Cosmas was different. He was a photographer like Mama. His wife had died some years before. He'd come to her studio, and he and Mama would talk for hours about lenses and camera gear and the advantages of film over digital photography. He said Mama was the best photographer he'd ever met.

For some reason Mama refused to put on her make-up or hair dye or tight-fitting dresses, but still Mr Cosmas continued to visit. They'd eat popcorn, photograph each other, tell jokes, and Mama would laugh for long stretches and indeed look like a twenty-something girl. She stopped smelling of must, her cooking had new somersaulting flavours, and at night she sang Whitney Houston. Weeks later, after Mr Cosmas refused to vanish, she began to invite him home. He'd buy me books and football jerseys; we'd argue about Messi and Ronaldo.

But everything changed the night she took him to her bedroom. They didn't last more than five minutes there. He came out of her room and walked out of the house and I've not seen him since.

For a few days after Mr Cosmas finally vanished, Mama didn't go to her studio. She lay all day in bed, and I made the charcoal fire and cooked us breakfast and dinner, took her food to her bed. I've asked her a couple times what happened between them, but of course she ain't saying shit. Maybe she told him about the botched caesarean.

Now, Mama adds some dry pepper to the soup. Stirs the mixture clockwise, then anticlockwise. She smiles at me.

'It smells so yummy, Ma,' I say in Ososo.

'Thanks,' she says.

'I wish I could cook as well as you do.'

'Really? Why not aim to be even better?'

'But, Ma, a chef is the last thing I want to become.'

'That's not the point.'

'What's it, Ma?'

'You need to be a great cook so that when you marry Fatima or whoever you choose to, you'll feed her very juicy meals.'

'You're funny.'

'Am I? I'd rather have you be the cook of your family than your wife.'

'Really?'

'Exactly. We women are done being servants or slaves. Those days are long gone.'

'But cooking isn't slavery.'

'You're not a girl, dear. You'll never understand.'

'But you used to do these things for Mr Cosmas.'

'What things?'

'You cooked for him. Even washed his clothes a couple times.'

'That's different.'

'How's it different?'

She sighs. I know a mini-sermon is coming. Although she's often silent, she won't pass a chance to dispense motherly tidbits.

'Andrew mè, the truth is that the women of my generation are still slaves. Sadly. Nothing we can do about it. We either choose to be slaves or choose not to exist. Those are our only choices. Worst is, we have to be slaves to find love. As hard as we try, we can't do without love. Love makes us feel less like slaves.' She adds a ladle of water to the soup. Stirs it a few more times. 'But your generation is different. You have computers, smartphones. You are educated. These days you don't need to physically meet someone to fall in love with them. Girls have access to many men, the opportunity to choose who they want. So if your generation still continues the violence of ours, then humanity is doomed.'

A Hausa girl knocks on our gate. 'Assalamu alaikum.' Our gate is actually a tiny iron door which amplifies taps better than it keeps hens out, but this little girl doesn't bang on it like others do. She lists her wares: fresh tomatoes, kuka, busheshen kubewa. Although I don't see her, I feel the impatience in her voice, the desire to sell all her stuff asap and return home. If she returns home by nightfall without selling all her wares, her mama will whip her ass and accuse her of playing around, of not knocking on enough doors.

'Allah ya kawo kasuwa,' Mama says.

'Ameen,' the girl mutters in disappointment and goes away.

'So, Mama . . .' I say.

'What?' she says.

'What about Mr Cosmas?'

'What about him?'

'Just wanted to know if you're still hearing from him.'

She's silent. I know she won't say anything. I feel bad for toying with her scars.

'No,' she says, rising. 'No, I haven't heard from him.'

She boils water, pours it into a large mortar, adds the garri, covers the mortar for five minutes, hums 'Into Your Sanctuary', nods, removes a mote from my hair, opens the mortar, pounds the garri with a pestle, cuts the resulting eba into oval cakes, wraps the cakes in polythene, puts the wrapped cakes in a thermal container, tells me to wash the mortar and pestle. I don't grumble, even though eba clings to surfaces, especially wooden ones, like superglue.

We move to the living room to eat. The door is open as wide as its hinges allow. The cream curtain flutters softly, lightening and darkening the room. Mama sits on the floor, splays her legs, balances her stainless-steel bowls of eba and egusi before her. She likes eating on the floor. She says it reminds her of when she was a girl, when the world was spinning normally. That food tastes better when you're closer to the earth.

She dips a finger into the soup. Takes it to her mouth. Yellow finger perches there for a whole minute. She nods. Asks me to get her drinking water from the clay pot.

I go to her room. Fetch the water. Only things kept in clay pots escape the mad heat of June.

She sips the cold water. 'Thanks.'

I sit on the sofa, feeling myself plunge into a valley older and deeper than Mama's dimples. I place my food on the centre table, dig in. I go slowly. Mould small balls of eba. Chew noiselessly, because Mama is watching. I chase off a fly. I try to imagine what pizza tastes like. Like bread dipped in tomato and curry. I wonder whether I'd like chips dipped in ketchup, whether lasagne and macaroni and cheese are actually the same thing. After a few swallows I *comment positively* on the food.

'It's very delicious, Ma.'

But this isn't enough. I have to say why and how. That's how you comment positively on Mama's cooking. So I add:

'I like how the onions and waterleaf are slightly raw. They spice the egusi nicely, very nicely. And the egusi is just so milky!'

Mama grins. 'Abi? Thanks, Andrew mè. Enjoy.'

She shows off the gap between her teeth which she got by paying two hundred naira to an old baba. Ydna says the gap makes her look younger, makes her smile sexy. I kinda think it's true, although I'll punch anybody, including myself, who dares to call Mama sexy.

Mama messed up the cooking once. I'd returned from school so pissed off that when I sat down and tasted the food, I told her the Truth, the whole Truth: that the soup was too salty, that it was as watery as a river, that it had no meat.

Mama just stared at me. A long, loud, mad stare. I saw her girlhood in it, when she walked barefoot to the forest with only a wrapper on; when she stubbed her toes and bruised her shins as she returned from the forest with firewood on her head; those countless mornings when she was chased from school for being unable to pay the fees, for being a girl. She smoothed her cornrows as she stared. As I sat there, breathless, unable to blink, unable to move my gaze away, I prayed to all the saints that Mama would never stare at me like that again.

Mama smiles, very pleased with my culinary review. 'Andrew mè, I think it's time you learnt a thing or two about your mama's trade. A few hours in the studio after you return from school? Right? You're grown now.'

In the past I often visited her studio. Helped her clean, ran errands. But about two years ago she banned my ass.

Her studio is a small shop on Sharp Corner, around the sudden bend in the road that knifes many lives. *Glory Bright Photos* is italicised in black just above the glass door. Stuck in the glass are photos which folks refused to pay for: topless babies crying on couches, mamas dancing in bubas and geles, new houses with colourful roofs shining in the sun. Kids returning from government schools usually stop to watch, scratching their sandy hair, ringworms underneath.

Opposite her studio is Queens Palace Guest Inn, one of the main brothels of our town. Fifteen-year-old girls and fifty-year-old women sashay in micro-skirts and bras. They call out to kids and old men amid the honking of cars and motorbikes. 'Bobo, you no wan fuck?' It's a Babel which our corrupt police, our holy sharia courts, our saintly pastors can't shut down. It doesn't look like any brothel you've seen, if you've even seen one before. It's simply a grey metal door that opens into a wide compound with small rooms on your left and right. Each room has just a tiny window to hide the sins inside. Condoms pour out of bins, fluids trickling out. The heavy perfumes of the hos protect your nose.

Inside Mama's studio there's a red carpet on which everything stands: lighting equipment, sofa, stool, folding chair. There are white, black, and red curtains hanging on lines which serve as backgrounds for shots. Behind the curtains is a door that opens into a darkroom where she used to develop black-and-white photos. Since the death of black-and-white photography, she develops her colour photos at Bob Shege along Lagos Road (swirl of cars, lines of shops) because their colour equipment produces the sharpest and sleekest photos in our town.

Mama banned me because one afternoon when I sat in her studio, drowsy, waiting for lunch, a ho in her twenties came to have her photo taken. She wore stilettos, a sports bra, tights, but no panties. As Mama got things ready, turning on the lighting, selecting the best background, the ho walked towards me. Tapping her Huawei screen, lost in thought, her pussy winking at me with each step.

'Hahaha!' she suddenly laughed at me. 'You dey look my vajayjay!' She turned to Mama, her laughter rising to a crescendo. 'Your boy wan fuck. He wan fuck. I go help you fuck am.'

She proposed a deal to Mama: three shots of her and she'd give me one hour of her time. 'I get expertise to disvirgin boys o.'

Mama asked her to leave.

The ho laughed. 'Na joke I dey joke o.'
Mama insisted.
'I no dey go anywhere. Till you snap me photo.'
Mama asked her to leave and called her Satan.
The ho slapped Mama.
Mama dropped her camera beside my feet. She pushed the ho with all she had, veins jutting out of her arms, out of her neck, till she and the ho were outside, till they landed on the ground, till they rolled and rolled in the sand.
Men gathered.
The ho got up. Tore Mama's dress. Ripped Mama's bra. Mama's breasts spilled out.

two
saggy
suns

two
black
suns

The men whistled. Forcing out third eyes from the centres of their foreheads.
I stood. Rooted. Useless. A Semi-Man.
Mama got up. Covered herself with her sandy hands. Walked back to the studio. As she reached the doorway, the ho sprang forward and slapped her butt. Called her a prostitute. Said her butt was big enough to earn her three times what she makes from her studio.
The men laughed.
I couldn't look at her that day.
Or the next one.
Or weeks after.

                    i
                  stepped
                        into
                          black

she
plunged
into
bl-

a

c

k

An abyss grew in my throat. I couldn't speak to her. My words kept falling and screaming as they fell. The Unspoken tapped me up at night. I gasped for air. Only found screaming silence.

I only greeted her good morning after prayer or good evening when I returned from school.

She looked at her feet when she replied with a sullen 'How are you?', not even mentioning my name. She stared at her plate when she asked me to get her drinking water, when she said thank you.

I woke up one night gasping on my cold mat. I heard a strange, croaky voice from her room. A voice weeping.

2

Mama wants to say something but stops herself. She smiles. Those dimples that kill me. Those dimples that become eyes. She has four eyes whenever she smiles. Two up, two down. Two shiny, two dark. Full, hollow. Her dimples are:

a
tunnel
that wouldn't
let me in either way

My Samsung beeps. It's a chat from Morocca:

> wassup, werdna. slim and i are cummin to c ya asap. we needta check out that whyte chick. im sure ya dick is already spillin yogurts for her. c ya

Mama and I wash our hands in a basin. Dry them on a towel. I take the basin and bowls to our store, a small room where we keep pots and plates and broken things, like my bike. Cobwebs wobble on the ceiling. A plump gecko clings to the unplastered wall, its tail forming a C.

Mama bought me the bike eight years ago after I'd received my First Holy Communion. The school principals of Model and Muazu had paid her for taking the WAEC photos of their final-year students, a contract other photographers pay huge bribes to get. I didn't even hug her thank you. I hopped on the bike and cycled like mad around the neighbourhood. Jumping piss streams from bathrooms and toilets. Dodging plastic bags and clucking hens. Raising my hands to the sky, screaming words only I could understand. Kids playing football stopped. They watched me with arms akimbo, shooting me Avada Kedavras with their eyes, sweat glistening on their shirtless bodies. I didn't mind because:

the wind
whistled promises
in my ears

Five minutes later I limped back home to Mama, hands and knees gushing blood, several spokes broken, neighbourhood kids laughing. They stuck out their dirty tongues at me, bleating like goats in heat, wishing I'd lost all my teeth.

Ydna couldn't stop laughing when I told him about it. Every night he asked me for updates about my bike, whether I'd fallen that day, how many bruises I'd had so far. I described the new stunts I'd learnt. How I could cycle backwards without holding the handles. How I became a flying bird whenever I did my favourite stunt: cycling on just the rear wheel, the front wheel raised high above my head. 'Cool,' he said. I spent one afternoon etching his name with a key on the rear mudguard. When Slim and Morocca saw it they begged me to tell them what it meant, even handed me their popcorn. I munched the popcorn very slowly, laughing at them, wasting their time, licking the milk on my lips. When they got fed up and tried to punch me, I told them that the writing was a secret between someone and me. 'Have you gotten a girlfriend?' they asked, jealous that I was already touching those Bouncy Objects On a Babe's Structure. When I told Ydna about it, about his name on the mudguard, he jumped around the room laughing, pulling my ears, my hair, my nose, ducking my slaps. I'd never seen him so wild, so happy.

I can't see his name on the mudguard anymore. I'll have to wipe the dust and cobwebs. The bike is slanted on the wall. Flattened tyres. Torn saddle. Dusty reflectors. Spiders own it now. Riding it every minute, spinning from web to web. They always take over everything, outlive everything, suck the memories buried in things. It's so unbelievable that I once rode such a tiny frame.

When I finish washing the basin and bowls, I return to the living room and stop in the doorway. Mama is still sitting on the floor, a photo album open on her lap. When she notices me she quickly flips past the page she's been staring at. It contains my baby photos. Those of me standing in t-shirt and jeans, Big Ben behind me. Those of me sitting, barefoot, shirtless, her ruby necklace hanging down my neck, my afro a springy garden, my finger pointing at the camera, at her, at you.

She quickly flips past the photo of her mama she took many years ago. The frail woman sits on a stool, in a lace blouse and gele, clutching a bag on her lap. She's facing the camera, leathery skin, Mona Lisa smile, sharp eyes reflecting the flash.

Mama settles on the photos of her siblings and cousins. I know their names and the towns where they live, but I've never met them. Neither have I met her mama. In fact, Mama has never taken me to Ososo, our hometown, where she claims her grandfather built a majestic two-storey house. There she suffered several miscarriages, spent most days on the bed thinking of hurting herself. One morning, when she was really close, she claims I suddenly appeared before her in a vision. I told her to wipe her eyes, that all would be fine, that I'd be with her soon.

Usually she enjoys telling me about the house. She says it contains over twenty rooms, a wooden staircase and wooden beams which support the upper floor. That there was nothing like concrete in the past, so Ososos used okpakpa wood for building houses with many levels:

'Our fathers even built huge bridges with okpakpa. Bridges that could carry pickups. Even two lorries. Side by side.'

I begin to doubt her whenever she gets to the lorry part. She could simply say that the okpakpa contains magical powers, that it's our own vibranium. That's a better way to make a lie truer, to make it more digestible.

But the weirdest shit she's ever told me about my great-grandfather's house is the graves. She says it contains over fifty graves: Those of my great-grandparents and their siblings. Those of my grandfather and his siblings and cousins. That of Ydna. She says that there's no cemetery in Ososo.

'Dead people are buried in their bedrooms or living rooms, or in their frontyards if their rooms are already full of graves. Their relatives dig a deep hole in the floor, and then they're laid to rest in it. The grave is cemented. Then the name and dates are written on it as the cement dries. And this will be the only sign that somebody is lying there. Every day in Ososo we sit and eat and sleep on graves.'

It's fucking insane. I punctuate her speech with 'Really?', 'Seriously?' whenever she talks about the graves. Although she changes the details each time, she never contradicts herself. Each retelling is new and old, fresh and dog-eared, like an old book.

I always wonder where Ydna is buried. Whether he's lying in the living room or frontyard of the house. Whether there's a flower around his head.

'We once had a cemetery,' Mama will always remind me. 'But only a few people were buried there. People whose spirits became candle flames at night. Roaming round the village. Scaring those returning from farms. People whose spirits threw knives and pots. Waking their families every night.'

Occasionally she pauses, roving her eyes over me, gauging my reaction. 'Since only a few people were buried there,' she'll continue, 'the government turned the cemetery into a market. Yes, they did. With stalls made of okpakpa and straw, where Ososos sell yellow garri and fish and palm oil, where—' She'll suddenly stop mid-sentence and sigh, shaking her head. 'Why can't you ever believe me?'

Whenever I ask her to take me to Ososo, she pretends not to hear or changes the subject.

That's also what she would do when I used to ask her about Papa. It was worse, actually. She'd go silent whenever I pestered her, avoiding my gaze even though we'd been laughing and teasing each other moments before. She'd begin to chew gum even though her mouth was empty. She'd lie or give flimsy excuses, but they never worked on me.

One evening, a few weeks after she'd gotten me the bicycle, I asked her again and again who Papa was.

She fell silent.

'Who is he, Mama?'

She began to chew gum.

'Where is he?'

She chuckled. Crossed her legs. Fell silent again.

'When will I see Papa?'

She sighed.

She got up, went to her room. Folded my clothes, placed them in my Ghana Must Go, zipped it up. She dragged it to the living room. Took my hand without looking at me.

'Let's go,' she said.

'Where are we going?' I said.

We walked to the gate. She released my hand. Dropped my Ghana Must Go before me. Opened the gate.

She turned, walked back to the house, her flip-flops making slap sounds.

'Mama!' I cried.

'Go find your papa,' she said.

She went into the living room and locked the door.

It was getting dark. A star pierced out of the sky, twinkling at me.

+

I'm in her room. I unzip my Ghana Must Go and take out my Jordan t-shirt and jeans. I dress up. Force my feet into my Adidas. This is the only designer stuff I own. I only wear them on special Sundays, such as when I serve Mass. Although I hate mirrors, I peek into Mama's round mirror hung on the wall. I finger the lone strand of beard under my chin. I smile. I don't know why I'm smiling. Maybe because I think Eileen will swoon when she sees my broad shoulders in Jordans, when she looks into my brown eyes. Even Zahrah can't stand my eyes when I look at her. She once paused in the middle of a lesson and said aloud,

'Andrew Aziza, stop looking at me like that!' The whole class turned to me, giggling, thinking I'd lost my soul to her, that I'd shot into my boxers.

I hear Slim and Morocca arguing and laughing in the distance. I zip up my Ghana Must Go, place it gently in the corner beside the sack of garri, and return to the living room.

'Your friends are here,' Mama says with the indifferent tone she uses when talking about my droogs. She rises, closes the album, goes to her room.

Slim and Morocca knock on our gate, and since our fence is low, they open the latch and come to our house. I go outside to welcome them.

'What's up, Scads?' I say, fist-bumping them.

'What's up, Werdna?'

'Cool, man. You?'

'Cool.'

'You're looking hip, bro,' Morocca says.

'Dressed to molok Eileen,' Slim says.

'Thanks, guys,' I say.

They're also hip. Slim in red Louis Vuitton t-shirt, black Armani jeans, red Nikes. Morocca in Prada shades pinned on Versace t-shirt. D&G jeans, a chain jiggling at the side. Black boots.

But all this stuff, including my Jordans and Adidas, are from charity shops in LA and London, sold in special sections in our boutiques.

'Come in, dawgs.'

In the living room my droogs scan around as though they haven't been here a billion times. Slim: our CRT TV with a hump, the crucifix and the crack beside it. Morocca: the gorges on our sofa, the white plastic chair, our plastic carpet torn in places.

I try not to look where they look.

Morocca sits in the plastic chair, Slim and I on the sofa.

'Fucking hot out there,' Slim says.

'Like the devil's asshole,' Morocca says.

We laugh.

'But how d'you know that?' Slim says.

'Know what?' Morocca says.

'About the devil's asshole?'

'I don't know. Just do.'

'I know why. Because you're the devil himself.'

'Fuck off.'

We laugh.

I point at the flowery curtain separating the living room from Mama's room and mouth to the Scads to mind their language, that the Queen is inside, eavesdropping as usual.

They cover their mouths, mocking shock.

Mama dislikes Morocca for the scorpion tattoo on his bicep, which he inked using his mama's sewing needles and hot cashew oil. She dislikes him for organising and performing in rap shows in Igbo Hall where thirteen-year-old girls grind their flat butts on twenty-year-old guys. She dislikes him for every fuck he's said, for every line of hip-hop he's rapped. I don't know why she dislikes Slim. He looks agreeable and innocent with his light skin and shaved head, unlike Morocca who wears a flat-top and an earring in his left ear, whose skin is darker than his shoes. Maybe she's put two and two together from all her eavesdropping and knows about Slim's paintings of men with snake-long dicks fucking each other in *Avatar*-like gardens of earthly delights.

I fetch them drinking water. Morocca drains the stainless-steel cup halfway and passes it to Slim. When Slim is done, I return the cup to the store and tell Mama that I'm going to the party with Michael and Thomas. She grunts okay.

+

This is my neighbourhood: Houses detached like dots. Facing east west north south. No pavements. No flowers. No bins.

A hen and her four chicks scratch the earth for seeds. Clucking, pecking. They don't find anything. They see ants marching in a queue, dragging white food. They eat the ants and the white food. A goat is beside them nibbling dry stubborn grass. They don't spare him a glance.

A dog is reclining yards away, watching kids play football, watching them jump thin streams reeking of piss and kitchen waste. The kids are playing shirtless, barefoot. One kicks a stone and yelps, a string of blood spitting out. Another is twirling with the ball, unstoppable, zigzagging past his friends, galloping, speeding. He steps on a plastic bag (they're everywhere) and slips, bashing his teeth on the ground. The other kids laugh and continue playing as though nothing has happened. The kid who has fallen rises up asap before he's called a silly girl and resumes playing, limping gently, hand on his mouth. He limps over a piss stream without even looking at it. When he's tired of pretending, he sneaks out to his house, an unplastered one-room apartment, the top half built of mud blocks, the bottom half built of cement blocks. He's panting, sweating. He dips a cup into the clay pot, drinks, dips, drinks. The water: a shifting, uncertain yellow like tea, a pupa twitching on it.

The dog sees other boys and girls enter or leave their one- or two-room apartments. Their movements make him notice the hen and her chicks and the goat. He jumps up. Chases them. The goat takes off without looking back. The hen stands her ground a bit, tells her chicks in her secret language to fucking run, flares her wings and feathers at the dog, tells him she'll widen his sores with her beak if he dares take one more step. He doesn't. He just barks on and on. The hen strolls away. One of the kids playing football picks a stone and throws it at the dog. He doesn't miss his target, one of the dog's sores. The dog shrieks and runs back home. To one of the houses facing south north west east.

+

We the Scadvengers are bouncing to Eileen's party. Me, Werdna, at the centre: superhero poet; Morocca the Sand Lord on my left: rapper extraordinaire; Slim T on my right: Black Picasso.

Girls check us out: girls in chadors and not in chadors.

Morocca puts on his shades.

'Fucking hot, man.'

'Devil's asshole.'

'Yep.'

Motorbikes rush past us. Blaring their horns, though nothing is in their way.

We bounce on. Past Hausa men sitting on mats, talking about Boko Haram and kafirai and elections, a small transistor radio chirping the news, none listening to it. One of them talks about how, an hour ago, a Christian man insulted the Prophet Muhammad in the market, and how all true Muslims must arise now before Kontagora is over-Christianised.

Past a dogonyaro tree with a conical speaker hanging on top, an old man sitting on a mat underneath, speaking into a mike, quoting from the Hadith. A little girl in a hijab comes to him. He asks her what he can do for her. She says, 'Mama na tace ka yi mata addu'a.' She gives him a wrinkled twenty naira. He prays for the girl and her mama, and the mama hopefully hears the prayer wherever she is over the speaker.

Past shops selling packaged stuff: Yale biscuits and Cowbell milk, purewater and Cokes, cigarettes and weed, their packets and bottles reflecting the yellow sun. Past a Mai Shayi frying Indomie and eggs, cooling tea by pouring it from a cup raised high in one hand into another cup held low in the other, without spilling a single drop. Past girls frying kosai on wood fires, giggling at customers; women roasting maize on charcoal fires with no customers; an old man fiddling the strings of his gurmi, no naira in his box.

We talk about the new *Star Wars* trailer. Slim thinks this year's instalment is going to be the best yet. Morocca disagrees, says everything in it is shit, even the new droid sidekick who talks like a lizard.

'Do lizards even talk?' Slim says.

'You didn't know?' Morocca says.

'Fuck you.'

We laugh.

I don't know who to support because I haven't seen the trailer yet. I don't like discussing *Star Wars* with Zahrah or Fatima. They don't ever see how cool the X-wings are or how funny the new droid is. They don't even give two fucks about the Force, a special energy field that connects Everything, Americans and Europeans and us on this crappy continent. They don't give a shit because 'it's not African'. Instead they see things that aren't there, such as how, in a galaxy so large and so far away, there are only two or three Blacks, 'and none of them are even African'.

We're on Model School Road, tarred, grainy, semis parked at intervals. There are fewer shops here. Zahrah lives down the road, just before the bend. A dirt road connects to the bend, forming a T, leading to the cemetery. The houses – two rooms, three rooms – are plastered. Some painted, others halfway. Green, yellow. There are stains on the walls, shaped like leprous hands and feet. There are also chalk and charcoal sketches: Mickey Mouse dancing on dollar signs. A father and a mother kissing, a baby coming out of her. Freaks with three heads screaming, tongues sticking out. The gutters are open, buzzing with flies, separating the doors from the road.

'Werdna, did you see that babe?' Morocca says.

'What babe?' I say.

'Just passed now.'

'Oh.' I'm tempted to look, but I don't.

'That ass, man. Like rubber.'

'Like seriously?'

'Seriously.'

'Anyhoo, I'm not an ass man,' I say.

'Come on, Werdna,' Morocca says. 'You keep saying that shit.'

'Seriously, bro.'

'Then why d'you watch Nicki and Bey?'

'Because I like them?'

'And there's a boy I like,' Slim says.

A bro is approaching us from the other side of the road. He's in Adidas and Prada, an earring in his left ear.

'And he's gay,' Slim says.

'How d'you know?' Morocca says.

'Gaydar.'

'Ha.'

I feel like changing the subject but I don't know what to say. I don't want to discuss Eileen with the Scads. I don't want to hear them joke about her hair, lips, or accent.

Behind us two men are approaching on a motorbike, riding slowly. Their beards are twisted, their faces creased and heavy with the unsaid. The man at the back has something like a log wrapped in a mat laid across his lap.

I know what's in the mat.

I shut my eyes. Red world. I want to go there. And remain.

I open my eyes when I'm sure the men have passed. The world: blurred, a translucent yellow. I feel the fingering of the breeze on my skin. It's rough, getting rougher, growing into an itch.

It's only when I stop fighting, when I allow my gaze to shoot to the men, that clarity returns. I see:

baby feet
peeking
out of the mat

All this happens in five seconds, five nano-infinities. My droogs don't notice.

Perhaps Ydna was once in such a mat.

'I don't like this road,' I say.

'Why?' Slim says.

'Don't know.'

'Because of the corpses?' Morocca says.

'Or the ghosts?' Slim says.

'I guess,' I say.

It was on this road that Slim Whispered.

Slim, Morocca, and I first met in Primary One at St Michael's, a school founded by Bishop Timothy Carroll SMA. Slim was slimmer then, bony, the tallest. Mama took a photo of us; my copy is tucked in A. E. Housman. We were dwarfs then. Tiny. Noisy. Magical. We backflipped and played karate during break. Broke teeth. Blood spurted from our noses. Spattered on our yellow-and-white-chequered uniforms. My blood on theirs, their blood on mine.

And in Primary Five, we touched each other's pricks as we returned from school. Amid bushes, no passers-by in sight:

'Andy, your prick is so big,' Slim would say, laughing, ducking the punch I threw because he'd touched me so suddenly. There was something wrong about a boy touching me.

'Mine is bigger!' Morocca would say.

'Shut up, Mikey. Andy's prick is the biggest. A small snake!'

And Morocca would tell us that the previous night some milk leaked out of his prick. That it was horrible. But sweet. That he'd seen his seatmate, Patience, in the dream. And while staring at my feet I'd describe how the same thing had happened to me. Although I hadn't seen my seatmate, Abidemi, in it. I'd seen Rose. Rose from *Titanic*.

But Slim never said anything. We never noticed that he never said anything until he Whispered.

And when he was done, I forced one of the brightest smiles I'd ever beamed. I patted him on the back. Forced my hand to linger a bit. Each second a scorching eternity.

In them, I rewound every moment I'd spent with him. Each handshake. Each touch on his neck, his hair, his prick. Those times we'd stopped to urinate in the bush. Did he feel something? Did I make it harder for him? How can I even be 100 per cent sure I'm not like him?

As my hand sizzled on his back, his Whisper became an echoing feedback. Each return louder, spiralling faster, growing into something, taking shape, like an inflating balloon. It became the whistle of whips and the pounds of sticks. It grew into cries for help. Ekene's cries as the mob flung him to the ground and booted his mouth, as they cried 'Dan daudu' and hit him with sticks. Slim's cries for help as my mind seized control, deleted Ekene from the centre of the mob, and slowly inserted him. I couldn't stop myself from hearing him cry out to me, 'Save me, Werdna!', from seeing myself walk away, afraid of the sticks and spit.

It was also on this road, years ago, before the Whisper, that Slim, Morocca, and I decided to become Africa's first superheroes. We'd just finished the pirated DVDs of *Iron Man* and

Captain America and *The Avengers*. We placed our left hands on our hearts, raised our rights to the sky. We vowed:

To kill all the corrupt leaders
To veil Africa from the sun
To feed every African kid chicken and ice cream every day

We took new names, new identities, new futures. We laughed.

+

Although Morocca is sixteen and has a two-year-old daughter at home, he talks about how cool it would be to date Eileen. To travel to the UK with her and live in London, a city without blackouts. To rap in pubs with her gazing at him. After all, whites love anyone with musical talent. He read that on Reddit.

We nod.

Slim says that a girl like Eileen could turn him straight. He whispers the 'straight'.

We laugh.

'Seriously, bro,' Slim says, 'there's no reason for a girl like that to like a guy like you. Like us.'

'I'll give you one,' Morocca says.

'What shitty reason is that?'

'Our dicks,' Morocca says. 'They're big. Fat. They're small lions.'

We laugh.

'That's a stupid myth, bro,' Slim says. 'Ain't scientific.'

'What science? Dick science?' Morocca says. 'Did the fucking scientists measure every fucking black dick?'

'They don't need to, fool.'

'They should've at least measured mine. It's a rhino.'

'It's a fucking millipede, shut up.'

We're very close to Zahrah's now. But first we must pass Oga Oliver's.

He's sitting, as usual, on a low stool outside his house. He's wearing a brown vest that used to be white, rusty glasses that used to be gold-rimmed, black shorts that used to be grey. Flies are eating the empty cup beside his feet. He's cleaner today, his face shaved, his jaw dotted with rashes. We pretend not to see him or to feel the guilt of taunting him when we were younger.

Years ago Oga Oliver tried travelling to Europe through the Sahara. He was kidnapped in Libya, where he could practically smell the garlic and Bolognese pasta coming from Italy. The Libyans tied him in chains, whipped his flat black ass, forced him to work like a bipedal donkey on their farms. Since his Return, or rather his lucky escape, he hasn't spoken a single word. Actually, he does speak one word: 'Water'. That's the only word in his mouth. That's the only language his navigator brain knows. Greet him, 'Good morning, sir', and he'll say, 'Water!' Ask him, 'What's your name, Oga Oliver?' and he'll say, 'Water!' Ask him, 'What planet are we on?' and he'll say, 'Water!'

As we pass him, each step blunting the blades in our stomachs, I turn. Our eyes meet. He stands. Raises his left hand. Points to me. 'Water,' he mutters. 'Water.'

II: The Scourging at the Pillar

Theorem: A permutation of odd order must be even.

3

Hey, Andy?
Hey, Ydna! Long time!
What's up?
Good, man. Sunny as hell, though.
I see.
On my way to Eileen's party. Thinking about stopping at Zahrah's.
Okay. So how's Mama?
I think she'll be alright.
What d'you mean?
She's fine, Ydna. That's all that matters.
Right.
She even wants me to start visiting the studio again.
Great. Aren't you happy?
I'm happy, yeah.
You're not.
Yeah.
But why?
Can't really say.
You think she hasn't forgiven you?
About what, Ydna?
You know what I mean.
Could we change the subject? If you don't mind?
. . .
. . .
. . .
Ydna, there's something I should tell you.

What?
Something just isn't right.
What's that?
It's been there a long time. Deep inside me. I see it this second. And next, it slips from my reach, like a fish.
But you feel it.
Yes. Just like I feel you.
Hmm.
And I think it's changing everything.
Like what?
Like Mama and me. Like you and me.
Okay.
It's changed you and me, Ydna.
Andy, let's not talk about that.
We need to, bro.
We don't.
We need to. We've not been the same.
. . .
Say something, Ydna.
. . .
Why d'you do that, Ydna?
Do what?
Leave me.
Look, Andy. I'm doing my best here. We're not supposed to be talking. Are we even talking? Aren't you faking it?
We are, Ydna. We're talking.
We aren't.
Because there's something binding us.
How could you be so sure?
You feel it, bro. In your heart, in your soul. I feel it too.
Is that a poem?
Maybe. You're funny.
. . .
You there, Ydna?
Yes?
I miss you.
. . .

40

I – I love you.

. . .

Say something.

. . .

Say something, Ydna.

. . .

Ydna!

. . .

+

Just as my droogs and I pass Zahrah's house, a voice from behind stops us:

'Andy Africa!'

The voice is high-pitched, slightly mocking. Everyone seems to have a nickname for me: Andy, Andiza, Andrew mè, Werdna . . . Most I don't mind, but I verbally crucify anyone who calls me that shit. That nickname is a switch to so many crappy memories.

My droogs and I turn: it's Fatima. She's smiling, her yellow hijab billowing in the breeze. I smile. We walk to her.

'Hey, Fatee,' I say. 'How's it going?'

'Good, good,' she says.

'How far, Fatee?' Slim says.

'What's up, pretty babe?' Morocca says.

She smiles. 'Very fine.'

Fatima is perhaps the smartest young person I know. She isn't a loud smartass like me. Although she's read almost all of Shakespeare and memorised Dante, she doesn't pepper her speech with their lines like I would. She and I have won several trophies for our school in state competitions, and we're the only students elected to our school's Club for the Gifted. We meet in Zahrah's office every day in the last period before break and discuss permutations and Frantz Fanon, although these days Zahrah spends most of the time in digressions about Anifuturism.

Fatima is in a tie-dye dress, a pimple reddening on her nose. She's light-skinned and her irises are like black beads, large, shiny, reflecting your entire body in them. When she smiles – chocolate sepal lips – you feel as though she's spinning about you, curving smoothly, like the colours in an impressionist painting. She keeps looking away when our eyes meet, her gaze flitting to Slim and Morocca before returning to me.

'I've been calling you guys for the past minute,' she says, her voice rich, evoking colours, like cello music.

'Sorry, we didn't hear,' I say.

'We've been thinking about the unbearable lightness of being,' Slim says, trying to sound sophisticated.

'And getting rich,' Morocca says.

We laugh.

'So you guys are heading to the party?'

'Yeah, yeah.'

'Did you hear about what happened in the market this afternoon?'

'What happened, Fatee?'

'A Christian man insulted the Prophet. He was nearly killed by a mob. Now some guys are planning a protest this evening. Fanatics, really. Hopefully nothing crazy will happen. Still, you guys should be careful. You know how these things can turn violent.'

'Don't worry about us, Fatee,' Slim says.

'We're superheroes,' Morocca says.

We laugh.

'Trust us,' I say.

'Alright. Still, be very careful,' she says.

I try not to think about the last riot two years ago. Because of me, a mob nearly whacked Mama with machetes.

'So you're not coming to the party?' I say to Fatee. 'I hear Zahrah's play will be staged.'

'I don't think I can make it,' she says. 'It's my mother. She wants to talk.'

Fatima has been living with Zahrah for weeks now. Her hijab covers a faint scar that snakes from her ear down to her neck. Before moving in with Zahrah, she sometimes came to school with her lips flaky and unoiled, her socks dirty, her uniform unironed. And during break we'd sit at the back of the class and she'd roll her sleeves or pull off her socks and show me the

42

latest: Long thin cuts on her arm dribbling water. Patches on her feet – red, burnt, swollen – that she bent to scratch at intervals. And I'd help her rub shea butter on her injuries, her body hot in my hands, pulsing, slippery, her moans quantifying my massage.

It began simply: Her alhaja mother pulling her ears, clicking her fingers at her, spitting on her when Fatima made the sign of the cross at the dining table.

Her mother throwing boiling water on her legs when she refused to wear her ankle-length chador.

Her mother whipping her with the dog chain when she caught her reading *The Portable Atheist.*

Sometimes Fatima fought back. Last time, she'd knocked away the pan of sizzling tomato sauce that her mother had tried to throw at her. In the process, the sauce had spattered on her mother's face, hair, breasts, covering her in fake blood.

A motorbike rushes past us, honking like hell. Sacks of rice are piled on its rear seat, none tied to the bike, none falling off. Two girls carrying trays of boiled peanuts on their heads stop to ask us whether we'll buy. The girls are our age-mates, dressed in faded ankara and chadors, and are clearly uneducated. They only address my droogs and me, and don't spare Fatima a glance even though she's the richest among us. Morocca tells them no thanks in English. They don't understand. Fatima says 'Mun gode' to them in a kind voice. They roll their eyes at her, at her hijab, because it isn't long enough. They hiss, murmur 'Kafiri', and walk away.

Morocca's gaze has been trailing the lace hem of Fatima's hijab which covers her bust. He once swore, hand raised to heaven, that she had the best boobs among all the girls and female teachers in our school.

He taps Slim. Mouths something to him. They laugh.

'Why're you guys laughing?' she says.

'Oh, nothing,' Slim says. 'We're just happy.'

'About what?'

'About you and Andy,' Morocca says.

'You're such a fine couple,' Slim says.

'Yep. Two cute geniuses.'

'One handsome, the other beautiful.'

'One chocolate, the other light-skinned.'

'We need to wed them asap,' Slim says, turning to Morocca. 'Do you have any ring in your pocket?'

We laugh, but I'm the first to stop, and she's the last, smiling shyly, cheeks glinting.

Many times I think about marrying Fatee, but I forcefully kill the thought immediately after starting it. It always sneaks up on me when I watch blondes on TV, remote in hand, thumb on the rewind button: She and I on a beach, her head on my lap, my fingers cruising in her hair. She and I lying next to each other, my hand under her clothes, our noses kissing. She and I licking each other's tongues, her mouth like strawberries, her large eyes tugging me into their fantasy lands.

But something about being with her just never feels right. I don't know what it is. It must be the It, the It I talked about with Ydna. And it's while thinking about her that I feel achingly different, that I feel I'm meant for something else, something shiny, pulsing, seismic . . . sleek, light, wavy . . . blue, dove-winged, icy. I like her so much and want to love her, but the It never lets me. And I hate myself for that. Because she's the only female friend I dream of. She's the only person my age who understands me when I say that *Hamlet* and *Blade Runner* and 'Bohemian Rhapsody' are actually the same thing. I've also caught her a few times staring unseeingly at me during our lessons with Zahrah.

Ydna would've loved her. I don't know why, but I'm sure. He'd agree with her that it matters that there isn't an African in *Star Wars*. That kinky hair and wavy hair are equal and the same. That my droogs and I should wear less Adidas and more tie-dye. But most times I can't stop myself from feeling that I'd have loved her if It hadn't permuted me, if I'd been Ydna and never become Andy, if HXVX had never existed . . .

Morocca is showing Slim a WhatsApp chat on his Samsung Galaxy. They're giggling, wide-eyed. It seems Morocca has baited some sugar mummy or something.

'I've just been out to get a recharge card,' Fatee says to me. 'Why don't you come in to say hi to Zahrah?'

'Another time,' I say. 'We're running late.'

'But you've got like an hour,' she says, glancing at her Apple Watch.

'Yeah, but—'

'Trust me, you really want to talk to Zahrah.'

'Why?'

'D'you know that she travelled to Ososo during the mid-term break?'

'Seriously?'

Zahrah is also from Ososo, like Mama and me. She'd never visited Ososo before she went to the Sahara, but since she Returned she visits periodically.

'Cool,' I say. 'So Zahrah saw all the hills and rocks and waterfalls?'

'Yes,' Fatee says. 'And the graves in bedrooms too.' She laughs.

Fatima is Hausa-Fulani, from Sokoto. It's unheard of in her culture for the dead to be buried in their bedrooms.

I make a face. I try to defend my culture, even though I feel no connection to it. I tell her that my people highly honour the dead, especially dead loved ones. So we cling to them even when they leave us.

'True,' she says. 'I understand. But it's still a little weird.'

'Yeah, it is.'

'And Zahrah has something for you.'

'Another proof of Cayley's theorem? No thanks.'

'No,' she laughs. 'She has something you'll really like.'

'Like what?'

'A letter.'

'From who?'

'Your grandma.'

'Seriously?'

For a moment I try to fathom why Grandma would write to me, but can't come up with any good guess. Mama and Grandma must have huge beef. Probably over me. That's why Mama never talks about her, never mentions her the rare times she talks about her childhood. Something must have happened, Grandma writing to me and all.

My droogs ask me to message them when I'm done with Zahrah. They were scared to shit the last time they went to her house, so they decide to check out one of their bros in the hood.

Most people in our town call Zahrah Suleiman a witch. They talk about her in the market, point and hiss at her when she passes in the neighbourhood, tell our principal Sister Lakefield to sack her. They call her a witch because they don't want to understand what she's up to. Sometimes I don't blame them.

Enter Zahrah's living room: No chairs. No tables. No TV.

Three yellow bulbs hang from the ceiling, equidistant from each other, forming a triangle.

Red candles gutter on the floor.

Busts and figurines line the walls. They're wooden, jet-black, open-mouthed, screaming. Some have whiskers, others have their tongues stuck out, others have triangular heads like freaks. One with a trapezium head is pointing its forefinger at me, a red LED flashing at the tip, its eyes empty holes, shaped like African maps.

This is her Temple Zero. Temple One is her office, Temple Two is in Ososo.

'Feel at home, Andy,' Fatima says.

On the terrazzo floor are formulas written in curly white font. $e^{i\pi} + 1 = 0$ is at the centre of the room, written in gold, reflecting the lights overhead.

The aroma of goat meat and garlic and onions wafts from the kitchen.

A thirty-something woman comes out of the kitchen. She closes the door behind her, goes to the statuette with the trapezium head. She bends her knees to it, touches its LED light, slips a thin roll of naira into its African eye slits. She turns, smiles at Fatima and me, and exits the house. She's familiar: a lawyer at JDPC.

On the wall opposite the door is a *Guernica*-sized painting. It depicts IQ City, the conurbation Africa will become in the year $2xyz$. Its red skyscrapers are statues of gods, some holding ankhs, others swinging lightning. Sahara is the capital. Its holy lakes wind round the city in concentric circles, millions of pilgrims swimming or bathing or fucking in it. Its beaches gleam with people kissing or laughing or dancing, others juggling fire, others stroking lions. And in mid-air, Zahrah flies around the city in a golden bikini.

Fatima and I enter the kitchen.

'Andy Africa!' Zahrah cries. 'Yay! Good to see you, boy!'

She's wearing a red apron over a red dress, stirring a pot of jollof rice on the gas cooker. The rice smells so good.

'Good afternoon, Aunty Zahrah,' I say.

She drops the ladle on a plate, rushes over, and gives me a hug. She stands on her toes, kisses my forehead. She gazes at me: large watery eyes rippling with delight.

Her afro, which is dyed red on top, is covered in a flowery scarf. Her forearms are tattooed. On the left she has *Every African is a witch, wizard, or superhero*, and on the right, *Every African has a halo circling over their heads*.

Since she Returned from the Sahara, she mostly wears red: Red leather jacket. A flowing red ankara or dashiki dress. Red gladiator heels. Her hoop earrings have stones and zigzags and flames etched along their rims. She's always in a hurry (I like fast women!), always smiling, snorting, with dimples that dig deep into her cheeks. And when she laughs, her earrings also laugh, swinging to and fro like pendulums, and her laughter also makes you laugh no matter what you feel about her.

'Andy Africa!' she says again, hand on her chest. 'I've been thinking about you all day.'

'He wouldn't have stopped by,' Fatima says, 'if I hadn't caught him passing.'

'Is that true, Andy?' Zahrah says.

'I – I . . . I thought I was . . .' I'll grill Fatima for this later.

'Are you still sore?' Zahrah says, her large eyes peering at me, screening for any fold of hostility.

'About what?' I pretend not to know what she's talking about.

'About your new name,' she says.

She and Fatima chuckle.

'N–no, I'm not sore.'

Three weeks ago Zahrah named me Andy Africa.

'Good. It's such a pretty name. I wish someone would call me Zahrah Africa.'

'Me too,' Fatima says. 'Fatee Africa.'

'But you're the lucky one, Andy,' Zahrah says. 'Your name fits it so well. *Aziza. Africa.* The first vowel of the alphabet begins and ends your name. The third vowel is at the centre. These numbers – one and three – are very special, very significant. You sure have powerful ancestors.'

I don't know whether to thank her or not. I just want the letter from Grandma.

Laughing, Zahrah tells us how five dogs chased her this morning at the market. Their owners had set them after her because she was dressed in her red regalia. The dogs followed her. Past meat stalls buzzing with flies. Past poultry shops with hens shrieking in their cages. She ran and ran. Flung the meat and honey she'd bought at the dogs, trying to appease them. But they roared and screeched and sped up. Were about to rip her to shreds.

Suddenly she stopped and turned to the dogs. She sang them a lullaby. They growled and became bored, turned and bounded away. Passers-by called her trick witchcraft. They edged away from her, clicking their fingers, muttering 'Holy Ghost fire' or 'Allah ya tsare'. Shopkeepers even refused to sell her tomatoes.

She laughs about how a lot of Africans call her a witch or wasted genius on Facebook. How they keep reporting her page to be blocked, how lots of white people (over a thousand now) have followed her page.

'Sadly,' she says, 'whites know the value of what we have better than we do. That's why they're always ahead.'

That's what she said the morning she named me Andy Africa.

Every morning in school we stand on the assembly grounds in male and female lines according to our classes. The teacher on duty presides over the gathering from the assembly platform. Standing behind the platform is our logo of a dove breathing fire onto an open book. We sing hymns like 'Colours of the Day' or 'All the Earth', the morning sun colouring our hymnbooks orange. We chant the prayer of the day, sing the national anthem, recite the Pledge, and greet our teachers good morning. Afterwards the teacher on duty makes the announcements ('Latecoming is becoming a big issue . . .' or 'Any boy and girl caught together in the school toilet will be . . .') and then dismisses the assembly. And we march to our classes, singing silly songs like 'Thread the Needle' or 'We are H.A.P.P.Y'.

Zahrah was the teacher on duty the week she named me Andy Africa. She branded her week 'Anifuturist Week', printed posters and pinned them on every noticeboard in our school. The posters had kids flying in mid-air or walking on water or juggling fire, their skin as dark as tar. Their speech bubbles said: 'You're a witch, wizard, or superhero!' 'Your blackness is your badass-ness!' 'You're fly!'

Morning assemblies usually take thirty minutes, but Zahrah's were an entire hour. She brought a whiteboard from her office and stood it on the platform. She wrote quantum formulas and BCE dates. Discussed how Africa is the future of civilisation. How she unfortunately discovered this very late in her life (although she's only thirty years old). She drew plane shapes and matchstick figures. Explained how Anifuturism is the fusion of animism and Afrofuturism. How all Africans will never find light or rest till they embrace their animist and futurist heritage. How animism (the belief in the god in things, in the ancestors) is in fact futurist.

'Animism isn't primitivity,' she said. 'We wouldn't have climate change today if we were all animists.'

By the third day of her week, everyone (except Fatima and Bro Magnus and a few dementors) was done with Anifuturism. But no one in the gathering of three hundred could stand up to her. Only our principal Sister Lakefield could, but she'd travelled to Rome for a meeting of her order.

Zahrah went on and on. Shared pamphlets and pages from scientific journals. She even discussed my idea about HXVX without giving me credit. She'd found it in one of my poems, expounded on it, and added it to her Anifuturist bible.

In my poem, HXVX is a being of planetary proportions. It hovers over us, its shadow darkening the continent. Its million million tentacles:

eye us

feed us bits
of its twisted soul

that we build fires
and step into them

guffawing

forgetting
the heat and hunger and yesterday

HXVX is like YHWH; it's the Tetragrammaton shorthand for the Curse of Africa. Mathematically,

$$HXVX = (Sauron + Thanos)^{\infty} = The\ Curse\ (of\ Africa),\ \text{where}\ \infty$$
is infinity.

Thus HXVX is fucking monstrous, fucking invincible, seriously. HXVX is why the Sahara is here and not in Europe, why we suffer most from the shitty sun. Its numberless tentacles control *every single thing* on this land: from the water we drink to who gets knocked by a car to each synapse our neurones make. Our births and the shades of our skin and our deaths are designed in its palms. These days I'm beginning to be convinced that even God cannot defeat it. Like, where would He start? Thus the only option is to flee from its reach, i.e. out of this shitty continent. Since HXVX and the Curse are equal, you could even say they're synonyms, so that *my Cursed life = my HXVX life.*

As we yawned and sighed and rubbed our eyes in the assembly ground, Zahrah went on and on. 'Every African child is a witch, wizard, or superhero,' she said. 'Yes. The power is there. Glowing under the black skin. The black pigment is the stopper.'

She paused for effect, and pointed at the sky, at our school gate. 'But They, especially HXVX, don't want us to know this.'

She described HXVX as a construct that is everything negative that has befallen Africa: slavery, colonialism, dictatorship, kleptocracy, xenocentrism. Even Fatima was yawning at this point, shifting her weight from one foot to the other.

'We've been on this continent for so long that we've forgotten what it really is. Our ancient mamas never forgot. Because they smelt it in stones. Saw it in the fires of their sacrifices. They saw it. Its real soul. As the Pulse of Existence.' She paused, nodding, sinking her point into us. 'Today, all by our fault, all by our conniving with HXVX, we've made Africa the heart of darkness. You and me. We're to blame. For failing her. For not believing in her.'

Suddenly, for no reason, I got fed up. I raised my hand and said, 'Excuse me, Aunty Zahrah. I have a question.'

She ignored me.

I raised my hand higher and spoke louder. 'Excuse me!'

She was silent for a long moment, expressionless. I'd done what no teacher could do: I'd dared to interrupt and challenge her. She was my second mama, her eyes said, and if I truly had any concerns I should've waited to ask her in person. She looked at me very coldly, as though I'd become HXVX, tentacles and all.

'Yes, Andrew Aziza?' she said, folding her arms.

'Africa as a construct and continent has failed us,' I said aloud. 'Why should we believe in it?'

The moment I spat my question I saw how foolish it was and how stupid I sounded.

The assembly laughed. Even Slim and Morocca who'd been sleeping on their feet woke.

Was it the It that pushed me this far?

'Come here, Andrew Aziza,' Zahrah said.

Slim and Morocca whistled.

'Andy don die today,' Okey whispered.

The assembly of three hundred was silent.

I climbed the steps of the platform and went to her.

She asked me to kneel facing the school. 'Close your eyes. Raise your hands to the sky. Yes, let our ancestors see them.'

She took a large paper and wrote in bold letters: *Andy Africa*. She made me hold it up to the school, told me to open my eyes and behold my shame. She motioned Bro Magnus. He came forward with his horsewhip.

'Give him twelve strokes,' she told him.

like cacti, like hooks, like nails

the whips came

a tear
oozed
from
my
eye

to the sands
and

they cried out

That evening Mama massaged my back with a towel soaked in hot water. She rubbed shea butter on my back, kneaded it, not listening to my whimpers as I lay on her lap.

'Who did this to you?' she asked.

'Zahrah,' I said.

She sighed.

If it had been another teacher she'd have stormed our school the next day. She'd have shaken her fists in the teacher's face, spat on their table, demanded that Sister Lakefield sack them. But Mama didn't do anything. She and Zahrah already had huge beef that neither of them wanted to tell me about.

+

Although I tell Zahrah I've already had lunch, she insists I eat something, that I haven't tasted her cooking in a long time. She asks me again if I'm still sore. I say no, of course.

Using my foot I trace one of the numbers painted on the floor. 6.02×10^{23}:

the rage
in
one
mole
of my blood

Zahrah dishes yellow-red jollof rice onto a large plate, forming a tower, pieces of fried meat clinging to its sides like climbers. 'We'll all eat from this plate,' she says. 'Anifuturism is about eating together. It's about that esoteric sense of community our ancestors had.'

Fatima takes the rice tower to the living room. I follow her with a plate of lettuce-cabbage-tomato salad, place it on the floor, sit beside her. She removes her hijab, folds it, lays it by her side.

We hear Zahrah's phone ring, hear her speaking to her father. It seems her fiancé has bought him some dope present.

As we wait for Zahrah, Fatee and I talk and laugh about Zahrah's forthcoming wedding, about her plan to feature masquerades. Fatee's voice sounds richer, soothes like a shoulder massage.

Once again I wish that we were an item. That I could take her hand this very second and kiss it. Our conversations are the best – they leave me renewed, refined, re-energised. In school we go on long strolls debating black holes and history and the continent. Sometimes we even talk about love. Everyone, even my droogs, claim we'd be perfect together. Still I refuse to make a move. In fact, these days, I no longer put my hand around her when we stroll. I'm sure she's noticed.

Zahrah joins us with a tray of cutlery, cups, bottles of water and orange juice. She sits down, hands us our spoons. Before we dig in, she cuts from the juiciest spot of the tower and casts some rice and a chunk of meat to the floor. 'Our ancestors,' she says. 'Yesterday, Today . . .'

Fatima chuckles. 'Ameen,' she says.

Zahrah sprinkles some orange juice to the floor. 'Our ancestors,' she says. 'Tomorrow.'

Fatima chuckles again. 'Ameen.'

It makes no sense, throwing food and drink on maths formulas, dirtying a pristine floor. Mama would slam our sofa at this. She'd rant about Zahrah sweeping the floor and throwing away such a juicy chunk of meat when so many kids on the streets have nothing to eat.

Zahrah is looking at me, unsmiling.

'So sad how we Africans have forgotten the power of symbols, of gesture,' she says. 'Of course, the gods won't descend from heaven to eat this. This simple act sends our hearts to heaven to meet them.'

I wonder how Fatima survives living with Zahrah, how the mini-lectures haven't barbecued her brain. Sometimes I pity Zahrah and think that Fatima and I don't fully engage her as an audience, that we haven't read enough, that she'd be better off teaching in a university. Although Zahrah graduated with a strong first-class degree, the best student in her year, and has published several papers on permutations (which she forces Fatima and me to read even though we mostly don't understand a thing), no Nigerian university gives a shit about her. They've all rejected her job applications because she doesn't know the son or daughter of a governor, because she doesn't have the money to bribe a dean or registrar, because she isn't a man. So Zahrah tries to turn Fatima and me into her intellectual colleagues, making us read journals on permutations and give alternate proofs to interesting theorems, cajoling us to read *Ulysses* and *The Brothers Karamazov* and write essays on them. These days, though, her research is getting weird. She's trying to use results in permutation theory to prove that Black power is thermodynamic. It's completely insane. She's shown Fatima and me the manuscripts and the rejection letters from journals. This is what she talks about as we eat.

'Those referees,' she says, munching meat, 'they don't know a thing. They can't find what's on their noses. This is the result of specialisation. Trust me, those referees don't even know who William Shakespeare is.'

We laugh, although I'm sure the referees made no mistake in rejecting her papers.

I fear the extent to which Zahrah has influenced Fatima and me. Because Fatima begins to tell us about a new theorem she's trying to prove that examines how the construct of Black power shaped the Big Bang.

Zahrah applauds her, gives her a high five. 'Yay, good girl. Keep it up.' She turns to me. 'What about you, Andy?'

'I – I ...' I say, googling my hippocampus for every big grammar I know. 'I'm thinking along the same lines as Fatee. But I'm trying to examine the duality of Black power ... as a wave and particle ... its quantum structure, et cetera. And most importantly, I'm thinking of its philosophical ramifications ... its ontology ...'

'Yay!' Zahrah says, giving me a high five, eyes glinting. 'Interesting.'

'Thanks.'

'Will it be a poem or a paper?'

'I'm not sure yet.'

'That's all right. In the end, poetry and maths are actually the same thing. The pathways to truth.'

Zahrah and Fatima pour themselves some orange juice. They sip.

Zahrah's fingernails and toenails are also painted red. I wonder what Okorie, her fiancé, thinks about her redmania. Maybe that's what actually draws him to her. Love can be so weird sometimes – aliens take note!

I've met Okorie a few times and he's really grand. He's tall, speaks with a very deep voice (like me!), and owns a Jaguar. He was a Rhodes Scholar at Oxford. He teaches maths at the University of Warwick and at the African University of Science and Technology in Abuja. He and Zahrah got engaged weeks ago and plan to marry in two months. He's always bemoaning the educational horrorshow in Nigeria. Zahrah's always warning him to be careful with his university activism, that, in case he's forgotten, assassinations are rife in this shithole.

'I heard you travelled to Ososo,' I say to Zahrah.

'Yes, yes,' she says. 'A long journey.'

'Wow.'

'Fatee told you, right? I went very secretly this time. I've been commissioned to write an article on Anifuturism for a British magazine.'

She says she's investigating a new interest: How the soul permutes the body. How the soul is split and distributed among the children of a set of parents. Spiritual twinhood, children sharing a soul with unborn siblings.

I look up at her, at her serrated brows and jiggling earrings. Does she know about Ydna?

Probably just a coincidence.

She says she's writing the article more from the standpoint of a sceptic. That all her life she's heard stories of dead people moving to towns far away from where they'd lived, to begin life afresh.

'In fact, it happened here recently,' she says.

'Seriously?' I say.

'Yes. There's a shop just around the corner. Turns out that the owner died years ago in Niger. Last week his wife and kids visited Kontagora and found him running the shop. When he saw them approaching, he jumped through the window and fled. Since then no one has seen him. In fact, the emir has seized the shop and handed it to one of his wives.'

We laugh. Fatima spills her orange juice. Zahrah stops and says that this isn't a laughing matter.

Fatima's iPhone buzzes: her mother is waiting for her at home.

'Thank you, Aunty Zahrah,' she says. 'I need to get ready.' She picks up her hijab and leaves for her room.

'So, Andy, I met your grandma,' Zahrah says, sipping water.

'Really?' I say, leaning forward.

'Yes. Lovely woman.'

'What's she like?'

'Old, of course. But tall. Taller than your mama.'

'Is she like Mama?'

Zahrah pauses. 'Andy, you've met her before.'

56

'No, I haven't.'

'You have.'

'I haven't.'

'She came here a few months ago. To see you.'

'Aunty Zahrah, you're—'

'She even went to school. To my office. We were inside talking – you, Fatima, and me.'

'I can't remember seeing anyone like her . . .'

'But she came. I assure you.'

'But why didn't you tell me? Or introduce her to me?'

'I didn't know her at the time.'

old woman
with an old stick
peeping
into an office
at me

'And Andy,' Zahrah says, 'she followed you and your friends as you walked home.'

'Seriously?'

'Yes, she did. She even stopped at a shop you and your friends stopped at. She bought you guys chocolate biscuits.'

'I remember . . .'

Vaguely.

Months ago Slim, Morocca, and I stopped at a shop to buy purewater and chocolate biscuits. The shopkeeper gave us the biscuits and we were about to open them when we realised we didn't have enough money. A tall old woman behind us offered to pay. She had a red leather handbag and stood very erect for a woman of her age. She held a stick playfully, not resting her weight on it, and it looked like an afterthought in her hand. My droogs and I simply thanked her and bounced on without giving her a second glance.

Mama often says that blood smells. That even if you travel to a distant country and meet an unknown relative there, you'd recognise them immediately. You'd feel some force pulling you to them, itching you under your skin, reminding you of something. I wonder whether this is true, whether I didn't recognise Grandma because Mama's blood was already smelling all over town.

Fatima emerges from her room in a black hijab and an ankara dress, a plump bag slung over her shoulder.

'See you later,' she says. 'Thanks, Aunty Zahrah.'

'Later, Fatee,' Zahrah says. 'Take care.'

'Bye, Andy Africa!' she calls, laughing.

'Bye, Fatee,' I say. But my tone is flat.

Fatima goes out the door slowly, shoulders slumped.

'But why?' I say to Zahrah. 'Why didn't she say anything?'

'Say what?' Zahrah says, picking bits of rice sprinkled on the floor. She throws them onto the plate.

'She could've introduced herself or something.'

'Yes, Andy. But it's not as simple as that.'

'What do you mean?'

'I don't know.'

'You're not telling me something.'

Zahrah's globe eyes beam at me.

'Come on, Andy,' she says. 'You're like a son to me. At least like a younger brother.' She places a hand on my cheek. It's warm. 'And I wouldn't do that to you.'

'Thanks,' I say.

But I still feel she's hiding something. Although she spins unending monologues, she's also secretive. Nobody knows why she went to the Sahara. She's evaded the question whenever Fatima and I have raised it. 'We can't talk about that,' she'll say. 'It was the darkest time of my entire life. Even my mother and her mother didn't suffer like I did.' Fatima and I have guessed that it must have involved a baby.

'Your grandma sent you a letter,' Zahrah says. 'She actually dictated it in Ososo, and I wrote it down in English. Give me a sec.'

She marches barefoot to her room.

The god with the trapezium head calls to me. Its African eye slits are like eyes with hot tears trickling down, permanently halted from dropping. It must be very shitty being such a god, suffering such eternal tears.

Suddenly I want to scream.

But I don't have it in me. Using my finger I write *It* on the floor. It stays a moment. But fades away. Like Everything.

Zahrah returns and hands me a white envelope.

'I need to get dressed for the party,' she says.

She places the plate dotted with rice on the tray. Then the empty bottles. Then the cups, the cutlery.

'Thanks,' I say.

'For what?'

'For the food.'

'Oh. You're such a lovely person, Andy.'

She leaves for the kitchen. Unloads the tray, emerges, goes to her room.

Very slowly, I open the envelope.

Andrew mè,

How are you?

I think about you. Always. I've even learnt how to spell your name. It's the only word I can write. It looks pretty when I look at it.

Andrew mè, forgive me, but I couldn't say a word to you. I couldn't cross all those boundaries. I was too weak inside. The more of you I saw, the more I wanted. Forgive me.

Your mama is one of the greatest people I know. She's done things for you that I can't do for my own child. Still, we disagree about basic things. For example, even though she has her reasons, she shouldn't keep your papa away from you for so long. I know he has hurt her so gravely. But still, she has to forgive him. And you have to forgive her. And you all have to embrace each other and be a family somehow. This was why I came to Kontagora to see her. And I hope to speak to her again about this soon. But Andrew mè, you mustn't stop loving her. You're her, she's you, I'm her,

I'm you. We're a chain. Only together can we spin. If we stop being together, we become scraps. Useless, aimless. Best dumped into a landfill. Please continue to be patient as we try to get your mama to let go of the past and let your papa into your life. He is so eager to see you, to hold you in his arms. In fact, he's vowed to visit you very soon.

When I think about you, everything in me leaps. And I'm happy. And I sing. Do you like singing? Did you enjoy those biscuits?

I'll sing you a song my mama used to sing to me. (I've asked Zahrah to translate it very carefully.)

Ọmọ e werọ	A child, sweet
Abi shi sugar	Like sugar
Osono yiwọ	There's so much suffering
Aki kunọ yin ugi	Lay them in a basket
Oghọghọ ọgbọ kpọ sé	And its weight overwhelms, overflows
Evesho dobọ obia ọmọ re enerhe ọmọ	God, help us enjoy their fruits
Osono mi minẹ uvu ma chi nẹ samina	Those thorns in my womb I could never forget
Debi kpedi bia bia o	But on the day you were born, you were born

I'll see you again.

Your Grandma Aziza

Scalds spinning in my eyes.
Mama … Her smell … Her goodnight sleep well musty scent. Her mysteries, her lies …
There's a note from Zahrah at the back of the letter:

I cried while writing this, while translating it. And I remembered your Ydna. Yes, I know who he is. How confusing things must be for you . . . Just know that you're never alone, Andy. You always have Ydna. Also know that most of us Africans have our Ydnas too. Hopefully, this realisation helps. Z.

4

On the fence of our church, *Post No Bill* is painted in black at intervals. But hundreds of bills are stuck on the fence, riffling in the breeze, advertising fake jobs. *Stop!* one says. *Earn 100k in two days!* Although many folks know the jobs are fake, they still apply, pay thousands in application fees. It kills me.

Slim, Morocca, and I walk through the gate into our church compound.

This is our cathedral: No domes. No spires. No arches. Just a large squat bungalow. Painted yellow up, brown down. Cracks of peeled paint peeping at us.

Dry yellowing bushes surround it, but one at the back entrance is blooming: an oasis, a saint, a flame at night. And inside, a bumblebee bumps and bumps against a dusty window.

The sun is milder, orange. A hand of cloud slowly covers it.

Leaves crunch under our feet. The air is cool in this shade of whistling gmelina trees. Fallen seeds smell like sweet urine.

Before I left her house, I asked Zahrah a ton of questions. How she learnt about Ydna. When I'll be seeing my papa. Why she was keeping a secret from me. She declined to answer, saying I should talk to Mama, that Mama would explain everything.

'So sad to learn about Ydna,' she said. 'Reminds me of mine . . . How she left me. How she sent me to the Sahara . . . Guess I'll rename her Harhaz.'

My droogs ask me why I've been downcast, why I'm not laughing at their jokes, what happened at Zahrah's. I tell them that all's fine, that we should continue walking before we're late. They try to raise my spirits, tickling my sides, rubbing my back. Morocca jokes that he knows Zahrah has a huge crush on me, the way she stares at me and all. That if I ever want to lose my precious virginity all I have to do is visit her at night. And she'll give me a hard titty fuck. I burst out laughing, throw him a punch.

'I'll kill you, dawg,' I say.

We laugh and walk on.

My phone begins to ring. I dig it out of my jeans.

It's Mama.

My heart jerks. I wait a moment. Take deep breaths.

I pick up the call. There's music in the earpiece. People shouting, laughing.

'Andrew mè,' she says.

I don't know whether to say 'Yes' or 'Yes, Ma', considering how she's selfishly hidden me away from my papa.

'Andrew mè?'

'Yes?' I say in Ososo.

There's a pause. I'm sure she noticed I didn't add 'Ma' to my response. She notices everything.

'Hope you're all right?' she says. 'Where are you?'

'I'm in the church compound. On my way to the Father's House.'

'Okay. I thought you were far away. Would have told you to go back home.'

Is my papa coming to the party? Is she trying to keep me away from him?

She says she just learnt that a riot is stirring in town. One of our church members got drunk, insulted the Prophet Muhammad, and burnt a Tasbih. Muslims took to the street, breaking windscreens, burning tyres. The police intervened, and so far the riot has quietened.

'Still, we cannot trust these people,' she says. 'All right, then. See you!'

And she ends the call before I say another word. Trust Mama. Always trying to save her airtime.

During the last riot churches and Christian-owned shops were broken into, looted, burnt. Women and children were hacked with machetes. I was at a party with Slim and Morocca. Mama had to run into the night amid all the screaming and 'Allahu akbar' to find me. Men chased her, whipped her, grabbed her breasts. To save herself she denied she was a Christian. Denied Christ. Said the Bible was fake, evil, despite reciting Psalm 23 and praying the rosary every day. She chanted, at the top of her voice, 'La ilaha illallah! Muhammadur rasulullah!' The men laughed at her.

I tell my droogs about the call. Morocca checks his phone and sees a message about the riot. We continue walking, hoping it won't reach the church, that the police continue to quell it.

Slim smiles and shakes his head.

'Why're you smiling like a bunny?' Morocca says.

'Just a thought,' he says.

'What effing thought?' Morocca says.

'I wish Eileen had a twin bro. So that I could also roll.'

'And a twin sis too,' Morocca says. 'So that we could all roll.'

We laugh.

We pass a grove of masquerade trees. The Father's House is at the eastern end of the compound, a minute away.

'Aren't we silly?' Slim says.

'How?' Morocca says.

'We're crushing on someone who can never like us.'

'Come on, man,' Morocca says. 'We've talked about this shit. And I proved you wrong.'

'Shut up. How?'

'About our dicks.'

'Yeah?'

'That they're small lions. That every white chick wants a bite.'

'Go bite a rat with your python dick, Morocca,' Slim says. 'Trust me, Eileen won't touch ya beyond a handshake.'

I want to change the subject. But I don't know what to say.

We hear the children's choir singing 'Lord of the Dance'. And Morocca begins to shake his flat black ass to the rhythm. Twisting left, right. Front, back.

We laugh.

But then we freeze. Because we can see the porch of the Father's House. It's partly covered by flamboyant trees. Someone stands there, shifting slowly: someone who should not exist here.

Time slows. Seconds expand.

There are infinities between every two numbers. There are millennia buried in seconds. Creatures are born and they die and they're reborn. The world ends and begins and begins. Blink, and the world you see is new.

A blonde girl is standing by the door. In a peach dress and sandals. She's waving at some children, smiling.

Platinum-blonde hair. Wavy. Waist-length. Each strand a long sweet sun.

The hand of cloud shifts from the orange sun. Warm brightness unfurls. Eileen looks up at it:

Ode to Eileen

gazing
at the sun

she sees herself

smiles at herself
beauty before a mirror

Ode to The Scream

every
african

    s

    c

    r

    e

    a

    m

    s

  at the
  sun

    at

    hxvx

whenever
they see a

white person

Time contracts.

We walk on. Silently. Not looking at each other. Not looking at her. Just staring at flamboyant trees. At their bleeding flowers. Some shaped like bleeding hearts.

We reach the steps of the house. The children's choir is very loud now. Their singing seems to come from the back garden.

We approach her.

She smiles. Green eyes. Like meadows in the breeze.

A ring glows on her nose. Her pendant too.

She seems to spin around us, wreathe us. Nothing else remains. Even when I look away, all I see is platinum. Whirling. Winking. Piercing.

She smiles at me.

Something in me ripples.

I smile at her.

'Hi,' I say.

'Hello,' she says.

'You must be Eileen.'

There's a soft sparkle in her.

'Oh, yes,' she says with a laugh.

'I'm Andy.'

'Oh, hello, Andy.'

Her 'oh' and 'hello' finger a string in me.

'Good to meet you, Eileen.'

'Nice to meet you, Andy.'

. . . The way her voice twirls up–down–up like a curve, turning words into song . . .

She gives me her hand. Pink sculpture. Do I kiss or shake it?

I shake it. Hold it a second longer. It's satiny, like a wet petal.

'And these are Tom and Mike,' I say, gesturing at my droogs.

I sound somewhat strange, deeper voice and all. More British? And I don't know why I shortened the names of my droogs. I've never done that before.

'Hi, Tom. Hi, Mike,' she says, giving them her hand.

'Hey, Eileen,' Slim says.

'Hiya, pretty Eileen,' Morocca says. 'How's you?'

She laughs. 'I'm great.'

I'm annoyed with Morocca for calling her pretty, for not giving me that honour. But I don't sweat it too much. Because her gaze keeps returning to me even as she glances at him and Slim.

... The way her lips coil to a rosy O when she laughs ...

'Good to meet you.'

'Thanks.'

'Nice.'

'Great.'

'Swell.'

... The way she blinks and her eyes return fresher ...

'How're you finding Kontagora?' I say, in full-blown Cockney.

'Say that again?' she says.

I repeat my question, a little ashamed, slower this time, trying to be more relaxed, more everyday.

'Oh,' she says. 'It's been great. Different from London, of course. But great.'

'Seriously?' I say. 'How d'you mean?'

'I like the vibe here. Everyone's friendly, happy, laughing ... And the scenery is just beautiful.'

'Really?'

'Yes. And I like the culture. Colourful dresses. Cool words and names.'

'Great.'

'What's "ya ki ke"?' she says. 'Did I say that right?'

'Yeah,' I say, even though she didn't.

'It means "How are you?"' Slim says.

'Oh, nice.'

'Cool.'

'Great.'

'You seem to like the arts,' Morocca says.

'Yes,' she says. 'Sure do.'

'D'you know I'm a rapper?' Morocca says. 'Like Kanye West? And Andy is a poet?'

She turns to me. 'Really? You write poetry?'

'Yeah,' I say. 'Some.'

'I love poetry,' she says.

'Really?'

'Yes. Emily Dickinson, the Brontës, especially Charlotte, Seamus Heaney, Sylvia Plath . . .'

'Perfect taste,' I say. 'I love them too.' Truth be told, I only like Dickinson and Plath.

Morocca is sad that Eileen doesn't give a damn about his rapping.

'And Andy's poem won first prize,' Slim says, 'in the state competition. It got published in newspapers round the country.'

'Wow, great,' she says. 'Really great. Congrats.'

'Thanks,' I say.

Eileen says that, although she's memorised lots of poems, she's never dared to write one before. I ask why. She says she's sure any attempt will be pure crap, or at best a redux of her favourite poems. I tell her not to be afraid of repetition, that all good art begins as imitation.

'True,' she says softly. 'Very true.'

Damn. Really crazy that we're already chit-chatting about poetry.

I want to hold her stone pendant. Finger it. Pick the bits of herself in its edges.

We look at each other. Seconds expand. My droogs disappear. I find myself in her meadow. She sailing above me. Calling me. Making me levitate to her.

'I'd like to read some of your work,' she says, 'if you don't mind.'

'Oh, very kind of you,' I say. 'Thanks.'

'I hope to read more African poetry while I'm here.'

'Great plan,' I say, hoping she won't ask for recommendations. I have few to give.

I suddenly notice that our church council chairman and his wife and children are behind us. In fact, a small crowd has formed around the steps, waiting to say hi to Eileen, to proceed to the party.

Eileen tells us that it has just begun, in the back garden. That we should go into the living room and take the back door. She'll be with us in a moment.

'See you in a minute,' she says to us. To me she adds, 'You'll read some of your poems to me, won't you?'

'Yeah. Sure. Later, Eileen.'

She steps forward, radiant, a halo flickering about her. She welcomes the guests, shakes their hands, hugs the women. Squats and lets little kids finger her platinum Strands of Power. The kids giggle.

'It's so soft!' they say. 'Like water!'

Their parents tell them to quit touching her hair. That they're messing with it, staining it.

I'm sure she's feeling very weird: like an angel stepping out of heaven, an alien princess landing on earth, a fish tossing and tossing on a beach.

Morocca tugs at me. I follow him and Slim to the living room, feeling light departing from me.

+

In the garden, platinum colours everything I see: The scores of people sitting in a circle in plastic chairs, smiling, sparky. The children's choir at the centre, hopping, twisting, pirouetting in unison to Panam Percy Paul's 'African Way'. They're little kids, aged five to twelve, dressed in white shirts and trousers and gloves. They raise their hands skyward when Panam croons about heaven and fall to their knees when he sings of earth. The audience wows and claps. Little kids at the rear stand atop their seats to see clearly.

Mama appears, her camera strapped to her neck. It's heaving on her chest like a third breast.

Riot of emotions in my blood. Here is the pillar between my papa and me. I want to hate her, to roar and spit and break

70

things. But Grandma's words continue to echo: *you mustn't stop loving her; you're her, she's you; we're a chain.* And when memories of Mama's smell confront me, I begin to submit, piece by piece.

Mama squats before the dancing choir. Fixes the camera on her face. Winds the lenses right left right. She smiles. Click, click. She falls on her knees, leans forward, smiles again. Click, click. Flash!

She's in a red–black tie–dye dress, a flowery scarf covering her greying cornrows. She gets up. Turns suddenly. Looks at me.

I die.

I'm standing amidst kids my age and many who are older. But Mama's gaze finds me in the throng. She smiles at me. Flashes the gap between her teeth. I do not know what her dimples say. I try not to, try very hard not to, but I fail:

I smile at her.

A breeze sweeps through the garden. Flowering plants wake. Filling our eyes with flaming red, pink, and peach: Flamboyant trees with bleeding flowers, swaying. Bougainvillea crawling about. Petite roses winking.

Mama moves to the high table. It's decorated with lace and rainbow balloons, and lining the top are Eva wine bottles and Five Alive cartons. Sitting behind it are the who's who of our church. In the middle are Father McMahon, Sister Lakefield, and Elder Paschal, our church council chairman. Just between McMahon and Lakefield is an ornate flowery throne for Eileen.

Mama snaps them. Stoops, smiles, snaps them again.

I really don't like Mama stooping before people while winding her lenses. It feels as if she's accepted who she is, who we are, as people who stoop, who have to stoop, who are condemned to stoop.

Father McMahon will pay her twenty thousand for this evening, plus other expenses like transport and lab fees. She's planned to buy two wrappers, some clothes for me, and to fill our store with food.

I wish we could talk in private. But she wouldn't talk to me now since she's working. 'Wait till we get home,' she'd say. I'll have to wait till after the party.

She retreats into the crowd. Disappears into a grove of frangipani trees.

The children's choir spin and stand on their toes like Michael Jackson.

'That's my boy!' a man in red cries.

Chief Onu, popularly called Mai Gemu (even though he's completely beardless), rises from his seat beside Elder Paschal. He's wearing a black tunic and a string of red beads, each bead like a goat horn. He's called Mai Gemu because he's very wealthy, because he makes at least five million every day from his spare-parts shop on Lagos Road. It's said that he's killed three people, including his first son, and offered their blood, private parts, and souls to the evil spirits of his village. It's also said that he has three live tortoises buried in the veranda of his shop, and that these evil spirits and tortoises cause car accidents and breakdowns in our town, make drivers suffer an irresistible itch to buy spare parts whenever they pass his shop.

He struts towards the dancing choir. Men hail him: 'Mai Gemu, Mai Gemu!' His shoulders broaden. He raises his staff at the audience as though it were the World Cup. They cheer. His polished staff flashes, reflecting lights as he swings it side to side, up and down.

'Mai Gemu!'

He gets to the dancing choir, dips his hand into his tunic, brings out a wad of shiny twenty-naira notes fresh from the Central Bank. The choir begins to dance wildly, the audience holds its breath. Suddenly he flings the money at the choir. A rain of green notes spatters on them. They miss steps, bump into each other; one crashes headfirst onto the ground.

The audience gets to its feet, roars.

Mama emerges, clicking away with her camera.

Mai Gemu falls into a dancing fit. He shakes his big buttocks up down, gripping his staff as though it were a dance pole. He's out of sync with the choir; they're dancing Western, he's dancing tribal. He flaps his shoulders, bending down slowly slowly till he's squatting.

The audience is mad.

Mai Gemu's friends race onto the grounds to join him. The MC encourages the audience to do the same. He says that today is the day of God, the day of our priest. 'Heaven shall fall down tonight. He who dances once prays twice.'

The audience rushes onto the grounds and begins dancing. Soon almost everyone is dancing, except Father McMahon and Sister Lakefield, both still at the high table. They hesitate a minute. Then they rise and walk awkwardly to the grounds. They stand another minute, uncertain how to move, whether to imitate the back-breaking tribal dance around them or to move in a slow, calculated, Western way. They settle for a clumsy swinging of arms and feet. In the frenzy, nobody seems to notice a little boy in the choir who slips one of the fallen notes into his pocket.

I check the back door for Eileen. Wonder why she isn't here yet. Can't wait to see how she'll dance.

Mr Calculator, our chief church warden, jostles through the crowd, his afro as huge as a bowler hat. He's clutching a plastic basket, picking up the fallen notes, throwing them into it. I'm sure he's tempted to pocket some, but he convinces himself otherwise, that this is God's money, even though it's Father McMahon who'll spend it afterwards.

The DJ switches to a praise-and-worship song:

> *Bouncing in the Lord*
> *I am bouncing in the Lord every day*
> *Bounce! Bounce! Bounce! . . .*

The crowd roars, hopping and rebounding and crashing into each other. Father McMahon and Sister Lakefield are completely lost. They stand, arms akimbo, gazing around at the alien dance steps, helpless, Sister Lakefield blushing slightly. She sees me and waves as though I were the helicopter that would take her out of this weirdoland.

I walk over to them, pushing through the twists and hops and sweat. Everywhere I turn there's the heavy smell of perspiration or camphor or some cheap perfume.

I pass Slim and Morocca. They're standing, arms folded, around an ixora bush, muttering that the dancing and music is nonsense, primitive, like we've gone back a hundred years.

'Whatcha up to, bro?' they say.

'Nothing much,' I say. 'Gimme a minute.'

Father McMahon and Sister Lakefield look like an old white couple, he in his sixties, she middle-aged, both greying and wrinkled and wearing glasses. He's in a white shirt tucked in jeans; she's in a blue knee-length flowery dress. They're the first whites I ever knew. In fact, it was Father McMahon who baptised me. He insisted Mama call me Andrew, the bro of the dude who founded Christianity, because I'd been born on St Andrew's feast day. He even told Mama that I'd grow up to be a great man like St Andrew. That Mama shouldn't worry but have faith.

That I'd transform her life.

Mama had wanted to call me something else, like Akpamè (my lamp) or Omokhafè (a child is home), but she reluctantly accepted Andrew when she heard the great man part. Still, she thinks Andrew is too raw and foreign on her tongue, so she calls me Andrew mè, my Andrew.

I'm sure I've only transformed Mama's life by making it worse.

children
are the curse
of things

'Hello, Andy,' Sister Lakefield says.

Updownup accent. Long thin nose. Producing impossible sound.

Wish I could talk like that.

'Good evening, Sister. Good evening, Father,' I say to them.

'Evening, Andy,' Father McMahon says.

Their accent always gives me a sweet jolt whenever I talk to them, reminding me to get outta here asap.

'Hope you're having a good time?' Sister Lakefield says.

'Yes, Sister.'

'And you've met Eileen?'

'Yes, Father. She's very . . . kind.'

I wanted to say pretty or beautiful, but I stopped myself because men don't like other men admiring their females.

I always feel like a bird (free, flying, floating) whenever I'm with Father McMahon and Sister Lakefield. I feel like my feet are inches out of this continent. And there's this beating of blood, this soothing spiral and strengthening around my shoulders whenever I talk to them, whenever passing people see us together. And in the eyes of these people there's this glint, this wishing to God they were in my place. It always kills me.

'How's your book coming along?' I ask Father McMahon. He's looking very bearded and sleepless these days.

'Good so far, Andy. Just that I've missed my deadline and my editor is cross.'

Father McMahon is writing a book about his archaeological excavations of communities along the River Niger, and how the creation stories of Northern Nigerian tribes parallel and dovetail that of Genesis. I visit him occasionally on weekends, and we spend evenings talking about Darwin (how his theory doesn't negate Genesis) and Georges Lemaître (how faith can guide and strengthen reason). We spend nights in his garden peering through his telescope at Alpha Scorpii and Proxima Centauri b, wondering about possible lives out there, whether they have that hole deep in them to understand things, whether they know God exists, God's plan for creating other planets apart from earth. Father McMahon's greatest wish (apart from making heaven!) is to be somehow reborn in a thousand years to discover how Everything has turned out.

Suddenly the music stops. And I know why. I turn to the back door. There stands the Queen of Platinum, in a peach dress, resting her weight on one foot. She's wide-eyed, amazed at how everyone has gone native, gone back to Eden, especially her uncle and prim Sister Lakefield.

The MC, pot-bellied Chief OZ, speaks into the mike. Feedback spirals through the garden like a spring.

'Praise the Lord!' he says. 'Praise the Lord o!'

'Hallelujah o!' the crowd answers, catching its breath.

Chief OZ says that this is the moment we've been waiting for, for the 'triumphant entry of our very distinguished guest of honour'. Mr Calculator steps forward to do what he does best. In half a minute, pushing and threatening people, he manages to clear a straight path through the crowd, between the back door and Eileen's throne at the high table.

The DJ plays 'Gloria in excelsis Deo'.

Hey, Ydna.
What's up, Andy?
Is this really happening?
Guess so, man.

'And now,' Chief OZ says, 'from London, UK . . . brothers and sisters . . . please welcome . . . Eileen Catherine Grosvenor!'

Men and women cheer. Boys whistle. Girls shriek. All singing 'Gloria in excelsis Deo', as though this were Palm Sunday, as though Eileen were Christ Himself.

Eileen blushes, hesitates a moment. Then she begins her entry, walking through the path, and it closes behind her.

I'm sure all the boys and men are hearing creaking beds in their heads, the pink in their mouths aching for the pink of her body, the jet-black between their legs craving to be whirled and bleached by the platinum waving down her back. The women must be cursing the sun, wishing they could spin back time, having sci-fi ideas about how to look like her.

Ydna?
Yes, bro?
I wanna look away.
Go on.
But I can't!
Seriously, man. You can. You can do anything.

Girls caress Eileen's hair, their mouths wide as the rim of a cup. They're wondering whether all this hair is real, is natural, why they weren't this lucky, whether the Universe and Everything is just. The older girls are wearing red or dark-blonde wigs made locally from petroleum (the cheapest ones) or imported from Brazil (the most expensive). Others have straightened their hair with relaxers or braided theirs with blonde attachments.

Mama is at the end of the path, clicking away with her camera.

Queen of Platinum gets to her throne, her halo flickering about her. She sits. The cheering climaxes.

Ydna, d'you really think we are?
Are what?
You know what. Them and us.
. . .
Answer me, Ydna. Tell me the truth. Are we? Are we . . . like the
same? Like the same level?
. . .
Ydna. Talk to me. Ydna!

Slowly, the crowd drift to their seats. I join other kids my age under a flamboyant tree. I know a few but I don't say a word to them. They mostly don't understand me when we talk. They don't ever get my references about *Dune* or Tarantino, and I don't get their chit-chat about the latest Tiwa Savage music video (how she danced naked) or the latest Tonto Dikeh film (how her skin is getting whiter).

+

Three little girls, dressed in white lace like angels, are in the centre of the grounds. They're singing Eileen a welcome song.

E for exquisite
I for infinite
L for—

My droogs join me, dragging our classmate Okey with them. Morocca's arm is round Okey's waist, Slim is running his hand round Okey's huge shiny skull. Okey's eyes are the biggest I've ever seen, seriously. They're like WALL-E's. In fact, if you want to get a punch or behold the full size of his eyes, just call him WALL-E. My droogs are so amped and I'm so 9-1-1 to know why they're giving him the girlfriend treatment.

'Wazzup, Scads,' I say. 'What's up, Okey?' I'm really itching to call him WALL-E.

'Okey, my nigga,' Morocca says, 'tell Andy what you just told us.'

Okey is giggling like a rat, licking his lower lip, feeling like a celeb.

'Come on, Okey,' Slim begs.

'Why una dey disturb me, na,' Okey laughs at my droogs.

'Please, Okey,' Morocca says.

'Okay,' Okey says to me. 'Long story short. Me and my uncle are travelling abroad very soon. We go go Spain.'

'Really?' I say. I'm sure he's lying. When it comes to lies, he's the Einstein. Although his grandfather is long deceased and worked as a cleaner throughout his life, Okey claims he in fact owns an engineering company in Abuja where he builds satellites. Okey has fooled all our teachers, including Zahrah, inventing rocket-science excuses for skipping school or not doing his assignments. Last time, he claimed that his grandfather found his name and the coordinates of our school in a strange message from one of the Nigerian satellites. Thus he was advised to stay away from school for at least a week until the message was properly investigated.

'Seriously, Okey?' I say.

He nods confidently, swagger about him, like some superstar.

'Cool,' I say, not believing him.

'Andy,' Morocca says, 'ask him how he'll be travelling.'

'How will you be travelling, Okey?'

Okey gives Morocca the red eye a bit, then smiles.

'When are you flying, Okey?' I say.

My droogs burst out laughing, pointing at me as though I've suddenly developed a dozen antennas on my head. They laugh hard for a minute. A church warden glares at them.

'Come on, Scads,' I say, wanting them to stop. 'Are you travelling by sea, then, on a ship?'

My droogs laugh harder. When they finally stop, Morocca says that Okey intends to travel by the third (or rather the first) means of transport: land.

'Seriously?' I say, becoming excited myself. 'Really, Okey?'

Okey gives his swagger nod.

'Damn,' I say. 'So you guys want to follow the Sahara?'

'Yep,' Okey says. 'What's wrong with that?'

'But it's effing dangerous, man.'

Okey hisses. 'Stay there make pant dey wear you, Andy. Me and my uncle are fucking following the desert to Spain.'

'But why would you want to follow the desert? See how Oga Oliver turned out.'

'You dey talk like a pussy, Andy.'

Another time I would've slapped his big mouth for such a comment. But now I'm too excited to really care.

'Make I tell you, Andy,' Okey says. 'About two of my cousins and one of my uncles are in Spain. They went through the desert, I dey tell you. They're sharp, bro, very sharp, not like Oga Oliver. They're doing very well there, man. Eating all kinds of goodies. Fucking all kinds of damsels.'

'Wow,' I say. My droogs and I gaze at him, hands on our hips.

'Many people who travel through the desert succeed, man. Only the cowards don't. As for me and my uncle, we're going. We can't stay in this mumu country any longer.'

A long silence. My droogs and I gawk at Okey, wishing we were in his place, despite the risks. We know that, if he succeeds, his life will be the opposite of ours. He smiles at us, a conceited smile, pitying our unfortunate souls.

The children's singing reaches a crescendo:

Miss Eileen, welcome
We are saying welcome

Eileen giggles. Takes out her iPhone. Photographs the girls.

'Andy,' Okey says, 'I hear say you and Morocca are fallin' in love with that innocent white girl!' He laughs. 'Are you guys even serious? You think say that white girl is gonna have anything to do with you boys? If you wanna taste white pussy you better get outta here soon, I dey tell you. You are just wasting your time with the chick.'

We gawk at him, not the least offended by his barbs.

He shakes his big head. 'I go leave you mumu boys for this mumu country!' he says, as though it's our fault we're stuck here. 'I bet you guys say I go taste white pussy before all of una!'

I excuse myself, go to use the toilet. When I return to the flamboyant tree I can't find my droogs or Okey.

A girl under the tree wearing a wig eyes me. But I don't meet her gaze. Mine sails and perches on the Queen of Platinum at the high table. She's scanning through the programme, her nose ring winking at me.

I seriously don't know what's wrong with me. I'm sure that girl is still staring at moi. Tbh, she ain't looking bad at all. Why can't I look back at her, begin a conversation, get her number? Is it simply because of her wig? And why am I the only one noticing wigs?

I continue watching the high table. I dig out my phone, pretend as though I'm reading some life-changing chat from my homies. And, very slowly, I move away from the flamboyant tree and stop when I'm under another, several yards away. Around me are fellas who're slightly older, many of whom I don't know. I look around: oui, I'm safe from the girl; oui, I can see the high table clearly.

Chief OZ taps the mike, says it's time for toast and breaking of kolanuts. At the high table the ushers serve kolanuts in saucers. Pour sparkling red wine in glasses. Place the glasses gently before our special guests. To the other guests they toss yellow-green aubergine and paper cups half-filled with orange juice.

Chief OZ hands the mike to Mai Gemu to pray over the kolanuts. Mai Gemu clears his throat, taps the mike repeatedly till feedback cuts through the garden. He prays for good health for Eileen, that she enjoys her stay, that the seed Father McMahon and other whites sowed in this country will grow and grow till it passes the stars. He prays for all men gathered (forgetting the women) that God opens all the windows of heaven and blesses their businesses, and blesses, especially, his own business, for he who prays shouldn't forget himself. People chuckle and cry, 'Amen.'

Chief OZ asks everyone to stand for the toast. They all do. He goes to the centre of the grounds, raises his drink high to the evening sun.

'J,' he says into the mike.

'J,' people respond.

'E,' he says.

'E.'

'S.'

'S.'

'U.'

'U.'

'S!'

'S!'

'Jesus!' he cries.

The audience cheers.

Eileen, Father McMahon, and Sister Lakefield are confused. They finally understand that the toast has been made when people on the high table begin clinking their glasses. Then they smile and clink their glasses too.

Eileen sips. Life drains out of her and returns. Her meadow eyes are greener, cheeks fuller balloons, lips redder. She glances at the kolanut in her saucer. Her nose twitches. She looks back to the audience, wearing a fresher smile, kola forgotten.

Her uncle takes a bite of the kola and returns it to the saucer. Sister Lakefield breaks a pinch. Throws it into her mouth. Grimaces. Smiles immediately before it's too late.

People bash paper cups on paper cups. Spills, stains. They drink. Smile. Bite into their aubergines. Laugh.

Chioma, Isaiah's wife, pushes a trolley to the front of the high table. It's carrying a three-tower cake with two statuettes atop, like a wedding cake. One is of a blonde in a peach dress, and the other a white man in a white cassock.

As the audience sits, Chief OZ says that today is a double feast. First, the church's grand welcoming of Eileen, and second, Father McMahon's thirty-ninth anniversary in Nigeria and Africa. He invites Father McMahon to give a speech.

People cheer, clap, whistle.

Father McMahon steps forward and takes the mike. His sleek greying hair ruffles in the breeze.

'Thank you, Ozoemenam,' he says, stressing the first syllable of OZ's name instead of the second. 'Thank you everyone for coming. It's such a thrilling event today. Eileen has really enjoyed herself, I'm sure.' His pronunciation of her name is effortless, as though he's among the league naturally endowed to pronounce her name correctly. 'I have some sad news, I'm afraid. But before that, I'd like to say how the past thirty-nine years have been the best I could've ever lived. It feels like only yesterday I came down a ship in Lagos. Like only yesterday all this began.'

5

I've tried several times to understand why Father McMahon left the Real Life in England – of potatoes and sleek roads and nine degrees Celsius – for this shithole Cursed continent of garri and potholes and forty degrees. What else is here for him but horror and scorching death? I've asked him this several times (in indirect ways), but he's been unable to answer me satisfactorily. I wish he could explain himself in this speech, but he seems uninterested in pursuing it.

'The very first moment I saw the Nigerian coast,' he says, 'I fell in love with Africa.'

The audience applauds. Screams, cheers.

He goes on, explaining how he spent hours and hours absorbing the beauty of this place. How he loved the special yellow of the African sun. The refreshing greenness of leaves as they absorbed and reflected it. How whirlwinds suddenly emerged from trees, formed a spinning mass of dust and leaves and dirty things, and disappeared back into them. The sound of the forest at night, the chirping of infinite creatures he couldn't see by flashlight or in sunlight. How in every moment he could smell and hear the Spirit of God in this place.

The audience applauds. Whistles.

He says all this looking very burnt and red and wrinkled and tired. If he'd been in England all this time he would definitely look younger, with more black in his hair and a glint in his eyes and cheeks.

Maybe he himself doesn't know what pushed him here. Maybe white people are so bored with their comfortable lives that they seek any adventure to give their existence meaning. That's why they do free solos. That's why they enter a reality horror film like Africa. What do white people even want?

'But most importantly,' he says, 'I've been able to carry my cross in my time here, and been reminded of the footsteps of Christ.'

He tells us how, when he and Father Tom Beckett docked, the military government demanded a bribe from them. And when they refused to pay, the soldiers seized the containers in which they had pickups and thousands and thousands of pounds they'd raised from donations to build churches in the Nigerian hinterlands. When he and Beckett eventually met their superiors in Ibadan, they had almost nothing on them except for their Bibles.

'And worse still, in the third week of our arrival to our station, my best friend Father Tom passed on. It was malaria . . . Tom and I were born on the same day in Yarmouth. Grew up on the same street. Were even ordained together. We'd hoped to grow old together . . . Like many missionaries, Father Tom never lived to see the fruits of his sacrifice. He was always more hardworking than me. More optimistic. He'd even foreseen this day despite all the doubts I had.'

He goes to the high table. Picks up his half-empty glass. Raises it to the audience.

'To Father Tom Beckett,' he says. 'Thank you for life, for friendship. Rest in the Peace of Christ.'

He sips.

Silence. Awkwardness.

Then people begin to stand. First those at the high table. Then the whole audience.

They clap. On and on for a long time. Those still having wine or orange juice drink to Father Beckett.

Eileen drinks. Looks in my direction. Looks away.

Strangely, I find myself clapping.

The audience sits and Father McMahon continues.

He talks about how some traditional rulers were unwelcoming to the beautiful words of the Gospel. That they only gave him abandoned graveyards or leper colonies to build his churches. That once he was even stoned and chased from a heathen village near Shafaci. To convince the king of Tudun Masara to accept Christ, he'd had to share his breakfast of a boiled snake and drink amber water from a stagnant pool.

'But the sun of the Gospel can never be hidden, and is never far. People still flocked to see me and hear the saving words of our Messiah.'

I'm sure people only went to see him because he had skin like sunlight, because they thought he was some sort of god. They must have also heard rumours that he dug supernatural wells and built clinics in villages that accepted him, villages that went on Sundays to his special shrine full of candles and white cloths and golden cups.

'In my thirty-nine years I've founded fourteen parishes and thirty-four outstations.'

The audience applauds. Some at the high table give him a standing ovation.

'But the world is changing very fast, especially in my country. Men are getting married to men. Children are being killed in the womb. Churches are empty or only have people my age. They are being closed down or turned into museums and cafés. Young men no longer answer the call of Christ to the priesthood. Even Father Tom never saw this coming. But it's clear now. That Africa is the future of Christ. And so I'll always be an African in my heart.'

Silence. Pungent, nauseating. Even babies in the audience seem to understand this irony of history.

Father McMahon clears his throat and announces that this is his last year in Nigeria and Africa. That he's recently been summoned to shepherd his home parish in Great Yarmouth where there hasn't been a priest in five years.

More silence. But bitter. Noisy with unuttered screams.

Father McMahon hands the mike to Chief OZ and goes to his seat. There's no feedback.

Finally, a baby girl cries out.

+

Eileen is sipping water, talking to Sister Lakefield. Now and then her hand rises gracefully to her platinum. Flicks it back. And it shines brighter. Her ear becomes exposed. Pinkish. Bearing two silvery earrings.

She laughs. Hahaha. Because she controls my spacetime, I find myself laughing too. Hahahaha.

Wish I could get her number. Wish my finger could crawl through the nirvana of her hair. And stop on her ear. So that she could hear the voices in my blood, singing her name.

eileen, eileen
eiqueen

nucleus

of
radioactive
ecstasy

It's drama time. I look around for Zahrah but can't find her. She's the director of the play the children's choir are about to stage. Sister Lakefield had asked her to prepare a playlet with them about the missionary experience suitable for performance on such a day. Zahrah had promised a light-hearted playlet that would also be topical but wouldn't feature any of her Anifuturist ideas. But trust Zahrah. She'll still try to slip some of her ideas into the play, I'm sure.

A girl in white ambles to the front of the high table to introduce the play.

'Good evening, Father, Sister, Eileen, and our beloved parents. We are about to stage a play called *Colours*. As you watch, may you remain blessed. Thank you.'

And she gives the female bow: bending forward her knees.

Sister Lakefield sits up, ready to end the play if it begins to go haywire.

First scene: At the centre of the stage six children are sitting in a semicircle. They're only wearing panties, with sand in their hair, sores on their bodies. They're praying to the statuettes of gods in their centre. Their leader beats a gong. Throws cowries. Calls on Amadioha and Ogun and Adikoriko. 'Save us o, save us. Hear us o, hear us!'

A boy in a white cassock and a girl in a habit come onto the stage. They're wearing blonde wigs, their bodies painted white with chalk. They speak to each other through their noses, sounding like horny birds.

The audience laughs. Eileen giggles. Sister Lakefield sighs in relief, Father McMahon grins.

The boy and the girl, our Father McMahon and Sister Lakefield, go to the heathens sitting in the centre. They preach the Gospel to them.

'Accept the One True God, the Father Almighty, maker of heaven and earth, of all things visible and invisible. Accept his Son, Jesus Christ, who died on the cross for your sins.'

After the preaching, three of the topless heathen children join Father McMahon and Sister Lakefield. Two beautiful angels in white robes fly onto the stage. They take Father McMahon, Sister Lakefield, and the three converted heathens to heaven. The DJ plays 'Gloria in excelsis Deo'.

The audience applauds, cheers.

Suddenly a tall devil gallops onto the stage. He has huge curved horns and a body painted black with charcoal. He draws out his long whip from his black tunic and whips the remaining heathens, especially their leader. He carts them offstage. To hell.

The audience gives a standing ovation, clapping, whistling.

'Great!' a pimply boy says.

'Serves them right!' a lanky woman says.

'Yes o!'

Second scene: At the centre of the stage six children are sitting comfortably in chairs. They're wearing blonde wigs, suits or evening dresses, their bodies shining with white chalk. They cross their legs. Take drags on their cigars. Sip their beer. Play their mobile games.

A Black boy in a white cassock (Father Achi?) timidly approaches them and tells them about the Gospel. He asks them to accept Christ as their Lord and Personal Saviour.

They don't listen to him. 'Go away,' one says to him in a very weird British accent that sounds like a goat bleating.

Sister Lakefield is on the edge of her seat.

As Father Achi turns to go, the black devil with horns sprints to the stage and approaches him. The devil draws out his whip, lashes Father Achi. Seizes him and drags him off to hell.

The two beautiful angels fly to the stage. They beckon the six men and women and lead them to heaven. The DJ plays 'Gloria in excelsis Deo'.

Everyone is stunned.

Father McMahon and Sister Lakefield are leaning forward, heads bent. Eileen is tapping and tapping her iPhone, biting her lip, pretending to seem unaffected.

Elder Paschal rises, fingering his long beard. He cancels the play. But it has already ended.

Zahrah is nowhere to be found.

+

The Zumunta Mata, our church's society of Northern women, are dancing at the centre of the gathering. They're about thirty women, ordered in five lines, chanting a praise song and swinging their bodies in unison. They raise their hands skyward to God. Bring them down to their hearts. Bend and twist their heavy backsides left and right.

> *Mun ba ka yabo Allah, ya Allah*
> *Mun ba ka babban yabo*

The instrumentalists, three greying women, are sitting a few yards behind them. One plays a percussion drum, another a pot bass, the third a tall gong. The gong player is very skilful. She runs her baton up and down her instrument, eyes closed, lost in the music. Her melodies zigzag the harmony of the other players, adding flesh and skin.

Mama appears and photographs the Zumunta. They've asked her a couple times to join their society. She's always declined, reminding them that she's a full-blooded Southerner despite having lived here in the North a long time. She is, of course, a member of CWO, the Catholic Women's Organisation, where she receives tips about pleasing the husband she doesn't have and building her family like that of Jesus, Mary, and Joseph.

Again I wish I had a papa. I wish Mama would tell me just one thing about him. If he's tall and handsome. If he spends nights dreaming about crossing the oceans. If he's ever wished she had blonde hair.

Mama goes to the high table and snaps Father McMahon, Eileen, and Sister Lakefield. They've looked grave since the drama, especially Father McMahon. Their displeasure, like an odour, has soured the vibe in the garden. It has also accelerated the sunset, the garden getting darker. Soon Mr Calculator will have to turn on the floodlights.

Father McMahon's expression softens when the Zumunta mention him in their song.

> *Father Pete, Allah ya aiko ka*
> *Don ka maishemu yaransa*
> *Muna godiya da aikinka*

One holds her nostrils tight and sounds an ear-piercing shriek: 'Errrirrrirrrrrriii!'

Father McMahon smiles, bows to the women, waves. Eileen whispers something to him. Sister Lakefield overhears it and chuckles.

The air lightens, becomes fresher. People sigh their relief and sit up. I move my weight from one foot to the other.

The women dance to the high table, taking a long step forward, a short step back, twisting their backsides, their motherly bosoms wobbling in response. The instrumentalists increase their tempo and the women speed up their steps. They spin in unison, flap their backs, wind their backsides till their wrappers begin to loosen. Holding their nostrils, they squeal so loud my ears hurt.

The audience claps. Mai Gemu rises and runs onto the grounds, throws a wad of ten-naira notes at them, joins the dance.

Soon the audience troops onto the grounds and begins dancing. After a minute, Father McMahon and Sister Lakefield reluctantly rise too. Eileen seems very uncertain. Her peeps have to reassure her, Father McMahon taking her hand. People cheer as they join the dance.

I get an idea. This is my moment. Okey can fucking go to hell with his jabs.

I push into the grounds and join the dance, my compass needle fixed on Eileen and Father McMahon.

People flap their backs, spin, hop, elbow the air, the smell of perspiration growing stronger.

Father McMahon and Sister Lakefield swing their arms and feet clumsily like before. At first Eileen stands unmoving, blushing slightly. Then she starts to imitate their moves. But hers are more fluid, energetic, elegant, like a seabird's. Her peeps gaze at her, wowing, realising they know only so much about her. She spins and spins. Giggles. Raises her iPhone to her face, sticks out her tongue, takes a selfie. Father McMahon, Sister Lakefield, and the weirdness are all captured in the background.

'Hi, Andy,' Father McMahon says, waving me over.

I rush to meet him and Eileen, pushing through the spinning and panting and sweat and smells.

Eileen sees me. Smiles. A real British smile, like a petal opening.

My heart flips. It spreads its wings, flies out of me. Fluttering left and right like a baby bird.

'Andy, hey,' she says.

She remembers my name! Gloria!

'Hiya, Eileen,' I say.

'Having a good time?' Father McMahon says.

'Yes, Father. It's been fantastic.'

'Nice.'

'Great.'

She smells like dates. Or is it almonds? Her voice is sweeter than either. In the light of dusk she looks otherworldly. Like a mermaid in a dream. She glows; her halo covers me. She smiles, and her platinum becomes fluorescent.

Sister Lakefield is behind her, speaking earnestly to Bro Magnus about Zahrah's drama. How it's completely unacceptable, how there will be consequences.

Eileen says something. I don't catch it due to the tribal craze all around.

'Sorry?' I say.

'The photographer. She's your mother, right?'

I freeze. Has she talked to Mama? Did she hear her English, see the stained gap between her teeth? Has she shaken her sandpaper hand, touched her blackberry skin?

And the contrast hits me. Eileen is a page, Mama the writing on it.

'Y-yes,' I say.

'Oh, great,' she says.

'But – but how?'

I'm sounding different to my own ears. British again? I'm enjoying it. But why do I feel guilty?

'How what?' she says.

'Did you know?'

'Guess!'

'We – we don't look alike, so . . .'

'Hmm. Okay. Not sure about that.'

'I know how! Father Pete told you!'

She raises her hands in surrender. 'You got me!'

Father McMahon turns to us when he hears his name.

'Yeah, I met her earlier this evening,' Eileen says. 'She was so lovely.'

I wonder whether Mama is really lovely, considering all she's kept from me. Is love not supposed to be like salt, pure, complete, and strong?

'Thank you, Eileen,' I say.

'Your mother is such an amazing photographer,' Father McMahon says. 'The best in town.'

'Oh, thank you, Father.'

My phone buzzes in my pocket. I don't give a damn. I only care about my Eiqueen, about how her furry brow flutters as she blinks and beams at me.

Sister Lakefield joins us.

'Oh, what have I missed?' she says.

'We're just talking about Andy's mother.'

'Oh. For some reason, I've not been privileged to know her well. But I understand she is a very hardworking woman.'

'Yes, she is.'

I wish they'd stop talking about Mama. I don't like seeing her with Father McMahon or Sister Lakefield. It's often when she's with them that I realise how poor her English really is. Now and then she says 'I' instead of 'me', 'was' instead of 'is'.

Father McMahon asks Eileen about some gift boxes. She says she hasn't seen them yet, that she thinks Isaiah forgot to bring them from her room.

I dig out my phone, pushing aside Grandma's letter. I've got a text from Fatima:

Hope you're okay, Andy? Things are heating up in town.
Just take care.

Fuck. Really hope the riot doesn't reach here. Hopefully Elder Paschal will get the army to protect our church if the police fail to quell it. That was what he did in the last riot. Problem is the new CO is a Muslim and might shirk.

As I'm about to reply to Fatee, Father McMahon says to me:

'Andy, could you and Eileen get the gift boxes? They're in her place. In the Garden of Eden.'

'Okay, Father,' I say without hesitation, pocketing my phone, pushing Fatee away.

And here comes my fantabulous chance. To be alone with Eileen. To be killed and resurrected by her petal smile. To get her number. Might never happen again in a thousand years!

Eileen and I turn to leave. I slow down till she's in front of me. Gentlemen are supposed to walk behind ladies, right?

The Garden of Eden is in the adjoining compound to the west of the Father's House. It's called Eden because of its roses and cashew trees and fountain. Wish it had an apple tree so that Eileen could feed me. So that a part of herself – her saliva, the print of her fingers on the fruit – could enter me.

We take the back door into the living room. Come out to the porch. Climb down the steps to the front garden. Insects are chirping, whispering to each other, saying Eileen is close.

She slows till I'm beside her. Her hand calls to me. It looks like a C at her side. Empty. Incomplete. And I want to hold it, squeeze it, fill its empty space.

'So, Andy,' she says.

'Yes, Eileen?'

'What're your poems about?'

Shocking question.

'Life?' I say. 'Death?'

I wanted to say love but stopped myself.

'Nice.'

But she doesn't seem impressed.

'And about my brother, Ydna.'

'Nice. Is he here?'

'Never met him. He was born dead.'

She pauses. Her meadow eyes caress me with green pity.

'Andy, I'm so sorry.'

We're under a flamboyant tree. A dry, blood-red petal falls on her shoulder. Rolls off.

'Thank you, Eileen.'

I don't know why I'm telling her about Ydna. I've never told even Fatima or my droogs about him.

'I miss him,' I say. 'All the time.'

'Yeah. I know what you mean. My friend Sophie died last winter. I dream of her all the time too.'

'Oh. I'm so sorry.'

'Thanks, mate.'

She just called me mate! Gloria in excelsis!

'I've written a sequence of ten poems for Ydna. On my blog.'

'You've got a blog? Great.'

'Thanks.'

'I'll check it out.'

'That's kind of you. Thanks!'

I pray she leaves a comment so that I can get her email from there.

We get to the grey gate that leads to the Garden. I rush forward and open it as though she were pointing a gun at me. And she is: the gun of her green eyes is killing the black dot in my soul.

'Thanks.'

Hiss of water from the fountain. A bird coos. A black cat flashes past, rustling leaves.

Red and white roses peering at us. Very still. A grove of cashew trees before us.

Wish the cashew were in season. So that I could pluck one. Eat a bite. Hand the rest to my queen of radioactive ecstasy. And then our eyes will open . . .

On our left is a cottage, and in the distance, the church council hall. She takes out a key and leads me to the cottage.

Strange fears rise to my neck. I realise that she and I are going to be alone indoors.

My pulse begins to race. Drumming of blood in my ears.

God, let me not do anything stupid. God, let me not do anything . . .

'Welcome to my humble abode!'

We step inside.

'Very nice.' I say. 'Golden curtains. Warm chandeliers. Is that a picture of you?'

She smiles. 'You have good eyes.'

I go to the picture frame on the shelf. She's younger there, hair more luxuriant, flashing the British smile, front teeth gleaming. Beside that is another frame of her. In it she's flanked by a middle-aged white couple.

'And these are your parents?'

'Yeah, Mum and Dad. Currently holidaying in Kenya.'

'Very cool.'

'Yeah.'

I wonder whether her parents would like me. Does her father own a gun? Does her mother have any Black friends?

Mama can't afford to feed me decently, let alone travel abroad for a holiday. To her it would be the most preposterous suggestion in the world: both of us meandering about and spending so much deng, sitting in a horrorcool hotel as though we've got no house or things to do. I'm sure Eileen's parents are employing someone like her to photograph them, to do their laundry and polish their shoes. I don't even want to imagine it, Mama working for Eileen's parents, asking me to assist her in cleaning Eileen's sandals, to be sure to remove the cattle dung from the soles.

Shame and guilt claw at my stomach. I shoo them asap, scan the rest of the shelf.

'You've got nice books here,' I say. 'Dante. Camus. Is that Proust? Heard it's a difficult read.'

'It really is,' she says, nodding gravely. 'Every sentence slips from your mind as soon as you finish it.'

'Oh, really?'

There are many books in French. Saint-Exupéry, Hugo, Verlaine.

'Do you speak French?'

'Yeah,' she says, sitting down on the sofa. 'Spent nine months in Paris.'

I turn to her in awe. For the first time ever I'm face to face with someone who's living the life I should've lived, who's eaten the food and visited the places I sigh about every night I cannot sleep. I always wonder why my soul or consciousness or whatever rejected all those bodies over there – bodies with futures, with beauty – and chose this Cursed one on this Cursed continent. It is the first and greatest mistake that ever happened in my life.

I sigh and turn back to the shelf.

'And these are German novels? Günter Grass?'

'I also know German.'

'Damn. You're so cool.'

'Thanks. I hope to become a translator someday.'

'Best plan.'

'Yeah.'

Although I've heard about these books, I'm seeing many of them for the first time. My school library is all stuff for children, donations from kids abroad. Our town doesn't even own a shelf despite its population of three hundred thousand, whereas I'm sure a village of five in Britain has a well-stocked library.

'And is that Kafka? In the original German? *Die Ver-wand-lung* ...'

'*The Metamorphosis*, yeah.'

'God. I love Kafka. Especially *The Metamorphosis*.'

'I love it too.'

'*One fine morning, when Gregor Samsa woke from uneasy dreams* ...'

She smiles. '... *he found himself transformed in his bed* ...'

'... *into a monstrous vermin*.'

We laugh.

'Best opening ever!'

'Yeah,' she says. 'Better in the original.'

'Everything is better in the original.'

'Yeah.'

'You've got many wonderful books, Eileen.'

Someday I'll shorten her name to Ei or Leen. *Eye lean. I lean.*

'Yeah, thanks. But actually I didn't bring many of my favourites. Didn't want to upset Uncle Pete.'

'What d'you mean? What favourites?'

'My books on atheism.'

'Wow.'

'He thinks I still pray. He's just realised I no longer receive communion.'

I want to say something. But I don't know what to say.

The books suddenly begin to smell stronger. My stomach growls.

I turn to the window for a bit, turn back to her.

'So – so you're an atheist?'

'Something like that, yeah.'

She must be the first atheist I've ever met. In Nigeria you're either Christian or Muslim. Anything else (Traditionalist, Eckankar) is frowned upon. But being completely unreligious? It's also shocking how she divulged something so private with such ease. A Black girl wouldn't do this.

'But – but why?' I say.

'Why what?'

For some reason I can't bring myself to ask her.

'Why I stopped believing in God?'

'Yes.'

'Dunno. It just doesn't make any sense. Why do we need a god?'

As an altar boy I'm supposed to tear my shirt at this. But I find myself smiling.

'Hmm. Why're you smiling, Andy?'

'You're very funny, Eileen.'

'How?'

'You wouldn't need a god in England. In Europe.'

'But why?'

'Because things are working there. Unlike here.'

She nods, folds her arms. 'Yeah, I understand . . .'

I tell her that everyone here learns to believe in God. That it's the only way we can survive. Because our existence is riddled with uncertainty. And only a superforce like God can control things like uncertainty. You leave your house praying there's electricity when you return, hoping that the sun doesn't burn you too much. On the road, you're praying not to be hit by a car because the roads are potholed and the drivers are unqualified to drive. When you're hit, you're praying that the doctors aren't on strike, that hospitals have the equipment needed for your treatment. When you die, you're praying that your family conquers this cycle. You know that, just like you, they won't, that your prayer will go unanswered. But you still pray.

'Life in Africa is a long prayer,' I say.

'It's sad,' she says. 'It's really sad.'

A long silence.

A moth is circling round the chandelier. It circles, perches. Circles, perches. Stuns itself against it.

Music from the garden filters into the room to and fro like a pendulum. People are shrieking, laughing, singing. And suddenly things become clear to me.

I want to tell Eileen that our propensity to always sing and dance shouldn't deceive her into thinking we're a happy people. Because we're not. We're a people of masks. Singing and dancing and laughing are our attempts to force forgetfulness on ourselves. To ignore the Horror. To own the happiness we can never afford. And, sometimes, it works.

But I don't say anything.

'Could you excuse me a minute?' she says.

She rises. Slowly. As though she's carrying the weight of the continent. As though there's nothing that can ever save us. She walks into the bedroom, shuts the door.

+

It's another Eileen that comes out to the living room. A walking, breathing rose. Sinfully red lips, wicked stabbing eyes. She's brushed her platinum, applied more lipstick, more mascara on her lashes. She smiles.

I die.

I want to kiss her.

Every black dot on me wants her. Stretch out to her. Like a plant to the sun.

If only I could know why colours exist. Why things must contrast. Why black must be on a white page. Then I'll stop looking at her.

'Are you okay, Andy?'

we'll go sailing
round the british isles

the breeze
on your brow

i'll put a spoonful
of ice cream in your mouth

you'll lick it, laugh
yes, andy, yes

'Andy, what's wrong?'

i'll melt
    you
in me
and melt
    me
in you

'You're beautiful,' I say.
'What did you say?'
'You're the most beautiful thing in the world.'
She seems not to understand what I've said. Neither do I.
Suddenly she goes very pale. Eyes twice bigger as though I've called her the devil, as though she could swallow me in their green flames, chain and punish me forever. She wants to say something. Stops herself. She smooths her platinum and returns to the bedroom.

god

    what
        have
            i
        done

            god?

She comes out to the living room, sees me standing, becomes startled.
She tells me that I can go now. Says thank you.

6

People are singing and dancing and cheering and clinking glasses and scanning phones and chatting and laughing and hugging.

I'm standing under the flamboyant tree, arms folded. It's dusk. The floodlights are on, screaming in my eyes. But there's nothing I can do.

I want to cry. But I don't want to look like a baby.

'I am a man,' I say. 'A man. A man. A man!'

Eileen and Father McMahon are talking to Elder Paschal and his wife. They're all clutching drinks, laughing. Eileen is facing my direction. But she doesn't look at me.

Mr Calculator and Chioma are distributing the stuffed unicorns and action figures Eileen brought from London. They hand them to little kids or their mamas. Some kids my age are holding out their silly hands to Mr Calculator, not wanting to miss out on the special stuff from Europe, but he barks 'No' in their faces. It was Chioma who wound up helping Eileen carry the boxes to the garden. I wonder what reason Eileen gave her uncle for why it wasn't me.

Yes, I've let myself be deceived. By her smiling. Her feathery voice, her updownup accent. The way she called me Andy. I've let them all fool me into believing that I've been transformed into a gigantic beauty when nothing has changed. When I'm still who I am. And everything still Everything. Colours. Contrasts. What our parents made us. Curses we can never change.

Maybe she doesn't hate me. Maybe I just made my comment too suddenly, too early, because my blood was somersaulting.

As I scan the party for my droogs, she glances fleetingly at me. $\frac{1}{10}$ of a second. Was she looking at me or something else? Was it anger in her eyes or simply pity?

+

Mama is everywhere. Camera fixed to her face like a new organ. Bending. Squatting. Kneeling. Click, click. Flash:

Mai Gemu and his wife, both dancing.
The children's choir. A boy singing off-key. A girl with a runny nose. Turning to the boy, telling him to shut up.
Eileen and Father McMahon, both laughing.
Eileen and Sister Lakefield, smiling softly.
Eileen with a little girl crying in her arms.

Click, click. Flash.

Mama laughs.
She tells people to lean closer. Hold it for her. Right there. You squat in front. Right. Great. Wait for it. Wait for it. Click, click. Flash.
Great!
She told me once while we were eating suya that it was one of her ex-husbands who taught her photography. She immediately regretted saying this. Because I've kept asking her about him ever since. Whether he's still a photographer. Whether he's my papa.
Click, click. Flash.
Soon it will be time for Eileen's speech. And then the cutting of the cake. The DJ plays Awilo and Flavour. People dance, clutching Cokes or La Casera or chicken wings. Spills, stains.
Mama laughs at funny poses. Her mirth cuts across the garden, punctures the music. Wish she could cut down on her hahahas. It's slightly irritating, makes her look as though she were happy, as though Everything were alright.
The back door opens. Zahrah comes into the garden. A man is beside her. He's short, stocky, very light-skinned, bald.

Mama is about to take a shot of three girls. But before the click, she turns and sees Zahrah and the man. The camera falls from her hands to her belly.

She hurries over to them. I've never seen Mama this blinding fast.

'Where are you going?' the three girls call to her. 'Snap us!'

Mama reaches Zahrah and the man. She addresses them in Ososo, her voice agitated. I can't hear her over the music.

Morocca is beside me, scanning through his phone.

'The riot is worse, man,' he says. 'It might get here soon.'

A few people are speaking anxiously into their phones. A woman carts her twin daughters out of the garden. But most people don't care very much because the barracks is nearby. It would be foolish of the mob to attack our church.

'Give me a minute,' I say.

I jostle through the crowd of dancers and stop when I'm close enough to hear Mama and the man. The conversation is getting heated. Mama is stabbing the air with her finger, her left earring missing.

'You've got no business here!' she spits at him.

'This is not your party, is it?' he says in Ososo.

'Didn't I warn you to stay out of our lives?'

'Out of my way, woman.'

'Get out. Leave.'

'I'm not going anywhere.'

'You monster. I don't want to see you. Ever.'

'You're not getting away this time.'

'Leave. Disappear.'

'I must see him.'

'Never.'

'I must.'

'Get lost.'

'He's mine.'

Mama slaps him.

'Monster. How dare you? How dare you call him yours?'

Her lips tremble, become ugly. Her cornrows look like horns.

The man holds his cheek. He turns to Zahrah.

'Where is he? Show him to me.'

'You demon!' Mama says to Zahrah, her voice croaky. 'You claim to be my friend. Is this how you betray me?'

'Show him to me. I'm taking him home.'

Mama screams.

Loud.

The party pauses.

Her arms are flailing, her chest heaving. The world becomes unbalanced, upending around us.

She tells the man in English to get out. Leave. Disappear.

All eyes turn to them. Father McMahon's, Sister Lakefield's, Eileen's.

But I don't care.

I go to my mama. Put my hand around her. Her old musty scent. Warm. Conjuring of her breast milk. Flashes of our sand-castlemoulding and our dimplecounting.

She calms. Hugs me. Smell of perspiration.

'Andrew mè,' she whispers. 'Tell him to leave. Please.'

'Is that him?' the man asks Zahrah in Ososo.

Zahrah is silent, expressionless.

A small crowd is forming around us. Children gaze at Mama as if she were a puzzle.

'Are you Andrew?' the man says to me in Ososo.

'Yes?' I say in Ososo.

'I'm your father,' he says. 'I've come to take you home.'

'What did you say?'

'I am your father. She – Gloria – is a terrible mother, a wicked wife. She kept you away from me for fifteen years. Fifteen years! Just because of one little disagreement.'

My hand falls down Mama's waist. I find myself edging away from her, from her ancient warm goodnight sleep well musty scent.

'And I can prove it to you,' the man says. 'You need to speak to your grandmother. To your uncles and aunties. They all know the truth.'

I look at the man who claims to be my father. At his large eyes. The pink in his mouth. The pimple underlip. Face broad.

Square. Sharp. And I don't know whether I can see myself in him. Smell myself in him.

I want to turn to Mama.

her old wrapper covering me
her laughter
her saggy breasts as she leans before me

But I look at the ground.

At a toad hopping past. Simple little life. No worries about a mama or a papa or crossing oceans. Just grass and water, ants and flies. A birth and a death:

Consciousness is a nightmare.

I look at Mama.

She wipes her eyes but tears trickle. Hair torn, scarf falling off, she looks wild. Undaunted. Ready to tear the world and stuff me in her pouch.

dusk, tears
dawn, tears

money wasted
sleep missed

breasts
emptied

and you still
want to be
my mama?

+

There's screaming in the distance. Drumming. Chanting. Taking shape, forming into words. It's coming from town. A mob is approaching the gate of our church.

We all turn towards the gate. The DJ quenches the music.

Panting all around me.

'Allahu akbar! Allahu akbar!' the mob chants.

They strike our gate with metal. Machetes, probably.

'Ku buɗe mu kashe ku!'

'Bude! Bude!'
'You all deserve to die!'
'Infidels!'
'Kafirai.'
'Sinners.'
'Open up! Open!'
Nobody moves.

They hurl stones into our church compound. Roofing sheets cry out. Glass crashes. Two stones travel the long distance from the gate to the garden. One misses a little boy by an inch. The other smashes into the uncut cake as though perfectly aimed. The top two towers slowly collapse. The statuettes of Eileen and Father McMahon crash to the ground. There's always precision in randomness.

This rouses everyone. Women call out to their children, men to their wives. Zahrah and the man duck from an approaching stone. Mama and I run to a frangipani tree. A few people rush to the back door.

Eileen coils into the embrace of Father McMahon.

'Stop!' Elder Paschal cries.

He says that we should all be calm. That the town is on fire. It's not safe to leave the church compound because they're every-where. Everywhere! That we should all silently file out through the back door to the Garden of Eden and hide in the council hall. There we'll be safe till the police and soldiers arrive. He and Father McMahon have called them and they're on their way. The barbed wire on our fence is electrified. So we still have some time before the mob figures out how to enter the compound.

He repeats his announcement over and over, his voice mask-ing anxiety, until we all choose to be convinced. He reminds us that the council hall is one of the safest places to be during a riot. In fact, in the last riot, many Christians flocked to our council hall to hide.

We rush to the back door. Into the living room. Out to the front garden.

Mama and I hold hands.

The moon is out. Clear. A crescent. It looks bored, unfazed by all the screaming below.

The stars are out. Just a single brush of blue left in the sky.

'Infidels!'

'Kafirai!'

They're ramming a section of the fence.

We run to the gate of the Garden of Eden. Leaves crunch under our feet. Crickets screech, children wail.

In the Garden the only lighting comes from Eileen's cottage and the council hall in the distance. Trees and shrubs look like monsters with weapons drawn.

Mr Calculator tells us to hurry.

'What are you looking at, eh? Do you want to die?'

Mama pulls me. We run to the hall.

Inside, people are hiding under tables and chairs. Praying to St Michael the Archangel. Reciting Psalm 23.

> *The Lord is my shepherd, I shall not want.*
> *He makes me lie down in . . .*

Mama and I join the Kayode family under a table. Mrs Kayode pauses her Prayer to My Guardian Angel, turns to us. She glares at us as though we were strangers, as though she hasn't visited our house several times and drunk our Cokes. Her frown tells us to disappear asap lest we draw the machetes to her children.

'Are you alright?' I ask Mama.

'Yes, Andrew mè,' she says. 'What about you?'

'I am, yes.'

'"I am, yes"?'

'Yes.'

'Is that how you address me?'

'What do you mean?'

She shakes her head. 'Andrew mè. Andrew mè . . .'

I didn't add 'Ma' or 'Mama' in my responses. I could now. Just one syllable, two syllables.

I close my eyes. How could those simple words carry so much?

+

We hear a heavy thud. And the panting and praying quieten. We know what has happened.

We hear their cursing and screaming as they race into the compound, as they enter the church.

Crashing of glass.
Denting of wood.
Booming of an eternal fire.
Smoke in our nostrils.

The lights go off in the hall. In the Garden outside.
People yelp. Then quieten again.

Elder Paschal's voice comes from his corner, shaky, unconvincing. Assures us that the soldiers are coming. That we'll hear their trucks and armoured vehicles soon.

A man whispers that Father McMahon had to bribe the CO of our barracks to send soldiers. Fifty thousand per soldier. That there's a possibility the CO won't help us because he's also a Muslim.

'Our country is held together by Sellotape,' the man says. 'When will God save us?'

Silence again. Except for the screaming coming from the church. Except for the crickets crying to the heavens.

+

An hour later. Absolute silence. The rioters seem to have had their fill of destruction. Even the crickets are spent.

A man whispers that the Father's House is on fire. That our pews, altar, and tabernacle have been hacked and burnt. The police and soldiers aren't coming. We'll have to wait here all night till the mobile police arrives from Abuja, a distance of 350 kilometres.

'This is it,' he says. 'Even Father Pete has given up. He's been crying all night.'

Suddenly we hear a loud whistle just outside in the Garden.

'Come! They're here! The kafirai are all here!'

'Kafirai su na nan! Ku zo mu kashe su!'

'Ku zo. Ku zo!'

'Ihu!'
'Allahu akbar. Allahu akbar!'

Smashes in the darkness.
Machetes striking tables.
People rushing out, bashing their heads on chairs and walls.
Screams. Wails. Children screeching.

'Father, into thy hands I commit my spirit . . . Into thy hands I commit . . . Into thy . . .'
'Come out, all of you,' they say. 'Don't think we can't see you under the tables.'
Flashes from their torches. Cutting across the hall.
I take Mama's hand. We creep to a far corner of the hall. Using my other hand, I search for one of the windows I always sit beside during altar boy practice. I find one. Push it open. Peep. No signs of anyone. I whisper to Mama to jump first. She says no, I should go first. Please. That they're so close. She wants to be sure I'm safe.
We argue for a moment.
'Just go,' she says. 'Please! They're here!'
I clamber up and jump, falling onto grass.
Mama is taking too long to climb, held back by her long dress. She finally makes it onto the windowsill. But somebody appears behind her.
'Kafiri,' he sneers.
Mama screams.
A cutting sound.
Blood.
The world stops.

III: The Crowning with Thorns

Theorem: The inverse of every even permutation is even . . .
The inverse of every odd permutation is odd.

7

Seven weeks now.
  And Everything has changed.
  And Everything is the same.

  Me.
  Mama and me.
  Town, church.

Father McMahon is standing by the makeshift altar, giving his final announcement. The altar is the ashen table which, before the riot, had been abandoned in the church compound, forgotten after a bazaar, left in the rain and sun. It used to be the love bed of Okey and Linda. He'd push her onto it, strum her nipples, thumb her panties. And she'd laugh aloud that he should stop despite still letting his hands wander. Now it's covered with white lace and placed at the centre of the sanctuary. Bread and wine become the body and blood of Christ on it.

My droogs and I are sitting in the sanctuary, Morocca beside me, Slim at the opposite end. We're dressed in cream cassocks and white surplices, our hands pressed together in holiness: The same hands we touch ourselves with at night. The same hands Morocca touches Patience and other girls with at his rap shows. Now they're sanctified. Held out like holy flames. At the end of the Mass these hands will revisit where they have been.

Our sanctuary used to be grand. On the wall behind it there was a large stained-glass mosaic which an anonymous donor in

Italy gifted our church. People came all the way from parishes in Abuja and Port Harcourt to see it. It showed a handsome Jesus Christ with a goatee ascending to heaven, his perforated hands blessing us, waving us goodbye, his macho smile saying he'd see us soon. Its pieces of glass were twinkling, winking, kaleidoscopic. Greens. Yellows. Blues. Lush, magical. Curling and changing as we turned our heads. Giving us a peek at the wonders of heaven.

Surrounding the mosaic was a fresco. It depicted biblical stories with black figures: Adam and Eve, butt naked, munching apples in Eden. Christ raising the dead, walking on blue waters, grinning like some cool dude. The Last Day, Christ stepping on a huge seven-headed dragon, crushing its ten horns, showing us that we could also defeat the most tempting of sins.

Now there's an ozone hole in the mosaic. Through the hole I can see the Father's House in the distance, burnt and blackened. A huge dragon of soot has coiled over the fresco. When I look at the hole and the dragon, cries of 'Allahu akbar!' fill my ears. Mama's scream pierces me again. And I awaken, jump in my skin.

Seven weeks.

I want to look for Mama in the congregation. But I stop myself. I know what I'll see. Everything I cannot change.

'We must hold firm in these trying times,' Father McMahon says, British accent still intact. 'We must remember that the Church was built on the blood of martyrs.'

Silence. The rustle of Sunday bulletins. Feet dragging on the floor. The smell of a smoke we cannot see.

The roofing sheets are sagging, screeching when a wind blows, threatening to fall on us. The iron pillars are bent, blackened like the walls around us.

'And we shall,' Father McMahon says. 'We shall triumph. We shall triumph through Christ our Lord.'

'Amen,' the congregation whispers, as though afraid that the Muslim mob might hear them and return with their machetes.

The church is surprisingly full. You'd expect only a few to turn up after eleven people were killed and two dozen injured on the night of 12 June. But a thousand of us are packed in between these crumbling walls. A thousand silent poor hungry stubborn souls.

We shall triumph.

Father McMahon begins the closing prayer and we all rise. He prays for peace. For the faithfully departed. Especially the Okeke and Oghene families. Maman Ibrahim. Hilary Adekunle.

'And we thank you for the lives of many others,' he says, 'for Simon Ibeh, Musa Yakubu, and Gloria Aziza. Complete your healing work within them. Radiate to them the fullness of your love.'

I want to turn to Mama. But I stop myself.

He blesses us: Father. Son. And the Holy Spirit.

'Go in the peace of Christ,' he says. 'This Mass is ended.'

'Thanks be to God,' we say.

The choir breaks into a hymn. No drums. No keyboard. Just scared, hungry voices.

> *Give me oil in my lamp, keep me burning*
> *Give me oil in my lamp, I pray*

I march to the centre of the sanctuary. Pick up the processional cross from the stand. Bow, climb down the steps of the sanctuary, wait. Slim and Morocca work simultaneously: they pick up their candlesticks, light their candles, bow, and come down the sanctuary to join me. Father McMahon kisses the altar and joins us. We bow and begin the procession down the main aisle to the sacristy.

Mama is sitting by the third row of the nave. I try very hard not to look at her. Yet she seems to be looking at me. Scanning my face. Seeing my struggle. I'm sure she wants me to look at her. Wants me to scream. That I love her. That I want her the way she is. That nothing has changed.

I try not to. Try very hard not to.

But some force pulls me. Rain to sand.

I turn.

Our eyes meet.

She's sitting in her wheelchair. In a tie-dye dress.

Everyone else is standing. Resting their weight on their feet. But Mama sits, clutching the arms of her chair. Like the Queen she's not. The Queen she'll never be.

+

She no longer talks to me. Since she woke from her six-day coma she chats with everyone else: Doctors and nurses about the huge lightning on her back. Aunty Lizzy her younger sister about some dead uncle or aunt. My droogs about their parents. She even spends hours talking to Zahrah, the same Zahrah who she claimed had betrayed her, about her fiancé and the benefits of a large family. But she never says a word to me. She looks away whenever I walk into a room. Takes back her hand after I've held it for a moment. Does not respond when I ask if she's in pain, if she needs anything.

It's very annoying whenever she takes back her hand. As though I were not a part of her. As though a body could do without its hands or feet. And I always want to slam her bed or chair whenever she says nothing to my promises. Of how I'll always be with her. How I'll forever protect her. How we'll be alright Together. Her silence makes me sound like a liar to myself. Like a con. Like a little foolish baby.

Every time I'm with her my neurones scream like car horns at me. Her silence makes their voices even more persuasive. Wake the fuck up, they say. This woman's done for, can't ya see? She couldn't hold a pen correctly, and now she can't even stand on her feet, something toddlers can do. You wanna spend ya entire life babysitting? You'd better check out asap, move in with your droogs, before it's too late. Let's face it, her life's Cursed. Don't worsen yours.

I'm sure the universe or HXVX or whatever is punishing me, making me pay for comparing her to Mama 2. They're taunting me by making her even less of who she's supposed to be, less Mama 2.

Her attacker struck her on the spine with a machete. The doctor said that no hospital in the country could help her. That our operating theatres are but cobbler workshops, not facilities where serious medical work can be done. Throughout her stay in the hospital and now at home she only sleeps while lying on her front. As if she were in an eternal prayer to some Pitiless Superforce who despite her pleas and groans does nothing to save her.

When the doctor told her that she might never walk again she tore the tubes off her hands. Wincing and wincing, she sat up on the bed. She dragged her feet off it, tried to stand them on the ground, but fell face-first to the floor. She didn't stop. She moved her parted insensate feet towards her. Propped herself on her knees, tried to walk. Again, she fell on her face. She repeated this over and over, groaning and groaning. No nurse or doctor could stop her. Zahrah couldn't. Aunty Lizzy neither. They were all crying, begging her to stop. That she shouldn't kill herself, that she still had a boy to raise. Her blood was everywhere. Dripping from her back, pouring from her nose. But Mama wouldn't stop.

'Tell your mother to stop,' one of the nurses begged me. 'Cry and beg her.'

But I was silent. I couldn't say a word. My eyes got even drier.

That wasn't the only time I didn't cry. I didn't even cry after her attacker struck her with his machete, after her Scream, after she fell down from the high window to my feet. My eyes remained dry even after we'd rushed her to the hospital. And all through those six blurry days when she lay stonily on the bed, oxygen mask on her face, lips bigger, ugly, face swollen, armpits hairy and smelly. I didn't cry during all those sponge baths Aunty Lizzy and I gave her. Not even one tear from my evil eyes.

Maybe she stopped talking to me because she couldn't forgive my stoniness, my stubbornness. What son would refuse to cry when his mother – his only parent – was in so much pain? What son wouldn't want to wear his mother's pain, give her his own legs, make her his Olympian?

I've stirred and stirred on my bed about it. I've paced around the house about it, rubbing her two gold medals in my hand, uncovering nothing. She won them in school for running a hundred metres. She used to boast about them, about how she could outrun me even now that she had some grey on her head.

I've asked Ydna about it. But he pretends not to exist and doesn't answer. He always takes her side, Ydna. As though he were closer to her than to me. As though one foot could be closer to the heart than the other.

I'm sure her silence isn't because she's trying to avoid talking about my papa. It's also not because I didn't call her 'Mama' just before she was struck.

It must be because of Eileen.

My desire for her must be Cursed. And Mama has become my lamb.

It must be because Mama knows I don't want this copy of herself that she's become. That I want my old Mama back. My mama with the musty smell and the palm oil stain on her teeth. Who loved money a little too much and overcharged our white priests. Who was always everywhere, always in a hurry, fighting and bending life, wrestling with the ho who propositioned me, slapping the man who claimed to be my father. I want that original back. Not this helpless version. She must have seen it in my eyes after she came out of her coma and wouldn't forgive me for it.

+

The sacristy. Smell of candle and incense. Yellow light filters from windows. Chalices and monstrances shine gold in glass shelves. Chasubles hang stiffly in wardrobes.

We say the prayer after Mass, reading it off a frame on the wall.

We thank thee, Lord Jesus
For the sacred grace to serve at thy Altar . . .

The sacristy is the only part of the church that was untouched during the riot. Although it was open during the macheting and inferno, not a single piece of glass was broken. The holy objects must have repelled all the psychos.

Maybe God does exist. He allows some sacrilege now and then to fan our scepticism. He allows us to tear down His temple and sin under His nose. But like every sensible being, He knows when to guard Himself.

At the end of the prayer, Father McMahon makes the sign of the cross over us and bows. 'Thank you,' he says.

We bow. 'Thank you, Father.'

I push the cross into its stand. My droogs and I wait for him to undress. He takes off his glasses, his chasuble. Puts on his glasses, undoes his cincture, eyes me briefly. That glint in his blue eyes. Full of counsel but also contempt. He knows. Eileen must have told him that I'll be visiting her tomorrow in Abuja, that we've become semi-besties. He takes off his stole, gives me a weird smile, leaves the sacristy.

'What's up, dawgs?' I say.

'Cool, man,' Slim says.

'Fuckin' hungry.' Morocca yawns. 'I'm sure there are vampire worms in my belly.'

'I'm sure there are,' Slim laughs.

Trust Morocca. He swears even when he's in the engine room of Jesus. He isn't afraid of thunderbolts or anything. Like me, he's a pendulum when it comes to God.

Today he's in good-boy mode. Not wearing any earrings or chains. But his lips are thick and black as though he's just finished three wraps of weed. Slim's lips are small and girlish. His face is very ashen as if he forgot to rub in some cream this morning.

'Why was old man looking at you like that, Andy?' Slim says.

'I'm sure he knows,' Morocca says.

'How?' Slim says.

Morocca gawks at him. 'Isn't he the homeboy of God? The Holy Spirit speaks to him in dreams!'

We laugh.

'Shut up,' Slim says. 'D'you know where we are, fool?'

'Room 101?'

'Watch your mouth. Please, I don't want some Holy Ghost fire to blast my ass.'

Morocca yawns aloud. Like the shark he is.

'Very hungry,' he says.

'Maybe that's why your cap hasn't been rising,' Slim says.

Morocca nods gravely, imitating Father McMahon. 'Flesh and blood didn't reveal that to you, boy.'

We laugh.

He goes to a cabinet, opens it, takes out the big container of altar bread.

'Like David in the wilderness,' he says.

He brings the container to me to take some of the unblessed communion. He always brings it to me first. Not because I'm the tallest or oldest. But because my eating first okays our act.

I take two pieces of bread. Throw them into my mouth. Stale. Slim takes five. Morocca fetches about a dozen and forces them into his big mouth. We laugh, watching him struggle to eat all that bread, wishing he could choke on them so that he'd stop making us sin in this holiest of places.

Morocca takes off his surplice and cassock. He's wearing a long-sleeved shirt today, probably because of his tats. I want to ask him why he bothers to attend church and serve at Mass, only to crack jokes and make us eat altar bread in the end. His parents and siblings don't ever attend Mass. They're always settling some beef among themselves. His brothers are often into one dirty shit or another. Scamming white people on the internet. Peddling fake government contracts around town. Like him, they've all fathered babies.

I tell him that I saw Serena, his two-year-old daughter, at Mass, with her mother Patience. That Serena is growing fast, looking beautiful.

'Nice,' he says, moving to the window. He never says nice. He clearly wants me to change the subject.

Silence.

Outside, people walk past the door of the sacristy. Father McMahon says 'God bless you' to them. A little boy parts the curtain of the sacristy and comes in. His mama pulls him back, laughs, says his time hasn't come yet. It's sad that someday he'll become like us, eat altar bread in the sacristy, talk about dicks and boobs amidst monstrances.

'You'll soon have your own Serena,' Morocca says, grinning wickedly. 'With Eileen.'

I don't know how to deal with this. I thought he'd let the topic go. I bend to retie my well-knotted shoelaces.

'I wonder what kind of hair or skin she'll have,' he adds.

I want to tell him to shut up. But I don't say anything.

I always bottle that Thought whenever it tries to jump into my consciousness. Just like I'm doing now. *Bottle. Bottle. Bottle.* The Thought of who Eileen and I could be. Of the kids we could have— *Bottle. Bottle. Bottle.*

'I also saw your mama,' Slim says, trying to come to my rescue. 'She's looking very good, Andy.'

'Yeah, thanks,' I say, wanting to change this subject too.

I'll have to leave the sacristy for her soon. Her sympathisers must have finished wishing her good health. I don't want to see them dipping their hands into their pockets or purses. Bringing out wads of cash, handing a note or two to her. As though she were a beggar, Cursed by God, sent to earth to suffer. As though she weren't the one who used to run around to make her own money, her camera slung down her neck, heaving before her, her third breast.

I try to think of Eileen. Picture her in Abuja. Wonder whether her skin is now red because of the sun.

She left Kontagora the day after the riot because her folks were worried there could be reprisal attacks. Before she left she came to the hospital with flowers and a get-well card for Mama. She met us all in the corridor of the theatre amidst the reek of disinfectant – me, my droogs, Fatima (who eyed her throughout), and Zahrah. She came with Father McMahon and a policeman who clutched his ancient rifle with a piece of red cloth tied around its barrel, and who kept scanning the corridors. The nurses called her 'ma' or 'madam'. I was sitting down, leaning forward, eyes tracing patterns on the terrazzo floor, creating futures for Mama and me, when Morocca whispered that Eileen was here.

I got up, feet trembling. And voilà, Eileen was before me. In a green dress. Meadow eyes moist with pity. She gave me the flowers, the card. She hugged me. And we stood as one for several moments, each an eternity of rainbows.

She said she was moving to Abuja. That she hoped to see me again. Doctors and nurses and passers-by gawked at me, wondering how a local nigga like me met her, earned this attention.

The next day she read my poems on my blog and posted a long glowing comment. 'The most touching poetry I've read in a while,' she said. 'This is so heart-wrenching, this twisted love between two brothers.' From her comment I got her email address and fired her a thank-you message with exclamation marks dancing everywhere. And since then we've been an item. Sort of. Day and night, our avatars chatting about books. And memory. And time. And love.

+

Slim and I pull off our surplices and cassocks and hang them in the wardrobe. Morocca tells us that the Honda is set for our journey tomorrow. That he had it serviced yesterday. Changed the engine oil, fixed the tail lights, poured some chilled water into the radiator.

'You'll have to pay me extra, Andy,' he says. 'It's because of you we're leaving so early.'

Zahrah's wedding is next week, and my droogs and I are travelling to Abuja to attend. We're planning to go with Serena, Patience, and Fatima. We're supposed to go three days before the wedding, but I pressured my droogs to go earlier. Eileen's leaving Nigeria next week to join her parents in Niger, where they're researching Ebola, and I want to spend as much time as possible with her. Because after this we might never see each other again.

'So what d'you plan to do with Eileen?' Morocca says, smirking. 'Fuck her?'

'Shut up,' I say.

'You've got a throne waiting for you in hell, Morocca,' Slim says.

We laugh.

'I still can't believe Zahrah's getting married so soon,' I say.

'Me neither.'

'Didn't know she was the marrying type.'

'But, man, she's so lucky.'

'Yeah.'

'Wish I were the one marrying her fiancé,' Slim says. 'So that I could cruise all those cars.'

Morocca and I chuckle, wishing Slim hadn't reminded us of his Whisper.

I've met Okorie, Zahrah's fiancé, twice in the past few weeks. Both times, he came with Zahrah in his Jaguar to visit Mama in the hospital. During the first visit they told Mama how they met. That it was two years ago, at an Afrofuturism conference in Lagos. They'd had a heated argument on a panel, and afterwards he couldn't stop eyeballing her. For months he kept asking her on a date and she kept turning him down. But despite how hard she tried, she kept thinking of him, dreaming of him . . . i.e. romantic fantasy of the decade.

Okorie's English is slightly weird: one moment he sounds like Father McMahon, the next like us. He and Zahrah recently visited Dubai to shop for their wedding.

We talk about Okorie's Mercedes and Audi and try to guess his net worth. We talk about the wedding, whether Zahrah will wear a red wedding dress, whether the ceremony will also be Anifuturist. We try to understand why, among all the millions of white girls in the UK that Okorie has met and maybe fucked, he chose our Zahrah.

'Love is like bouncing on a trampoline,' Morocca says. 'Fucking senseless.'

As we're about to bounce outta the sacristy, Morocca's phone rings. It's silent outside – Father McMahon has finished greeting the parishioners and gone home.

'What fucking strange number is this,' Morocca says. 'It's foreign.'

In this country if a strange number calls you, you gotta hesitate picking up. Because there are countless tales of people who died in their sleep after taking calls from strange numbers.

But Morocca picks up the call.

'Hello? Who is this?'

Seconds later, he begins to hyperventilate.

'What the fuck,' he says. 'What the fuck.'

'Who is it?' Slim and I say.

'What the fuck. Impossible.'

'Who is it?'

'It's WALL-E! He's in Spain!'

'Fuck.'

'Goddam.'

Slim and I say fuck and goddam a hundred more times, becoming like Morocca, not giving a fuckdam about the chalices and monstrances. If God didn't stop Okey from crossing the desert, then His existence is highly doubtful.

Morocca puts the phone on loudspeaker. Okey rambles on and on in his weird smoothie of Pidgin and English. He says he and his uncle have been given a cool room to stay in while the immigration officers sort their asylum applications. 'Guys, since me and my uncle land, dem dey treat us like kings. Dem dey give us three in fact four square meals every day, I dey tell you. Guys, there's always water in the tap, and our light neva blink even once. Since my mama born me, I neva see this kind thing, seriously. Dis na the best decision I ever take for my mumu life.'

There are no syllables in our Cursed mouths. Even Morocca is dead silent.

When Okey hangs up, promising to call later, we just gaze at each other. At the monstrances in the shelves which have lost their shine. The cement floor. The fire ant crawling under the curtain into the room.

+

Elder Paschal and his wife are the only ones left greeting Mama. There are still people in the nave, talking in low tones in groups of twos or threes. Fingers of sunlight slant into the church. Mama's wheelchair shines back, reminding me to create a space in my chest for it, a place it hasn't earned. Elder Paschal makes the sign of the cross on her forehead. He dips his hand into his tunic, brings out a roll of notes, hands her two. She says thank you, sir. God bless you, sir. No hint of emotion in her voice. Still, it shatters glass in me.

The Paschals see me. They're both grey-haired and slightly hunched.

'Oh, Andy,' Mrs Paschal says, knotting the end of her wrapper.

'Happy Sunday, sir. Happy Sunday, ma,' I say.

'Good work with your mama,' she says.

'The Lord will be with you, my son,' Elder Paschal says. 'Always.'

The Lord whose host (and pre-self) I eat in His sacristy; the Lord who I really think is not out there.

I smile. 'Thank you, sir. Thank you, ma.'

Wish I could reverse the order of my statement.

The Paschals bid us goodbye. Leave us. Taking with them their minty smell.

It's Mama before me now. And the Silence begins.

Her cornrows are falling out of her headtie. There is more black in her hair than there was before. Fewer creases on her face. Eyes bigger, whites more watery, lids thicker and hardly closing.

She looks at me. Her lips part.

Say anything, Mama.
Call me a monkey.
Say I'm an idiot.
Call me ungrateful.

But she says nothing.

A greeting tries to force itself out of me. I fight it, bend it, twist it.

I walk to the back of the wheelchair, place my trembling hands on the handles.

You'd expect some change to have happened to her legs. That they'd be slightly bent, bear a long scar, have braces supporting them. But they are the same legs from our previous life. The same legs that ran from room to room, from our house to the studio. That were spread sturdily before her while she sat and cooked us egusi.

I wheel her down the main aisle and out to the church compound.

Yellow sun. Gmelina trees whistling. Cool breeze.

But there's a whiff of smoke in it. Twitch your nose and you'll miss it. There's screaming in the whistling of the gmelina. The sniffling of the dead. The wailing of those scheduled to be born on this land.

+

I finally cried about Mama the afternoon she was discharged from the hospital. That was the first time I saw her in the wheelchair.

I was in Zahrah's living room – our living room. She'd made Aunty Lizzy and me move to her place because there are fewer Muslims in her neighbourhood. I sat cross-legged on the floor amidst Zahrah's formulas, having an email chat with Eileen. We were talking about love. How it's arbitrary. Entropic. An illogical coincidence. An x and a y from different sets, unalike in any way, that sum to one and have a difference of zero, that are basically halves of the same thing.

A van outside honked. I got up to check it out, nose still buried in my phone. I chuckled about something funny Eileen had said. Replied with a long stream of emojis. And for the first time I saw our relationship rising from all fours to its feet.

Outside in the sun, Zahrah and the driver came out of the white van. The driver slid the side door open. Brought it out. The wheelchair. Placed it on the road – it sparkled in the sun. The acid smell of its steel called to me, told me to see what I had done.

Zahrah's phone rang. She took it and begged her caller not to be offended, that she was on her way now.

She and the driver carried Mama out. Placed her in the wheelchair. Mama winced now and then, but her face was mostly expressionless.

The smell grew stronger. I began to smell the smoke in it. Nauseating. Hear some of the screams. The wheelchair shone too brightly in my eyes.

The driver shut the side door. Went into the van.

Zahrah and Mama were left on the road. Mama shaded her eyes from the sun with a hand. Zahrah's phone rang again. She hissed.

'Andy,' she called, 'I'm so late. Help me wheel your mama into the house.'

But I did not move. Could not move. Because it was then that it sank into me. Deep into me. Head and all.

'Andy.'

Mama will be an infant forever.

'Andy!'

Forever!

Mama unshaded her eyes, hate coiling in them.

The wheelchair too bright. The smell too nauseating.

'What are you doing, Andy? Why have you dropped your phone?'

Get up, Mama.

Get up!

'Get up, Mama!' I screamed.

And the world paused.

Zahrah and Mama stared at me. Passers-by murmured. A passing goat eyed me.

8

At home at Zahrah's, sweating and burnt by the sun, I wheel Mama into her room. Although the stones and pools of sand on our unpaved roads caused delays, our journey from the church took too long mainly because we stopped to gaze at her photo studio. It's blackened now, darker than the shade of our skin, smells like rotten egg. Its roof is nowhere to be found. The walls are dented, pouring black stuff when you touch them, the glass door strewn in a thousand pieces on the porch. The name *Glory Bright Photos* is indecipherable, mixed with soot, forming a new word only demons can understand. The shops beside it and the brothel opposite – all owned by Christians – suffered the same fate. But unlike them, nothing in Mama's studio is salvageable. It's all burnt and deformed and turned to shit. Her cameras and flash stands. Furniture and backgrounds. Negatives. All unprovable memory.

Aunty Lizzy has placed Mama's lunch on a low table beside the bed. Mama wheels herself to it, opens the stainless-steel plates of yam porridge and fish stew – the smell of fish assailing me. She stares at the silvery bell beside the plates. Looks out the window at three girls playing tsallake, as they leap across squares drawn in the sand, shiny buttons on the backs of their hands. She gazes at them as though she wants to join them.

It's been shitty sun and sun since the riot. Some nights and mornings clouds gather, and there's rolling winds and paper and plastic bags tossing in mid-air, but still no rain even though it's July. This time of year the rains are supposed to be heavy, the roads muddy and covered in stagnant pools, houses collecting drinking water by placing basins under the eaves. Bullfrogs in pools are supposed to be croaking at night, telling their lovers tales of their previous lives, creating the drowsy ambience for an easy dreamless sleep. It rains almost everywhere, even in Sokoto, where you can practically smell the Sahara. The corn and peanuts our farmers planted in May and June are now small yellow flags, but the weeds around them are still sturdy and green. Many people in our town – especially those affected by the riot – claim that it's the blood of the twenty-two killed on that night that are crying to the heavens for justice and stopping our rain. You might well wonder whether the God over there – if He's there – is a just one, and why He's punishing His saints as well as His sinners whom He didn't stop from sinning in the first place. Or is the God over there actually HXVX, orchestrating the riot to drink the blood of those killed, and stealing our rain for His dessert? (Hint: *dessert* – *s* = *desert*.)

Since Mama returned from the hospital, I wheel her wherever she wants to go. She rings the bell and I appear. I wonder how she'll cope when I leave for Abuja tomorrow. I haven't even told her yet. But I'm sure Aunty Lizzy has, probably while laughing about something else. She's always laughing, that woman, a loud false laughter that doesn't come from her heart but from a secret place even she might never know.

My phone begins to ring. It's a videocall from Zahrah.

'Yay, Andy Africa,' she laughs. 'How're you doing?'

'Good afternoon, Aunty Zahrah,' I say.

She's looking good. Dressed in red as usual, but this time in a tightly fitting top with lace trimmings. Her hair is really nice, neatly done and shiny, plaited in thin long braids, bunched together and curled into a tall donut on her head. One of the braids, the topmost one, is coloured red. Trust Zahrah.

She asks about Mama, about my journey tomorrow. She says that Kelani, the man who claimed to be my papa at Eileen's party, will visit us this evening. That he wants to have a conversation with Mama and me now that she's out of the hospital. I've asked Zahrah about him, how she met him, why she brought him to the party. She told me that she met him in Ososo but refused to say any more. 'I've already caused enough damage,' she said. 'Speak to your mama. She'll explain everything.'

He visited Mama once in the hospital, the day after the riot. He sat opposite me, staring at Mama as she lay stonily on the bed, no drop of pity in his evil eyes. I wanted to punch him and tear at his stupid bald skull. He didn't say much or stay long. He kept glancing at me, as though I were a pet he liked and was deciding on buying, wondering whether I'd someday go rabid and bite his flat black ass. He dropped some money on Mama's table and left. I've not heard from him since. But I'm sure he isn't my father. He just can't be. I'd rather be fatherless than have such a zombie as my papa.

'Hmm, Andy,' Zahrah says. 'I've just finished reading one of your new poems.'

'Which one?'

'The one about Africa being a computer simulation.'

'Oh, I like that one.'

She leans forward. 'Andy, hmm ... Sometimes I wonder where you get your ideas ... So you're claiming that this simulation was orchestrated and/or is being exploited by HXVX.'

'Yes, yes.'

How else could we explain the sun and hunger vs our laughter and dancing, the corruption and killings vs the churches and mosques in every corner of every neighbourhood? How else could we explain the lightning on Mama's back?

'I must confess that it's a great idea,' Zahrah says, 'even if it's unsettling at the same time. I'll read it again and give you some notes.'

I ask about her Anifuturism article in the British magazine. She says it received a mixed response (I ain't surprised!), that one commenter even called her a hungry author and promised to pay her bills if she vowed never to write again. She laughs; I join her. She says she's currently researching quantum Anifuturism, that it provides the clearest path for establishing many Anifuturist tenets. To do this, she's been trying to advance Nick Herbert's idea of 'quantum animism'. Herbert argues that everything in the universe is a quantum as well as an animistic system. So that, using quantum theory, the consciousness (and even life) of 'inanimate' objects could be glimpsed and mathematically proven. But the maths and theory to do this didn't exist until now. Thanks to Anifuturism and its configuration of permutation theory, a key isomorphism between quantum mechanics and animism can be established. If done, it will open the floodgates to understanding consciousness and proving the life of 'inanimate' things.

'And guess what, Andy. I've just read a revolutionary preprint by Hummels and Adegoke who used Anifuturist theory to do just that. That's what I've been struggling to prove for months! Isn't it just amazing?'

I don't give the littlest damn, but I nod and nod. 'It's really, really amazing.'

She asks again about Mama and I tell her that she's here. I give Mama the phone. She takes it without saying thanks and talks to Zahrah in Ososo. Zahrah asks her a couple times if she's fine, whether she needs anything.

'Mi só, Zahrah,' Mama says, smiling a little. 'I'm really fine. Just a little tiredness here and there. Because of the sun, I guess. But I'm all good. Soon I'll be able to start doing things on my own. For myself. Figuring what's left for me.'

'That's great to hear, aunty mè,' Zahrah says. 'Okorie sends his regards.'

'Hope he's fine?'

'He is, thanks. He just can't wait for our big day!'

For a while, Mama is silent.

'So sad that I won't be attending,' she says.

'Yes, really sad. How we used to look forward to this time. All the things we said.'

+

There are now chairs in Zahrah's living room, two white plastic unremarkable ones. Zahrah bought them for Mama's visitors after Aunty Lizzy called her names and told Mama and me to pack and leave her house. Zahrah also bought a plasma screen.

The chairs and the screen are placed in the most boring part of the room, where there are only a few maths formulas on the floor and no statuettes of gods on the walls. I'm sure Zahrah wouldn't have relented if she were still living here. She'll try to convince us to align our corporeal selves with their copies in the spirit world. To live as sparely as our ancient ancestors whose communion with the stones and universe was undisturbed by Western colonial tech. That this sacrifice would yield an ascension in our souls, make us establish an advanced equilibrium with existence.

But Zahrah didn't try too hard. Maybe because she'd already moved to Abuja to live with Okorie in his huge two-storey house. I'm sure she's turned it into the biggest Anifuturist temple on the continent and filled even the hallways with freakish statuettes.

There's a hijab placed over one of the chairs, and on the other books on permutations and atheism. I've scanned through a couple before: *Patterns in Permutations and Words* by Sergey Kitaev, *The Blind Watchmaker* by Richard Dawkins. Fatima must be around. She visits occasionally and sleeps in Zahrah's old room. Aunty Lizzy always peeps in whenever I'm inside with Fatee. She laughs and creates weird excuses for why she's come. Once she stormed in claiming to have seen a rat's shadow entering the room. Since rats salivate about books, she came to ensure that none of Zahrah's textbooks were harmed, as though she gave a shit about Zahrah and her books. It's funny to see how low she'll stoop to stop Fatee and me from fucking. She doesn't know that she needn't bother, that although I think Fatee is hot I can mostly control myself around her because she doesn't have green eyes or a platinum ponytail.

Aunty Lizzy's whistling comes from the kitchen. The smell of fried plantains wafts into the living room. I begin to feel hungry. But first I must take off my expensive Nikes lest they get stained or begin to smell of plantains. Okorie bought them for me from Dubai. He called them 'cheering-up stuff' in the wake of the riot.

As I turn towards my room, Aunty Lizzy calls Fatee from the kitchen. She's so crazy loud, that woman. I'm sure her whisper would be heard by everyone in a stadium.

'I'm waiting for you o!' she says.

The door of my room opens and Fatee comes out, eyes on the floor.

'Hiya, Fatee,' I say, deep voice charming as hell, trying to show off my Nikes.

'Hi, Andy,' she says, eyes still on the floor.

She never calls me plain Andy in greeting. She's the one other person in the universe who's permitted to call me that most hateful construction – Andy Africa – and the only one who gives it a velvety feel.

'What's up, Fatee? Hope all's well?'

I like her long-sleeved ankara blouse and her black trousers.

'All's well, yes yes,' she says, forcing a smile. It's as droopy as her eyelids. 'I only went to your room to get this.' She shows me the bowl I made cornflakes in last night. I forgot to return it to the kitchen afterwards. Her fingers are trembling, as though I've just caught her stealing.

'Aunty Lizzy wants to use it,' she adds.

'Oh, alright. Sorry for not washing it.'

'No worries.'

'Hope you're alright? You look—'

'Oh, I'm fine. The sun's just something today.'

'Yeah, it is,' I say, wondering why everyone's blaming the innocent sun. Is it even innocent? Isn't it letting itself be used by HXVX?

Fatee isn't wearing a headtie or anything. Her hair is plaited in cornrows that fall to the front and back of her head. They're rough, one or two a bit loose, as though she's been pulling or scratching at them.

She keeps looking away when I look at her, as though I've hurt her, and she prefers to wade in the hurt a little more. This isn't my Fatee who'll smile shyly whenever she sees me. Who'll play eye games with me, her eyes large unblinking mirrors. In them I'll usually find a secret glee, a secret yes! when she's around me. I'm sure that yes! doesn't appear when she's with other people, even her bestie Zahrah.

'But are you sure, Fatee? Can I get you anything?'

'Seriously, I'm good,' she says, a little of the shy glee returning to her.

'Alright. You down for a movie?'

'Sure.'

'I got something mad yesterday.'

'Another pirated disc?' she says, chuckling.

'Yeah. Sadly. A collection of all Aronofsky. Imagine!'

'Cool.'

'Zahrah would kill herself.'

'Yeah.'

Although Zahrah seems to disapprove of TV screens, she watches a lot of movies on her laptop or the TV in her room. She'll say that she isn't against cinematic arts per se, that although they can be especially informative, they must be controlled in the African context, not put before or beside our gods and culture and existence.

Fatee and I go to the kitchen.

'Good afternoon, Aunty,' I say to Aunty Lizzy.

'Andy Andy,' she says. 'Biggest boy in town.'

She always calls me that crap and I never have a proper response. I either smile when I'm not feeling like it or chuckle and hail her when I feel like playacting. Now I don't feel like molokoing about, especially given what she said yesterday evening.

She's tall, taller than Mama, same height as me. Although she's as dark as Mama, her blackberry skin glows brighter, and is more toned than that of many women I know. She likes wearing tank tops and shorts to show off her sleek arms and legs, as though she were Lupita Nyong'o or something. Although I'll kill myself for thinking this, I think she's more beautiful than Mama. Maybe it's because of her youth; maybe Mama looked even better at her age. Anyhoo, she's completely unlike Mama. She can be very loud, very bossy, controlling conversations without giving her listener any say. Sometimes she talks to Mama as though Mama isn't her older sister by ten years. Sometimes she snaps at her. And when she does I grab my seat tightly so I don't jump and click my fingers in her face.

Unsurprisingly, Aunty Lizzy and Zahrah often clash. They've argued about money and food and religion, and Aunty Lizzy has called Zahrah a witch countless times. Maybe that's why Zahrah ran away to Abuja and left us here to tussle with her.

Aunty Lizzy immediately rushed to Kontagora when Zahrah called to inform her about Mama. She spent three days and nights at the hospital without showering, waiting for Mama to come out of her coma. It took Zahrah and Fatee and me to beg her to go home and shower and sleep.

'So, Andy,' Aunty Lizzy says. 'How was Mass? That's what you Catholics call it, right? As in, anything that has weight and occupies space?'

That's Aunty Lizzy. She can be quite silly.

Fatee washes the bowl. When she's done, she places it on a rack to dry and watches Aunty Lizzy and me.

'Mass was cool,' I say.

'Cool? How could you describe a covenant between God and man like that?'

I'm not one bit in a Lizzy mood today.

'Mass was quite moving, spiritual, and nourishing,' I say.

'Okay o. Speak all the big English you know. After all, that's what Zahrah teaches you people, abi? But did you get to pray for your mama?'

Classic Aunty Lizzy, deftly salvaging a dead conversation.

'Yes, I did. I even served Mass and held the communion plate.'

'Cool,' she says, as though she hasn't just ripped me for saying that. 'So how does the communion even taste? That white stuff? You Catholics are so white.'

And I'm instantly put off again.

She attends a Pentecostal church whose name I can't remember. They meet on Saturdays. They claim it's the real sabbath, that we Catholics are fake Christians who think we can change things to suit ourselves just because we have billions of followers worldwide. Yesterday she came back from church with a plastic doll she called 'Spiritual Watchman'. It has huge eyes and a big cross painted across its face, and it's supposed to repel evil spirits. She hung it in the living room just above the plasma. She believes Zahrah's Anifuturist statuettes are crammed with evil spirits, that they're hindering Mama from fully recovering. She claims that Mama had been recovering at an exponential rate while she was in the hospital, but that things have slowed down since she moved to Zahrah's place.

I'm still hurt by the names she called me those few days I didn't visit Mama in the hospital. But none of that is as traumatising as what she said yesterday evening while I made cornflakes in the kitchen.

She asked me whether I'd forgiven Mama for keeping my papa, Kelani, from me. It was out of nowhere – we'd been talking about her fishponds and catfish in Kaduna. After a pause, I told her that I didn't think Kelani was my papa, that we have nothing in common, we don't even look alike, and that I believe Mama, she wouldn't lie about such a thing. Aunty Lizzy placed her hand on my shoulder and said that growing up must have been difficult for me.

'You'll have to accept him, Andy,' she said.

'Why?' I said.

'He's your father. Your true father. A boy can never do without his papa,' she said, as though I were a toddler who couldn't find his zipper. 'He'll never fully become a man.'

'What did you say?' I asked, removing her hand. It felt like a slug on my body.

She repeated herself.

'He's your true papa, Andy. Your mother selfishly hid you from him just because of a disagreement they had. Believe me, I'm on your side. It's my job to protect you, including from your own mother. Yes, it's difficult. But you must try to embrace Kelani. If you don't, you'll have a very sorrowful adulthood, trust me. You're still too young to understand all you've missed.'

'Can you shut up?'

'Andy,' she said, her voice very gentle, 'I understand how hard it must be for you. I don't even know how I'd have survived if I were in your situation. I would've run mad or something. Because how could I live if my mother was so cruel to me, to keep me away from my true father?'

'Shut up!'

'I'm sorry, Andy dear. So sorry. Please don't cry. Please know I'm—'

'Shut up. Shut up. Shut up!'

And I threw the carton of cornflakes at her.

Now, as I finish dishing out my food, she asks if I feel better today, as if she gives a shit. 'You know, you still haven't apologised for what you did yesterday. I was only trying to help.'

I don't say anything. I pick up my plates of porridge and fish stew and plantains and bounce out of the kitchen. I feel bad for leaving Fatee with her.

I place the plates on the floor in front of the plasma and sit, balancing them between my legs. Zahrah would be proud. She'd say that, although she isn't around, I'm still true to my Anifuturist roots.

I can't stop thinking about what Aunty Lizzy said yesterday. And about Grandma's letter. What if I'm truly Kelani's child? Maybe Mama broke up with him just before he realised she was pregnant with me. Maybe he did something terrible to her that she wouldn't forgive.

But still, there should have been something, even a bit of it, when I first met Kelani. It should have come up. Woken in me. Stirred and opened its eyes after fifteen years. Flown out of me the very second I saw him.

But there was nothing.

Zero.

Zip.

+

Fatee sits beside me on the floor. It's Ramadan, and she's forbidden from eating or drinking until dusk. I feel bad for her, for the flakiness of her lips, the slowness of her arms, the shadows in her eyes. I wonder if these are because of the fast or something else or both.

During Ramadan everyone in our town fasts in some way. At three every morning Muslim kids move from house to house beating dead plastic jerrycans, chanting 'A tashi!', rousing everyone from their *Legend of Zelda* dreams. And our Muslim neighbours will get up and eat their fill, telling stories and laughing, the moon a platinum C in the sky, peeping into rooms. They'll all stop eating at five, immediately after the salah is called. Many return to bed after the prayer, to rise at noon, so shops don't open until afternoon. Muslims are really cool during Ramadan. They greet you 'Assalamu alaikum' when they see you, give alms to beggars on the streets, and are absolutely honest when you buy stuff from their shops.

A mosque behind our house calls for prayer. The speakers of other mosques in the neighbourhood crackle to life. Feedback springs around us.

Fatee rises, goes to Zahrah's room, returns with a prayer mat and a plastic kettle. She takes the kettle outdoors to do her ablution. Minutes later she shambles into the living room, her face and hair dripping water. She picks up her hijab from the chair, puts it on slowly. Rolls the mat towards east, stands before it, places her open hands behind her ears.

'Allahu akbar,' she says.

She prays for a minute, bowing, standing straight. She goes down on her knees and pushes her forehead to the floor. 'Allahu akbar.' She whispers more prayers, her voice sibilant.

Moments later her whispering begins to change. It begins to sound like cawing. Like a bird yearning to fly to the peak of the world but falling repeatedly. Pushed back not by the storms outside but by those coiling in the heart.

Suddenly she smacks and smacks the floor with her hand. Rises. Sees her shoe. Picks it up and flings it across the room.

When she realises I'm staring at her, she mutters inaudibly. She picks up the mat, goes to fetch the shoe, marches to Zahrah's room, dragging the mat behind her. She stays there long enough for me to finish half of my porridge before she returns to the living room.

I wish I could get up and hug her, but I remain stuck to the floor. She sits down beside me, pretending nothing has happened. She's not wearing her hijab. Her smell is different, yeasty, as though she's undergone some fermentation.

139

'And where's our film?' she says, trying to sound normal.

'Fatee, what happened?' I say.

'I don't want to talk about it.'

'Alright.'

Again, this isn't my Fatee. Or maybe I don't really know her, despite all the books we've exchanged and the walks we've taken and the arguments about black holes we've had. It's sad and embarrassing that I've wasted all my time learning the blurbs about her life, thinking about her figure and boobs, being a passer-by in her world.

I get up and insert the DVD into the machine.

'What should we start with?'

As I fetch the remote I notice she's eating some of my plantains.

'You don't mind, do you?' she says.

'Feel free, babe.'

I wish she could just talk to me. Not that I haven't been like this all my life too, hooks tearing in my chest but saying nothing to anyone. All peeps my age are like this. Adults think we're mostly fine, without problems, just because we haven't tried using a noose before.

'Thanks,' she says. 'Let's start with *Pi*.'

We begin watching. We eat our plantains and chat about the actors and laugh about funny scenes. FYI, Fatee handles the remote when you watch a film with her. She pauses a million times. Rewinds to rewatch a scene, to rehear witty lines of dialogue (which she repeats to herself), and fast-forwards afterwards. She says all this aids her memory as she can't stand watching the same movie twice.

I go to the kitchen to get more porridge and plantains. When I return, the electricity goes off.

'Oh, NEPA,' we say simultaneously.

'Those fuckers,' I say.

'Yeah,' she says, helping herself to another plantain.

When we finish eating, she goes to Zahrah's room and returns with a skipping rope.

'But you just finished eating,' I say.

'I won't die,' she laughs.

We go to the backyard and she begins to skip on the sand. Afterwards she gets on all fours and does a headstand. She goes from that to a forearm handstand, then to a simple handstand, leaving hand and leg prints in the sand. She laughs and I laugh, watching her do things I wouldn't dare.

'Come on, Andy. You can do it!'

And for one tiny tiny second I wish again that I could marry her. If I did, we'd spend our lives doing yoga, eating plantains, laughing, and watching experimental films. But Northern Muslims don't marry Southern Christians, like ever. Such a match is as rare as finding an extraterrestrial couple snogging in your backyard. The relationship is doomed from Day Zero, because, for example, where would the wedding take place? Would the children become Muslim Christians or Christian Muslims, Northern Southerners or Southern Northerners?

But hey, I shouldn't be worrying about marriage just yet – it's centuries away. If the time comes, Fatee and I would think of something. E.g. we'd become full-fledged Anifuturists or maybe even create our own religion that'll allow us to be together. Hence there's nada stopping us from holding on to each other like clamps, kissing when no one's watching, putting our hands under each other's clothes.

I bite my small finger, comparing her to Eileen. Who's smarter? Who's funnier? As I watch Fatee, wanting to dip my fingers into her hand- and footprints, I can't help wondering what really holds me back from her. I always thought I understood it. That it's because she's a Muslim and I'm a Christian. That she's from the North and I'm from the South. That it's because of the It, because of HXVX. But now I wonder whether it's actually just me. Maybe I haven't tried hard enough to love her. Because every time, I feel I'll regret not being with her when I'm older. For she's: *Fatee − e = Fate*. My Fatee. My Fate.

She switches to a side plank and I try not to look at her boobs. I tell her about my simulation poem, that Zahrah thinks it's a good idea, albeit unsettling.

'Still, I believe we're definitely in a simulation, Fatee, everything on this continent. We must be in a computer powered by a black hole or something. This simulation is so deep and power-ful that we can even come out of it into the real world outside the continent.'

She says nothing. She stands on one foot, wobbling a little. She places her hands together, her foot in her thigh.

'I don't agree, Andy.'

'Why?'

'You're saying that only the world outside the continent is real?'

'Fatee, I'm talking about a powerful computer here. One that is powered by a huge black hole. The kind at the centre of our galaxy.'

'Sagittarius A*?'

'Yeah.'

'I don't agree. This is all there is to it, Andy.'

'Why are you so sure?'

She's silent. That's what she does when she's got no answer.

'I think the Sagan standard answers your problem,' she says.

'How?'

'Such a huge assumption must be backed with equally huge evidence, which you don't have. So, by Occam's razor, this is all there is to it, Andy. No simulation or anything like it. Plus everything on the continent makes cause–effect sense. Although a simulation is possible, I highly doubt it, from the experiential aspect and all, from the complexity of consciousness, which a computer might never be able to simulate.'

'But, Fatee, the Sagan standard and Occam's razor are not science.'

'Is that so? Then your proposition is also not science. It's unverifiable.'

'Come on, Fatee. A computer with infinite input and process-ing power could easily do it. Can't you see?'

'You're raising your voice, Andy.'

'We're in a simulation, Fatee.'

'So if we're in a simulation, where did its input come from? Who set up such a computer? Are they also in a simulation? You've not even shown that such a computer can exist.'

'But computers are getting better and better!'

'Of course they are.'

'Give them a thousand years. They'll do anything.'

'You're still raising your voice. Why're you taking this personally?'

Is she simply evading my points? She never argues unfairly.

I dig out my phone. No chats from Eileen. I wonder what she's up to now. A siesta, perhaps. She's the only real thing in this land of simulations.

Fatee doesn't understand how important this is. That we're probably not in love because we're in a simulation. My desire for crossing oceans, for Eileen's hair, must have been installed in me at the moment of conception.

As Fatee switches to a meditation pose, the electricity is restored.

'Up NEPA,' she says.

I also want to hail NEPA, but I stop myself. I've spent my life hailing them and they've kept seizing the electricity. If Fatee needs any proof that it's all bullshit, they're the paragon.

We return to the living room, sit on the floor, resume our film. She thinks it should've gotten at least an Oscar nom, if not for its cinematography then for its screenplay, since it managed to bridge science and faith so effortlessly. I would argue under different circumstances, but I just nod.

+

We switch to *Requiem for a Dream*. The first scene is about a mother and son fighting. As I try to recall when I last had such a scuffle with Mama, I feel Fatee stiffen. She gets up and leaves for Zahrah's room. She must have remembered – and suffered again – those times her mother whipped her with the dog chain and poured boiling water on her. That's how trauma is, I guess. The brush of a feather can cause a landslide in us.

This time I get up and go after her.

She's lying on the bed. Face buried in a pillow. I shut the door.

A fan is whirring above, moving the smell of books around the room. They line the walls, neatly arranged in bookcases, books on permutations, voodooism, prehistory, futurism, Afrofeminism, and plant anatomy.

I sit on the bed, scan her body for new scars but don't find any. The thin scar on her neck is still visible, though fainter now. Those on her hands seem to have disappeared.

I shift closer to her. Place my hand softly on her shoulder.

She stiffens again. Turns and glares at me. Serpents coil in her eyes, their fangs poised to strike.

I take back my hand and she pushes her face into the pillow again. I don't know what to say. Vets must be the smartest people on the planet. How do you treat someone who doesn't describe their pain?

'Fatee,' I say.

She doesn't respond.

I place my hand on her back. 'Fatima.'

'Don't touch me. Get out.'

I don't remove my hand.

In a flash she turns and slaps my hand off her, then slaps me in the face.

'Come on, Fatee,' I say, grabbing her hands, my face stinging like hell.

She struggles for a moment, breaks free, slaps me again.

I get up. Walk to the door. Open it. But I cannot leave.

Her face is buried back in the pillow. This time she's clutching it, her veins jutting out, as though she's trying to suffocate herself.

My face still stinging, I shut the door.

'Come on, Fatima. Don't choke yourself. Please.'

She moves away from the pillow. Curls into a foetal position. She looks like an old woman, the old woman she'll become. Bony, face wrinkled, hair tattered, ugly. How could my slim, smiling Fatee gather so much rage? Where did she store all this in her delicate frame? This is my proof that there've been other Fatees, Fatee $\beta, \gamma, \delta, \ldots, \chi, \psi, \omega$, and this is just one of the litany coming out, jutting out of her neck, thrashing out of her hands.

I go to the bed and stand behind her, vowing to leave if she slaps me again.

'What's wrong, Fatee?'

She turns, eyes closed. 'You,' she whispers.

'Me? What d'you mean?'

She shakes her head. 'I miss Zahrah.'

'We all miss Zahrah. But why are you so—'

'She's my only friend. The only person I trust. The only one I can talk to.'

'But I'm your friend, Fatee,' I say, sitting down. 'We've been friends since Primary One, way before you met her.'

'Yes, we were friends.'

'What d'you mean *were*? I'm still your friend.'

'You're not.'

'I am, Fatee.'

'You've been lying to me.'

'Come on, Fatee. What are you talking about?'

'You've been claiming to be who you're not.'

'Claiming what?'

'To be my friend.'

'Fatee? Why're you doing this? What have I done wrong? I apologise. I'm sorry.'

She straightens her legs. Rubs her face with the back of her hand.

I lie on the bed beside her. I tell her I'm sorry. That she should forgive me. That she should tell me what happened.

'It happened again yesterday,' she says.

'What happened yesterday?'

'I miss Zahrah.'

'Why?'

'Only she can understand.'

'Understand what?'

She tells me that last night her father came into her room. She was asleep. It had been a long time since it last happened, months ago when her mother almost caught him, almost caught them. She never sleeps when he's around. She keeps seeing the same shadow on the wall, the shadow with the big head, crawling towards her. But since he's always away at work in Abuja, she's been mostly fine. But yesterday he suddenly returned after she'd gone to bed. She'd had an intense yoga session and had gone to bed early and was sleeping soundly when he walked into her room. He didn't go far this time. How she screamed! She threatened to report him to her mother. He laughed, knowing she wouldn't dare. They both knew her mother would blame her and splash boiling water on her if she mentioned it. After all, she'd done worse as a result of minor things.

'What I still can't believe,' Fatee says, 'is that he's the same person who preaches in our neighbourhood mosque. He likes talking about holiness, about faithfulness. He even talks about how parents no longer set good examples for their children.'

I put a hand around her and she pushes it off. I move my face towards her and tell her I'm so sorry, so very sorry, that it will never ever happen again, that I promise this from the bottom of my heart.

We both know that my promises are crap, the assurances of a baby. That I'm powerless to cause any change. I could go to the police, but what would it lead to? They'd ask for bribes, take statements, and do nothing, just as they did when I went to report the attack on Mama after the riot. 'Are you the only boy whose mother was injured?' the sergeant said, tapping my head with his truncheon. 'The mothers of others were even killed, but they haven't woken us at night about it.' Worse still is that Fatee's father is an adviser to a minister in Abuja and has many political connections. The police would probably arrest me for reporting him, for slandering such a faultless and diligent public servant.

The most painful thing of all, Fatee says, is that it's only when her father is at home that she's free. She could choose not to pray, even refuse to fast, and her father would silence her mother if she complained. She could demand the latest iPhone and her father would buy it immediately. She always taunts and disobeys her mother to retaliate for the slaps and beatings she receives while her father is away, knowing her mother will seek a worse payback when he departs.

'I've been bad,' she says. 'I've been very bad.'

She blows her nose in a handkerchief.

'For a long time,' she says, 'I thought all men were the same. Liars, tricksters, evil. All out to hurt me. Until I became close to you. You were kind. Caring. Always helping me treat my injuries. Always listening to me. Unlike many boys at school. And I began to like you. And I began to imagine a future with both of us in it. Where we'd be together and you'd never hurt me. Only for me to see today what you wrote in your diary. Blonde girls? Pigtails? Eileen? I don't understand. What do you see in her? In white girls? What is it about their colour? Are you hearing me? I've just asked you a question, Andy. Talk to me. Talk!'

+

Mama, Aunty Lizzy, and I are in Zahrah's living room waiting for Kelani to arrive. It's sunset. Outside, daylight is mimicking morning, but it's a spent, drowsy light that's hovering on things. Little girls in hijabs pass our house carrying trays of onions and tomatoes on their heads, hawking them from door to door. Two stop and announce their wares. Aunty Lizzy tells them that we ain't buying, that they shouldn't bother coming here again because we won't ever be needing their vegetables. The girls don't shout back. Although they're just five or six years old, they're already used to this. They'll return tomorrow. Someday they'll be fourteen or fifteen, get married, stop hawking, and begin to live in purdah.

Mama is in her wheelchair, chewing something. Her watery eyes roam across the room. She stares at Kelani's chair, placed as far as possible from us, and then at the statuette of the god with eyes like African maps. Her gaze darts to the *Guernica*-sized painting at the end of the room, to the formulas on the floor, and settles on the Schrödinger equation at her feet. She squints hard at it, as though she's finally understanding it and feeling its power, recognising how scientists use it for calculating the wave function of a particle, for finding the most invisible of things.

$$H\Psi(x) = E\Psi(x)$$

She's wearing a green t-shirt, and underneath it her fallen breasts are like a pair of flip-flops. Since the riot they sag even more and I really don't like seeing them. Those milliseconds

I accidentally do, a barbed shame crawls through me. Their L-shapes will refuse to leave my head, and I'll begin to hear their angry voices in my ear. *You're the cause of all this, Andy Africa,* they say. *You've been ruining Everything since your shitty birth, wasting all her sweat and blood.*

Aunty Lizzy, in a pair of combat shorts, slaps a mosquito dead on her leg. She tells Mama that she saw me lying beside Fatee a few hours ago. That she's sure I'm up to something bad because Fatee was crying and all. So Mama better talk to me since I'm clearly keeping a huge secret from her. If not, I could make a giant mistake that I'll spend the rest of my life trying to correct, just as she did.

Mama looks at me and I wish she could say something. *Criticise me, Ma. Ask me to confess. Tell me to clean the floors of the whole house as punishment.* If she asks, I'll tell her everything. About Eileen. About the blonde porn clips I've been watching. About the guilt I feel when I look at her, my comparisons of her to Mama 2. But she doesn't say anything. In fact, she seems to be smiling covertly to herself as though she already knows the secret and has more important things to worry about. *You don't, Ma. Seriously. Talk to me.*

Aunty Lizzy frowns. She expected some chastisement, if not a full-blown exorcism. When she realises Mama isn't going to do anything she snaps at me to get Mama some cold drinking water.

I get up, bounce to the kitchen. Someday I'll grow older and sport a full beard and own my own place, and nobody will send me on petty errands. But I wonder what mistake she was referring to. Mama must have mentioned it. Aunty Lizzy must be the sister who trusted her geography teacher and followed him to his house. . .

I fetch the water and stand in the doorway of the kitchen to eavesdrop. But Mama and Aunty Lizzy ain't talking about me. Mama is telling Aunty Lizzy about the dream she keeps having. That she had it again an hour ago while she was napping. And yes, it was more real this time.

She's about to say more but sees me in the doorway and stops.

I hand her the glass. She takes it without saying thanks, sips from it, places it on a side table, her hand shaky.

I sit and they're silent for a while.

Since Mama regained consciousness she's been going on about this dream. Not to me, of course, but to Aunty Lizzy and Zahrah. I've only learnt a few details about it. Mama claims she's seeing somebody in the dream, somebody she isn't supposed to be dreaming about. She claims she hasn't actually seen the person's face yet, so she isn't sure of anything.

Aunty Lizzy leans towards Mama. 'Tell me more, aunty mè,' she says.

'It was different this time,' Mama says.

'How?'

'It was clearer.'

'Hmm.'

'I think I now know what it means.'

'Really? You saw the person's face this time?'

Mama nods. Aunty Lizzy glances at me. I take out my phone and pretend I'm reading some breaking news.

Aunty Lizzy turns back to Mama. 'Tell me, aunty mè. Please.'

Mama shakes her head.

I also want to know who this person is. So I get up and walk to the kitchen, leaving my ears in the living room. I open the fridge and steal a small piece of cake. Minutes later I leave the kitchen, stop by Zahrah's door, turn the handle. It's still locked. There's no sound through the keyhole. I hope Fatee will at least come out to get some dinner later.

It's crazy what she's been through. All evening shards of thoughts assail me – I bottle them all. Still, I know that somehow I'm the cause. My being a man already makes me complicit. If only she hadn't read the damn diary!

I return to the living room and Aunty Lizzy is still pestering Mama about who she sees in the dream. Mama ain't saying shit. She's staring at the floor, at Schrödinger.

I'm sure that person is my Ydna. He left me and went to her. He must be gossiping to her about me, telling her all my secrets. Maybe that's why she isn't talking to me anymore.

'Is this person male or female?' Aunty Lizzy asks, her final try.

'Male,' Mama says decisively. Nothing walking or crawling on earth will make her say any more.

I wonder where in herself she stores all these secrets. When she leaves this world (and I hate myself for thinking this!), wouldn't she still owe the living? All those babies she's lost. The husbands she's had. The father of her son . . . Wouldn't they make the process of leaving less easy?

+

Just as Kelani sits down, Mama tells him in Ososo that if he's come all this way to claim he's the father of her son, then he better get up and leave. He's wearing a suit and tie, as though hoping they will aid his claim.

He apologises for coming late. He tells us he left Abuja this morning after church, and he'll return tonight because of work tomorrow. He glances at his fake gold watch, tries to reset it.

Outside, the last orange of the sun disappears. A greyness settles on things.

Aunty Lizzy tells me to get Kelani some drinking water. As I get up, Mama points back at my seat. I return to it without question.

'So you won't even offer me water?' he says.

Mama frowns.

'This is very simple,' he says. 'Five minutes and we're done. First, Andy needs to know a few facts.'

'What facts?' she says.

'The full story.'

'And what's that?'

'Andrew, eighteen years ago I married your mother,' he says, loosening his tie a little. 'We had many good times together. We were in love, we were happy, I assure you. But seventeen years ago, in the month of October, we had a disagreement.'

'And what was it about?' Mama says.

'I won't go into all that.'

'I thought you were telling the full story.'

'I'm not interested in pointing fingers,' he says. 'I have a good heart in me, and so I forgive and forget. I let bygones be bygones. Unlike you, Gloria.'

Mama seethes but remains silent.

'So, as I was saying,' Kelani says, 'she and I had a disagreement. Like all couples do. I wanted us to resolve this disagreement, to return to our loving, happy relationship. But for some reason your mother didn't want to continue with our marriage. She lost faith in us. And when I finally let her go, I suspected that she must be pregnant with our child, that—'

'Shut up,' Mama spits. 'Stop your mindless lies, you monster. You stole everything from me. You ruined even the little we had. You demon, you were—'

He ignores Mama. 'So, I suspected she was pregnant. My suspicion was confirmed a year later when I heard she'd fled to the North and had a son, my boy. And Andrew,' he says, gazing at me with reddening eyes, 'for the past fifteen years I've been searching everywhere for you. My search finally ended some months ago when your grandmother and I tracked Gloria and came to Kontagora to see her, to see you, to take my rightful place in your life.'

He wipes his face with a filthy white handkerchief.

He adds that, since he and Mama separated, he's been married to two other women, but unfortunately neither could give him a child.

'And when I think about you, Andrew, I am overjoyed. I am grateful to God. He has endowed me with such a kind, hard-working, and brilliant son. I can't wait to finally be in your life, to give you a better life, to show you all the wonders of Abuja.'

Mama is frowning harder than ever.

'What do you think?' he asks Aunty Lizzy.

'I think all you've said sounds reasonable,' she says. 'I even think you look alike, you and Andy.'

A part of me wants to hug him, the answer to all my teary nights, and the other wants to slap Aunty Lizzy for claiming I resemble him. I do not see myself in him, smell myself in him. His red eyes are like those of a beast. His blue suit is fake, his handkerchief slimy. His chuckles sound as though he's escaped from a psych ward. I wonder why Mama would marry such a man. Was she very desperate? Did society force him onto her?

Surprisingly, Mama smiles at me.

A firefly glides into the room. Flies past me, past Mama. Settles on the handle of her wheelchair.

'Wait,' Aunty Lizzy says to Kelani. 'You said you and Gloria separated in October. It means your child should have been born at most eight months later, in June. But Andy was born in November . . .'

'She lied,' he says. 'She changed his date of birth to keep me away from him. You don't know Gloria, I swear. She can be so wilful, so unforgiving. She has kept my son away from me for fifteen years. Fifteen years!'

I wonder whether it's possible for a person to feel their age. Is age not a construct and an approximation? How can I be sure that I'm not fourteen or even seventeen?

Mama laughs, for the first time since the riot. She laughs long and hard and I'm afraid she might burst open her scars.

'How could a mother lie about when she gave birth to her son?' she says.

'This isn't a laughing matter, sister,' Aunty Lizzy says to her.

Mama laughs even louder. As though she's laughing all the laughter she's hoarded since the Change.

'Stop all this nonsense, Gloria,' Aunty Lizzy says. 'This has got to stop. We all know who Andy's father is.'

Mama is now staring at Schrödinger on the floor.

'Yes,' Aunty Lizzy continues, 'admit it! You've been deceiving Andy all these years. How do you think you're helping him? You're so secretive. You have a heart of stone. You've stopped talking to everybody. To Mother. To your twin brother. To your very own twin! For all these years! Every day he calls me and asks about Andy. I'm sure Andy doesn't even know who he is.'

Mama's lower lip widens, elongates, becomes ugly. She starts to weep.

'Look at him. Look at who you call your son. There's a hole in him. Maybe this thing that's happened to you is punishment for all you've done.'

And that is when I snap.
That is when I fly to my feet.
That is when I fling Aunty Lizzy with all that's in me.
That is when I go to Mama.
That is when she hugs me.
That is when she calls me by my name.
That is when I know I'm her, and she's me.

9

Somebody's disturbing my sleep. Telling me to wake up. Like a voice underwater. Leave me here. I don't want to go back. Wake up, Andy. It's Aunty Lizzy. All's not well. Your mama is ill. She's been wailing all night. About her back, her sides. Didn't you hear it? Even Fatima at the other end of the house heard. I've called Elder Paschal. He's coming to take her to the hospital. He'll be here soon. You'll have to cancel your journey today.

'Andy? Did you hear me, Andy? I said your mother . . .'

Slowly slowly, life flows back to my heavy limbs and I regain control. 'What's the time?' I say, sitting up on the bed.

'Around five. Day hasn't broken.'

I jump up, put on my flip-flops, and that's when I hear Mama. Crying like an infant. I hurry. As I pass the living room, Aunty Lizzy scuttling behind me, I see in the darkness flashes of people in black flocking around a long box, singing a slow tune. Behind them, dunes of sand.

In the room, an LED lamp beams from the wall. Mama is lying face down on the bed, Fatima sitting beside her. Mama is almost naked except for a wrapper covering her bottom, and when Fatima sees me she tries to cover her back with another wrapper. Mama screams and yanks the wrappers away as though they were blankets of fire. Instantly her nakedness and tar skin hit me like a slap, wring my stomach.

'Evesho mè!' she screams, calling on God. 'Evesho. Evesho. Evesho!'

She thrashes her arms about the bed, but her legs and feet are dead. She wails and wails:

'My back. My back. My back!'

'Why me? Eni mi shi khè? Why me? This is just too much. O kpini mè. O kpini mè!'

'What have I – what have I – what have I done?'

Fatima covers Mama's bottom and I move closer to her. I stare at her back. There's live lightning there. Or is it a spiderweb? Or is it a whip? An eternal whip?

There are so many things I want to say. Sorry, Ma. Please don't cry. It will be alright. Elder Paschal will be here soon. This will be over soon.

But nothing comes out.

Why am I like this?

Fatima looks at me. Do something, her eyes say. She's your mama. Contribute. Pay your debt.

I move to place my cold hand on Mama's hot shoulder. She stiffens, slowly relaxes, quietens. She takes deep breaths, eyes closed, like she's asleep.

She must know I'm the one touching her. She begins to feed me her memories; they seep from her shoulder to my hand and down to my chest. And I sit beside her, and I begin to unpack them.

Outside, half-moon in clear sky. Insects still chirping. A car speeds to the front of the house, honks.

+

At nine I come out of our house and begin the thirty-minute walk to Morocca's, sun like a blowtorch on my skin. I stop for a moment and adjust the strap of my bag containing my Abuja stuff till the bag is comfortable. I continue bouncing, past girls and women carrying basins of water on their heads, the girls checking me out, the women telling the girls to hurry, that they are lazy, like all children nowadays. Morocca calls me and I tell him to chill, that Mama is mostly alright and we don't have to cancel the journey.

Mama and Aunty Lizzy are still in Dr Rapha's clinic. I left them an hour ago after the doctor said he didn't know what was wrong with her, that he thought she was mostly fine, but that he'd run some tests during the week. He gave her an injection, and she was receiving her second drip by the time I left. Elder Paschal didn't take her to General Hospital, our only hospital, because recently folks have been dying there like flies from simple ailments like chickenpox or appendicitis. It's said that the doctors have joined secret cults and are using the blood and the heartbeats of peeps to make blood money to cover their unpaid salaries.

When I rose to leave Mama my forefinger began to tremble. I crazily wanted to touch her. To dip my finger in the places where her dimples used to appear. To trace every vein on that blackberry skin. I kept moving forward and back, trying to understand this desire, this ancient musty trap, this rope tying me to this woman. I left the room, wiped my eyes, stopped in the front porch of the clinic. Aunty Lizzy came out to join me, and we stood on the steps watching a passing cobbler sing and wink and smile at passers-by, his tools piled in a basket on his head. She shook her head and said she hadn't forgiven me for what I did last night. 'I was only trying to help,' she said, as if I needed her shitty help. 'Despite all you do, Andy, I'll continue to help you however I can. That's the least I can do as a good Christian. Even though your mother has kept you from us all your life, you are still one of us. You are part of our big loving family. In fact, since you're going to Abuja, I want you to meet our brother, your mother's twin. I know your mother will be angry with me, but please try and visit him. He called me this morning to ask about you and her. He's a big man. You must see him. I'm sure he'll give you some money. Do you know his name? Monsignor William Aziza? And give my regards to Zahrah. Although we don't see eye to eye about many things, I still wish her well.'

I continue bouncing, past a hen and her chicks digging out white food on the road, past a man in a kaftan selling touch-and-follow in bottles. Morocca's bro and Okey can't do without that shit. They spray it under their dirty armpits and claim it helps them attract any chick, no matter how classy she is. That with just a single tap on her shoulder she'll swoon and follow them instantly, laugh at whatever they say, lick whatever they wish.

Past Model School, a government school with most of its windows and roof stolen or blown away in rainstorms. During term time two hundred pupils sit cross-legged on the floor of each classroom, holes in their shorts and shirts, and they are taught one or two lessons every day, the same 1-2-3 and A-B-C, with little variation. The pupils only know how to read and write their names. They can't tell you the name of the first president of Nigeria or what continent they are on. They haven't heard of Lewis Carroll or even Lord Lugard. They grow up to become the cobblers or housewives or drug dealers of our town. I used to attend this school and draw Bruce Lee in my exercise books and make paper planes with their dog-eared pages until Father McMahon awarded me a scholarship to St Michael's, a school with real teachers and real lessons and real desks and real blackboards and twenty real pupils per class.

Past a Fulani woman in beads and lipstick hawking nono in a covered calabash placed on her head. Past an old man selling alewa on a wheelbarrow. Many Southerners in our town don't buy nono because they claim the milk is from cows suffering weird diseases, that Fulanis are dirty people who rub shea butter as cream and adulterate their milk with dirty water. They also don't buy alewa because it's practically sugar melted, dyed, and moulded into bars.

Approaching me on the road is Oga Oliver in a grey suit and tie. During the riot, right in front of him, the rioters beat his daughter to death with thorny sticks, calling her the neighbourhood slut, her blood splashing onto his glasses. He must have snapped back to his senses as a result, because now he resembles the man he was before he set out for Europe through the Sahara. Since his recovery, despite the heat, he mostly wears creased old-fashioned suits and ties, as though he's trying to reclaim the reputation he's lost since his Return. He used his former connections to get a job in the local government and has been the leader of the Christian organisation of folks who lost family or property during the riot. I've attended one of the meetings, and last week I heard rumours that a reprisal was being planned.

He's directly in front of me. We both slow down, stop.

'Good morning, sir,' I say to him. It's weird greeting him now after all those years my droogs and I taunted him.

He doesn't answer. This is the third time since his recovery that he's not answered my greeting. He stares hard at me, as though he could glimpse my jet-black soul, could spot the entire tan curve of my life and the great ditch I'm about to plunge into. His stony eyes make Ydna hop inside me and try to jump out.

I wish I could tell Oga Oliver that I'm sorry for all those years my droogs and I mocked him, calling him a freak doll who said only 'Water'. That I'm proud of him for being bold enough to abandon this Cursed land which our parents forced us onto, for challenging the Sahara in the ring of fate and failing honourably.

I turn away from him and bounce on. But he seems to have muttered something. A single word. Sounds like 'Don't'.

+

In front of Morocca's house, my phone buzzes. It's Eiqueen. She's just replied to my chat about what she's up to today, that she hopes to finally watch *La Vie en Rose* and finish *Notes from Underground*. Most importantly she says she's madly looking forward to our fantabulous reunion! She's added *xx* at the end of her chat and two beauteous emojis. I smile and smile. I'm sure I look like some cool goat. But what does she really mean by her *xx*? Is she saying that she's ... that she's ... sending me – *say it, Andy* – kisses? I always try not to imagine her kissing me. The feeling is just too much. Her rosy lips will burn and burn me till it's only the soot of my red heart left on her pinky palms.

As I proceed to Morocca's house, I freeze. In the frontyard Serena is playing in the sand. With a blonde doll. Cradled in her arms. She unbuttons her shirt and smooths the tresses of the doll. Brings its mouth to her nipple. She smiles, the doll sucking from her. Suck. Suck. Suck.

I look away. Think about a theorem. Gödel. Cayley. Euler. Thoughts perform press-ups in my head, and I bottle them all – *Bottle. Bottle. Bottle.*

Haha, Andy.
Shut up, Ydna.
Hahaha.
Shut up.
How long d'you think you can do this for?
For as long as required, bro.

She sees me but doesn't run to me. She continues her game, picks a teaspoon from a cup, and feeds her baby water. Her hair is bunched in three pigtails. I go to her and squat. I place a hand on her front pigtail, bring my hand down to her silky fat cheek, rub it a little. I really love her. A couple times I've even wished she were mine.

She smiles. 'Andy.'

Voice like a cat's. Eyes like one too.

'How are you, baby?'

'Fine.'

I hear her parents arguing in the house, a door slamming. They're always arguing, Morocca and Patience, about an ant or Serena's lost earring or the boy Morocca caught her smiling at or the girl Morocca fucked in his last show. I'm such a psychotic fuckhead, I swear, because whenever I look at Serena I remember the night she was conceived. The memory is eternally there in her face, in the movement of her sweet choco lips, in the blinking of her cat eyes. I don't know why I'm like this, seriously, why I can't unsee the unutterable in people.

She was conceived three years ago during one of Morocca's shows in De Amsterdam Plaza on Barracks Road. The plaza is famous for selling the most expensive booze in town and for pimping the youngest chicks. Pot-bellied men from New Bussa and even Minna, the state capital, travel to the plaza to fuck thirteen- or fourteen-year-old girls. Our catechism teachers call it a Gomorrah. They warn us never to 'go near there' or fantasise about 'going near there', for that alone is a hellish mortal sin. The queens of the plaza are known for throwing away babies in the pit toilets or dumpsites of our town.

The King Kong of the plaza paid Morocca a couple thousand to bring his boys and throw a small show for some Big Oga in government who was spending the night in Kontagora. As a bonus he gave Morocca an hour with Aunty Christy, his cheapest ho, who was in her late thirties, old enough to be our mother. That night, as we arrived with other rappers, Morocca promised to give me fifteen minutes of his time with Aunty Christy so that I could lose that shit called virginity. 'It's for the birds,' he laughed. He'd lost his virginity to Aunty Christy, like many other boys in my class. He and Okey claim she's the woman they've had the best sex with, that she's a rider extraordinaire well versed in the subtle art of reawakening a limp dick. Part of his entourage was Patience, whom he'd recently signed as his backup singer.

Before Morocca and Patience began their performance, a waitress in a bikini handed them what she called 'sweet drink'. They gulped it and climbed onstage, and the DJ played the beat and Morocca spat his lines and Patience punctuated them with 'yeah' and 'oh yeah'. Between the stage and the audience was a swimming pool with disco lights that gave the place the feel of *Blade Runner*. As they performed, they gradually became wild: Morocca leaping to the sky with sci-fi energy as though his feet were nuclear reactors; Patience spinning acrobatics, twisting seductively as though she'd become a twenty-something video vixen, when she was only thirteen. Suddenly she yanked off her top and tossed it to the pool. The big men cheered. She sashayed to Morocca and grinded his front with her big back – the audience cheering – and used her free hand to unzip his jeans. Moments later she had his dick in her hands and was to-froing in her mouth. He was still rapping, she making slurping sounds in the mike. The men were on their feet now, neighing, braying, screaming like dinosaurs, horns appearing on their heads, splashing vodka at each other, tossing naira into the pool. He stopped his song mid-verse, tossed the mike, grabbed her, and doggy-styled her right there.

When they were done, they picked up their mikes and continued making music. My brow was itching, and when I rubbed away the sweat, I realised I'd been crying. My ears hurt, my throat burnt. I should've done something, bust the bellies of these men, dragged my droog home. Instead I sat like a sack and did nothing. As I considered leaving, a woman whispered in my ear. 'Hello, darling,' she said. 'Your turn don come.' It was Aunty Christy. She repeated herself. Smiling sheepishly. Shaking her fat tits. Taking my hand, placing it on her ice-cream ass. My jet-black snake flared, saying Go Andy, go Andy, go!

In her room she took off her bra and panties and fell onto the bed. She smiled. Motioned me with her big finger. 'Come. Come, my boy. Come make I teach you sometin.'

I stood by the door, still fully dressed. She was the first woman I'd ever seen naked. She was sweating around her neck, swaying softly on the bed.

Suddenly she began to look like a beast. Like a tar-skinned rhino. Like a black hole that could swallow even the fastest light.

'Come,' she said. 'Put your big prick inside my mouth. I go make am big big.' She giggled, pushed her tit and nipple into her mouth. Sucked.

Moments later she propped her head on her hand, began to frown. 'Wetin dey worry you sef? No be fuck you wan fuck?'

I turned the handle of the door and went out. Back to the music and cheering. In the spinning light I saw Morocca and Patience fucking amid some bushes. Onstage was another schoolmate rapping and a girl grinding him. I hurried to the gate of the plaza.

+

'Andy,' Serena says, scratching her eye. 'I'm hungry!'

'Okay,' I say. 'Let's go to the house and get you something.'

I hold out my hand. She doesn't take it. Maybe I should take her hand, carry her in my arms. Children don't like to be given options.

Patience comes out of the house in a short skirt and tank top. She sees me, waves feebly. 'How far, Andy?'

That's how she always greets me, and I'm always tempted to give her my estimated distance in four decimal places.

'I'm cool,' I say. 'How's it going?'

She doesn't respond, her attention fixed on her child. She's skinny, her hair braided with attachments. The cornrows fall to her back, nearly reaching her big butt.

'What're you doing, baby girl?' she says. 'Oya, come to the house now.'

'She says she's hungry.'

'Don't mind the silly girl. I've just given her a plate of Indomie and she didn't even touch it.'

'I want mango!' Serena says with conviction.

Patience chuckles. 'How will you eat a mango with those teeth, eh, Seree? And the moment you give her a mango she'll begin to ask for a watermelon.'

I smile at Serena, hold out my hand to her. She still doesn't take it. She's always rejecting me, this baby girl. Every time I hold her she begins to cry. As though I've got some disease under my skin which she senses with her microscope body. As though she's blaming me for her existence, for not having Morocca's back the moment it most mattered. Before she was born, Morocca kept denying he was the father. But the moment he first saw her, he called her his little lovely bird and fell so in love with her that he refused to let anybody touch her, including his mama, who cried, wanting to carry her first female grandchild. And because he refused to part with her, Patience gradually became an unofficial member of his family. He insisted that the baby be named Serena, after Serena Williams, so that when she grows up, she'll become a superstar who'll save his family from poverty. Not that his family is as poor as mine. For example, his poppa owns an old Benz that farts clouds and breaks down at least twice a week. His mama owns a Starlet which she struggles to climb into every morning because of her trunk-sized thighs and parachute-like behind. Men become drooling babies when she walks past. Her male students call her Aunty Big Nyash or Mrs Zygote, and she retaliates by scoring them $\frac{1/2}{70}$ in their biology exams.

For some reason I sometimes worry that Serena will become like her in a couple years despite how skinny Patience is.

'Oya, oya, come here,' Patience says, taking Serena's hand. I follow them to the house.

It's a large cream bungalow with a grey chimney on top that has never been used. The door opens into a wide living room with brown couches surrounding a plasma on the wall. Slim, in a *Jurassic Park* t-shirt, is lying on one of the couches, a hand placed over his face as though he's asleep, but he's clearly not. His big toe squeezes into the couch; his phone is playing Adele on his bag. Morocca's dog comes out of a room and begins to bark, its tail aloft, but Slim doesn't budge. Patience sits on the couch opposite him and places Serena on her lap, her free hand scrolling through her phone.

The dog is still barking. Morocca swaggers into the living room, freestyling, and it quietens, wags its furry tail.

'Wazzup, Werdna!' Morocca says. He's wearing a durag and a Lakers jersey.

We bump our fists and shake hands.

'Nice kit,' I say. 'When did you get it?'

'Oh. I've always had it. Bout a year now. Razorboy stole it for me.' He chuckles.

Razorboy is his immediate older bro who uses way too much touch-and-follow. He recently hacked an American redhead's emails and blackmailed her into paying him a couple thousand dollars. Word on the street is that he's begun a new venture, fucking teen girls in the neighbourhood and streaming it live for crisp dollars, performing on them the dictates of his white viewers. The girls agree to work with him because he promises not to show their faces, and because the ten or so dollars they receive go to buying new undies or foodstuffs for their families. He's applied five times for an American visa and been denied each time. He's constantly boasting about how he'll set the country ablaze if the embassy 'makes the mistake' of granting him a visa. I always hate seeing him. He moves about shirtless, showing his centenarian abs, his two phones in one hand and a joint in the other. He speaks in a low drawl, thinks he sounds like Lil Wayne, and tells me I'm wasting my time reading all those books and following Zahrah around like a fucking pussy.

Morocca leans forward and begins to whisper. 'Boy Slim ain't feeling grand today, man. Homeboy dumped his ass this morning. Says he's planning to join the seminary. Tread with care.'

I sigh. 'Sad.'

'Yeah.'

Slim's boyfriend is in SS 3, a year our senior in school. They've been dating *very secretly* for two years. In fact, Morocca and I didn't know jack till a few months ago when Bro Magnus – acting on what he called 'divine inspiration' – caught them kissing in the smelly toilet during break. He dragged them to the evening assembly where Sister Lakefield gave an everlasting homily full of Bible quotes about the 'iniquity of sodomy', told and retold the sad story of Sodom and Gomorrah, and described in acute detail in her British accent the dark crannies of hell, where seven suns cannot shine, where people like Thomas and Wisdom will be banished to. Some silly boys and girls began to weep because of her descriptions. She thanked and rethanked Bro Magnus, even gave him a British hug for unearthing this 'rot of sodomy' in her school. She ordered him to give each of the 'shameless' boys fifty strokes. Afterwards she handed them suspension letters with *three weeks* printed in bold font. It's the same Sister Lakefield who allowed Morocca to return to the classroom after she'd learnt about Patience's pregnancy, the same Sister Lakefield who allowed Patience to promote to the next class with us after she'd missed a year of school, because, in her words, 'Patience is a courageous young woman who carried her mistake with pride and didn't think of aborting it.'

But it was after Slim received the fifty strokes and the suspension letter that the Drama really began. First, his boy Wisdom distanced himself from him and started bouncing around with a Jerusalem Bible under his armpit and a fifteen-decade rosary hanging down his neck. Next, Slim's poppa dragged Slim to Queens Palace Guest Inn and locked him up with two hos for two whole days. When his poppa failed, his momma and her prayer-warrior gang and Evangelist Okonkwo took him to the mountain near Koko. They spent eight full days atop it, fasting till dusk and saying the Prayer of Manasseh like non-stop. And when they returned, looking like walking sticks, Slim turned to a pillar of salt each time we asked him about it. But Okey's mother, Mama Amebo as she's called, spilled the beans on my droog. She claimed that, on the first day, Slim fell on his knees and begged them to do whatever it took so that he could become like every other boy. They made him confess every stare he'd made at boys, his paintings of male buttocks, all the shirtless bodybuilders he'd looked at on his phone. But as they performed their novena/exorcism, bathing him with spittle and holy water and Goya olive oil, Slim became even more 'hardened', as if a 'worse spirit' was possessing him. He stopped saying amen to their prayers, kept trying to run away, poured out their jerrycan of holy water, even handed their food to monkeys in the bush. They had to cut short their novena because of starvation.

When they returned, Slim came straight to Morocca's and spent a week here. I wonder why he didn't come to my place. Was it because my house was small and Mama often cooked without meat to save money? Or did he – in the faintest way – fancy me? He does claim my brown eyes can get me any girl. Also, some of the bodybuilders I've caught him watching are white, some even blonde. I must have infected him.

'Mo-ro-cca,' Serena calls. 'Mo-ro-cca.' She's just so cute, this baby girl.

'Yes, love?' he says.

'I'm hungry.'

'Good gracious. What d'you wanna eat?'

'Watermelon. I want watermelon!'

'See what I said?' Patience says, laughing, eyes still buried in her phone.

'I'll get ya some on the way,' he says.

I wish he'd stop saying ya and wanna and gotta to Serena. She's just so cute, so saintly with her fat cheeks and big eyes. I don't want her to speak like us when she grows up. The idea makes me really sad.

'Where's the car?' I say to him. 'I didn't see it outside.'

'Oh. It's Razorboy. Took it to drop his new bird. Will return soon.'

'Oh, okay.'

'Why dontcha sit down, bro? I wanna put on some real threads. Patience, why dontcha get Werdna something to drink?'

She doesn't respond.

'I'm talking to you,' he says, his voice rising.

'K,' Patience says, eyes still on her phone.

Morocca shakes his head and bounces to his room.

I go to the free couch and sit. I want to reach out to Slim, but I stop myself. He must be feeling very shitty, worms crawling in his chest and all, his happy memories with Wisdom now agonies. It's insane how the plus of love can become a series subtracting to infinity.

Serena jumps down Patience's thigh and goes to Slim, staring at him as though she's checking to see whether he's still alive. She removes his hand from his eye but he places it back. Removes it, he places it back. Patience looks up from her phone, motions to her to return to her thigh. Such a brave girl, Serena, doing what I couldn't dare.

'Andy,' Patience says, leaning forward to me, handing me her phone. 'Do you know this girl?'

On her phone is an Instagram photo of my droogs and a plump girl. She's in a pink crop top and miniskirt, standing amidst my droogs, their hands round her hips. I recognise her instantly. But I tell Patience that no, I haven't seen her before.

'Are you sure?' she says, sitting back.

'Yeah, I'm sure,' I say.

'You haven't seen her with Morocca before?'

'No. Why?'

'Someone told me she saw them kissing.'

'Oh. Have you asked Morocca about it?'

'Not really. He's just a liar, like all men. But you're different, Andy. Sometimes I wish he were like you. You wouldn't do to Fatee what he does to me.'

'Oh.' And that's all I can say. Guilty thoughts flutter in my chest. I bottle them all.

The girl in the photo is Kosi. Last December, during a party in Safara Motel, Morocca boned her on a table in the conference room. Afterwards he laughed and claimed it was the sickest one-night stand he's ever had. Subsequently, Kosi and Slim became close, taking long walks, exchanging books, painting together. One evening I dropped by Slim's place and found her cowgirling him in his room, his hands clasping her ass. As I left the house, he ran and begged me never to tell anyone, kept stuttering as though he'd robbed a bank. He claimed that it was all Kosi's fault, that he didn't even enjoy it and was only 'experimenting'.

Every time I think about the James Bonding of my droogs, I feel ashamed of my virginity. Among the sixteen boys of my class, only Jonaldo and I haven't done it. In Jonaldo's case it's because he's this skyscrapingly obese kid who all the girls laugh at, including Funmi who's always reading a Bible and refusing to shake the hands of boys. My own virginity is more of a mystery. Often I have this fear that I'll cum the very second I come near a vagina, and the girl – a blonde? – will slap me with a pillow for being such a toddler. But today I feel lucky, even privileged, for not having done it. Why? I don't know, and don't want to think about it. Understanding why will sour the cool of being lucky, of being privileged.

10

We're on Lagos Road, heading to Fatima's place. She lives in GRA, the Government Reserved Area, where the babanrigas and agbadas and politicians of our town live. Behind the wheel is Morocca the Sand Lord, nodding to 2Pac. In the passenger seat is his faux-wife, Patience, and love-of-his-life Serena the Sand Lady. Patience is scrolling through her phone as usual, responding to chats, giggling now and then. On my left is Slim T, head on the headrest, eyes closed. I nod a bit with Morocca, gaze out the window. At the small shops on our left and right, their roofs brown from acid rain, selling generators and vehicle parts, cement and mattresses, shoes and shedas and onions and garri, fake movies, fake drugs. There are hundreds of people on the street, thousands even, in shirts and shorts and jellabiyas and chadors, trooping in or out of the market, pushing wheelbarrows, carrying toddlers strapped to their backs, laughing and patting each other, shrieking spitting punching praying squatting snoring. Despite all the pomp, all the blood and spittle and sweat, most will return home tonight with the equivalent of a dollar or two.

Horns blare. Grinding mills screech. Speakers scream Qur'anic recitations.

We approach the roundabout at Emir's Palace, circle left, and a minute later we're cruising in the silent boulevards of GRA. We all sigh, finally free from the Babel and the sun. The GRA is always a bomb to look at: Houses left and right, two storeys, three storeys. Painted white with blue or red aluminium roofing. Tall dogonyaro or gmelina trees shading them. Pavements in front, bins everywhere, and wherever you turn, no shitty plastic bags or bottles, just sweet fallen leaves and broomstick markings in the ground.

Fatima's crib is a two-storey house with large glass windows. An old gateman is sitting outside the blue gate amidst trim bushes, clutching a truncheon and a torchlight as though he's expecting an eclipse. She's standing beside the gateman with a backpack and purse, looking pretty in a white lacy hijab and cream dress, face powdered, lashes mascaraed, lips pencilled. Morocca goes out to help her put the backpack in the boot. The gateman tells him again and again to drive her safely, that Fatee is a First Lady, his First Lady, to make sure we all use a seatbelt. FYI, nobody in our town or the entire country uses a seatbelt. Only peeps like Father McMahon and Okorie do. Seatbelts are only enforced in Abuja because, hey, that's the backyard of our president and his ministers.

Fatee gets into the car from the right door. I move closer to Slim to give her room.

'Hi, guys,' she says, flashing a small smile.

'Hey, Fatee,' Patience says, looking up from her phone. Even Slim wakes up a sec and says hey to her. But I don't dare.

She reaches out to Serena, squeezes her hand, smooths her hair. 'Hi, Seree!'

'Aunty Fatee!' Serena giggles.

She likes Fatima a lot. Fatima is her supplier of chocolates and candies. The few times I've gotten her chocolate, she's refused to take it. Each time, her mama had to scold her and force her to say thank you. But when it's Fatima presenting her choco and candy, she'll hop around and hug Fatima's nice toned legs.

'How are you, baby girl?'

'Fine.'

Fatima settles back and we take off. She doesn't say anything to me. She doesn't even spare me a glance. She's wearing perfume (it smells very expensive!), and is weirdly chewing gum (my Fatee hates that stuff). Her hijab clings to her body and her bust pushes out, jolly and hemispherical and big. I can't remember when her boobs grew to this size. Have I simply stopped noticing her? Is she wearing a padded bra or something? Trying to get back at me? Like, Hey Andy, you're going after platinum, right? Guess what, look at me! I'm very hot, very smart. Proof: see my perfect body, remember my medals. Yeah, bite your finger, loser.

We're looking in the same direction, at the meters on the dashboard, but we're not seeing the same thing. She's so resolute, chewing her gum, daring me to talk to her, waiting for the opportunity and the delight of ignoring me. This morning as Mama, Aunty Lizzy, Elder Paschal, and I were about to leave for the hospital, I told her goodbye, see ya later, but she stared at me as though I were empty breeze, as though I had slugs peeping out of my ears.

+

Outside town Morocca picks up speed, zigzagging past potholes, some filled with clay. The road ahead is such a shitty patchwork of craters that often he has to steer into the clayey paths beside it. We pass our first village, Farin-Shinge. Pass boys and men in rags sitting on the ground under trees or outside their mud huts, having a late-morning chat. Women carrying calabashes on their heads, some in chadors, a few topless, their breasts like old socks. A shirtless boy pumping water from a grimy borehole installed by the World Bank. Shirtless kids in panties kicking a plastic container beside a stream, laughing and screaming. We pass Machanga, Beri, Mariga. The scenery the same: the corn and groundnut farms, the scanty trees, the lightbulbs hanging from the roofs of huts, shining yellow in the sun.

Since we left, no one has said a word.

We don't comment on the hatchbacks that speed past us, carrying five passengers in the rear, two in the passenger seat. A few have an eighth passenger sharing the driver's seat. The passengers are huddled like sardines, sweating on each other, heaving together when they hit a pothole. But this is how the driver will turn a good profit.

Patience looks up from her phone and turns to Fatima and me. 'Why are you guys so silent today?'

'You think everyone is like you?' Morocca says.

She hisses, yawns.

Silence. Noisy. Itchy. Amplifying the sound of breathing.

Patience yawns aloud again. 'This stupid sun.' She has this nagging tone when she speaks as though she's quarrelling with her listener. 'Stupid, stupid sun,' she hisses.

'Yeah,' Morocca says.

'Why doesn't this car have an AC?'

'Who told ya it doesn't?'

'Can't you see I'm sweating like a rat?'

'You're always complaining, Patience.'

'And so what?'

'Why don't you wind down the glass a lil bit?'

'The breeze is even worse. It's like a dragon is blowing it.'

Morocca laughs. Fatima chuckles. Slim stirs. We're fingering the sores in his chest. He looks so pitiful I want to cry.

'I wonder,' Patience says, looking out the window, 'why do these tiny villages always have electricity?'

'You don't want them to have?' Morocca says.

'They have too much of it. We've got none back at home.'

We begin to circle a hill. We emerge onto straight road, see two policemen standing ahead.

Morocca hisses. Patience too. 'I don't effing have any change,' he says, dipping his hand into his back pocket. 'Anyone have some change?'

The policemen are in black uniforms, sweating and grilling like pigs, each standing on a separate lane. They're clutching rusty tenth-century rifles with red cloths tied around the barrels. Morocca stops before the one in our lane.

'Officer!' Morocca greets him, brimming with smiles, adding more bass to his voice. 'My oga, my oga. I dey hail you o! How work?'

Trust Morocca. He knows when to stop mimicking Eminem.

Policemen love to be called officers, though most aren't and don't even know how to read. You could be delayed for hours if you try to speak English to them, what they call 'grammar'.

'How work, oga sah?' Morocca says, smiling like Eddie Murphy in *Dr. Dolittle*.

'Fine, fine,' the policeman says, poking his sweaty leathery skull into the car, scanning our faces.

'My oga, my oga.'

He asks Morocca for his licence, and Morocca hands him his fake licence with his fake age, and the policeman holds the card high in the air as though he needs glasses. I'm sure he can't read.

He tells us to come out of the car, that he needs to search it. That's his tactic for getting some cool cash.

'Oga, we dey hurry fa,' Morocca says. 'Ana jiran mu a kasuwa.'

I almost burst out laughing. Fatima is chuckling silently into my ear, indirectly mocking me, I'm sure.

Morocca digs a hand into his jeans and hands the policeman a hundred-naira note. The policeman squeezes the money into a ball. He laughs.

'You dis boy,' he says, his laughter making him sound like the pig he is. 'Oya dey go. Ku wuce. Allah ya kiyaye.'

'Ameen,' Morocca says and we zoom off. 'Thieving mother-fucker,' he hisses.

Moments later he becomes alarmed, slowing down the car. 'What the fuck . . . What the fuck . . .' he mutters.

'What's happening?' Patience shrieks, pointing.

There are girls our age and women sitting or lying on the road. They are topless, dresses and bras torn, weeping. A woman is wailing before three of the girls. A man lies unconscious in front of them, blood spurting from his arm. Cars are parked on both sides of the road, people standing outside them, the women weeping, the men with hands on their heads. A couple of them are dial-ling phones, making frantic calls, trying to reach the police. As we approach, we see a severed head lying in dry grass and a man's torso beside it. Patience covers Serena's eyes with her hand.

Morocca parks the car and goes out. He asks a man to tell him what really happened.

'Armed robbers,' he says, refusing to say any more.

+

An hour passes, and two rusty, grimy ambulances arrive. A dozen women, a few with blood coursing down their legs, get into the first. The second takes away the corpses of four men. People return to their vehicles.

Beside me in the car, Fatee is dabbing her eyes with a handkerchief. In the passenger seat Patience hugs Serena, smooths her hair, tells her to stop crying. Morocca gets into the car and we resume our journey. Patience tells Morocca that maybe we should turn back home, that the robbers might be up ahead. Morocca says that, since the ambulances came from Minna, he's sure the road is safe.

'What I can't understand,' he says, 'is that such a thing happened near a police checkpoint. Who can tell me that the police ain't working with these robbers? In fact, how did we have them robbers in the first place? This is such a shitty country. Very, very shitty. Don't know what I'm still doin' here. Don't want Serena to grow up in such a place.'

Silence.

I know that, just like me, my droogs are thinking about Okey, wishing they were in his place.

'Guys,' I say, 'the very first chance we get, we have to get out of here.'

Patience shakes her head, clucks.

'Okay, Morocca,' she says. 'If you don't want us to turn back, then we have to pray. We must. I don't want anything to happen to my baby girl.'

'Who's stopping ya from praying?'

She opens her purse, brings out a finger rosary. I didn't know she was this religious. Suddenly I'm feeling bad for having always thought her shallow.

'Let us pray. Hope you don't mind?' she says to Fatima, though she doesn't wait for a response. 'For a safe journey, let us pray the Five Sorrowful Mysteries. In the name of the Father, and of the Son, and of the . . .'

Andy?
Yes, bro.
Why don't you write a poem about me?

Wow, Ydna. I've written dozens about you.
No, I don't mean those kinds of poems.
So what d'you mean?
A poem about me fighting . . .
Fighting?
Yeah.
That's mad, Ydna. Dope.
Yeah. Won't you ask me who I'll be fighting?
Right, who will ya be fighting?
Your HXVX.
HXVX?!
HXVX.
But — but why d'you wanna fight HXVX?
You know why.
Why?
Use your head, Andy. You claim to be a genius, right?
Because of Mama?
Yes.
Because HXVX caused all that she's been through?
Yes.
Hmm.
And because of you too.
Hmm. D'you know what Slim did yesterday?
You're changing the topic, Andy.
I'm not.
You are.
I'm really not.
Why d'you like things as they are?
I don't.
You do.
*You know I don't. You know I really don't. That I'm always
thinking about spinning stuff. Changing stuff. Permutations and all.
That's why lately I've been reading lots about cloning, about flight,
about escape artists like Houdini. Escape is the only way HXVX
can be defeated, you know. Anything else is just deferral of the
inevitable.*
Hmm.

. . .
So will you write the poem or not?
How d'you think you can beat HXVX, Ydna? He's planetary,
man. So fucking huge. And you, you're just, you're . . .
I'm what?
Very . . .
Very what?
I can't say it.
I'm surprised, Andy.
About what?
. . .
Ydna?
. . .
Ydna!
. . .
. . .

+

Patience is still praying: 'The Third Sorrowful Mystery: The Crowning with Thorns. Our Father who art in heaven . . .'

I look at Slim, then out the window, at a gaunt old woman with wood piled on her back. Wish I could say the Sorrowful Mysteries for her, for myself, for everyone on this land. And just like that it becomes clear to me. The lives of everyone on this Cursed land mirror the prayer: from the agonies of our shitty births to our crowning with thorns and to our eventual shittier crucifixions and deaths.

Our father who art in heaven . . . Our father HXVX?

+.

I'm in a taxi heading to the Central Business District to meet Eileen. It's four, and she's asked me to meet her by five in the lobby of the Chelsea Hotel. Due to multiple delays (more bad roads, more police checkpoints, Serena suddenly feeling sick), we arrived at Zahrah and Okorie's house late in the evening, so I couldn't visit her yesterday. It's Tuesday today, and Eileen says she'll be leaving Nigeria in exactly one week, on the eve of Zahrah's wedding. Hopefully I'll get her to stay longer.

Abuja is the centre of dreams. The streets are multilane and tarred. So smooth you could play snooker on them. There are these sweet clean banging pavements and hedges and lawns everywhere, and lots of trees. On your left and right are these cool tall glass buildings as though you're cruising in NYC. Drivers wear seatbelts, obey traffic lights, and don't honk like psychos. No plastic bags or refuse dumps or hens in sight. It's as though you've left Nigeria and West Africa and Africa.

But it's all on the surface.

Because on the street are student protesters from universities all over the country. They've congregated here and painted themselves in chalk or charcoal or the green-white-green of the Nigerian flag, and they're hopping and dancing and singing with placards raised over their heads. They are everywhere. Blocking the traffic. Chanting 'A luta continua, vitória é certa.' Drivers are cheering or cursing them. We're tired of the strikes, the students say. Tired of the embezzlement and mismanagement and sectarianism and nepotism. We want change in this country. C-H-A-N-G-E. We want a revolution. R-E-V-O-L-U-T-I-O-N.

There've been stories of students assaulting senators outside the National Assembly. Throwing eggs and purewater at them. Screaming that they resign. Okorie is one of the lecturers advising the SUG on the protest. At dinner yesterday Zahrah repeatedly warned him to be careful, that he might run into trouble. 'You know this country is rife with extrajudicial killings, right?' she said, her forehead creased, afraid that his years studying in England have loosened his grip on reality.

The protesters have been in the news since we arrived. In fact, my driver and I are listening to the national president of the SUG being interviewed by Sowore, foremost activist and founder of saharareporters.com, the only newspaper that peeps trust. The president is speaking very animatedly, decrying how the government has been censoring the press. That three students were shot yesterday near the CBN when they were protesting. 'This is why

I say we need a revolution. A *peaceful* revolution. We the students and future of this country are saying enough is enough. We're tired of these old kleptocratic fools ruling us. We're tired of this democrazy.'

The driver sighs. I look at him, adjusting my seatbelt. He shakes his head and turns down the volume.

'What do you think?' I say.

'Hmm hmm,' he says, clucking. 'Hmm hmm. This boy should be very careful o. See how he's talking. Does he know what he's even saying?'

'What do you mean?'

He wipes the sweat off his brow, deftly overtakes a car.

'I don't think this boy is long for this world,' he says. 'I pity his parents. I pity them. Parents are not supposed to bury their children.'

For some reason I feel like slapping him, burning up his taxi, this sleek road, Everything.

I pick up *The Metamorphosis* from my lap. I took it from Zahrah and Okorie's shelf to keep me company in the lobby while I wait for Eileen. I also brought it because she and I had that cool chat about it at her party. I feel this book brought us together somehow, connects us, even explains us. Anyhoo, I won't lie, I also brought it because I'm sure we'll have silent moments, and it will def give us something to talk about, something with which I can impress her. I don't know why this Queen of Platinum makes me dishonest to my own self!

The Chelsea Hotel appears in the distance. The driver glances at me and says:

'So you don't agree with what I said?'

'What?'

'You think he did the right thing by going on the radio and saying all that?'

'I don't think—'

'I don't blame you,' he says, shaking his head in that pitiful way that gives me the creeps. 'You're still too young. You don't know that there are things that should be left unsaid.'

I shut the door of the taxi, and standing on the pavement of
the Chelsea, I check myself. My white YSL shirt tucked in blue
D&G jeans, black Nikes gleaming like hell. Before me and in
the distance, cars are zooming left and right on snooker road, on
flyovers. Sprinkled around are towers of hotels and government
buildings, painted white or cream, surrounded by trim hedges.
No girls in chadors hawking groundnuts on their heads. No
old women roasting corn or yams on charcoal fires. No hens or
goats or rams meandering like demons. Just men and women in
suits or expensive kaftans and ankara.

I message Eileen that I've arrived and set out for the entrance.
God, these hedges, flat like tennis tables. I want to lie on them, to
be one of the gambolling bees, to drink from the spinning sprinklers and never thirst again. As I approach the glass doors I'm
afraid someone will stop me and send me back to the shithole
where I belong.

'Welcome, sir,' the doorman says.

I'm shocked and undecided for a moment. This is the first
time I've been called sir in my entire Cursed life.

I decide to respond, inflecting my voice with my fake British
accent:

'Thank you.'

Inside, the temperature nosedives instantly as if this is Norway.
My feet are sleek on the glassy marble; the glint of silver and
polished wood and elevators and couches almost scares me
away. Too much light, that of chandeliers, of exit signs. I scan for
Eileen. She told me she's here but I can't spot her. I pull out my
phone and begin typing a message to her.

'Andy!' an updown British accent calls me from behind. 'So
great to see you again!'

For a moment I think I'm in the wrong place, that the voice
is a hallucination. But it's Eileen. Completely changed. Wearing
a dashiki dress. Hair bundled up and hidden in a flowery headtie
like a proper Nigerian lady. She's even wearing glasses. For a sec

I fear that something has happened to her platinum. Was she playing with fire or something?

'Eileen,' I say, my voice cracking, sounding somewhat disappointed. 'Eileen! Didn't recognise you at all.'

She laughs, gives me a tight hug, the kind I haven't had all my Pitiful Life.

Her nose ring is gone too. But now I'm sure her platinum is safe: a curl is peeking out of her headtie, saying hello.

'I wanted to surprise you,' she says. Her sparkle is also intact. Her smell like almonds, like dates, still intact. The black dot in my chest begins to stir, beats its wings.

She takes off her glasses. 'Oh,' she says, looking at them strangely, as though she hasn't just been wearing them. 'Oh. These would have confused you. Even Aunt Joan couldn't recognise me in them.' She looks at me, smiles. Thankfully her meadow eyes are still intact. 'They're more like my visors or something. I wear them when I go walking because of dust and flying stuff.'

I smile as broadly as I can. 'Great.'

'Come on, mate,' she says, taking my hand:

pink white
    on
black black

I die.

Although she's holding a small part of me, I feel her all around me, her fingers creeping into my chest, rubbing my soul.

'Let's get something to eat. I'm starving here.'

She laughs. She's always laughing, this soft, feathery Meadow-Eyed Queen.

I mentally count the dead presidents in my shitty wallet, wondering if I have enough cheddar to buy a Coke here. And because we're meant for each other, because she can read my mind, she says:

'Don't worry, Andy. It's my treat.'

She gives me an embarrassed smile. I smile back, embarrassed too.

We walk past couches and flowerpots, through the glass doors of the restaurant. She: leading me. Carpet: soft as my bed at

Zahrah's. People: turning to look at us, wondering who this little nigga thinks he is, moving around with this superhot Africanised white chick.

'Nice, nice,' she says. 'Let's . . . sit . . . over . . . there.' Stone pendant still intact, rosy lips . . . partly intact.

We sit and I glance at her headtie, wondering what has come over her. Just seven weeks. 1,176 hours.

'We've got so, so much to talk about,' she says, placing her phone in her purse, putting it on one side. 'Where should we start?'

The waiter hurries to us in a black waistcoat and bow tie. 'Hello, madam,' he says to her with a broad fake smile. He turns to me, almost scowling. 'Hello, sir.' He hands each of us a black-bound volume. I open it, wondering what the hell it is. It's a menu! He asks us – Eileen, that is – what we'll drink, tells her that we should take our time.

Eileen beams at him. 'Thank you!'

I flip through the menu, ask for a lemonade. Eileen orders an apple juice, punctuating her statement with please, please, as though she isn't going to pay in the end. He gives her a small bow and sets off.

'Isn't he lovely,' she says.

'Yeah. I guess.'

She scans through the pages, the colour of her hands. Meadow eyes roving, blinking, coming out fresher. I look at her headtie again.

'Wow, Eileen.'

'What, Andy?'

'Your dress, your headgear.'

'Yeah?' She looks concerned, as though she's done something wrong. 'D'you like them?'

'Oh yes, yes. I love them. Really do. What a cool surprise!'

She beams again, like a little girl. 'Oh, thank you, Andy. Thanks. I made Aunt Joan get them for me. I've got a wardrobe full of them. Mum will hang herself!' She laughs.

This is the first thing she's said about her mother.

'You look good too,' she says.

'Oh, thank you,' I say.

Eileen thinks I look good! Gloria! Gloria in excelsis!

But I still can't understand what got into her that made her hide those fantasy tresses, her platinum Strands of Power, so that she's slightly less powerful now. What does she know about this dashiki in which she's hidden her trim figure? She thinks she's experimenting, making a statement, becoming 'better', not knowing it's just pointless. It's like a queen deciding to wear rags but clinging to her throne. Maybe she's suffering from the same stuff that sent her uncle to Africa to become a red golem. Maybe it flows in the family or something. But whatever she does, my Eileen will remain my Eileen, my Eiqueen, my Eimpress of radioEitive Eicstasy. She could wear rags like St Assisi and I'd still kiss those mesmerising Eitoes.

'Why are people looking at us?' she says.

'Oh. Are they?' I say.

'Yeah.'

I look at the tables around us. There are two ladies in geles flashing us weird glances.

I smile very broadly to reassure her.

'Oh,' I say, 'they aren't trying to be rude or anything. They admire you. They find us interesting, that's all. They wish they could see more of this.'

'Oh. More of this? Hmm. Cool.'

I want to think of something, but my head is blank.

'They'll stop looking in a moment.'

'Alright.'

The waiter brings our drinks on a tray, places them before us. There's a lemon (or is it an orange?) floating on mine. Wow.

'Thanks,' she says to him.

'Thanks,' I say.

'You're welcome, madam,' he says. 'Please take your time with the menu.' He bows to her and walks away. If I'd come with Fatima, I'm sure he wouldn't grant us even a nod.

I wait for Eileen to take a sip. She does. I sip.

'Mmmm,' she says.

'Mmmm,' I say.

11

We're halfway into the dessert. I scoop some salted caramel ice cream into my mouth. I wish I could feed Eileen some; I wish she could feed me some of her pineapple tarte Tatin. I push my hands into my pockets before they rebel, force myself to sit back in my chair.

The jerk chicken I had is still playing karate in my head. It was just so soft, so juicy, flavours that made me see bands of colours, hear guitar chords. The damn fork and knife almost ruined my shit, though. Apart from Father McMahon and Okorie, everyone I know eats with a spoon or their bare hands and never with a fork and knife. In fact, until today, I've never tried this combo before. But because I didn't want to look like a Homo erectus before her, I kept fooling around with the meat like a toddler. She feigned ignorance, pretending not to see my cat-and-mouse chases around the plate. She kept asking me, 'D'you like the food, are you sure?' Now I only have to use this teaspoon in my right hand to eat my ice cream. Thank Jah.

But as for her, she eats slowly, softly, her back mostly straight like the queen she is. She's just so cool, my Eileen, so special, exactly what my Dead Life needs. Perhaps this is the first of many dinners, and with time I'll eat as elegantly as her. With time I'll become a better person, a real man.

She had vegetarian stuff, falafels and a bowl of peas and other things I don't know or want to taste. She kept blinking and nodding and gushing about the falafels, that they're some of the best she's ever had, and that's why she always comes here to have dinner. I wish she hadn't said that because her meal costs about twenty grand, twice the cost of mine. Her meal could feed Mama and Aunty Lizzy and me for two whole months.

She finishes her plate, places her fork and knife together, and the waiter suddenly appears and clears the table. He doesn't ask me if I'm done. He places my bowl on his tray even though it still has a quarter ice cream in it. Eileen doesn't seem to notice.

'Thanks very much,' she says to him. 'It was delicious.'

He smiles and thanks her. Disappears again.

'Thanks, Eileen,' I say. 'For the meal.'

She nods, flushes, sips her water.

'So, Andy,' she says, meadows on me, greener because of the falafels. 'Tell me everything. Everything. Your mum. Kontagora. It still pains me that I couldn't stay.'

I tell her that Mama is fine, or mostly fine, at least when I called her this morning. That Kontagora is somewhat changed. Christians no longer trust Muslims and vice versa, fearing another attack or a reprisal, so they've mostly boycotted each other's businesses. Plus, a funny thing: there's been a drought since the riot, and many townsfolk believe it's the blood of the massacred stopping the rains, crying to the heavens for justice.

'Oh,' she says, chuckling. She quickly stops after realising she isn't supposed to laugh. Although it's funny, it ain't funny-funny.

'Do you think they might be right?' she says.

'No, I don't,' I say. 'I don't see how the dead can exert agency.'

'True, true. But you should still give their theory a second thought, I think.'

'Alright, I guess.'

I'm kinda surprised I'm the one who's being scientific here. Has she stopped being an atheist or something? Is she just compensating for her chuckle?

She crosses her legs. A button of her dashiki comes undone, and I catch a glimpse of her cleavage. The bro between my thighs springs alive. My pulse begins to boom and bam.

I hiss at myself. Look at her face, you sinful altar boy. Look look look. Bottle. Bottle. Bottle. You don't want her walking away from you again, do you? And as though her dashiki can hear me, it opens up even more. Cleavage like quarter-oranges.

I look away, out the glass doors of the restaurant at an old man fiddling with a gurmi in the distance. When I return my gaze to her, cleavage is no more. The bro between my thighs sadly deflates.

'It must have been difficult,' she says. 'It must have been very difficult for you.'

'Yeah,' I say. 'And I haven't told you the worst part yet.'

'What's that?'

'My mother. She's . . . she's now in a wheelchair.'

She covers her mouth in shock. Says sorry and sorry and sorry. For some reason I never told her about Mama in our chats. All those times she asked, I kept telling her that Mama was recovering fine.

'Thank you, Eileen,' I say.

She reaches for my hand. Squeezes. Her hand is silky, like warm water. This gesture – or something else – makes my eyes begin to go wet.

I wipe my eyes quickly, but they come faster, even hotter. Am I crying? Am I really crying? Can I please stop? Please stop, Andy. Please.

Yes, Andy. Please stop.
I can't.
You can.
I just can't.
. . .
Help me, Ydna.

wheelchair
spokes glinting

mama in it
staring at me
saying nothing

dimples dead
breasts deformed

Eileen gets up. Pushes her chair to me. Sits down. Wraps her
arm around me.
  'Oh, Andy. Oh, Andy.'

+

We're still sitting side by side. We've never been this close before.
Her arms are on the table, each a long, toned nirvana. I wish I
could take that pinkish hand, trace every blue vein on it, kiss it.
But I'll never dare. She'll banish me before I blink. Send me to
the dungeons of hell. I'm sure her aunt knows people in government, knows the Inspector General.
  I'm still surprised by how she squeezed my hand and put her
arm around me. Was she not in a hurry to break free from me
asap? Is she not afraid I might stain her, my colour jump onto
her like in those monster horror films?
  She tells me that she invited me here because she has two
things to show me. 'First,' she says, bringing out her phone from
her purse and scrolling to a photo. It's a poem in a picture frame,
flowers and hills sketched around the lines. The poem is very
familiar.
  'It's my poem!' I say.
  She laughs, glad she's finally cheering me up. 'Yes!'
  She begins to read it to me. It sounds much better, takes new
meaning, her accent and cadence giving it a life it never had.
It sounds as though it's her own words, her own experiences.
Amazing how a work of art can live beyond its creator.

because of me
you are gone
and lost and
have become sand
like me, me sandman
broad, empty, of the wind

She swipes to the next photo. Another picture frame of my poem. She reads it:

yes, i did, i did, i did it
but you'll free me
if you're who you are
which you are, which
      i'll be

They're old poems I wrote on my blog for Ydna. I'd almost forgotten about them, and I cringe a little at their amateurish phrasings. Now I'd almost not call them poems.

But her eyes are moist. She quickly wipes them. A tear or two cling to her hand.

'The first is a wall,' she says, swiping to it, 'pouring sand. The second a signboard. They're brilliant!'

A few more tears drop down her eyes. Do I wipe them for her? Isn't that too much?

'Andy,' she says, meadows soft, sad. 'Andy, these poems really affected me. I read them when I needed a little help, a little push. Thank you for them. I didn't expect to find poetry like this here. It's so amazing, given how hard you've had it.'

'I don't know what to say, Eileen. Thank you.'

Wish she'd left out the bit about hardship, though. And why's she so surprised to find such poetry here – does she think we ain't that good?

Still, I've never met anyone who's reacted this personally to my work. Zahrah, perhaps my biggest fan (and plagiarist?), only gives me thoughtful nods and pats on the back. I wonder what Eileen has been through, what help she means.

'Eileen, please feel free to tell me anything. I've also been through shitty times myself, as you know. Talking always helps.'

She smiles weakly. 'Thank you, Andy.'

She stares at me a moment. 'There's something on your hair, I think. Looks like a speck of something. Should I take it out?'

Shocking. Has it been there all along?

'Oh. That's kind of you. Thanks.'

She moves closer to me, reaches for the centre of my head. Her fingers scrape through the hair, pick out something, flick it away. But she doesn't stop. She keeps touching my hair, her hand gliding across, her fingers sticking deeper, gripping strands. She keeps touching, on and on and on. Wish she would stop. What is she looking for in there?

'What happens when water touches your hair,' she says.

'Oh, nothing. Nothing, I guess.'

'Nothing?'

Now she's touching the back of my hair.

I lose track of time. Has a year passed?

'Wow,' she says and sits back.

Wow what?

I wish she would say more but she doesn't. Say you like my hair, Eileen. Say the haircut is cool. Say it reminds you of something. She's still silent. I look at the floor, a strange shame creeping into my chest. She's staring at me; I just know it. My pulse begins to race. She thinks my hair is rough, dirty, strange. She thinks it's like fur, like that of the furry sheep they breed in her country. So I must be some kind of cat or dog or sheep, lovely, but weird. Although I wash the hair daily, I don't like looking at it much myself.

She smiles.

Maybe her removing the speck is supposed to mean something, that she digs me, that she wants me to look perfect. Can't remember seeing that in a Hollywood film, though. Maybe it's a British thing.

'Andy, would you like to see a couple of photos? I've been quite busy.'

She picks up her phone, swipes to a folder, hands it to me.

She's indeed been busy. I swipe across photos of Abuja: The Welcome to Abuja gate and the Nigerian flag atop. Aerial views of the city. Shirtless muscular men playing the Hausa wrestling called kokuwa. Turbaned men on horses. An emir. Naked boys diving into an amber pool. Topless teenage girls wearing beads and dancing. A pineapple farm. I punctuate each photo – except those of the naked boys and topless girls – with 'nice', 'very nice', 'cool', even though they're mundane to me.

It's surprising how she's only interested in the mundanities. She's clearly ignored all the grand government and hotel towers around the city. She didn't even photograph the Millennium Tower, the tallest structure in Abuja, one of the tallest structures in the country.

I continue swiping till I stop at a photo of her. She's sitting on a lawn in a red dress, posing like a supermodel. Skin like marble, legs long and crossed and bare, arms so smooth, platinum long and angled like a waterfall. She's meditative, staring at something distant.

'Wow,' I say.

She looks at the photo. 'Oh. That's in a park behind my house in London. You like it?'

'Very much.'

I try not to, but I just can't stop looking.

'Thanks,' she says.

'Wow. Great dress.'

'Really?'

'Yeah.'

'Oh. I almost wore it today. Would you like to see me in it?'

'Yes. Yes. I would really love to see you in it.'

'Okay, then.'

She says she has some presents for Mama and me. That in her hurry she forgot them at home. Her place is five minutes' walk away, if I don't mind coming to pick up the items. And if I do, she'll put on the dress for me to see.

'I don't mind, Eileen. Thank you!'

I wonder what she has for Mama, for Mama mè. What is Mama up to now? Anyway, it will be so LSD to go to Eileen's place, to spend some personal time with her. Juicy thoughts flash through my head – I bottle them all. I remind myself that Aunt Joan will be there, chaperoning us like aunts of old.

+

We get up to go see Eileen's second surprise. I pick up *The Metamorphosis* from my side on the chair. She's not seen it since we met. She still doesn't notice it now.

We go out of the restaurant and walk past peeps sitting in the plush couches of the lobby, their gazes trailing us, the men wishing they were me, the women shaking their heads. We stop before the gurmi player. He's middle-aged, sitting on a low stool, dressed in a clean white kaftan and hula. He runs his hands across his instrument, playing a complicated tune.

'Gosh,' Eileen says.

Another white woman joins us. Unlike Eileen, she's plump and wearing a cream knee-length dress and ballerinas. She also says gosh (in an American accent), brings out her phone and begins to video the man. Eileen also takes out her phone and videos him. I don't know why they're doing this. We have scores of these men in our towns, sitting along alleys and wasting their lives on their gurmis. Everyone thinks they're losers and only spares them five or ten naira so that they don't starve to death.

He finishes playing, and Eileen and the American woman applaud him. I reluctantly join in at the end. He gives a small bow. They each drop shiny thousand-naira notes into his box. I almost bite my tongue.

'Na gode, na gode,' he says, his eyeballs popping at their generosity. He places his palms together. 'Na gode sosai.'

This evening I'm sure his children will have a good dinner, and his wife will allow him to touch her.

'Ba komai,' Eileen says in flawless Hausa. 'Sai anjima.'

We all freeze: the American, the man, me.

'Wow, really impressive,' the woman says in her R-ry accent. 'You gotta teach me!'

'And me too,' I say.

Eileen giggles. 'Thanks very much.'

We continue walking.

'Wow, Eileen,' I say. 'When did you learn Hausa so well?'

'Hang on a moment.'

She leads me to the library of the hotel. There's no one around, as expected. The fluorescent lights overhead are insanely bright, beaming on the rows and rows of shelves stacked with books.

'Ta-da!' she says.

Is this her surprise? The room is full of Hausa literature and has a couple Nok figurines in glass cases. The terracotta statuettes have huge heads and fancy hairdos, their chins resting on their knees as though they're counting the stars or developing Anifuturist ideas. I won't lie, they look really cool. It's amazing how, thousands of years ago, the Nok sculptors used ancient methods to craft clay so exquisitely and depict these sad, meditative faces. Still, I'm kinda disappointed that this is the surprise she's been hyping about.

She tells me she's been intensively studying Hausa these past weeks, that it's such a unique and precise language, one that you write the way you speak it, very historical and more Arabian than she'd thought. She shows me around the library, gushes about this book and that, names authors I've never heard of, says Western literature is missing huge chunks disguised in local African languages. She brings out two books, reading their titles effortlessly like a bona fide Malu babe. One is *Ruwan Bagaja* by Abubakar Imam, the other is a book of Hausa folk tales by Ismail Ahmed.

'You've got to read these, Andy. Brilliant, subterranean storytelling. In fact, I'm going to translate them into English. Dad knows a couple of editors in London.'

God. I'm speechless. I'm so in awe of this lady.

'That's really great, innit?' I say.

'Did you just say "innit"?'

'Yeah.'

She laughs for a long minute.

I don't know what to do. I force a short chuckle.

'Don't say that,' she says.

'Why?'

'Don't know,' she says with a shrug. She laughs again. I'm completely lost.

I pick another Abubakar Imam: *Magana Jari Ce*. Stare at the weird parrot on the cover. Flip to the title page.

'You're different, you know,' she says.

'What d'you mean?'

'Oh. Since I came here I've met lots of people. But there's so much that's different about you.'

'Really? Like what?'

'Don't know where to begin. Thought you already knew.'

'So – so am I different in a good way?'

'Yeah. Everyone here is very . . . is more . . . but you're not. You're quite cool, reserved.'

Am I to feel grand about this? What does she mean everybody here is something, as if she's met all of us? Does she mean that everybody here is . . . – *Bottle, bottle, bottle.*

'Thanks, Eileen,' I say.

And the moment I say it, a hook tears deep into my chest.

A woman in a waistcoat walks into the library, carrying a stack of new books. She smiles brightly at Eileen, a well-wrought fake smile, but doesn't spare me a glance. She proceeds further into the room, shelves the books.

Eileen's phone beeps twice. She takes it out, scans it.

'It's Aunt Joan. Looks like the FCT minister is imposing a curfew because of the protests. It begins in three hours. Seems the SUG president has been arrested by the army.'

Five minutes later, after looking at a few more books, we leave the library. As we set out for the exit of the hotel, Eileen asks what I think about the protests.

Instantly I've got a million things to say, but I just can't find the right words or images to convey them. I google and google my feelings, and then I realise – wait for it – that I'm holding Kafka! Kafka! I almost cry eureka.

'You won't believe what I'm about to say,' I say to Eileen. 'But it's true.'

'Try me,' she says.

'Kafka must have been an African.'

She looks at me as though smoke is pouring out of my nose and ears.

'Are you serious, Andy?'

'Yeah.'

'But that's not true.'

'Everything Kafka wrote is about here, about us.'

'Hang on. Are you saying that the African experience is Kafkaesque?'

'Exactly,' I say. 'The protest. The riot. The heat. Everything. Like something Kafka would've dreamt up. The metamorphosis of this land into the dirt it has become. Our own metamorphosis, what Zahrah calls our permutations. Kafka saw it all coming over a century ago. Kafka is an African.'

She's silent. She still doesn't believe me.

Even though Fatima and I have our disagreements, she'd believe me, I'm sure.

+

As Eileen shows me around the paintings at Aunt Joan's, she tells me that her aunt is actually not in Abuja. That she travelled this morning to Lagos for an FCO meeting.

'She works at the British High Commission,' she says. 'She's always working. Always saying she dislikes the job.'

This news changes my breathing, my heartbeat. I take deep breaths to slow down the bangs in my chest, the haze spreading across my face, around my head. Suddenly I feel intensely sad. Why, I don't know. I feel her so near me – too near, as though she's right inside my lungs. Her smell is strong. My fingers begin to tremble. Now that her aunt is not around, I could lose myself, I could do something really bad, like at her party.

God, I don't want to do anything I'll regret. God, I don't want to do anything . . .

I step away from her, move to the étagère. She's supposed to move further away from me. But she follows me. Draws closer.

God, I don't want to do anything . . .

I force myself to stare at the figurines, at the miniature masks. I begin to count numbers, to restate Cayley's theorem. She steps even closer. So close. I could take her hand. I could kiss her. Maybe she'll kiss me back. Maybe this is how we'll fall in love, like in the movies. Is she not feeling the electricity sparking under my skin?

Such perfect skin. Such red lips. Such eyes.

God.

I'm about to touch her.

She's staring hard at the masks. She thinks I'm looking at them.

'Isn't it just amazing,' she says, 'how the artisans managed to craft these tiny pieces?'

I make a horrible sound. My throat is a vice.

'Sorry?'

'Yes, yes,' I croak.

She moves away. Sighs.

'Wish you could stay a little longer. You'd like some tea, right?'

I nod.

'Right. First I should get you your presents! And yes, try that dress! Right. Right. Give me a few minutes.'

She heads to the serpentine stairs. Midway she pauses, turns back to me.

'Hope you're alright,' she says.

I nod. Nod again. Nod so that she can see me clearly. Like the lizard I am. The creature she's turned me into.

'Right.' She continues climbing, disappears.

I stand, completely lost, as if I'm in a dream. I regain my senses and walk to the black couch facing the plasma. I sink into it. Glance at the warm chandelier above. Drop *The Metamorphosis* on the table.

And right there is another Eileen. A picture frame of her. She's in a swimsuit. Shades hiked on her head. She's running, her platinum fluttering behind her. In the background, waves of water frothing.

My fingers are really shaking now. A sob is hovering in my throat, waiting for the slightest nudge. I fight it. Fight it.

I made a mistake. I should not have come to this city. I should have stayed at home with Mama. Now I'm trapped. What can I do to convince this girl to like me? She'll just ban me. Call the police. Her aunt has the connections.

I hear her on the stairs. I should leave now.

But my chest is banging, clunking. I am breathless. Insensate.

I can see her now. It's too late. I can't look away.

She's in the red dress.

She's so otherworldly.

I die.

She's climbing down. Long legs, bare perfect arms. Lush platinum. Winking cleavage.

She's holding a small bag. She's coming closer, closer. She drops the bag on the table. Stops in front of me. Spins. Round round round. Laughs.

Now I can't see her again. Something is wrong with me.

My chest is bursting.

My eyes are bursting.

My head is bursting.

Am I having a panic attack?

She stops laughing. Looks at me. Very scared.

'Andy. Are you alright?'

'Eileen,' I gasp. Is this my voice? 'Eileen.'

My fingers are shaking like mad. I try to stop them. I try and try.

'What's wrong, Andy? Are you alright? Why are you crying?'

Look at me. I am pitiful. I should get up and leave.

But my hands and feet are unsteady. I fall on my knees, a dog before his mistress.

I try to get up, but can't. I turn to the couch. Push my face into it.

'Andy, please. Please talk to me. Should I call an ambulance?'

I weep.

She is right behind me now. Is her hand on my back? Why is she so tentative with it? Doesn't she know she's got all the power? That she can summon even lightning?

'Andrew. Please. Did I do something wrong?'

I don't answer.

'Please, Andrew. Please talk to me. Please stop crying.'

'I'm sorry, Andrew. I'm so sorry. Forgive me for whatever I've done.'

I shake my head.

'What? Did you get some bad news, then?'

I shake my head.

'Please, Andrew. Please, I'm scared. Talk to me.'

I speak. She does not hear. I repeat. She says she can't hear me.

'It's me,' I say. 'It's my fault. I am to blame.'

'To blame? For what? Look at me.'

'It's my fault.'

'What is your fault? You haven't done anything wrong.'

I hear myself blurt: 'I am in love with you. It's my fault.'

I feel her stiffen, even though she's no longer touching me. She takes a couple steps away from me.

I begin to regain some control. My arms and hands become steadier. I can feel the floor under my knees. I wiggle my toes.

I wipe my eyes. She's turned her back to me. She's staring at the blank wall.

I know what she wants. She wants me out of her house. This is the end. When I walk out the door she'll delete my number, block me on Facebook and WhatsApp. I've betrayed what we had by loving her.

She's completely motionless, a statue of herself.

I wipe my eyes. Pick up my book. Walk to the door.

This is the end.

I shut the door. Walk into the front garden.

There's a little blue in the sky. The moon is almost full, fluffs of cloud creeping away from it.

I walk through the low gate, out to the pavement. The road is deserted. I walk a little more. Stop when I see a car approaching. I wave at it. It does not stop.

I'm tempted to throw rocks at the car, but I feel very calm. If we're in a simulation, we have to play by its rules. Else we'll worsen our condition fast since there's no coming out of it.

Minutes pass.

The sky is almost dark now. The few cars passing refuse to stop. But I'm not in a hurry.

A figure emerges from the shadows. Stops under the beam of a streetlight.

It's her.

We stare at each other.

+

I enter the living room. She shuts the door, locks it.

I return to the couch opposite the screen. Sit down. Place my book on the table.

She comes, sits down on the couch, a cushion between us.

Silence.

We stare at the screen. Our reflections – our freer digital selves – stare back. Someday, when everything becomes ones and zeros, the things of the heart will be easier.

She crosses her legs, folds her arms.

'Eileen,' I say.

She doesn't respond.

'Eileen. I really like you.'

No response.

I move closer to her. Closer. A strange confidence in my bones. If she called me back, it means she feels something, a seed in the bud of a rose. But what if it's just pity? The pity for a cute furry crying dog?

She does not move away. She does not slap me.

I take her hand. She does not resist. Instantly, we become: blackwhite, whiteblack.

'Eileen, you don't know what you mean to me.'

I want to kiss her hand, but I fear that might be too much.

'Andy,' she says, 'you didn't even ask if I have a boyfriend.'

I stiffen. 'I'm so sorry. Please tell me, do you have a boyfriend?'

She doesn't answer.

'Why do you like me?' she says.

Strange question. Why do I like her? Because she's beautiful? Because she has meadow eyes and platinum hair? Because I dream of her every night?

'I don't know.'

She shakes her head.

'I like you more than anything, Eileen. Since I first saw you, I've not been the same.'

'Andy, you don't even know me. You don't know a thing about me.'

I freeze.

'Yes, Eileen. I don't. But there's something I do know. You are everything. Everything. All that matters to me. My life was nothing until I met you.'

Again she shakes her head. 'Andy, you don't know anything about me. You don't know the real me. To be honest, I'm not who you think I am.'

'No, Eileen.'

'That is the truth. You had better stay away from me.'

'No, no, Eileen. I disagree. I disagree because evil cannot hide. For example, you came to visit my mother in the hospital. You paid for my dinner today. You even invited me here to give me and my mother presents. This is because you're a good person.

'Eileen, I used to hate myself before I met you. I was a shadow. I was nothing. But now I can dream. Now I can look at myself in the mirror. Now I feel like somebody.'

I move closer to her. Her halo covers me. Her smell too.

'You don't know what I've done, Andy.'

'I don't, yes. But I know you're a good person.'

'You don't. You don't want to hear. Let's just end this now.'

'I really like you.'

'No, you can't.'

'Please.'

'I'm an evil person. I'm vile.'

'No, you're not.'

'Yes, I am. It's my fault, my fault.'

'What's your fault?'

'It's my fault that my friend Sophie died! I'd wanted to tell you in the restaurant. It's my fault. You don't want to hear.'

I hold her in my arms.

'Her parents say it isn't my fault. But I know the truth. I caused everything. I was never truly there for her. I'm not a good person.'

She wipes her eyes with the back of her hand. For a moment we listen to the faint hum of the air conditioning, to the chirping of insects coming from outside.

'For weeks I couldn't sleep,' she says. 'It was horrible. When I managed to sleep I had sweaty nightmares and panic attacks. I'm so glad I came here. Uncle Pete says the sun here has healing properties. I think it's true. I haven't felt this good in ages.

'Andy, I find and delight in the worst in people. I really do. And that's why Mum hates me, always blames me for everything. Calls me ugly, lazy, incompetent. Every time, I'm thinking about travelling to the past, about changing things. Every time, I'm thinking about the other version of me, the one that didn't do all these things, the one that is beautiful, that Mum loves.'

I don't know what to think.

She rests her head on my chest, like a little girl.

'It's going to be alright, Eileen,' I say. 'It's going to be alright.'

+

Eileen and I are kissing.
I'm clutching her in my arms. Like she's mine.
She's holding the back of my neck.
My hands tremble. Tremble.

I kiss her cheek.
Kiss her lips.

She kisses me back.

We roll on the couch. We are gasping for air.

I kiss her again, my hand in her hair, on her back.
I kiss her neck. Her chest. Her boob.

She moans. Runs her hand round my chest.

We kiss. Kiss.

My fingers are in her bra. On her nipple.
My mouth is on her other nipple.

She moans. Moans.
Places her hand on my dick.
Moans.

We kiss and kiss.

I move my hand down her navel. Down to her pubic hair.
Down, down.
She stiffens. Holds my hand.
'Not today,' she whispers in my ear. 'Not today. I'm not
ready. I'm sorry.'
My voice comes cracking. 'That's fine. That's fine. Let's just
lie down here.'
She kisses me again. Places my hands on her boobs. Her
hands return to my dick. She takes it out.
'Wow,' she giggles. 'This is really something.' She strokes it.
Laughs. 'It's like a truncheon!'
I don't know whether to be happy or not.
But her body is red in my arms. It's amazing.

We keep playing, keep playing, until I shoot into her hand.
She laughs. Brings it to her nose. Says it smells very strongly.
Like sextuplets.
We laugh.

12

I pay the driver. Come out of the taxi.

'Thank you,' he says. 'Have a great day, my friend.'

I wait for the road to clear a bit, then cross to the other side. Five protesters walk past me, placards held low, sweating in the sun. Their feet are dusty, clothes muddy, faces downcast. I wish I could tell them to cheer up, to not give up now.

The hedges and bushes on this street are cute and trim. Everywhere you turn are white mansions, giant metal gates shielding them. This street is famous for being the residence of Nollywood stars, and I can't believe Mama's twin lives here. Aunty Lizzy gave me the wrong address or something.

I pause to double-check the address on my phone. From the mansion on my left a black SUV emerges. I step back to give way. I stare and stare at its sexy curves, its bling-bling wheels. And then I realise – wait for it – that it's a Porsche! A fucking Porsche! Seriously! I almost scream off my brains. Even God shouldn't afford such a ride. This is the first supercar I've ever seen. Suddenly I'm afraid a policeman might appear from nowhere and arrest me.

If indeed Uncle William lives here, then he must be the worst uncle on the planet, a miser extraordinaire. He probably wouldn't want to see me. Maybe that's why Mama kept me away from him. Still, it's really cool that my uncle is a priest – a monsignor, in fact.

The gate is green, huge, engraved with sphinxes. I knock on it, waiting for the gateman to shoo my ass.

The gateman peers through a hole, opens a door by the side of the gate, asks me what he can do for me. He's middle-aged, wearing a blue uniform, fanning himself with a newspaper.

I tell him that I'm here to see Monsignor William Aziza. 'He's my uncle. My name is Andrew Aziza.'

This has to be Uncle William's house because the gateman eyes me from head to toe, wondering how this boy in jeans and sneakers can be the nephew of such a great man.

'Wait outside,' he says, shutting the door in my face.

It's effing fantabulous that Uncle William lives here. I wonder who he really is, whether he looks like Mama, why he and Mama ain't close. Maybe he's actually cool, and the fault is all Mama's. She can be very tough, very stiff. Although I hate to admit it, Aunty Lizzy is right: Mama shouldn't have kept me away from her family. It's crazy that she'd do such a thing and refuse to explain herself. If Mama hadn't kept me from Uncle William, I would've spent some ice-creamy holidays here, attended the dope schools in the city, participated in competitions abroad. I'd have known how to eat with forks and knives, and thus reduced the gap between Eileen and me.

I stare at the protesters in the distance. One of them already has her placard torn in two. They're walking slower, taking heavier steps, finally realising that Hopelessness is where they've been headed for a long time, since their shitty births. One takes the hand of another. Better to walk into failure together.

Someday I'll be like them, assuring myself of a Hope that doesn't exist. Question is, whose hand will I be holding?

Eileen's smell comes to me again. The date smell of her skin. The apple flavour of her mouth. All night, I kept stirring and stirring on the bed, reanimating the feel of my lips on hers, my fingers in her platinum. Despite the darkness of the room, all items beamed at me with a strange blonde light. Can't wait to see her tonight and taste her mouth again.

The gateman opens the side door. 'Please come in, Mister Andrew,' he says with a small bow. 'Sorry o. So sorry for keeping you outside.'

Inside the compound: a white mansion with a garden on the roof. Red yellow ivory roses, sprinklers spitting threads of water at them. Bronze statues of centaurs and harpies and satyrs. A small domed chapel with a huge cross atop. And in the shed two Range Rovers and a Mercedes are snoozing.

Damn. Uncle William's palace is way cooler than Okorie's. He must be worth millions. When I return home to Kontagora, I'll grill Mama for selfishly stunting my life just because of some disagreement she had with her family. Again, I wish she were Mama 2. Hopefully, she'll recover soon – she told me this morning in a phone call that she's feeling much better.

The gateman leads me to the block of offices adjacent to the chapel.

'So, Mister Andrew, how are you, sir? I didn't know the monsignor had a nephew. He is a great man, the monsignor.'

'Oh, really?'

'Yes. Don't you know him very well?'

'I've never met him before.'

'How come? He is your uncle.'

'Yes, he is.'

'Na wa o. That's okay. You will like him, I tell you. He is really a great man, Mister Andrew. He has taught in universities abroad, won many awards too.'

'Wow.'

'Yes, sir. In fact, he has written many, many books.'

'Seriously?'

'He even added my name to the latest one. There's nothing as sweet as seeing your name in a book! And he's so generous, very generous.' He stops and clucks his tongue. 'God is such a miracle worker. Just look at you. May the Lord be praised!'

He leads me to an office, knocks on the polished wooden door, opens it.

'Please go in, sir.'

There's a man sitting behind the desk. He's in a black shirt and clerical collar.

He's exactly like me!

My doppelgänger.

Almost.

Except for the plump figure. Mama's eyes. The greying beard. He's stroking it, cheek on his palm, gazing at me.

We stare at each other a long time.

His pupils are thick and strong and overshadowing, enveloping me. Is that a frown under his eyes? Are his hands shaking?

'Jesus,' he says under his breath. 'Oh my God.' He makes the sign of the cross.

He grins. His smile is the most charming I've ever seen. I find myself smiling too.

He gets up, rushes to me. He's an inch or so taller than me, the height I'll attain.

He hugs me. Pushes himself into me.

I push myself into him – me.

We stand hugging for a long time.

I open my eyes, wanting to break off, but he doesn't let go. His smell is like Mama's, but without the perspiration, the mustiness, the poverty. On his shelf are philosophy and theology books. But one of them is a novel, *The Sorrows of Young Werther*. I've seen it on lists of greatest German novels but haven't read it.

I already dig Uncle William. We obviously have things in common, things to chat about. He even has the name of a king! Whether Mama likes it or not, I'll continue to visit him. Soon enough I'll move here permanently. His books will become mine, and his cars – partly mine.

Again I wonder why Mama would keep me away from Uncle William the Conqueror, someone who I could've learnt loads from. Maybe he disagreed with her life choices (such as marrying that slug called Kelani) and she decided to cut him off.

When Uncle William the Conqueror finally breaks away, he's crying.

We go out. His arm around me. This man who I have never known. Who I feel is me, and I'm him. Interesting how twinship is so powerful. So much of him is in me: his forehead, his lips, his laugh.

We go to the garden behind the block of offices, his arm still around me. We sit on a bench. He starts asking me questions, nodding. He's a fantastic listener!

He checks his watch. We rise, head to the white mansion. Inside, I stand gazing at the horrorcool of it all: cherubic chandeliers and mahogany panelling and furry red carpets. It's just so glitzy shiny dreamy; anything I turn to reflects me.

In the dining room, we sit. A middle-aged man in glasses and a white apron pushes the food on a trolley into the room.

'Welcome, sir,' he says to me.

He places before us a platter of fried rice and chicken and plantains. Places beside it a large bowl of coleslaw. A basket of apples and bananas. A bottle of orange juice. He bows at the monsignor.

'Thank you, Mr Okon,' Uncle William the Conqueror says, his voice slightly deeper than mine, the depth I'll attain. It's amazing the little things we share – the way he moves his hands, nods, or blinks, his sitting posture – as though I'd learnt them from him, as though he'd been around. Mr Okon returns to the kitchen.

Uncle William the Conqueror asks me to say grace.

When I finish, he stares at me, his eyes red and moist.

'Andrew,' he says, 'I'm sure you don't understand. Don't understand how I've been feeling all these years. But I've greatly wronged you . . . beyond any level you could ever know. I don't . . . I don't . . .'

He brings out his handkerchief. Blows his nose.

'I don't deserve to sit at a table with you. Tell me, should I leave?'

Silence.

He must be feeling very shitty for being Mama's twin and never contributing to my life, never paying my school fees or buying Mama and me clothes. He must be feeling like a very bad uncle when as a priest he preaches daily about selflessness. He seems very intense, though, flagellating himself more than the average person would. Maybe that's why he's a priest.

'I don't understand anything you've said,' I say in Ososo. He looks up, surprised that I know the language. 'The past is in the past. Why don't we just eat?'

'All right, Andrew,' he says in Ososo. 'All right.'

We talk. He tells me that, many years ago, he and Mama had a disagreement. At first it seemed trivial, but gradually it became this mountain between them and they stopped talking. But it was all his fault, his immaturity, his foolishness. I ask him to tell me about the disagreement.

'I am so ashamed even to think about it. But, with time, your mother and I will tell you everything.'

I nod. Hope it is soon.

I'm eager to ask him about my papa, but I'm guessing he knows nothing since he and Mama have been estranged for such a long time. Like Aunty Lizzy and Grandma, he probably thinks I'm Kelani's child.

Growing up was very difficult, he says. Grandpa could only pay the fees of one child, so he withdrew Mama from school and asked her to work on the farm with Grandma and sell their produce in the market. For a long time, William bemoaned how this was unfair, his going to school while Mama went to the farm when it was supposed to be the other way around, but Mama embraced the farm and refused to take his place even though she was the smarter twin. And because she had poor education, she drifted from one abusive husband to another, men who exploited her, seized her money, kicked her into the street, and married younger women when they got tired of her, when she suffered miscarriages, when she couldn't give them a child.

One particular instance still depresses him. Mama once owned a successful fabric business in Oshodi when they were in their late twenties. One morning, after another miscarriage, her husband Kelani brought a teenage girl from Ososo to their home and took her straight to their bed. He called Mama a man and said she was no longer his wife, that the teen would thenceforth take her place and her business. He handed the teen the key to her fabric store and the girl laughed at Mama. When Mama fought back for her business, her marriage, Kelani called the police and they locked her up for two days amidst rats and pails of urine and shit. When she was released she went back home to fight for her business, her possessions. Kelani beat her and dumped her in a smelly gutter full of flies and rotten food a mile away from home. One of her customers found her a day later and contacted William. He was in his eighth year in the seminary in Ibadan. He hurried to Oshodi with his savings, paltry amounts he'd received from parishioners. For three whole days Mama was unconscious. When she finally recovered, he couldn't even afford to pay her hospital bills, so he called some friends who were priests. A couple were very generous, and he rented her a place in Ibadan and helped her begin afresh. They became close again after years of being distant. And at this time, because of their closeness, they had the disagreement, and The Mountain began to grow between them. One afternoon he came to visit and discovered she'd left, that she was married again and had moved to the North and no longer wanted to speak to him. A year or so later, on his priestly ordination, he learnt she had separated from her husband and had a son, her first child, me.

'Your mother is the strongest woman I've ever met,' he says. 'The most optimistic. She never stopped believing in love even though it failed her several times. And I can see a lot of her in you. That unwavering strength. That proclivity to do the impossible, to make the best of whatever life has handed you.'

+

In the evening I put on my Ralph Lauren polo shirt and my New Balance sneakers and go to the mirror. I stand till Christ comes, removing the tiniest fluff from the shirt, fingering the four strands of beard under my chin. Yep, I look dope. Yep, I'm Eiqueen-worthy. I pray she says I look good today. If I stand here long enough, she might. Problem is, the longer I stand, the more I notice the things I don't wanna see, namely: My springy hair. My fat lips. My dead irises. Why are my irises so darkbrown? They could've, for example, been yellow or the colour of my inner lip or of my palms – i.e. any pumping colour. I sigh. Pocket my phone and keys and handkerchief. Go out the door.

I immediately freeze. Because Fatima's coming upstairs – I can smell and hear her. My genius babe with mirror eyes, who before Eiqueen used to make me see colours of impressionist paintings and hear guitar riffs whenever I was around her. We haven't spoken since she refused to answer my goodbye two days ago. Somehow I've managed to evade one-on-one meetings with her, and only see her at breakfast or dinner, my droogs and Zahrah and Okorie insulating me.

· She reaches the upstairs hallway. Will walk past me in a few secs. I really want to chat with her, but she'll ignore me if not slap me again. She's in a black abaya, hair in neat shiny cornrows, earrings pretty. I move back to let her pass freely. She smells of mint. Enters her room without glancing at me, shuts the door.

I stand undecided for several minutes.

Then I begin to inch towards her room, two steps forward, one step back, forward, back, until I'm at the door. I stand for another minute, tap the door gently like a thief, go in.

Fatima is reclining on the couch with a book but sits up when she sees me. She eyes me a bit, crosses her legs, returns to her book. The cover and spine are blank. I wish I knew what she was up to these days.

I clear my throat. Again and again. She doesn't budge.

'What are you reading?' I say.

She's silent for a few moments, then she says:

'*The Sorrows of Young Werther.*'

'Oh, really?'

I sound too excited. I hiss at myself, threaten lobotomy if I don't calm down asap.

'How're you finding the book?'

She doesn't respond, eyes still buried in it.

'Right. Well, I guess I should get going now. Sorry for distracting your reading.'

She looks up.

'You've read *Werther* before?' she says, her voice gentle.

'No, sadly. Wish I had.'

She places the book on her lap. Her eyes are soft, her cheekbones sharp, complementing her earrings. Despite her silence earlier, it doesn't seem like she wants to slap me right now. She might even want to have a chat, surprisingly. But why is that surprising, really? What did I do to her? Can't I write about loving blondes in my diary? Anyhoo, I wish I could sit beside her like old times.

'So how's the book?'

'Okay so far.'

'Great.'

'The narrator tends to digress a lot, though. He's really intense.'

'Wow . . . Interesting.'

A plane flies past, very low, the pilots visible. Planes are so rare in Kontagora that kids, even adults, run outdoors to wave and sing at them whenever they fly past. I point out the plane, say we should maybe go out to wave at it.

She chuckles.

The room feels brighter, begins to smell of flowers. I take a few steps towards her.

'It's kinda strange, though,' I say.

'What's strange?' she says.

'You don't believe in fate, right?'

'Yes, so . . .'

'You said chaos and randomness make more sense.'

She looks at me suspiciously. 'What are you getting at, Andy?'

I tell her I've just visited Uncle William and found a copy of *Werther* on his shelf.

'Oh,' she says, uncrossing her legs. 'Really? You have an uncle here?'

'Yeah. He's a priest. A monsignor, in fact. He's my mother's twin.'

'So your mama has a twin. Cool.'

I take a few more steps closer, look at the space beside her and decide to risk it. I sit, pick up the book, flip to the title page. She's wearing a thin silvery bangle. I stare at her hand. Although her skin is lighter than mine, our hands are so similar. Pink nails, dark knuckles. But in contrast Eileen's hand is a half-moon, ours the darkness around it.

I have a sudden urge to take Fatee's hand. To caress it, maybe even kiss it. With the bangle it looks different, pretty, even sexy. Didn't know my Fatee had such hands even though I've held them countless times.

'So how's your uncle?' she says.

'He's great. Gave me some money and said I should visit again asap. And d'you know what?'

'What?'

'We look a lot like each other.'

She smiles. 'What did you expect?'

'Don't know. And his house is really classy. Like top-notch. Hogwarts. I felt like Harry Potter in it.'

She's silent – doesn't even chuckle at my joke.

I don't know what to say. All possibilities – Zahrah, maths – lead back to Our Life before the Platinum, before the diary.

'So, Andy . . .'

'What, Fatee?'

'Why are you here?'

Shocking question.

'Oh. I – I . . . I just came to say hi. To check on you.'

She nods. 'To check on me.'

'Yeah.'

And a flood of guilt rushes into my chest.

I want to tell her I'm sorry about the diary. That something is wrong with me, and it's only she who can save me, because she's my Fatee, my fate. I want to fall on my knees and weep onto her hand. But somehow I remain sitting.

Her hand. Soft. Birthmark on the little finger.

I move my hand towards hers.

I take it.

Sleek.

Something begins to stir in me. Am I getting hard?

Suddenly Fatee takes back her hand.

'Don't think you can fool me, Andy.'

My voice comes croaking. 'What're you saying, Fatee?'

'Why don't you just come clean for once?'

'About what?'

'We both know where you're going to.'

'Where? I'm confused.'

'You're going to her place.'

A billion lies race to me. I don't bother taking any.

'I know you don't give a damn about what I say. But I hope someday you'll find a way out of your zigzags. I hope you find it soon.

'I'll keep being your friend, Andy. But don't come here and begin to pretend and play sweet as if nothing has changed between us. In fact, I think you should leave. I've got things to do.'

Slowly, I rise and walk out of the room. Out of the house. Boulders tied to my neck.

I stand watching the road, but I see nothing, hear nothing. I can't think, can't move – my head is blank.

Several minutes later, I begin to regain my senses. I feel the earth under my feet; I hear kids playing football in the distance. The road before me is empty. The sky is yellows and browns, full darkness in an hour.

I take out my phone. Eileen has sent me some lines full of emojis.

> Got really bored and decided to try this Madagascan wine.
> Now I'm a bit drunk!!
> You can come though. If you don't mind seeing me slightly wild.
> We could maybe watch a movie. Then I'll go to bed early.

+

At her door, I knock and she opens instantly. My Eimpress. In a tank top and bum shorts. Platinum wavy and twinkling. My chest explodes; the black dot in me leaps. Although there's a whiff of alcohol in the air, she doesn't look drunk or anything. For a few moments we stand looking at each other uncertainly, as though we didn't see each other's naked bodies just yesterday, as though we're trying to remember where we left off. Is she eyeing my hair? Has she changed her mind? Is she trying to shoo me? Suddenly she laughs and says:

'Hop in.'

We hug. Am I supposed to kiss her? Like in British films? I decide to risk it. I move my lips towards her. Left cheek, right cheek. She doesn't seem to respond. I move to her chin, her mouth. No response. I freeze. Move away from her.

'So sorry,' I say.

She laughs, higher-pitched than I expected. 'Go on. I'm enjoying it.'

I return to her cheek. Then her neck, her mouth, like in the movies. Yes, there's def some alcohol on her breath. I move down to her neck again.

She kisses me back, in fact becomes suddenly sparky, bubblier than I've known her, giggling in my ear, fingers prodding into my back. Yep, she's a little drunk. Was her earlier stoniness her attempt to mask it?

She whispers something in my ear. I tell her I didn't hear.

She laughs. 'You did.'

'No, I didn't.'

'Alright, I'll try again.'

She hugs me, whispers:

'I'm so y-n-r-o-h.'

'Oh. Really?' My chest almost explodes again. 'I – I ...' What's the proper response? 'I am too.'

She laughs. Moves her hand round my chest. Down to my stomach. Down, down.

'Wow. It's rising in my hand! Like a monster.'

Am I supposed to laugh? I laugh. Is it really that big, like a monster?

'You're so hard. Come on.'

She breaks off, holds me by my shirt, like I'm a criminal, like I'm a pet, and drags me into the living room. She laughs. I laugh. She tells me to take off her shorts. I do. To spank her bum cheeks. I hesitate, tap her green panties instead. Her ass is quite flat. Still, it's amazing.

'Don't be shy,' she says.

I try to change the subject. 'You've got a great bum.'

'That's not true.'

'It's true.'

'You know it's not. The women here have far better arses.'

She laughs and falls onto the sofa.

'Come and kiss me.'

We kiss for a minute. She moves my head to her stomach, to between her legs, parts her panties.

'Kiss me there.'

Down there, she's shaven and smells like a mixture of fish and syrup. I kiss. Lick. Savour the fishsyrup. She cries out, like the songbird she is. Minutes later, my tongue begins to itch, to become sore. I raise my head, but she cries out:

'Don't stop. It feels amazing.'

I get back to it. Continue licking and licking, my tongue sorer and sorer, my mouth drier. I know we're not doing BDSM; still I feel like a sub. To forget the soreness, to shoo comparisons to Fatee and how she wouldn't make me do this, I try to think of something. As a little boy, whenever I was sinning – e.g. stealing meat from the pot – I always feared that trumpets from heaven would sound that very moment, and I'd be banished instantly to hell. The fear of the eternal fire and the weeping and grinding of teeth would make me return the meat, usually after a nibble or two. I wonder why I don't feel that way anymore.

I raise my head again. She protests she's so close. 'Please don't stop.'

I continue licking, very feebly now.

'Aren't you enjoying it?' she says.

'I am,' I say.

She laughs, sits up, says she knows I'm dying to stick it in, that's why I keep stopping.

She takes off her panties, asks me to kiss her again. I do.

'You're a great kisser,' she says. 'You've got amazing lips.'

She unzips me, takes it, licks it.

'Wow,' she says. 'It's so big. Biggest I've ever seen. That's what you've always wanted, right? To put it inside of me?'

I'm afraid this is the real Eileen, this uncensored self. As I approach her, it begins to deflate slightly. I beg and beg it not to. Not to shame me just when it's Time.

+

I wake up before her. The sleep was quite hollow. My eyes are heavy, but I can't return. My tongue is still sore. There's a weird smell in the air. The smell of my sin? The purity I've lost?

I feel so sad. Why? I can't say. But I badly need to weep. That's how these eyelids will lighten.

Ydna?
. . .
Ydna?
. . .
Ydna?
. . .
. . .

Silence. Except for her breathing. Snoring, even. Didn't know white girls snored. Guess the movies leave those parts out.

I don't want to look at her. I should get up and leave. I can weep along the way.

I sit up. But I can't move. Best I can do is turn my entire back to her. Retract from the source of the radiation.

I try one more time:

Ydna?
. . .
. . .
. . .

I feel emptier than I came.
There are holes inside of me.
Wastelands inside of me.
Just soreness and shame to fill up.

There's daylight in the curtains before me, but it's weak, like my muscles. My muscles feel like they've received slaps punches kicks even though there's no wound to show. I pick up my phone to bottle everything.

I know what I'm supposed to do: message Fatee, beg her forgiveness, schedule a meeting to discuss us. Instead I flip through apps, refusing to open those that lead me back to her.

If I tell her I'm sorry, what would it lead to? Won't we simply end up like every couple on this land, living doomed lives, patching up our love daily?

She claimed I was moving in zigzags, but isn't that the direction of the universe and Everything? And when she took back her hand it all became clear. For all its softness, her hand isn't close to being as soft as Eileen's. And it will never be. It will instead get tougher, spongier, darker with age. Like Zahrah's. Like Mama's. Like those of every woman on this land. Worse still, with Fatee, my blood doesn't vaporise as much as it does around Miss Platinum. The jet-black between my legs seems scared, at crossroads, stagnation all before it, but with the Platinum it somersaults, hikes across the wonderland around it, stands atop the tallest hill, and sees some future peeking in the fog.

I drop the phone on the side table. The sound makes Eileen stir.

'Hi, Andy,' she yawns. 'Is it morning already? My head is sort of banging.'

I don't know why, but I don't respond.

'Andy, can you hear me?' She sits up. 'What's wrong? Why aren't you answering me?'

I know that if I look at her the black dot will pacify me, make me grovel before her again.

'Did I say something yesterday? I did warn you I was drunk, remember?'

Minutes pass. Why is it so hard for her to accept she treated me weird, to say sorry?

She sighs. Draws closer to me. Places her hands on my shoulders. Rubs my neck.

'Are you mad at me?'
Slowly, reluctantly, I shake my head.
'Great.'
She massages my shoulders, my arms.
'Kiss me.'
I kiss her. She kisses me back. Tickles my sides. I laugh.
'So you're ticklish too?'
I gaze at her.

the

    poetry

      of

        her

          body

+

Sun is up now. We're still sitting on the bed. A rope of sunlight crawls over our legs, showing the contrast. Her skin is evenly coloured, no stretch or spot of red or pink. It's so unreal how her skin is perfectly marble everywhere, from eyelids to toes, unlike mine that's a multitude of black shades: black here, black black there, black black black there. And all about her are these little translucent hairs, her halo. Wish I could finger every single one.

As I look away, I realise she's staring at me again. Not checking me out. Just pure staring. Probably at my fat nose. The springs of hair on my head. She must have Reawakened again, must be wondering what the hell she's doing with me. I smile, but she doesn't stop.

'What's on your mind?' I say.

'Nothing,' she says.

'Then why're you staring at me?'

'Aren't you the one staring?'

I chuckle, wishing to change the subject. She chuckles too.

I caress her face, smell her bun, untie it. Instantly her hair cascades on us.

'Amazing,' I say.

'What's amazing?'

I want to tell her that if you take out the braids from Mama's or Zahrah's or Fatima's hair, it will remain standing like Eiffel. But this explanation is so long-winded and tame that I don't bother.

I move the curls from her face, her ear. I hold and stare at them until my thoughts become as manifold as the strands.

I realise her hair is just hair – sleek, colourful, of course – but hair still, not something extraordinary, beyond human imagination or attainment, not a piece of vibranium or unobtainium. Still, there's something magical about it, an x in the strands that calls to me, that makes my fingers tremble and miss holding them the very second I let go. I'm sure that if given infinite time, I'd still be unable to find what I'm looking for in the hair, to satiate this craving I'll never understand.

'Take off your shirt,' she says.

Does she want to check if I have a six-pack? If my chest is as beefy as those of Elba and Foxx?

'Wow, your stomach is so flat.'

Is she saying something about my poverty?

She ties her hair back into a bun, makes me lie down and begins to examine my body with her fingers. My stomach, my ribs, my chest. She plants a kiss on my neck – warm, moist – and scans my lips, my nose, pries my eyelids open. Now she's on my hair. She spends an eternity gazing at it, fingering it. Why is she so obsessed with it? Is she composing an elaborate proof for why hers is sleeker and shinier? Isn't that obvious enough?

'What's up, Eileen?'

'Nothing.'

'What are you doing?'

'Trying to memorise your body.'

She lies down on the bed afterwards, says she's feeling unwell and dizzy, that her head is still banging.

'I'm so sorry, Andy. But is there a tiny tiny chance that you could get me breakfast? Please? Coffee would be nice. And an avocado toast. Shouldn't take you long.'

'Yeah, I can get you breakfast, Eileen.'

'Everything is in the kitchen. You can get yourself whatever you want.'

'No worries.'

'Thanks, Andy. Just too hungover to get up.'

I put on my shirt, go to the door.

'Andy? D'you know you've got a cute bum?' She laughs.

'Oh. Thanks.'

In the kitchen I spend a full minute checking out the super-sleek counter and microwave and gas cooker and toaster and sink. I've only used a microwave twice in my entire life, both times at Zahrah and Okorie's here in Abuja. The box is really dope – how can you warm or cook food without fire and water, without stirring smoke? I check out other devices which I don't know, then take out the bread and avocado from the fridge.

I've never made an avocado toast before. In fact, I've never made any kind of toast, ever. Although avocados are grown in the South, we rarely eat them at home. Mama considers buying them a waste of money because it could go to getting important foodstuffs like rice and garri. We only eat avocados when parishioners returning from the South give them to us.

I stare at the items on the counter without knowing what to do. Maybe I should've been humble and told her I didn't know shit, have never known shit. But what would that achieve? She'd think I'm a Homo habilis or something. Even cave dwellers in ancient Britain knew how to make toast. I pace about a bit, realise that Fatima or any female schoolmate wouldn't make me do this. In fact, I'm supposed to become offended, even angry, if they make such a request. Cooking is supposed to 'make a man less a man' – very silly indeed.

Suddenly I get a techrrific idea. Google! YouTube! I take out my phone, search how to make the shit. Halfway into the video I hear her coming downstairs. I pause the video asap. A tsunami of shame inundates me – the Shame Mama and her mother and everybody on this land has ever felt. She comes into the kitchen. I can't look at her. I don't know where to look. Everything in the kitchen screams at me with its shine, its newness, its artificiality. She flicks on switches, turns on the toaster and coffee maker, takes out a knife from the rack and begins to prep two plates. Wish she would say something, but she's silent, as if she isn't surprised by my failure. I must be the dumbest person she's ever met. She probably thinks everyone here is so dumb. I can picture the scene: she and her Brit friends sitting in a park, legs crossed, cackling at a joke she's just told them, of a boy she met in Africa who couldn't even make toast.

In two minutes she's done: two plates of yummy avocado toast, two steaming cups of coffee. She takes her plate and cup and marches upstairs. I take mine and trudge after her.

In her room she's sitting on the bed, chewing quietly. The curtains are parted. Sunlight pours in, particles frolicking along the beam. Outside in the distance, dudes and gals with bodies painted in charcoal are dancing, placards held high above their heads. A couple are around my age. I move quickly from the window to a chair under the air conditioner. She takes a remote, turns on the screen opposite the bed.

'Sorry about that,' I say.

'It's alright,' she says.

Wish she would smile, but she doesn't, eyes glued to the documentary on the screen.

+

We are watching Eileen's favourite film, *Avant la lettre*. It's about two biologists, a man and a woman, who meet at a science exhibition. They move around Paris, drinking in bars, having conversations about extraterrestrials, the multiverse, the reasons for their existence, their fetishes. The man believes the universe has brought them together for a reason, but the woman thinks their meeting is simply random. They spend the rest of the evening in a hotel trying to re-enact all the positions of the *Kama Sutra* while drinking and laughing.

Eileen and I are kissing again. We close the curtains, take off our clothes, fall onto the bed. Like in the film, she gets on all fours. Says I should spank her bum and do it from behind, her favourite position. I ask if she's sure about the spanking. She says I shouldn't be shy, that she gets really turned on when she's spanked. With my hands trembling, head bursting, armpits sweating, I do as she asked. Harder, she says, harder. But with each spank it begins to grow smaller, smaller, and when it's time, I can't get in. It deflates so fast, shrivels, takes a new toe shape and size that it's never been. Each of my pleas seems to accelerate its betrayal. I tell her sorry and sorry and sorry and sorry and sorry and sorry. She says nothing. I sit back on the bed. Stare at nothing. Through a small hole in the curtain, I see a protester with a placard, her body painted green-white-green. The guilt I felt earlier rouses inside me, metastasises.

We put on our clothes, sit on opposite sides of the bed. She turns off the screen, picks up her phone, replies to a couple chats. The only sounds are the taps of her fingers on the screen.

Perhaps to make up for failing her, I tell her I like her, really really like her.

She's silent for a long time.

'Are you sure?' she says.

'What do you mean?'

'You've said that a couple of times now.'

'Because I mean it.'

'Let's assume you mean it. Then why do you like me?'

'I don't know.'

'You keep saying that.'

'Because it's true.'

'No, it's not.'

'I really, really like you, Eileen.'

'Every time you say that, something about it feels off. Like there's something unreal about it all.'

'So you don't like me.'

'That's not what I'm saying, Andy.'

'No, you don't. You don't like me.'

'Andy, I'm still getting to know you.'

'So do you like the little you've got to know?'

'I do, obviously.'

A long silence.

'Do you like my skin, Eileen?'

'What?'

'You heard me.'

She drops the phone on the bed. Folds her arms.

'Andy, why are you asking me all these questions?'

I get up. Pick up my phone. Walk out of the room, out of the house.

On the street I begin to stalk a group of seven protesters. The three girls and four guys, in chalk or charcoal body paint, are smelly, dishevelled, look like they haven't slept in a week. Their bodies are caked in mud, their noses dripping phlegm. One of the girls has flies chasing her armpits and trousers. Still I continue to follow them. Cars honk at them, drivers squeal. Little boys and girls in the backs of SUVs spit at them, their parents saying nothing. At a side street one of the girls suddenly turns and walks away. The six pretend not to notice, their placards still held high, dog-eared in the wind. I follow and follow them until only one is left, until I can no longer walk.

At home at Zahrah and Okorie's, I walk into the living room and meet Fatima. She's all dressed up, wearing an ankara dress and a golden necklace, but no make-up. She's sitting, legs crossed, typing on her phone. On the walls are a legion of Zahrah's freakish statuettes, many exact copies of the ones in her house in KNT. I wonder whether Fatima will talk to me, considering how she sent me packing from her room yesterday.

She notices me and smiles.

'Hi, Andy, what's up?' she says.

'I'm great,' I say, walking to her.

'You're sweating.'

'Am I?' I touch my face. 'I guess, yeah.'

'Why are your clothes so dusty?'

'Oh. I saw a couple protesters. Decided to follow them a bit.'

'Really?'

She pulls out a handkerchief from her purse, hands it to me.

'Oh. Thanks, Fatee.'

I wipe my face, my eyes, my ears. I instantly feel better. In fact, I begin to smell a bit like her. Minty.

'So you followed the protesters.'

'Yeah.'

'Why didn't you join them instead?'

'Don't really know.'

She rises, picks up her purse. I wonder where she's heading to. Probably to see some relative in the city or shop for the wedding. It's so unbelievable that in six days Zahrah will be married.

I hear my droogs' laughter from upstairs. She says they're playing Xbox with Okorie.

'Anyway, I'm about to head out myself,' she says.

'Oh, great,' I say. 'Where are you going to?'

'The cinema.'

'Really? Alone?'

'Oh, not really. You remember Nicholas Oti? From the National Maths Competition? Last year?'

'Yes, yes, I remember him.'

'We're going out to see the new *Fast and Furious* film.'

But before I can say anything, her phone begins to ring.

'I think he's here,' she says. 'I've got to go. See you, Andy!'

And she rushes out of the house, shuts the door.

I stand staring at the door for several minutes. Numb. Haze all around me.

The laughter of my droogs rouses me. I realise I'm still holding Fatima's handkerchief. Although it's terribly soiled now.

13

A day passes. Another. No chat from Eileen.
I turn off the phone. Toss it wherever.
Jump onto the bed. Cry my eyes out.
Still I don't feel better.

Another day, the door is still locked.
I don't eat, don't sleep, don't wake.
Papers, soiled handkerchiefs, broken pencils on the floor.
Phone beside them. Still turned off. Screen facing down.
I know that if I turn it on, there'll be nothing.
On the bedsheet, the table, pens leaking ink.
Ink on my hands, my neck, my hair.
Ink on my pubic hair, my dick.
Night and day, stir and stir on the bed.
Ignore the droogs, Zahrah's calls to breakfast or dinner.
Once, I hear someone beside the door.
I know who it is.
I want her to knock.
She doesn't.
Because she doesn't, because she's given up on us, I cry my
eyes out again.

Piece by piece, I pick each scrap of paper.
Throw it in the basket, wipe the ink.
Piece by piece, I don't get better.

'Things will be fine again,' Zahrah says.
'Your mama will fully recover. You will recover. You will see.'

+

I turn on my phone. Her messages flood in.

+

We are back at the Chelsea. We're sitting opposite each other. She's in a wine-red dress. I laugh and laugh at something she says. We do not talk of that night, that morning, as though they never happened. I laugh and laugh again. We're silent for a moment, and she says, I love and love your skin. I really do. Can't you see? You must believe me. I say thanks, although I don't believe her. *Believe* $- b - e - v - e = lie$.

We go to a club. Everyone gawks at us, but we (i.e. I) don't give a fuck. We eat grilled chicken wings and gulp drinks and go to the floor. She begins to twerk and twerk and peeps clap and clap, even though she isn't that great a dancer. Under the spinning lights, we hug each other for so long that I want to believe her believe, one without a b and e and v and e.

We go to the park; she takes my hand. I do not take it back. We walk around and sketch dragons and unicorns with the stars. We stop under a floodlight and take selfies and selfies and selfies and selfies. We laugh and laugh and laugh and laugh. Still I try to believe her believe, one without b and e and v and e.

+

We are in the lobby of the National Gallery: Zahrah, Okorie, Fatima, my droogs, and me. It's two days before the wedding. Eileen's on her way. She asked if she could come and I said yeah of course. Patience and Serena couldn't come because the lil gal sadly got the plasmodium. It's four, and we're sitting round a table in the café of the lobby drinking milkshakes and eating croissants. Yep, I'm eating croissants for the first time in my life!

Yay! This crescent loaf is dope, seriously. I love how the crust flakes out and gives you a horrorshock in the oblongata when you chew it, and love the spectrum of buttery flavours that ballet into your tongue as you close your eyes, and love and love the perfection of the outer folds and inner layers when you just stare at it. The French or whoever invented this shit know the nucleus of having a good time, and I'm supposed to be with them, in those cities where magic is made, not in this shithole where only protests are made. It's sad that Eileen in her country gets to eat this every day for breakfast. Yeah, enviously sad.

People in twos and threes troop into or out of the building, wearing chic shirts and suits and dresses, only a few in kaftans and ankara. Zahrah at the head of the table is in her usual red dress, and beside her Okorie is in an expensive Louis Vuitton shirt and jeans. For the past few minutes they've been chatting quietly about his involvement in the protests. Once again Zahrah warns him to be very careful.

On my left and right are Slim and Morocca. Slim leans towards me and says:

'Are you sure Eileen is coming?'

Fatima is on his left. I glance at her hoping she didn't hear.

'Of course. Hundred per cent,' I say.

Morocca leans towards us and says:

'Andy, why don't you tell us what you did with her? Don't tell us you didn't eff her . . .'

'Guys, I ain't saying shit.'

Zahrah turns to us. 'What are you guys talking about? Why don't you share?'

My droogs and I burst out laughing. Zahrah and Okorie become even more interested. We think of a sweet lie to drop. Grown-ups never know better.

Fatima stares hard at her chocolate milkshake. 'They're talking about Andrew's time with his white girlfriend, Eileen. Apparently she's on her way here.'

'Woah, woah, woah,' Okorie says in his British accent. 'Wow. So you've got a girlfriend. And she's . . . she's . . .'

Zahrah is dead with shock, eyes like golf balls. She rests her chin on her palm, looks at me as though she's never seen me before, as though she's finally recognising the Darth Vader I am, her little smiling disciple maths genius Ososo boy. She opens her mouth and closes it. Opens, closes.

Long sweltering silence. I don't know where to look. I feel like real shit.

'Wow,' Okorie says, chuckling. He takes Zahrah's hand. 'Wow. Why don't you tell us about her, Andy Africa?' He's learnt that hateful concoction from Zahrah. 'Come on, man. Don't mind Zahrah. She wouldn't understand.'

Zahrah turns and gives him a very bad eye. She takes back her hand, her Africanness. She opens her purse and brings out her phone.

My droogs are staring at the table, at the floor, wishing Fatima had kept her mouth shut.

Just then, Eileen walks into the lobby. In a leopard-print dress. In gladiator heels. Her platinum waving from side to side. Taking different peeks at me.

My leopardess.

The whole lobby pauses to look at her. Hands and cups freeze in mid-air. Statements hang incomplete on tongues.

She approaches us. 'Hi, everyone,' she says.

And then we reawaken.

Fatima gets up. 'Excuse me,' she says to no one in particular. She marches to the toilet, not looking back.

We all rise.

'Hi, Eileen,' Zahrah says to her with a smile, as though she hasn't just heard the biggest reveal of her life. 'Good to meet you again.' She gives Eileen a hug. Eileen told me they had a nice chat during her welcome party.

'Hello, Eileen,' Okorie says, shaking her hand, suave as hell. 'I'm Okorie.'

'Wow,' Eileen says, 'so you're Zahrah's fiancé? Really pleased to meet you.'

'Pleased to meet you too.'

My droogs say hello and hey to her, shake her hand, with Morocca holding her hand a second too long. I almost Accio a saw to cut off his stupid hand.

Eileen gives me a hug. 'Hey, Andy.'

Her smell is a nirvana.

Zahrah rolls her big eyes.

We leave our table for the lift, with Morocca running back to steal my remaining croissant. He manages to get into the lift before the door closes.

On the second floor we look at paintings in their glass cases: Trees with babies as roots. Waterfalls pouring from the earth to the sky. Creatures without heads, without tails. Gradually we become three pairs: Zahrah and Okorie in front, Slim and Morocca before us, Eileen and me at the rear.

'You alright, Andy?' she says.

'I'm good. You?'

'Great, thanks.'

We stop at an abstract by Bruce Onobrakpeya: a ghost-like figure clutching a machete and floating over a crocodile of fire, and underneath, a sea of squids and sea snakes.

'Wow, this is something,' she says.

'Yeah.'

Who's the ghost among us? And who's the fire?

I try not to think of her departure tomorrow. Since I came to Abuja, I've failed at many things, but worst at getting her to stay longer.

We watch some abstracts of supernatural scenes by Yusuf Grillo, some portraits of women in geles by Ben Enwonwu. One of the women looks like Mama, her younger self, her expression just after losing Ydna.

We're the only ones in the corridor now. There's a door to my right, marked *Storage* with faded ink. I open it, peer inside. Light pours in from a distant window. The room is full of broken pottery and busts, and on the ceiling cobwebs wobble. I call Eileen to come check it out.

She walks in, picks up a sliver of pottery, raises it to the light. She drops it.

I hug her from behind, stroke her neck, rub her marble arms. She turns. Our lips find each other. We kiss. Our tongues playing seesaw. My hands running round her back, round her bum.

We must be kissing Forever. We're suddenly roused by a knock on the door. The floor becomes solid again, the world unfurls, reawakens.

'Andy,' Slim whispers. 'Zahrah is looking for you.'

Eileen and I come out, holding hands.

Fatima sees us come out, sees us holding hands. She turns to Onobrakpeya. At the ghost and fire.

Slim leads the way, Fatima still staring at the painting.

We take the lift to another floor, meet Zahrah and Okorie and Morocca.

'Where have you been, Andy Africa?' she says, but she isn't mad. 'Congratulations, Andy. I'm so proud of you,' she says, extending her phone to me.

I read the email. My poem, the one about HXVX, has won first prize in a West African contest for teenage poets.

'How?' I say.

'I submitted it on your behalf. I didn't want to raise your expectations.'

'Congrats, Andy Africa,' Okorie says, holding something behind him. He shows his hands: it's a crown, made of golden paper and ribbons. He must have bought it at the souvenir kiosk. He puts it on me, laughing. 'You are our king, Andy. King Andy Africa!' He bows deeply before me, chuckling.

My droogs begin to clap. People staring at artworks turn to see what the hell is happening.

I turn to Eileen. She is clapping too.

+

It's Tuesday evening. When I finish dressing I smell her again. Almonds, dates. Feel her hair between my fingers. Sleek, therapeutic. In a couple hours she'll be leaving for the airport. In a couple hours I might never see her again.

almonds, dates
dates, almonds
datalmond
diamond

I pocket my phone and go out the door. In the opposite room Slim, Morocca, Patience, and Serena are watching a comedy. I wonder what Fatima is doing in the next room. She's probably chatting with Nicholas, and he's telling her how she's the smartest and most beautiful thing in the world. Hooks tear in my chest, blaming me for losing her. I sigh and bottle everything.

As I walk down the stairs I hear Zahrah and her women friends in the living room. It's her hen party. Through my window I saw the women arrive in white dresses, some strapless, each bearing wrapped presents and a candle. A few even came out of flashy SUVs with chauffeurs opening the doors for them. Zahrah welcomed each with a hug and a kiss on the cheek. She looked very motherly in her expensive red George wrapper with golden patterns. Her top was made of shiny red beads, and her afro hung tall and trim, a shade of red on one side. Even though I ain't no fan of her attire, she looked real pretty.

In her short time in Abuja, she's managed to convert several high-profile peeps. She's even entrapped Shola Badmus and Mike Ighalo. We saw Shola's latest exhibition yesterday at the National Gallery, and Mike is the new Afrobeat sensation everyone is molokoing about.

I stop in the hallway to watch a little of the party. A dozen women are sitting on the floor in two semicircles on either side of Zahrah. The room is lit by their candle flames, and this light is reflected off the freakish statuettes of gods lining the room. She is talking about herself, and about permutations, of course. That they explain everything: change and invariance, flux and stagnation, the initial and final stages of a system. That the moment she discovered permutations and their applications to the complicated systems of life – growth and history and class and race and guilt and forgiveness – she became obsessed with studying them. In fact, permutation theory is at the heart of Anifuturism.

To demonstrate what she means, she takes a piece of chalk and begins to write and draw on the floor:

Given a set of three elements, say $\{\bullet, o, \Delta\}$:

permutation	maths repre.	rmk
$\bullet \ o \ \Delta$	$\begin{pmatrix} 1 & 2 & 3 \\ 1 & 2 & 3 \end{pmatrix}$	identity
$\bullet \ \Delta \ o$	$\begin{pmatrix} 1 & 2 & 3 \\ 1 & 3 & 2 \end{pmatrix}$	involution
$o \ \bullet \ \Delta$	$\begin{pmatrix} 1 & 2 & 3 \\ 2 & 1 & 3 \end{pmatrix}$	invol.
$o \ \Delta \ \bullet$	$\begin{pmatrix} 1 & 2 & 3 \\ 2 & 3 & 1 \end{pmatrix}$	inverse
$\Delta \ \bullet \ o$	$\begin{pmatrix} 1 & 2 & 3 \\ 3 & 1 & 2 \end{pmatrix}$	inverse
$\Delta \ o \ \bullet$	$\begin{pmatrix} 1 & 2 & 3 \\ 3 & 2 & 1 \end{pmatrix}$	invol.

This is the same table she used to introduce Fatima and me to permutation theory.

'And since mathematics gives us tools for theorising about complex abstract structures,' she says, 'permutations thus provide a concise medium for theorising, analysing, and understanding these complex systems of life, even our very own movement, Anifuturism.

'As I was saying earlier, we're living in a sacred place, one which we don't understand yet. Someday we'll learn exactly why we're here, why there are these particular laws of physics, why the earth is made this way. That is when as a species we'll truly become intelligent beings – gods, in fact. As you must have seen, this is only possible through Anifuturism. Anifuturism is the cure for the continent, for the world.'

She turns and sees me. Stares. A knowing, accusatory look. She turns back to her audience.

I reach asap for the door and bounce.

Yesterday as Okorie drove us home in his Jaguar, I received a weird text from her:

> For as the disobedience of one man made many sinners,
> so shall the obedience of one make many righteous.

I recognised the passage instantly, from St Paul's letter to the Romans. We all had to learn it in catechism. Bro Magnus always chants it in his moral instruction lessons to explain the person of Jesus as the Suffering Servant the Prophet Isaiah referred to when he talked about the lamb led to the slaughter, spat on by many, who obeyed till the end and didn't open his mouth. I read the message over and over, wondering why Zahrah was quoting the Bible, she who stopped attending church when she Returned from the Sahara. I could only extract a simple gist from her message: that I'm being 'disobedient' to my race or something. And so? Should I tie myself to a tree and lash my flat black ass? Last night I found myself horsing around with the text, perhaps just to spite her:

> For as the obedience of many men made all sinners, so
> shall the disobedience of one make many righteous.

And instantly the message looked much better.

+

In Eileen's living room, I watch her pack. I help her load some books into a suitcase, zip it. Outside, illuminated by streetlights, protesters are meandering with torchlights on their heads, placards held high, screaming. We can't hear them because of the closed windows and the distance. Suddenly, from nowhere, policemen descend on them. They wallop them with clubs, chase them into the darkness. They are especially ferocious because this is where expats live, where Eileen's people live.

Aunt Joan calls her, says her driver will be here in an hour, apologises for having been away for so long, promises to meet her in Niger.

Eileen is in a blouse and jeans, hair in a ponytail. Still she's otherworldly, my Eiqueen, the only Real Thing in this land of simulations. We go upstairs and I help her bring down her other suitcases. We sit on sofas opposite each other. She crosses her legs.

'Eileen, you don't have to go,' I say.

'I do have to,' she says.

'No, you don't.'

'Mum doesn't want me here any longer.'

'Why?'

'Because of the protests and all.'

'But don't you want to stay?'

'Wish I could, but my visa expires next week anyway. So we'll be in Niger for a few weeks and then we'll be going back home.'

'Stay, Eileen.'

'I'll have to go eventually, Andy. I'll have to go home. You know I don't belong here.'

She smiles, to show she doesn't mean to be disparaging. These days she's become very careful about what she says, especially when it's about here. Most times I don't really like it, the tiptoe-ing and all. There's a tiny chance it's simply a mask, a masque.

'So when are we going to see each other again?' I say.

'Maybe if you come to Niger,' she says. 'It's really not far away from here.'

I nod. In the painting behind her two fishermen in straw hats are launching a canoe, and in the horizon the sun is sinking into the waters. In fifty or a million years they'll still be there together, launching the canoe. They'll still be alive, laughing, unchanged. 'Static' and 'happy' must be equal, perfect synonyms.

'Alright,' I say. 'Could you please do me a favour, then?'

'Okay.' She eyes me, uncrosses her legs, thinks I'm about to ask her another Difficult Question, one about me, about us. I'm sure the Questions are part of the reason she's running away.

'Go on, Andy.'

232

'Don't worry. Forget it.'

'Come on. What's on your mind?'

'You'll think I'm a creep or something.'

'No, I won't.'

'Are you sure?'

'Feel free,' she says, glancing at her watch.

Still I don't ask my favour.

'Please ask me, Andy. I'll be leaving in an hour. We might not meet for a while. Might never meet again. So ask me.'

I go to her. Whisper it in her ear. She looks at me, surprised.

'Wow, you really like my hair,' she says.

She rises, goes to get a pair of scissors, cuts a small lock from the side, hands it to me.

'Take good care of it, then,' she laughs.

I push it into my pocket, the Real Thing. With each downward push, I sink in shame. Outside, under a streetlight, the protesters gather again.

'Kiss me, Andy,' she says. 'One more time. One last time.'

IV: The Carrying of the Cross

Theorem (Cayley): Every finite group is isomorphic to a group of permutations.

14

I smell her again.

I awaken.

From my window upstairs I look at the front garden, at the hundreds of guests all the way from Ososo and Kaduna and Lagos and Kontagora, gathered to dance and eat and drink with Zahrah and Okorie. Everyone is in white – white kaftan, babanriga, buba, agbada, gele – even the three huge masquerades who are hopping about making a helluva noise with their silly whistles and their tails that whip left and right as though chasing away flies. Zahrah insisted everyone – except her and her bae – wear white, for an Anifuturist wedding is a 'communal event' where everyone must mirror the 'transubstantiation' of the bride/groom to renew or contemplate the 'object of love'. For the purposes of differentiation the bride/groom could wear other colours – in particular red, the colour of Anifuturism. On the gate there's a red banner that says *First Anifuturist Wedding*. I don't know who put it there. I wonder if the notice is erroneous, for weren't the mothers of old Anifuturist?

But among the scores of people standing sitting laughing chatting, I can see someone nobody sees: my Eiqueen, a plume of her standing amidst the bougainvillea, staring at me, winking.

I sigh.

I put on my white sheda trousers and shirt. Button up, pick up the hula from my bed, and push it onto my head. I peep into the mirror. Yep, I look like some hot Hausa bloke. I smile, quickly looking away from the mirror. I decided to dress like a Hausa dude because I couldn't think of anything else to wear. Although I'm from the South, from Ososo, I couldn't figure out what Ososo men wear, because – spoiler alert – I've never been there before.

I peek at my phone. Sad, Eiqueen hasn't responded to my status report chats. But Aunty Lizzy has answered my texts. She says Mama is doing very cool, that Mama wants me to congratulate Zahrah for her.

I bounce out of my room to the Slim and Morocca villa. They're still dressing, Morocca laughing at Slim, saying he looks like a mosquito in his white lace kaftan.

'Andy, man, doesn't Slim look like the mosquito that bit you last night?' Morocca says.

'Yep,' I say. 'I recognise him.'

We laugh. Morocca smooths the straps of his singlet and dons his white agbada.

'Look at him,' Slim retorts. 'Doesn't he look like an armed robber?'

'Like the armed robber he is?' I suggest.

We laugh.

'Honestly, though, you guys look dope,' I say.

'Especially you,' Morocca says to me.

'When you walked in I thought it was Ali Nuhu,' Slim says.

'Exactly, boy Slim,' Morocca says.

'Don't compare me to that guy,' I say.

They laugh. Slim must have thought I'd be cool with the comparison to the most famous Kannywood actor.

'So, Werdna?' Morocca says.

'What's up, bro?'

'How's your babe?'

'Oh,' I say, looking away, smelling her skin again.

'How's she?'

'Is she gone?'

I nod.

'Eiyaa,' Slim says, like some market woman.

I know what's coming next.

'So did you get to . . .' Morocca says, eyes bigger.

I play along. 'Get to what?'

'You know what I'm talkin bout, nigga.'

'Don't know what you're talkin bout, nigga.'

I glance out the window, at the swinging tails of the masquerades.

'Fuck it. Did you get to eff her?'

'No comment,' I say.

Morocca laughs, hops around, turns to Slim.

'What did I tell ya? Told ya to trust my nigga Werdna! See how he made us proud!'

He and Slim laugh for a long minute. I try to force a frown. Force force force. Nothing seems to be happening.

They're still laughing. Patience peeps into the room and asks why they're laughing so loud. They don't answer her. 'Fools,' she hisses and slams the door.

Morocca comes to me and places his arm round my shoulders, like a good bro.

'Congratulations, Andy,' he says in a silly Cockney. 'Congrats. You've finally lost your baby boxers.'

'Go to hell,' I say.

'And with a white babe, Andy! You're so fucking lucky!'

'Shut up,' I say, smiling.

'I noticed it,' Morocca says. 'He came walking into the room with these broad shoulders, and I said "Man"!'

'So what will ya do,' Slim says, 'now that she's gone?'

'Don't know, bro.'

'She'll come back for my nigga,' Morocca says. 'That's if he didn't use a rubber.'

'Did you use one, Andy?' Slim says.

I don't fucking know what to do with these boys. I want to slap them, but I find myself laughing.

'Fuck off, you two,' I say. 'Get lost!'

They laugh even louder.

Slim's phone beeps. He takes it out.

'Man, things are still heating up in town,' he says.

'What now?' Morocca says.

'Thirty students have just been arrested,' Slim says, scrolling through the phone. 'They tried burning up a government building with flamethrowers and explosives and stuff. They were protesting the death of their president.'

'Death of what president?' I say.

They both look at me as though I'm from Pluto.

'Don't you know what's been happening? The president of the SUG was found dead last night. The government says he hanged himself in prison. They even published his suicide note.'

'What the fuck.'

'Yeah. Folks think he's been assassinated.'

'Seriously?' I say, remembering my encounter with the taxi driver.

'Whatever happened, it's clearly working.'

'Many students have already given up because their leader lost faith and all.'

'Just a few still holding on.'

'Yeah.'

'Look at this, Morocca,' Slim says, showing the phone to him. 'People are tweeting about police arresting lecturers.'

'Damn.'

Morocca and I also take out our phones and scroll through Twitter. Minutes later Morocca's phone starts to ring.

'Woah,' he says. 'WALL-E. It's Okey!'

He takes the call, puts it on loudspeaker.

'I get news for you guys,' Okey says.

'What news?' we say.

'O boy, the government here don grant me and my uncle asylum o.'

'Seriously, Okey?'

'Damn.'

'Fuck.'

'Seriously, guys,' Okey says. 'It's like a fuckin dream, man, I dey tell you. Last week they even move us to this cool banging neighbourhood. Now we dey drink fresh milk and eat sausages like water every day. See, they even full our fridge with every goody you fit imagine. The chicken pizza is so sweet, I like it so much, I can't get enough of the shit. I even start work for one Caribbean restaurant last week. Dem dey pay me well well. Now I dey make cool euros like a real nigga. I'm even liking one of the co-workers, sef. She be Spanish, redhead. Things might work for us, and through her I go become citizen. Anyways, I'm sure I go get her number very soon. You guys know say I be ladies' man. And when I get her, I go show her every inch of my lollipop.' He laughs.

We laugh too, our eyes big as doughnuts.

Morocca and I ask him to expatiate on his new life, our doughnut eyes growing bigger. 'Mumu boys,' Okey says. 'Just check my Facebook. You go see stuff.' He plans on sending his wages to his sis and bro and connecting them to the man in Niger who transported him and his uncle across the special easier route to Europe. 'The journey is mad and difficult o,' he says. 'But man, e worth am. E worth am.'

We ask him to send us the number of The Man, to introduce us to him. Okey says okay, no problem, that The Man is very hungry and very kind, it's amazing. 'Man, the girls here are dead sexy o, I dey tell you. You know it's summer and all. They're wearing all sorts of bikinis and boob tubes. Something funny happened yesterday. One girl with fat juggs came to our restaurant to eat. She didn't tie her boob tube well, and o boy, her juggies poured out like a waterfall.' He laughs. We laugh with him like silly dinosaurs. 'O boy, the life here is the opposite of Naija, I dey tell you. Do you know how these oyinbos waste food? They throw food away after eating just two forks. Even their eggs and oranges have expiry dates! Their buses move around with a single passenger just because they want to keep to schedule. Anyways, my uncle and I are thinking of moving to Germany or Sweden or the UK. They say life is even better there than here. But to do that we need to save a lot of pepper, o boy.'

When Morocca hangs up we sit in silence. I know we're all thinking the same thing. That it's all so simple, that Niger is so nearby. If Okey could do it, we can too. If we do, we'll be far away from the sun, from hunger and blackouts and protests and assassinations.

The beep of Morocca's phone rouses us. Okey has sent him The Man's number and a photo. It's a selfie of Okey standing outside a restaurant with *Pollo del Tirón* painted above the glass door. The sun on his face is different, less yellow, and there's more flesh to his cheeks.

'What the fuck,' Morocca says.

'So this shit is really real?' Slim says.

We check Okey's Facebook and see more photos: Okey and his uncle smiling amidst three white men in suits; Okey and an Arab girl on a busy street with many white people and brick houses in the background; Okey and two Arab girls eating pizza on a bench outside a restaurant; Okey laughing and pushing a trolley in a brightly lit supermarket with many white shoppers in the background.

'We have to call The Man,' I say. 'We fucking have to!'

+

We troop outside. It's a sea of white everywhere: men and women sitting under almond trees, under tarp pavilions, fanning themselves with programmes; little children sitting on the thighs of their parents, on small chairs, pointing at the masquerades; the tails of the masquerades swaying left and right, the bells on them clanging. And at the centre of the gathering, Zahrah and Okorie are dancing with two middle-aged men and women, their parents, Zahrah beautiful in her red-beads top and George wrapper, Okorie in a red tunic decorated with golden animal patterns. The audience claps and wows. The instrumentalists increase tempo, beating their percussion drums and pot bass and tall gongs like psychos. Zahrah and Okorie dance faster, kicking their feet forward and back, spinning, bending till they are almost squatting, all in perfect unison. The audience shrieks. It's so cool watching Zahrah dance – tbh, she's effing amazing. The audience applauds and I join them, whistle like a freak. My droogs also whistle, Morocca braying like the shark he is. The drummers reduce tempo and Zahrah and Okorie and their parents take a break. They move to the high table: Zahrah and Okorie sit on their golden thrones, their parents on the polished wooden chairs behind them.

Morocca points at a man. 'You see that nigga? In the designer suit? Beside Okorie's poppa?'

'Aye?' I say.

'He followed the Sahara to Europe. Was nothing before he left. Now he's a designer at Volkswagen.'

'Really? Art thou sure, man?'

'Too sure, bro.'

Fatima is sitting in the second row of the high table, wearing a pretty silk dress. Beside her is Nicholas Oti. He's looking flashy in his agbada. He whispers something to her and she chuckles shyly. He takes her hand, squeezes it. She doesn't take it back.

I wonder how he managed to get an IV to the party, and in fact a seat at the high table. He probably knows Zahrah. He's quite famous, having won several gold medals at national competitions and published a poetry collection. I wish I could march to the high table, saw off his silly hand, feed him millipedes to stopper his irritating laugh. Then tear off his agbada, set it ablaze.

The MC rises and thanks everyone for supporting the couple in their introductory dance. 'To perfectly begin the union of Zahrah Omowero Suleiman and Okorie Mark Osondu,' he says into the mike, 'we must first feed the ancestors some kolanuts and invite their blessings on the bride and groom. I hereby invite Assistant Priestess Ronke Adewale-Johnson to lead the breaking of the kolanuts and the libation thenceforth.'

The audience cheers as a woman in glasses and buba steps forward and takes the mike. I've seen her a couple times with Zahrah. She's an anthropology lecturer at UNILAG and the head of the Southern province of the Anifuturist movement. A cameraman who has been following the dancing and MC trails behind Ronke and moves his lens round the faces of the crowd. On his camera are logos of YouTube and Twitter and Facebook. The wedding is being live-streamed to Zahrah's fans worldwide.

The audience rises to its feet. Ronke closes her eyes and prays in Yoruba, Hausa, Igbo, and Ososo, calling on the ancestors to arise, to bless Zahrah and Okorie, to prove to everyone gathered here the transcendence of love.

As we say amen in different languages, we hear the blare of sirens. Everyone looks towards the gate, towards town.

A minute passes. The sound draws closer and closer. Then the gate bursts open. A dozen mobile policemen pour into the compound wielding rifles.

'Get down on your knees. Get down!' they say.

'Lie down.'

'Lie down quick.'

'On your faces.'

'Oya. On your faces.'

'Quick!'

A man tries to run away and a shot is fired in the air. He halts immediately and falls on his face. Children shriek, women wail. One of the policemen yanks the camera off the cameraman and bashes it on the ground. It shatters. My droogs and I lie on our faces asap, the earth rumbling from the boots of the policemen. Everyone is lying on the ground: Zahrah, Fatima, the MC with his mike.

The policemen seize and handcuff Okorie. They jeer at him, call him traitor and terrorist. Zahrah says please and please to them as though they were her gods. 'Please release him, sir. Please. Please, sir. He has done nothing. He has done nothing wrong!' They don't listen to her. It's gruesome hearing Zahrah so helpless, she the boldest woman in the world, the same teacher who ordered Bro Magnus to lash me twelve strokes.

One of the policemen slaps Okorie in the face. Zahrah yelps as though she's the one who was slapped.

'You think you can come and spoil our country for us, eh?' the policeman says. 'You should have remained abroad, you fool. What even brought you here? You're just giving us extra labour.'

'What have I done wrong?' Okorie says.

'Shut your trap, young man. Or we will shut it for you.'

'See how he sounds like an oyinbo.'

Okorie's mother and father cry that the policemen should release their son.

'Shut up, oga. Quiet, madam. Now lie down.'

'Don't you touch my parents.'

'Are you threatening us?'

'We will touch them and what can you do?'

'Take him away.'

They take Okorie out of the gate. The masquerades, the ancient ancestral spirits, do not come to save their host. They are also on their knees, perhaps too huge to lie down on their faces like us.

One of the policemen whistles, asks their officer: 'What about the boys, sir?'

'Why are you asking me about the boys? Can't you remember your orders? Arrest them all.'

They begin dragging men off the ground. They slap one of the drummers who tries to fight, kick his mouth with their boots. A string of blood shoots onto the ground.

Minutes pass, and they cart away a dozen men.

'What about these ones, sir?'

'I said take them all. How else can we know who is who?'

They drag me off the ground. Slap me in the face, on the head, whip my butt with a truncheon. Pull my hands behind my back, fasten the hot metal around them. One with a thick scar on his neck pulls me by the collar towards the gate. I hear Morocca wailing and protesting behind me, hear their boots thudding his body.

15

Andy. Andy. Wake up.
What's up, bro?
It's Mama.
What's up with Mama?
Just get up. Do something.
What should I do?
Anything. Pray. Pray for her.
I don't even know how to pray anymore.
What d'you mean you don't know how to pray?
See, Ydna, I'm in this shitty dark cell.
Yeah, but—
Rats are eating me up, man.
But you should—
They're eating my toes, my fingers, my eyelids! I haven't seen sun in days now. There's poop everywhere around me! And you are telling me to pray?
Do you love Mama?
What?
Do you love her?
Of course I do!
Then you must pray. You have to.
. . .
Andy? Come on.
. . .
Come on, Andy.
Hey, I've committed all these sins.

Just do something. Pray.
I'm tired of praying.
You're tired of praying?
Yeah.
Why?
God isn't out there.
He is.
He isn't.
He is!
He isn't. He's old. Tired. Retired.
. . .
HXVX is now in charge.
Do something, Andy.
. . .
Just say this one prayer.
. . .
Just this prayer for her.
. . .
Come on, Andy!

+

Policemen come with flashlights and drag Slim and me outside.
Sunlight. Like a punch. They toss us on the floor like rags. I
cover my eyes, fireworks exploding all around me, piercing sibilant noises in my ears, my skull. The floor is ice, gnawing on
my bare skin. Each flinch hurts, drills pins into my neck, my
back, my calves. So I curl like a small millipede, like their millipede. They're laughing at us. Hahahaha. They're laughing at me.
Hahahahaha. They think I'm playing dead. They don't know
death is easier.

'See them. Like crayfish,' one says.

'Dem never see anything sef.'

'Mumu children.'

'Idiots.'

I open my eyes. Two policemen are carrying Morocca on a
stretcher across the corridor towards an exit. He isn't whimpering or moving, but he seems to be breathing. He was beaten

248

really bad, and throughout our time in that huge dank emptiness, Slim and I couldn't get him to say anything. He was either groaning or snoring or both.

A policeman marches to us with our clothes and shoes. He flings them at us, tells us to put them on real quick. I look at my hands, my arms, my feet. Scabs and bite marks everywhere. From rats, cockroaches, truncheons.

Has it really been two days? Or three?

Slim and I finish dressing and they drag us to the front counter. On the other side of the grille and netting, Uncle William and Zahrah are sitting on a bench. They rise as soon as they see us. Uncle William is wearing a black cassock and a golden chain cross, and has a purple sash wound round his waist. I scan around for Fatima, but she isn't here. For some reason I've imagined she'd come, imagined her sorrow at seeing me so broken.

The policeman at the counter hands Slim and me each a paper and a pen and tells us to sign. I begin reading the paper, but he spits at me to just sign it. I do. He unlocks the grille door and says we can go.

'You boys should just tank your God for Fada William,' he says. 'If not because of him, we for take all of you to the prison. Una tink say you can come to de capital and burn government building?'

Zahrah hugs us, crying silently, and then Uncle William. He smells so much like Mama that I almost think I'm hugging her.

With his handkerchief he wipes my eyes. He's very kind, Uncle William, Uncle William my Conqueror. Wish he'd been there. And when I think about Fatima, about her absence, my eyes go wet again.

We troop out into the mad sun. My eyes are burning, blood thumping around my temples. Nobody says a word. What is there to say? They know we aren't fine.

Blare of cars and tricycles zooming left and right on the road. Policemen sitting on benches under trees pointing at us. Passers-by stopping and staring at the horns and tails on Slim and me, the horns and tails we've developed since our arrest. The policemen are right. We are crayfish. We are game. I should use it in Ydna's poem. I began composing it yesterday.

We walk to a black Range Rover in the car park. The driver alights, opens the door of the passenger seat for the monsignor, opens the back doors for us. We drive out to the exit, wait for traffic to ease, swerve onto the road.

Uncle William turns to me. 'Andrew, are you hungry?'

I shake my head.

He asks Slim. Slim mutters no thanks.

'Won't you like something to drink, at least?'

We shake our heads.

He sighs.

The road is smooth, and on both sides tall grasses are reclaiming uncompleted buildings and fallen electric poles. Now and then the driver deftly overtakes a hatchback or semi. The wound-up glass and air conditioning keep out the heavy fumes of the semis and the heat and dust.

Uncle William turns around again. 'But, Andrew, you have to eat something. We have a long journey ahead. We need to leave for Kontagora immediately after dropping off Zahrah and your friend.'

'Why?' I say.

'Your mother. She is critically ill and will undergo surgery this afternoon. Elizabeth says she has been asking for you.'

The car begins to smell like dead rats, like a tower of poop, like a tower of dead rat poop. I'm madly nauseous. Things want to pour out of me. I leap towards the window, but I'm late. I douse the car seat and door with slime.

+

We come out of the car. Aunty Lizzy is waiting for us outside the clinic. She says that the surgery will begin in an hour and asks us to follow her to the doctor's office for a briefing.

The sky is black and thick, but there's no rain. The wind swishes past us, sweeping plastic bags and paper into the air, making Uncle William's sash flap left and right, his cape rise and cover his face. A flash of lightning. Another. Both like the Curse on Mama's back. If it rains today it will be the first time since the riot, the first time in eight weeks, an end to the drought in the raining season. Maybe Mama's surgery is all that's needed to appease the skies. A drop of her blood and then a rainstorm.

This is Hamdala Clinic: a cream duplex converted into a medical centre. In the reception: old people in chairs gawking at the plasma screen, a few peering through windows at the clouds. On the corridors: fluorescent lights; nurses in white entering or coming out of doors; sweaty people on benches wincing or frowning or reclining, eyes closed, looking gloomy and helpless. Aunty Lizzy and Elder Paschal brought Mama here after Dr Rapha couldn't diagnose her resurgent pain. Hamdala is the newest and most expensive clinic in town, founded three years ago by Dr Farouk who had studied in Ghana. This is the first medical centre I've visited without that reek of Dettol and Izal and injections. Maybe I'm not smelling them because the clinic is already pungent with Mama, and my senses are starving to see her again, to smell her mustiness, to touch the hollows of her dimples.

Aunty Lizzy stops at a door and turns the handle. The doctor is not in, so we sit and wait.

Aunty Lizzy is greatly changed. The sheen of her blackberry skin is gone, her figure bony and veiny, her gaze so distant as though she can see creatures from other dimensions hovering. She smells like she hasn't had a shower in weeks.

We hear a man and a woman in the corridor begging the rain to please finally come, for they're tired of the heat and hunger, and Allah should forgive us for our transgressions.

A young nurse walks in and says the doctor will be with us soon. She eyes Uncle William a bit, surprised to see someone in such attire here, then hands Aunty Lizzy a paper. 'That's the invoice,' she says. Aunty Lizzy says okay, she'll go to the ATM after speaking to the doctor. The nurse thanks her and leaves.

I wonder where she's getting the money for Mama's treatment – maybe Elder Paschal?

'Thank you, Aunty,' I say to her.

She gives me the distant look. 'For what?'

'For all you've done for Mama.'

Still that distant look. She seems not to hear me. I repeat myself. I begin to feel guilty even though I called her every day since I left (except while in the maggoty police cell!), and she kept saying that Mama was fine, that she was getting better.

'I heard you the first time,' she says, looking at the invoice. 'Don't thank me. Thank your uncle. He's been the one taking care of your mother.'

He smiles a little and looks away, scratching the hair behind his neck.

I tell him thank you. Thank you, Uncle. He simply nods, paragon of modesty.

I really like Uncle William the Conqueror. He's so well read. We spent most of our journey talking about the big questions: Why there's something rather than nothing. Why there are these laws of physics and not other laws – for example, why the speed of light is 3×10^8 ms^{-1} and the Avogadro constant is 6.022×10^{23} mol^{-1}. We even talked about Hilbert's paradox of the infinite hotel and the Fermi paradox. It's amazing that, all through our chat, he didn't mention God or employ any theological explanation. He's also very cool. For example, he knows who Taylor Swift is and is a fan of Lady Gaga. Imagine! He claimed Gaga is the most creative and talented music artist currently working. I wanted to disagree with him, but I didn't because he's just so cool. And minutes before we arrived in Kontagora, I asked him about *The Sorrows of Young Werther*, since it stood out on his shelf of philosophy and theology texts. 'Oh,' he laughed. 'A friend in Germany gave it to me while I was there studying for my doctorate.' I almost died of envy! He's so fucking cool: he's lived where Beethoven and Einstein and Martin Luther come from, the country that produced Kafka's language! He said *Werther* is an epistolary novel about unrequited love: a painter pining for a woman who is already betrothed to a powerful upper-class man, and when he fails to convince her to marry him, he shoots himself. Uncle William says it's a good book, that although he thinks *Buddenbrooks* is the best German novel, he keeps returning to *Werther*. He's in fact written a theological article about

Werther, and the article is one of his favourites among all his published theological research.

A fly is playing around Aunty Lizzy's face as though testing her patience. She doesn't do anything, just stares. Outside, the wind is howling louder, trees screeching in agony, but there's still no drop.

The doctor walks in. Uncle William and I rise to greet him. Aunty Lizzy is still sitting, staring at nothing.

Uncle William shakes the doctor's hand and says he's Mama's twin.

'It's a pleasure to meet you, sir,' the doctor says. He turns to me. 'You must be the son.'

'Yes, sir,' I say. 'My name is Andrew.'

'Good to meet you, Andrew.'

He peers at me through his glasses. He looks too thin for a doctor.

We sit, and he sips tea from a small black flask, clears his throat.

'Yes,' he says, 'we have done many tests. We think we know what the problem is. But there are many other things we don't know. They are all in Allah's hands.'

He says that his team found a pair of surgical needles buried in Mama's spine. That they appear to have lacerated and infected her dura and other tissues. This was from her last surgery, but now and then these things happen, objects forgotten inside patients. Mama appears to be bleeding internally, having blood clots in the region, and it's a miracle she's still alive. He tells us to pray, that he's one of those doctors who practises medicine with spirituality, and Mama's case is very complicated.

'In her case,' he says, 'I would say that there is only a fifty per cent chance that this operation will be successful. It is that complicated, I'm afraid.'

Aunty Lizzy gets up, face in her hands. She walks out of the room, butts her head against the doorframe. She doesn't groan or look back.

Uncle William sighs deeply. 'Doctor, in the name of God, please do your very best.'

'Yes. That is exactly our intention.'

I want to cry.

I want to cry.

I want to cry.

But I can't.

+

Uncle William and I rise, and the doctor rings his bell and tells a nurse to take us to Mama. We follow the nurse into a wide room with my mama lying on the bed on her side. Her eyes are closed, her hand connected to a drip. She's sweating, but there seems to be a little smile on her face. As I approach her I notice that Uncle William has remained by the door.

I dig out my white handkerchief from my pocket and dab her face.

I feel better. She looks cleaner. Fresher. Younger. She likes it when I say she looks young. She'll smile, so broadly, dimples and all, and she'll indeed look young. Now her smile is clearer, free from the stain and weight of sweat.

She opens her eyes. 'Andrew mè.'

I die.

'Mama,' I say.

'Andrew mè.'

Things shatter in me.

'Mama.'

'Andrew mè.'

'How are you, Mama?'

'How are you, Andrew mè?'

I place my hand on her shoulder. It's slippery. But she likes it. She breathes deeper. My palm soaks up her sweat, transfers it to me. I have flashes of her and me moulding sandcastles after rainfalls, her dimples sucking me in.

She doesn't look too bad for somebody who's about to undergo surgery. Unlike Aunty Lizzy, she doesn't seem to have lost any weight. Just the tiredness in her eyes, the tiredness of Everything.

She opens her eyes wider. 'Who's at the door?'

She tries to raise her neck, to sit up, but can't. She winces.

'Andrew mè, am I not talking to you?'

I turn to look at him, back at her. They have so much in common: their chins, their lips, their eyes. It's almost funny.

'It's Uncle William,' I say.

'No, it's not,' she says.

'Yes, it is.'

She raises her neck, squinting, wincing. Sees him.

She screams.

Loud.

'Get out of here,' she says in Ososo. 'Get out.'

A nurse runs into the room. 'What is it?'

'Get out!'

'Leave.'

'Ki vèrà!'

'Ma choro mi minẹ!'

'What is it?' the nurse pleads with Mama.

Uncle William leaves the room. She calms immediately, lying back on her pillow, looking spent.

'Why is she shouting?' the nurse asks me.

I don't say anything. The nurse stares at each of us a moment, then walks out.

'Tell me the truth,' Mama says. 'Was it Elizabeth who told you about him?'

'È, Mama.'

She gnashes her teeth. 'That girl . . . That girl . . .'

If she could use her legs she'd have kicked away the linen trapping her, raced outside, and fought Aunty Lizzy for betraying her.

She asks me about Zahrah's wedding. I tell her that it didn't actually happen, that the mobile police arrested Okorie. I don't tell her about my arrest or my time in the dank cell.

'This country . . .' she says.

I draw up a chair. Hold her hand. Smell her mustiness.

'Have you been praying for me?' she says.

I want to lie. I want to say I've been praying every second for you, Mama. But I can't, with her spread out before me like a baby and all. I look at the clock on the opposite wall – it's 2:43.

'So you've not been praying for me, Andrew mè? Why?'

I stare at the terrazzo floor. I want to melt into it, to become that ant meandering around my foot.

'Why?'

'I'm sorry, Mama.'

'You're sorry?'

Silence.

'So what are your plans, then?' she says.

'What?'

'Your plans.'

'I don't understand.'

'Andrew mè, I am not a coward. I am not lying to myself. I know this is it. This is how far I'll come.'

'No, Mama. No.'

'Why are you shouting?'

'Everything will be fine, Mama.'

'Stop shouting.'

'You'll get better. Get back on your feet. All this will pass.'

'I said stop shouting. Just shut up.'

Silence, full of unuttered screams. Outside, the trees scream for us, branches gyrating. The branch of a son tree reaches towards its mother tree. The mother flings him away.

+

Minutes later Aunty Lizzy plods into the room. Mama opens her eyes, asks her to call William. Okay, Aunty Lizzy says. She tells me she's about to go to the bank, that I should take care of Mama while she's away. I sit up straight, nod. She leaves.

When Uncle William walks in, his eyes are on the floor. He looks so emasculated, my tall huge cool Uncle William the Conqueror. I wish I could take his hand. Catenate it with hers. Become their superhero. Flatten whatever's between them. But as usual I am weak. A sack of flesh. I only become a superhero when blonde strands are involved, when it comes to spitting on this land.

For a long minute nobody says a word.

Then Uncle William falls on his knees. He leans forward till his forehead is on the floor. He remains like that for a long time, as though he's performing some solemn function in church.

Mama doesn't flinch. In fact, she seems irritated by his gesture, as if it's a trick she's seen him pull off countless times.

Outside, webs of lightning. The mother tree flings her son away again. And now she flings away her brother, her twin.

'Andrew mè,' Mama says, 'whatever somebody does to you, you must forgive them. Even if they take your very life, you must forgive. This is what the Lord teaches us. But look at me. I am not like anybody. My life has never been like anybody's. Each moment has been like drowning. Don't think I am wicked. But I will never be able to forgive him. He can do whatever he wants, even wear a mountain around his neck, and I still won't forgive him. I can't.'

He raises his head, still on his knees. They stare at each other.

'I just have one favour to ask,' she says. 'I don't even know if it's a favour. It's simple. Take care of Andrew for me.'

'I will,' he says. 'We will, you and I, by the grace of God.'

He rises and starts towards the door.

'I've always wanted to ask you something,' she says to him. 'How is Luisa? How old is she now?'

He freezes. 'She died six years ago.'

'Oh. I'm sorry,' she says.

He doesn't respond. He leaves the room, shutting the door silently.

She closes her eyes. Scratches the skin around the needle.

'Who is Luisa?' I say.

She winces. I ask if she's okay, realising the folly of my question. Of course, I know she won't answer me. She'll change the topic as usual.

'Luisa is his daughter. Was his daughter. He had her while studying in Germany.'

'Seriously? I thought he was a priest then.'

'He was, yes.'

'Really?'

'She was really beautiful. Had long, wavy hair.'
'Golden hair? Was it golden?'
'Yes. Why? Why do you ask?'

+

Three nurses in green come for Mama. They remove the drip needle from her and place her on a wheeled stretcher. Although there's nothing to clean, I take out my handkerchief and dab her face again. Dab, dab. What is that in your pocket, she says. Oh, it's nothing, I say. It's my phone. She wants to say more but doesn't. They take her away. As I return the handkerchief into my pocket, I realise that some platinum strands are peeking out: my thin shiny rippling lies.

+

I go outside the clinic. It's dark and cloudy and windy, but there's still no rain. Across the road there's a kiosk lighted by LED lamps, a man behind the counter. It's been four hours since Mama went into surgery. There's no official news yet, but all seems to be fine. The nurses who came out of the theatre said all's going as planned.

My stomach growls. I cross the dirt road to the kiosk, buy a digestive and a Coke. I turn to go, but the shopkeeper says I've forgotten my change. 'Na gode,' I say to him and pocket the money. A piece of paper blown by the wind slaps me in the face. The wind makes weird noises, sounding like an old woman this moment, like a baby the next.

I tear the wrapper, push the digestive into my mouth. It's like sandpaper. I chew a little but completely lose my appetite. I pop open the can of Coke – some sugar might tempt my tongue to stop being silly. I take a gulp. No change. Now I feel like throwing up.

A blinding flash of lightning. Another. A bomb of thunder.

I still can't believe what Mama said about Uncle William. I pace about, trying to sketch each variable of the equation. But surrounding me are a crowd of thoughts. Each peeping at me. Looking away when I turn to them.

My phone rings. It's a videocall from Eileen. Perfect timing.

'Hey, Eileen,' I say, raising the phone to my face, putting on my headphones.

She's looking pretty, as always. Marble skin, flaring meadows, platinum in a neat bun. She's sitting on her bed, a pillow propped up behind her.

'Hiya, Andy!'

'Great to see you, cariad.'

'Did you just speak some Welsh?'

'Yes!'

'Sounds great. Anyway, I've been trying to reach you for days now. I've sent you like twenty messages without getting any response.'

'I'm so sorry. Things have been mad.'

'Where are you? I can't see you clearly. It's fine, though. Is that thunder?'

'Yes, yes.'

I tell her that I'm outside a clinic, that Mama is in surgery, but all seems to be well.

'Wow, so sorry to hear that. Hope it continues to go well.'

'Yes. Hope so too. Thanks.'

Another bomb of thunder.

'You won't believe it, Eileen. But things have been so crazy these past days.'

'What things?'

'D'you know that the police crashed into Zahrah's wedding? Arrested her fiancé? Arrested me and my friends?'

'What? What?'

I add that I spent three whole nights in a shitty dark cell and was given scraps to eat. She keeps asking me to repeat myself, unable to believe my sci-fi.

'I'm so sad to hear about that, Andy. God, I hate that such stuff happens here. Why – why do you think they happen here?'

'Don't know. Don't know at all, Eiqueen.'

'Did you just say "Eiqueen"?'

'Yeah.'

She laughs. 'Very funny. Really cool. Anyway, I'm so glad we're getting to catch up.'

'Yeah, glad too.'

'Great.'

'I really miss you, Eiqueen.'

'Really?'

'Been unable to get you out of my head.'

'Wow. Do you know what?'

'What?'

'Hmm. Forget it.'

'Tell me, Eileen.'

'I'm . . .'

'Feel free. I don't scare you, right?'

She laughs.

'Okay. Alright. Do you know that I dreamt of you last night?'

'Really?' I can't believe her.

'Yes. Sort of.'

'Are you sure?'

'Oh yeah, I'm sure.'

But why the reluctance to say she dreamt of me? And why the 'sort of'? I try to picture her dreaming of me. Each step. Her head on the pillow, her eyes closed, her dreamscape. Still it's unreal, more sci-fi than my arrest. A girl like her isn't supposed to dream of a guy like me.

'You said you miss me. I hope to see you before I leave Niger, then.'

'Yes, Eileen. I miss you more than everything.'

Instantly I feel ashamed, wish I could revise my statement. How could I say such a thing while my mama lies on a table being torn with forceps? As if the skies heard my betrayal, they finally release the rain.

they
    pour
from
    the
sky

needles

each sent
to impale me

'Do you know what, Eileen,' I say, trying to seek some cover, moving backwards to the side of the kiosk. 'Do you know that I've been smelling your skin over and over?'

'Really?'

'Yeah. Your smell wakes me up every day.'

And again I smell her. In the rain. In the dust mixed with rain.

'Wow,' she says. 'What's it like? My smell?'

'Like dates. Like almonds.'

The rain is spurting heavier and heavier, crystal needles seeking the thirsty fabric they've shunned for so long.

A figure comes out to the porch of the clinic. It's Uncle William. He's looking left and right into the rain. He sees me beside the kiosk. Waves at me. His hand says come. Come, Andy. Is that a smile on his face?

'Wow,' Eileen says. 'I'm speechless.'

'Excuse me, Eileen. I'll call you shortly.'

'Alright, then.'

I end the call, pocket my phone and headphones. Come out to the rain. Cross the road to Uncle William.

'Ehe'o, Uncle,' I say in greeting.

He moves closer to me, expressionless. Hugs me. Strange. Hugs me ever so tightly. He's whispering. Saying something. Something he should never dare say.

'Andrew. Andrew. I am so sorry. So sorry.'

'So sorry for what?'

'So, so sorry.'

'For what, Uncle? Tell me. Tell me, Uncle.'

'Your mother. She is gone.'

His body is trembling. Like the flash of lightning above.

'Andrew? Andrew? Did you hear me? Do you want to sit? Do you want to sit down? Should I get you something?'

'Andrew? You want to see her?'

'Why don't you sit down?'

'She is in the ward. She is right there.'

I push him away. Run into the clinic. A woman is screeching on the floor. She's kicking about her feet, hitting nothing. Flailing about her arms, grappling nothing. Tearing at her hair, her eyes. Men and women are gathered around her. Not touching her, not helping her. As I approach, I see that she's Aunty Lizzy.

I run into the room. A human figure is lying on the bed. White linen covering it from head to toe. A toe peeking out. Her toe, my toe.

I pull down the linen.

It is you, my mama.

Your dimples gone.

Forever.

'She's sleeping,' I say. 'She's only sleeping.'

I shake her shoulder. 'Mama. Mama. Wake up.'

She doesn't hear me.

I slap her shoulder. Raise her arm. Leave it. But it falls back.

With my fingers, I pry open her mouth, her eyes. She doesn't close them back.

I shake her neck. Shake her so hard. Shake her so very hard.

And she awakens. She tells me to leave her alone. To close back up her mouth and eyes. To cover her entire body with the linen. To tuck her toes in too.

People in the neighbourhood are laughing screaming bleating braying. To the skies. To Allah. For the rain.

16

The 5 battles and sorrows of ydna

(i)

You watch your mother being washed.
They scrub her nostrils.
Behind her ear.
Her collarbones.
Her chest.
Her black breasts.

The soap suds.
Each a breath.
None wakes her.

(ii)

In the backyard at Grandma's, two men are digging.
You've never seen them before.
Their sweat rain on the fresh scenting earth.
They keep going deeper, deeper.
Deeper. Deeper. Deeper.
You tell them, Stop. Stop!
They keep going deeper, deeper.
Deeper. Deeper. Deeper.

It is time.
The two men jump into the hole.
It swallows them.
Two other men hoist the box onto them.
Stop, you say. Open it up. I need to see her one last time.
They don't hear you.
Are you deaf, you say. I need to see her one last time.
And then you realise you've just said
'last'.

It is time.
They're all waiting for you to throw your sand.
Go on, they say.
You fear that if you throw you'll miss.
Go on, they say. Throw it. You won't miss.
If you do, she'll understand.
She'll know you're not yet a man.
You throw. You—

(iii)

In the evening Uncle William comes into the room.
'I have something to tell you,' he says.
'What?' you say.
'I hope you can forgive me.'
'About what?'

And then he tells you the four words.

You leap onto him.
You slap his face.
You punch his jaw, his chest.
You tear the buttons off his shirt.

He falls on his knees. Forehead on the floor. Asks you to
forgive him.

You want to puncture his big eyes with your fingers.
You want to peel off his black skin with your nails.
You want to tear out his heart and bite it a million times.

'I am your father. I am your father.'

Those four words. Carrying infinity along their axis.
Those four words. Despite their planetary size, that can only
be uttered in a whisper.

(iv)

and this is how ydna's firesword is made
he flies on the great black bird zephyra to null island
circles seven times for seven nights
and the old gods emerge from the wind
adikoriko, amadioha, anansi, and ala
ogun and osun and osai and odun
and the new gods too
mansa musa, haile selassie, jaja of opobo, ken saro-wiwa
and ydna cries unto them
now or never, now or never, i'll
not leave until it's now
and saro-wiwa hands him the blade
and musa turns it to gold
and amadioha turns the sky crystal
        and a flame plants on the sword
        and its beauty blinds eyes
and adikoriko and anansi and ala
and ogun and osai and odun
and selassie and opobo
        blow winds from their mouths
        and the flame becomes a million fires
and osun says unto ydna
we have thus given you all you asked
now you must hurry hence
now you must not slumber
now you must pluck us victory
and ydna spins round the sky in fires
and he sets fast for kilimanjaro
to battle god hxvx

(v)

ydna spins round kilimanjaro
seventy-seven times
crying to the skies
hxvx, hxvx
you owe me battle
bring your planetary self here
i summon you with the firesword
of the gods, with their breaths
and blood, their sighs
and sweat

and for
seventy-seven times
hxvx does not come

V: The Crucifixion

Theorem: The composition of an odd and an even permutation is odd.

17

Nine days now.
And Everything is complete.

the sand
complete

my eyes
complete

It is funny. This mound of sand. How can a full human lie underneath? Let alone you?

I'm standing beside her sand. It's full of her dimples. See them. Everywhere. In a few weeks Grandma and Mama's siblings will level and cement the mound. For now they prefer to see her raw in the backyard. It meets those cravings the photos of her cannot satisfy.

They hung one at the entrance of Great-Grandpa's two-storey house, and stood a large one on the floor of the living room. They wanted to put her there, but it was already full of people. They asked me where I would prefer, the frontyard or backyard, even though both places were already getting full. I told them to put her beside Ydna. Who is Ydna? they said. Oh, I said, he's my older brother, the one who left before I came. Oh, you mean The Unnamed, the one in the backyard? We call him The Unnamed here. We didn't want a name for him because we wanted your mother to move on, but she didn't listen. She said it was the first one that came out of her without pouring out as blood. That it was somebody, that it was hers. How could you say it shouldn't have a name? So we decided to call him The Unnamed.

I'm standing beside your sand, you The Unnamed, my Unnamed, my Ydna. Surprisingly, you're really small. You're just a tiny block of cement beside our Mama. You should have remained longer to become as big as her.

There's a picture frame of Mama on the backyard wall. She's younger there, flashing deep dimples and the gap between her teeth. She took it on the day she bought me the bike, a year before I began to watch superhero movies, a year before Ydna left.

I return to Ydna, to *The Unnamed* written in the cement, to the year below it. Just one year, when everyone has two. Since Mama left I've been screaming and screaming his name, but it's just silence on the other end. No matter how hard I try, I no longer feel his concentric presence around me or his breath rippling under my skin. It's just blank. As though he's been surviving on her blood and not mine. As though he and I aren't One and the Same.

Grandma comes out of the house. She's wearing a black wrapper, her neck and upper chest bare. For nine days now, since Mama was placed here, we've all been wearing black. Because of Grandma's similarities with Mama – skin tone, voice, musty smell – my senses always delude me that she's her. I've even called her Mama a few times, for example late last night when she came to my room with a kerosene lantern saying I was shouting in my sleep. She checked my tongue, said it was bleeding. We went downstairs and she gave me some water to rinse my mouth and some herbs to chew. Just before she came, I was eating eba and egusi with Mama and Ydna. We were laughing, and Mama was boasting to us that she could outrun us, especially me who runs like a duck. Ydna laughed at me real silly and then toppled his bowl of soup.

Grandma is not with her walking stick. There's a phone in her hand instead. The slap sounds of her flip-flops are too loud, like a bell clanging in my ears. These days everything is too loud, too bright, too blurred.

'Andrew,' she says.

I don't respond.

'Your uncle is on the phone. He wants to talk to you. Uncle William.'

I don't budge.

She repeats herself. Her voice is a lighter version of Mama's.

'No,' I say. 'No. I don't want to talk to him.'

'Please.'

'No.'

'Please, Andrew mè.'

'No.'

She ends the call, plods to me. She raises her hand to my face, wipes my eyes. Have I been crying?

She joins me in staring at Mama. At Ydna.

'Andrew,' she says.

'È, nyo?'

'I know that it's hard. That it's the hardest thing in the world for you now. But you have to try. You have to try to forgive him.'

I'm silent.

'You have to accept him.'

'Whatever you feel about him does not change who he is to you. It does not change who he truly is. He is a good person. Mistakes happen. The world is like this because of mistakes.'

A black ant is clambering on Mama. I want to kill it, tear it to pieces, burn it.

'Andrew. Why don't you go out? Please go out. Visit the Tourist Centre. Do something with your friends. You think your mother would like you doing this, standing by her grave all the time? Maybe it's time we cover it with cement. Please, let her rest. Leave her be. She's earned it.'

She hurries back to the house. This is like the tenth time she's given me this lecture.

Three black ants are now meandering on Mama. Maybe they mean well. Maybe they want to carry a message from me to her. Maybe she's talking to me through them. But what's she saying?

After all these years of Mama sealing her secret in her chest, it's now become semi-public. Grandma and Aunty Lizzy and

Uncle Odafe know. Even Zahrah knows. Knows that Uncle William is the devil himself.

That evening, he begged me to forgive him, said he loved me, that he wanted to be a part of my life. That it was all a mistake, a huge good mistake. I didn't know what he wanted me to forgive him for. For the eternal shame and Curse he's cast on me? For never being there? I didn't know what to do. I just wanted to kill him right there as he grovelled on his knees. I wanted to report him to the nuncio and archbishops before they ordained him a bishop in Sokoto. At the same time I wanted to hug him, to rest my head on his chest, to kiss his cheek. In the end I picked up my phone and went out of the house into the chill dark night. I listened to the chirping of the insects. Their voices often convey Mama's Whispers, relaying words she never got to say. He left Ososo the next day, and since then I've not seen him. How could life make your greatest desire completely useless on attainment?

Yes, Uncle William the Conqueror is the devil, the agent of the Curse, of HXVX. He goes to Mama in the guise of the cure, promising to save her from her abusive husbands, to help her start afresh. Instead, like Fatima's father, he causes the Curse, aggravates it, with his hands, his accursed dick. Like Father McMahon, he puts on his vestment and his smile, but turns us against each other, causing riots, Mama's injury and her wheelchair and her mound of sand and her Curse. He permutes me in Mama's womb, makes me Andy instead of Ydna, plants in me the desire for blondes, the burden of the Curse. (Hint: *Curse* − *s* = *Cure*.)

+

Zahrah comes into the backyard, sees me standing beside Mama. She's in a red top and black skirt. Her hair is tied in a bun. There's no streak of red in it.

'Hi, Andy,' she says. Nowadays she doesn't add 'Africa'.

'Aunty Zahrah,' I say.

She takes my hand, drags me from Mama, past other cement graves, to a rock amidst a banana and papaya tree. We sit. She brings out a chocolate bar from her purse. Breaks it in two, hands me the bigger half.

'No, thank you,' I say.

'I insist,' she says.

I take it. Roll and roll it in my hand. In Kontagora it would've become sticky because of the heat. But Ososo is much cooler, the sun less vile, because of the hills and rocks on which the town stands.

She takes a bite of her half. I catch the shine of a wedding ring.

'So, Andy, how are you doing?'

'Fine. I'm doing fine.'

On a tall rock in the next compound, a dwarf goat with an A-yoke round its neck gazes at us, regurgitating food. Ososo goats are super climbers; they can even scale Everest, I'm sure. The goat gazes round the neighbourhood, looking for something. What's it looking for? What does it think it knows? It bleats and climbs down the rock.

'Have you been up to anything lately?' Zahrah says.

'No. Not really.'

'So you're not writing or anything?'

'Just something little, I guess.'

'Tell me about it.'

'It's a poem.'

'About what?'

'The final battle.'

She looks intently at me. 'What final battle?'

I give her the unfailing poet mantra: 'Too soon to talk about, I guess.'

Again I remember Ydna. Again I remember Uncle William, Daddy William. I'll never be able to understand what Mama went through for me. Every night she must have gone to sleep thinking she'd forgotten about it, that she was free from her twin. But in the morning, the moment she saw me, she'd relive it all – his hands on her body, their grip, his motions as he cursed her. Like snakes, they'd all reawaken, hissing and coiling and piercing.

For I was the proof of his existence; my face was his face, my smile his smile, the smile he wore throughout the cursing. Each day must have been a drowning. I sunk her deeper each time I complained about her cooking, each time I asked her about my papa. She had four husbands, and none could give her a child. But it was when he, priest and devil and twin, took advantage of her that she finally had me.

Zahrah looks at me and sighs. 'Andy, you can't spend every minute here with your mother. You've got a huge interesting life ahead of you.'

I don't say anything.

'I understand a bit about how you feel. I really do.'

No, you don't. No, you don't, Aunty Zahrah.

'It was exactly what drove me to the Sahara three years ago. It was loss. Loss of what I loved beyond everything, loss of what came out of me. It was all I could do not to hurt myself. My other self – my Ydna – saved me. She sent me to the desert to find me. Seriously, Andy, you'll be fine. You are very strong for your age. Quite strong, even stronger than me. I believe in you.'

But my Ydna has abandoned me. Or am I the one who abandoned him?

Maybe she's right, maybe it's through Anifuturism that HXVX can be defeated. But how? I'm sure Zahrah herself doesn't know. If she did, HXVX would be past tense.

'Thank you,' I say.

'Oh, don't thank me.'

Grandma walks into the yard, this time with her stick. She scans around. Sees what she's looking for, a tomato plant growing under an orange tree. She peers at it. Plucks a red fruit. Walks back to the house.

'You're wearing a wedding ring,' I say.

'Yes. Are you just noticing it?'

'Yes.'

'Really? You've seen it several times, Andy. I've had it on for ten days now. Okorie and I had a small ceremony in prison, just before I came.'

I force a smile. 'That's really great. Congrats.'

'Thank you.'

The government has still not released Okorie. They claim he masterminded the protests and vandalism in Abuja with support from covert operations in Europe to unseat the current president. That he taught students how to make flamethrowers and rifles and high explosives. They froze all his accounts, including his British one, and seized all his cars. They're also trying to seize his house, and Zahrah and his lawyer have been fighting to retain it. The government keeps postponing his appearance in court, claiming it's for security reasons.

'I'm really happy for you both,' I say.

'Oh, thank you, Andy Africa,' she says, nudging me.

I smile. I don't know why, but for the first time I'm not irritated by that name.

'So how's your white girlfriend Eileen?'

In the next compound the goat is back on the rock. Beside it Mama and Ydna are holding hands, watching me.

'She's fine,' I say.

'To be honest, Andy, I'm still amazed. Seriously.'

I don't say anything. I know what's coming.

'Why her, Andy? You of all people? I can't understand it. Why not Fatee?'

I look at the ground, pick a fallen papaya leaf, plant it into the dark earth. It falls to the ground again.

'Perhaps the continent is a simulation after all, as you claim,' she says. 'That way, everything makes sense, right?

'Anyway, I've come to talk about Monsignor William. Elizabeth tells me that you're considering reporting him to his archbishop and stopping his ordination.'

She peers into my face.

'I'm not here to tell you to reconsider or not. Just to tell you to accept who you are. Your luck. Your destiny.'

Fatima comes out to the yard in a white abaya. She walks towards us, pretty feet in sandals. She comes to me. 'Hi, Andy. Mind if I join you?'

'Not at all,' I say.

For the past nine days we've been mostly so-so friends, exchanging small talk about the rocks and hills and woods of

Ososo, how they're different from the savannah of Kontagora. Still, I'm so grateful she's here.

+

Late afternoon, my droogs show up and drag me out of the house. Some air, they say. Some sights. 'Ososo is so dope, Werdna,' Slim says. 'Yeah,' Morocca says, 'it's a natural amusement park, innit?'

For a moment I stop and look back at the house. Great-Grandpa's legendary two-storey house, teeming with graves. It's surrounded by other buildings like it, tall grey perfect cuboids with rusty roofs. Their grey plaster masks red clay and straw and stones and rows of okpakpa wood, a few of which protrude out of the walls. The buildings are strangely beautiful, their form perfect, their materials ingenious. They look like the crafts of an ancient and futuristic civilisation – excellent demos of Anifuturism. Hey, why am I sounding like Zahrah?

Rocks and hills of various sizes and shapes are sprinkled around the neighbourhood and in the distance: Granitic boulders mounted on each other like dinosaurs playing games. Twenty-storey slabs with noses pointed skyward like starships at take-off. Domed hills with smooth, striped sides like habitats of stranded extraterrestrials. Amidst these are groves of palm and banana and papaya trees. Every corner you turn, it's green against grey.

Aunty Lizzy comes to her upstairs window. She sees me. Waves. I wave back.

'Ososo is seriously dope, man,' Slim says again. 'There's like magic everywhere.'

'*Lord of the Rings*?' Morocca says.

'*Lord of the Rings* times ten.'

'Thanks, Scads,' I say.

'Yeah. It's dope as fuck,' Morocca says.

I shoot him a look, wanting to spank his flat butt for the f-word. No effing in my hometown, please. He's wearing a durag and still has a plaster on his neck.

'Let's bounce.'

'Where are we going?'

'The Tourist Centre?'

'Very cool,' Morocca says. 'Patience and Fatee went there with Zahrah. They were raving like giraffes afterwards.'

'Calm down, Sand Lord,' Slim says. 'You lie too much, you coal-skinned nigga. Do giraffes even rave?'

'That's not the point, blockhead. It's a metaphor.'

'I know a metaphor when I see one, bush.'

'Shut up, skinny-ass. I'm the blacksmith of metaphors.'

We laugh.

'Wait a minute, Scads,' I say. 'I haven't seen Patience in a while.'

'Oh,' Morocca says, 'why're you asking about her? We told you last time you asked – wasn't it yesterday? – that she's gone east to see her folks.'

'Really?'

'Hell, she even told ya herself. A day before she left.'

'Oh. Guess I wasn't listening . . .'

They stare at me a bit to verify that my two ears are intact. They know I never forget stuff. I've been racing alone in a world without a sun. For the first time I see the skies and trees outside it.

We bounce on in silence. Up a road leading to the market. Past women with basins on their heads laden with vegetables and cassava and yellow garri. Motorbikes with double silencers booming as they navigate hills. Bearded goats with dwarf legs and wooden A-yokes around their necks. Drinking joints with MTN umbrellas and plastic chairs and makossa shrieking from speakers, guys chilling, legs crossed, girls twerking like Nicki Minaj.

We pause at a roundabout to look at the statues of two naked girls. Their breasts are like ice cream cones. Strings of beads adorn their necks, their skin red with camwood. Aunty Lizzy calls them oviko, says they represent a coming-of-age ritual all Ososo girls must partake in during their early teens. The story is that, hundreds of years ago, a powerful witch cursed Ososo women with infertility, and now girls must undergo this cleansing lest they become childless wives. In the past week I've seen a dozen oviko girls. They wear wrappers and beads and camwood and sit on low stools all day in front of their houses, clutching walking sticks. They do no chores and are given hearty meals and treated like queens. Family and friends give them gifts of cash or shoes or expensive wrappers. Many of the girls are quite shy and don't like you staring at them. After a week they clean up and become Homo sapiens again, having gained a kg or two. What's funny is that, even though Aunty Lizzy's church considers this a heathen practice, she herself doesn't. Maybe because the stakes are quite high – lifelong infertility? I wonder: if I were a girl, would Mama have brought me to Ososo to do this, or doomed me to eternal infertility in the North?

We scale rocks and small hills, cross a dirt road, and reach the concrete steps. They spiral round monster boulders and lead to the Tourist Centre. It was built decades ago by colonial peeps as a getaway from the sun and dust and madness. We begin the long climb, glancing left and right at the large igneous beauties perfectly sculpted and stacked as though by some alien life form. We peek at the grasses, at the little lives crawling or flying around them.

'What's up with these steps?' Slim says. 'Will they never end?'

'Keep walking, lazy puppy,' Morocca says. 'When it comes to playing with ya pencil dick, ya never want it to end.'

We climb for another minute and reach the top, a plateau from which we can see the brilliant grey and green of Ososo. And far far in the distance, pieces of silver are shining in the sun. They are the roofs of distant towns – perhaps Makeke, perhaps Okene – surrounded by a shifting green. We stand gazing for a while.

'Fuck,' we say simultaneously.

'Fuck,' Morocca says.

'We fucking need to build three tents here, man,' Slim says. 'One for you, one for me, one for millipede-dick Morocca.'

I smile. 'Yeah.'

Suddenly Morocca begins to jump up and down and scream.

'Hey, you nigs in Okene! Can you hear me? I'm Morocca the Sand Lord!'

'Are you mad?'

'Has a nut gone loose in your head?'

Two girls are laughing behind us. They're about our age, in leggings and denim jackets, eating ice cream. They're laughing at Morocca. He gives them the red eye. They don't stop.

'Why are you trying to sound like an American, eh?' the taller one says.

'Because you don't sound like one,' the other one says. 'Trust me.'

'Go to hell and mind your fucking business, bitches,' Morocca says.

They freeze, their ice cream hanging in their throats. They mutter something under their breaths and walk back to the bungalow of the centre. They join a dozen or so young peeps drinking beer or Maltina, balling in plastic chairs. My droogs and I dig out our phones and take selfies and shots of the horror-shock views of palms and fruit trees and rocks. We take shots of the Oruku, the tallest monolith in Ososo, and several selfies with it in the background.

We walk to the centre, part the bead curtains, enter the bar. P-Square booms from speakers; nude statuettes line the walls. At the counter we buy fried chicken and drinks: Slim a Guinness, Morocca a Heineken, I a Schweppes. I take out my wallet and pay. Since winning the contest, I've got several times more cash than my droogs have combined. We go outside and sit in plastic chairs and cross our legs and eat our marinated fried chicken and sip our icy drinks. Mmmm, we say. Girls eye us, especially the twosome who laughed at Morocca. Flashes of Mama and Ydna peer at me. I try not to peer back.

Morocca says he wishes he'd been kinder to the girls. If he'd been, he'd have gotten their numbers and tonight would've tasted some moist Ososo pussy. I shoot him a look. He laughs. 'You're so protective of your girls, right?' he says.

'Right,' I say.

'So, Andy, what's up with Eileen?' Slim says.

'She's alright.'

'Cool.'

'She's leaving Niger with her parents very soon. They're leaving this shithole for good.'

'Sad.'

'Yeah.'

'We plan to meet before she goes, though.'

'So she's coming back here? To Naija?'

'No.'

'You're going to Niger to meet her?' Morocca says.

'Yeah, man.'

'Can we go with you? It would be so cool to see the desert.'

'Of course you can come.'

'When are you leaving?'

'Next week. Monday or so. First I'll need to stop in Sokoto to see Mama's twin. I don't even know why I want to see him, but still I want to. He's been appointed as the new bishop of Sokoto. He'll be ordained there next Tuesday. Sokoto is close to Niamey where Eileen is. So it should be easy.'

'Perfect.'

'Great plan.'

Once again Mama and Ydna peer at me. I try and try not to peer back. I blink away their expressionless faces.

Even though I've been surrounded by people since Mama left, I've felt a strange dismemberment, like a trunk without branches or leaves. And Everything has become clear: I don't belong here. Not in Ososo, and definitely not in Kontagora, a town which has become a dump. There was a huge riot on the night Mama left. Several people from our church were killed, including Mai Gemu and Oga Oliver. In fact, our school and one of Morocca's father's mattress stores were looted and burnt. A mob beat Slim's ex Wisdom for being 'possessed', for being a 'lover of boys'. Doctors are still patching him up in hospital. Yesterday Slim told us he was afraid of returning home lest he's treated like Wisdom. I realise that, for several days now, I've been so submerged in Mama that I've failed to confront the recent Sorrows of my droogs.

We watch Morocca's girls bring out their phones, take selfies with duck faces, take shots of the trees and hills and the towns in the distance.

Suddenly I feel incredibly sad.

I tell my droogs that everything here is simply a façade: the rocks, the hills, the magical green. It's all a mask, an obstruction of what this land truly is, of what it's become: a place of prayer where we must ask the skies for food and electricity and good roads and functioning hospitals, where Mama dies of the needles in her back.

'Even if we say Ososo is an oasis because it looks cool, it's still not worth living in the desert for,' I say. 'And it ain't no oasis, bro. Don't let all this stuff deceive you. It still suffers from the same Curse the entire shithole suffers from.'

For a sec I ramble on about the riots in KNT, the robbers on our way to Abuja, the protests, Zahrah's ruined wedding, our time in the dank cell. I remind Morocca about his father's razed store and Slim about his incapacitated ex Wisdom. I go on and on, dabbing and dabbing my eyes with my sleeves. How, in comparison to when we were little, Everything is worse now, and will exponentially worsen the older we grow.

'We're doomed,' Slim says. 'We're all doomed.'

'We've got no future, man,' Morocca says.

'Exactly,' I say. 'All of us in this country, on this land.'

'Wish we were Okey,' Slim says. 'Really, really wish we were him.'

'Yeah.'

We talk about Okey's life, how it's now and forever the opposite of ours. Slim says that he's had night sweats since Wisdom was beaten. That if he were abroad he wouldn't have to look over his shoulder. Morocca talks about Serena, how he doesn't want her to live the life he's lived. How if he goes abroad, he'll quickly land a record deal.

'We need to call The Man,' I say. 'After all, we're going to Niger.'

'Yeah, yeah,' the Scads say.

'In fact, let's call him right now.'

I take out my phone and dial his number.

The phone rings for half a minute, but he doesn't pick up. I dial again. The same. I dial and dial and dial, until he picks up. We talk in Hausa. He says he doesn't do business over the phone, that if we want to talk we must come to Niamey to meet him, that way he'll know we're serious and aren't the police or something. Before I can say more, he hangs up.

'We'll meet him in Niger, then,' I say to the Scads. 'Maybe things will check out and we'll leave this shithole.'

'Yeah, yeah,' they say.

+

It's a quarter-moon this starry night. We're sitting in a circle outside the house: me, my droogs, Fatima, Zahrah, dozens of cousins, grey-haired uncles, chatty or sighing aunts, Grandma. One person is noticeably absent: Mama's twin, my father. But no one wants to talk about it. Like a trapped animal, it's screaming amidst us, at the few of us in the know, but we all choose to look away, to chat about other things. A lightbulb on a nearby pole illuminates us. A generator is blaring yards behind it, wobbling, trying to fly. We're all gathered to celebrate Mama, to share stories about her, to dance and say goodbye.

Nine days ago I knew almost none of these people. But Mama connects us all. She is also with us. Her large photo frame is in our centre, leaning on a stool. The light from the pole reflects off her dimple.

Aunty Omotayo breaks into a song. Everyone — except me and Fatima and my droogs — knows the song. They clap, sing in a slow, droning tune. It's a song about motherhood, but I don't understand a lot of the words. As soon as I arrived that afternoon in Ososo with Mama lying in the back of the bus, I realised that my Ososo is different from the one spoken here, that theirs is more rugged, multi-layered and poetic than the one Mama taught me, that mine is corrupt, full of Hausa words and phrases. For example, I asked Grandma for 'ashana' to light my lantern, and she didn't understand what I meant. I had to tell her 'matches' in English. It was quite shameful. But Grandma was still impressed and thrilled that, despite everything, Mama had taught me Ososo.

When I think of what Mama did, hiding me in the North away from these people to conceal her secret, I don't know whether to forgive her or even blame her in the first place. She thought she was protecting me. But wasn't she protecting herself?

Grandma told me that, just before I was born, Mama privately told her who my true papa was. She couldn't believe Mama because, to her, William was the most faultless son in the world. To be sure, Grandma asked William and he strongly denied it and convinced her otherwise. Soon enough Mama cut off the family completely. The rest of the family thought that Mama's hostility towards them (and William in particular) was from Mama's lifelong bitterness about being denied the educational opportunities William had had. Thus, when Kelani came to Grandma claiming he was my papa, it was easier to believe his lie than Mama's truth. So Grandma went to Kontagora to pressure Mama to introduce me to him. When she didn't succeed, she wrote the letter. But now she hates herself for it, for disbelieving her brave daughter. 'Every day,' she said, 'I try not to hate William. Because of you, Andrew. I know mistakes happen. I'm just so glad you're the result of it.'

Uncle TJ and two boys bring crates of beer and Cokes and Fanta from the house. They place them before Mama's photo as though asking her to see the extent to which they're celebrating her, telling her not to be thirsty wherever she is. A boy trudges into the centre with a plastic jerrycan on his head. Another helps him bring the can down. It contains ato, the Ososo booze made from fermented sorghum. A strong, sickly smell fills the air. Another boy brings a stack of calabashes and places them on the ground beside the can. Some aunts and female cousins rise and begin to distribute the drinks. I'm the first they serve. I take a Coke, and a cousin with an opener helps me with the cap. I hold the bottle, unable to drink, my tongue tasting like wood.

Aunty Omotayo goes to the centre and tells us about Mama. How Mama helped her with her school assignments and, years later, her children. How, after each miscarriage, she told Mama not to lose hope but try again, that one day she'd have a son who'd bury her. She looks at me, smiles softly. Aunty Lizzy wails. Bony Aunty Lizzy. She flings her Fanta and falls off her chair to the ground. A cousin squats beside her, whispering to her that all is well, that Mama is in a better place now.

Several relatives who I don't know rise to talk about Mama, retelling how she paid their children's school fees or lent them money which they couldn't repay or gave them life-changing advice. Aunty Lizzy bursts into sobs each time. That woman. She seems to be the one who misses Mama most. Her sorrows make me more Sorrowful. Remind me of how everything here is Cursed, why I should leave asap.

Aunty Omotayo asks me if I have anything to say. I shift in my seat and my Coke spills to the earth – my libation to Mama. 'No,' I say, shaking my head. She invites Grandma to give the final speech.

'Gloria is the strongest amongst my eight children,' Grandma says. She clears her throat. 'She is the strongest person I've ever met. Despite all that happened to her she is a mother for mothers. She wasn't perfect, I can tell you that. But look at her imperfections today. They have become her legacy. They have become great things. I must confess that, despite how hard I tried, I failed her as a mother. I never truly knew her. Daily, her greatest pain stared at me, but I couldn't see it, wouldn't see it. I will go to the grave with this bleeding sore of failure, my failure of not believing in her, of not knowing her. When a mother does not truly know her child, her bond to the child is a dry stem. Pulseless. Purposeless. Passionless. She becomes unable to truly partake in the child's life. Each breath the mother takes is useless. Time becomes meaningless, irrelevant, a clock without hands. Even if she and her child live for eternity, every second of it is futile, a piece of refuse. So for nine days now I've been sad. Not just because Gloria is gone. But because I failed to know her, failed to partake in her short life, failed to share her pain.'

She gazes unseeingly at us for a minute. Then she picks up her walking stick, walks out of the gathering to the house.

It's time to dance, to send Mama away. They call me to the centre and begin singing and clapping and stamping their feet. They tell me to shake my body, to sing aloud so that Mama will hear. They're singing the song Grandma sent in her letter.

Ọmọ e werọ
Abi shi sugar
Osono yiwọ
Aki kunọ yin ugi
Oghọghọ ọgbọ kpọ sé

I don't know how to dance, where to start. I look at Mama in the frame smiling at me. All eyes are on me. Every mouth singing, hand clapping, foot stamping.

I look up at the moon.

At its craters, its dimples.

It winks.

It hears the scream that I don't utter.

It echoes my Sorrow.

18

Kontagora is full of shadows now. Shadows of trees, of weeds, of the army patrolling in Humvees and tanks. Every day Southerners are leaving. Packing their couches and mats and pots and loading them in semis and speeding back the way they came decades ago. The only difference is that the roads are worse now, and the skin is leathery, flaky, baggy. There's nothing to show for the decades of sweat and blood, decades of being mocked for being Ososo or Igbo, for worshipping wooden crosses and plastic icons.

I'm standing outside Zahrah's house, formerly our house, watching an Igbo family pack. They lost their spare-parts shops and twin sons in the last riot. Now and then the father and mother glance at the sky, hoping the rains won't disrupt their packing.

The skies have been pouring endlessly since Mama left. The town is so battered and full of collapsed buildings and stagnant pools that it smells faintly of fish. In fact, some folks claim they saw small fish and crabs falling from the sky the night Mama died.

That same night, as we departed for Ososo with her body, the Christians launched their reprisal. They stormed the Central Mosque in Ungwan Nasarawa, wielding guns and machetes. But the Muslims were already expecting them, for a Christian who claimed to be a disciple of Jesus' lesson about turning the other cheek had alerted them. The clash lasted just ten minutes, and in the end the Muslims only sustained scratches. The police came later to pack the two dozen headless trunks and torsoless heads.

Afterwards the Muslims went to Lagos Road and burnt kilo-metres of shops owned by Christians and every major church in town, including our cathedral. Luckily Father McMahon was in Niger visiting Eileen's parents, after which he finally fled to Great Yarmouth.

The man yells at his twenty-something daughters. He tells them to hurry, that they cannot take everything, that they must leave before noon so that they'll arrive in Onitsha by tomorrow morning. There is a helplessness in his voice. He must greatly despise himself. He has lived all these decades, toiled and hoped, only to accrue a banality by middle age: that failure is the final stop in every life.

This is why I have to leave this dump of a town, this shithole of a continent. Mama was the only candle flame in its darkness. Now she's gone, taken Ydna with her. And soon Eileen, the only Real Thing, will vanish too. If I don't leave, there'll be no rest for me. Only lifelong regret, one which will eventually lead me to my noose.

I return to the house and continue my own packing. I throw a couple books into my bag, zip it.

My droogs and I are hitting the road for Niamey this morn-ing. When we arrive tomorrow we'll meet Eileen, and afterwards The Man. If for some reason we're unable to leave this shithole, I hope to visit this house one last time, pack up Mama's things, and move to Abuja to live with Zahrah. She insisted I move in with her, that there's nothing here for me. Fatima is already living with her, and if I move in too I wonder what will happen between us. Maybe we'll finally fall in love; maybe we'll become worse enemies. Either way we'll sit for WAEC and JAMB next year and attend one of the shitty unis in the country, and in the end become like Zahrah and Bro Magnus and Elder Paschal.

When I finish packing, I bring out the platinum, finger the strands, raise it to my nose. It still smells fresh, smells like my Eiqueen. I don't spare the house a goodbye glance. I don't look at the *Guernica*-sized painting of Africa in 2*xyz* or the freakish statuettes or the formulae on the floor. I lock the door and bounce past the packing family, my compass fixed on Morocca's. An army

Humvee is approaching. I quickly jump off the road, almost falling into the gutter, and wait for it to pass. I don't fucking want to be arrested again.

+

At Morocca's, Patience insists that she and Serena must come with us. She rants for several minutes, says she's fed up with this dead town. Besides, has Morocca forgotten she's the mother of his girl? What kind of father is he?

'I always care about you and our future,' she says, 'but you don't ever give a shit about me. Instead you're always chasing other girls, other futures.'

Morocca frowns at her. 'It's very risky, Patience,' he says. 'When I go to Europe, I'll come back for you and Serena.'

'Risky my foot,' Patience says. 'My cousin Amaka followed the desert three years ago with her son. Now they're Italian citizens, I swear.'

'Fine,' he says. 'You can come. Just hurry up.'

He takes his bag out to the car. Patience takes Serena to their room to pack and change. Slim is still on the couch, sketching abstract figures on a notepad, applying techniques he learnt from the paintings we saw in Abuja. I bring out my phone and reply to a chat from Eileen. I tell her that yes, I'll see her tomorrow Tuesday. Her flight to Heathrow is on Wednesday morning. I wish we had like a week to shack up together. She says she's booked us (i.e. including my droogs) a dinner at a wicked Mediterranean restaurant near the hotel where she's chillaxing with her parents.

Morocca swaggers into the room, freestyling some red-hot bars, insulting the government and police for fucking him up in Abuja. He sits and we call WALL-E and give him spoilers of our plans. Okey says it's the best plan ever! But he'll call us later 'cause a couple customers just walked into the restaurant. We spend the next several minutes scrolling through his Facebook, deleting him from his pix, and inserting ourselves, until Patience brings us back to shitty reality. She lumbers into the living room dragging a huge Ghana Must Go. Morocca shouts bloody hell, tells her to reduce the items, that we must go as light as possible.

'When we get to Europe,' he says, 'clothes ain't gonna be a problem.'

+

For a long time on the road, it's Okey we talk about.

'How did that nigga with those mosquito legs go abroad before us?' Morocca says. 'I can't fucking understand it.'

'It's not that he's smart or has a talent,' Slim says.

He's in the passenger seat, and beside me are Serena and Patience. Serena is reading an abridged version of *The Swiss Family Robinson*, Patience is skimming social media on her phone. Now and then Serena disregards us and reads aloud, giving us updates about the voyage of the Swiss family. I wish I could tell Morocca to cut down on his swearing because of her.

'This life makes no fucking sense,' Morocca says. 'How could such a nigga make it and we're still here eating eba and drinking this hot sun?'

'Don't know, man,' Slim says, yawning.

Morocca yawns after him. Patience too, hers loud and annoying. I try to stifle mine, but I fail. We laugh. Morocca yawns again, loud like the shark he is. Serena doesn't yawn, her eyes on the page.

We're close to Yauri. From here we can see the River Niger in the distance running across town, a long gleaming diamond in the horizon. It's really cool, the way it ripples in the sun like numberless ballerinas pirouetting. Again I remember Eileen, the diamonds of her body, her smell.

In Yauri we stop at a Mai Shayi joint. It's nearly noon, and a few peeps are still on the benches drinking tea and eating omelettes. We sit on a long bench facing the tall table stacked with bread and crates of eggs and towers of tin Peak milk and sachets of Cowbell chocolate drinks. The Mai Shayi, in faded t-shirt and trousers, is ecstatic. He asks us what he'll prepare for us. I order tea and two packets of Indomie and two-egg omelettes for the four of us. For Serena I order a tea, a small

Indomie, and a one-egg omelette. The Mai Shayi laughs and lights his two kerosene stoves and begins to process the order, whistling a soyayya tune. He soaks the Indomie in hot water, drips oil into a pan, chops tomatoes and peppers. When he's done he serves us with plastic plates and forks, and we dig into the hot yummy noodles swimming in tomatoes and rings of onions. The Indomie is simply dynamite. Tbh, Mai Shayis are the best cooks of noodles in the entire solar system! Sad that we'll miss this when we get to Europe. Still, it's effing worth it. My droogs hammer into their plates, and in a minute they're already halfway. Cars zoom past us, hurrying to Jega and Sokoto. I excuse myself and go to a Mai Suya a couple yards away and buy a thousand-naira suya and take it to my droogs. Patience says thank you, thank you, pushing away her Indomie and delving into the barbecued meat, her favourite Hausa dish. She mocks Morocca, says he doesn't take care of her, never buys her suya like a dude should do for his babe. We laugh. Serena doesn't like the suya, can't even finish her first bite. She returns to her book, reading in the glare of the sun, none of us discouraging her. I give a passing almajiri some money to get us Cokes and Sprites, and when he returns I tip him. We eat and laugh and drink and hope we'll soon be like Okey. Morocca says that the first thing he'll do when he goes abroad is to buy a giant chocolate sundae for his little girl. Soon after that he'll land a job and buy her lots of clothes, lots of shoes. Take her to the lush islands and beaches in Spain. Take her to watch Real Madrid matches. He asks her whether she wants all these things. 'Yes,' she says. 'I want clothes and shoes and books and teddy bears. I want plenty, plenty money!' We laugh.

I pay the Mai Shayi and we walk to the River Niger, stand, hands on our hips, gazing at its endlessness, at the little shirtless boys fishing in canoes in the distance. The wind blows and the water ripples, crystals in the sun, and I go to a fisherman on the shore and ask him how much he'll charge to give us a short ride.

Slim, Patience, and I help the fisherman launch the canoe into the river. The water laps so sweetly around my legs. We jump into the canoe after the fisherman and he paddles further into the water with his great oar. The world wobbles around us; it's so cool. Morocca is on the shore holding Serena by the hand. We laugh at him. 'Y'all should come back here real quick,' he says, looking very scared. 'You'll drown!' We laugh louder at him, at his childish fear of water. The fisherman also laughs at him, wondering how a grown-up boy like him could be so afraid of water. I laugh, the wind singing in my ear, sounding like Eileen. I laugh and laugh.

+

We drive past Jega, Tambuwal, broken bridges, mud houses, market stalls. Suddenly the engine begins to hoot and cluck cluck cluck, the car shooting forward, dying, shooting forward, dying. The engine utters a loud fart and dies completely. We jump out, while Patience and Serena remain in the car, Patience hissing and fanning herself with her hand. We push the car to the side of the road. Morocca says fuck fuck fuck and crawls under it as though he's lived a secret life as an engineer. Slim rests his back on the car, takes out his phone. I pace around a little, finger the platinum in my pocket, take out my phone. It's almost five. We spent too much time in Yauri. Five minutes pass, then ten, then fifteen. Morocca is banging something under the car.

Patience comes out, sunglasses in hand. 'Why are we not moving?' she says. 'What are you doing there, eh, Morocca? When did you become a mechanic? I don't want to spend the night here o! Better come out of there now. Better find some-one who will repair this mumu motor o.'

Morocca comes out without arguing. He's panting, dripping sweat like a Christmas goat. His hands are darker than tar, the back of his shirt has thorns and leaves and dirt clinging to it.

We decide to get help. For forty minutes no car passes. 'This is strange,' Morocca keeps saying. 'This is so strange. This is supposed to be one of the busiest roads in Naija.' As if to prove him right the cars start to rush past, their speed riffling our brows and shirts. We wave and cry out. But none stop.

'It's the rain,' Slim says. 'They think it's about to rain. The roads are bad and they're trying to reach their destinations asap.'

We gaze at the clouds, mascara-dark and bulbous, as though seeing them for the first time.

The skies begin to pour. We cram in the car, our breaths steaming on the glass. Morocca wipes it now and then with a dashiki rag. Outside, it thunders. The skies hurl buckets on us without pause. Lightning lashes at us as though we've committed some huge mortal sin for embarking on this journey. We lose signal on our phones, and we begin to drift off to sleep.

A vibration in my pocket wakes me. I see a chat from Eileen. It's almost four in the morning. I wipe the glass. Now it's just a lazy drizzle outside. I scratch the sleep from my eyes and read the chat. Eileen says that her flight has been rescheduled, and she'll be leaving by six this evening. She asks if I can still make it in time, make our grand parting dinner.

I reply that I can, even though I don't know how to make the miracle happen. From our studies of Google Maps, it would take at least seven hours to drive from Sokoto to Niamey, not including obstacles such as bad roads and checkpoints. In fact, we aren't even in Sokoto yet and this bloody car has died in our hands.

My giant hiss wakes everyone. They ask me what's wrong and I feed them the news.

'Don't give up yet, man,' Morocca says.

'I don't think this is gonna work,' Slim says.

'Shut up, you. What d'you know about driving?'

'I know simple maths, at least.'

'The problem is how to get this car running again.'

I drum my fingers. 'Okay,' I say. 'First, we'll have to skip our stop in Sokoto. I'll see my . . . my mother's twin some other time, I guess.'

'Yeah, yeah.'

'But, Morocca,' I continue, 'you must have someone to call. Call some drivers you know in KNT. Get them to call their contacts. At least one of them should know how to find us a mechanic.'

'Good idea, Werdna.'

Morocca takes out his phone and starts to ring a driver.

I look out the window, at the numberless cascading needles. I think of Mama, of her teeth stained with palm oil. During early-morning rainfalls while I slept, she'd shoo her sleep, get up. Using a torchlight she'd take our empty basins outside, place them below the eaves to catch the rain. And this is the water we'd drink and cook with afterwards. The water often had a sweet acid taste, like the taste of her fingers those times she put some food in my mouth. Now, I want to put out my hand. Catch some of the rain. Taste Mama in it. But I stop myself. If she were around she wouldn't let me travel to Niger, of course. But now that she's on the same infinite dimension as HXVX, I'm sure she's cheering me on as I flee from its reach.

+

Two hours later, cars still swishing past, the drizzle unceasing, a car full of passengers parks in front of us. The driver comes out with a toolbox, walks to our car, asks Morocca in Hausa if he's Morocca. 'Na'am,' Morocca says, getting out. Together they open the bonnet, work for several minutes. Meanwhile I dip in and out of sleep. Patience and Serena are sleeping, the latter resting her head on her mama's lap.

There's daylight now. But it's droopy. Because of the thick swirling leaky clouds.

The driver shuts the bonnet, tells Morocca he's confident of his work. He says goodbye to us, returns to his car, and drives away.

Patience and Serena wake up, both yawning. Morocca gets back in, cursing the driver under his breath, doubting his work. He starts the engine and it roars to life. He smiles. Deep sigh.

I laugh, slam the seat. We take off, flying in the rain, headlights illuminating the drops. We pass Sokoto, its multilane streets which remind us of Abuja, pass Gidan Madi and Bamgi and Kafin Sarki, Morocca tossing twenty-naira notes to police at checkpoints. 'These police,' he says. 'They ain't even turned off by the rain.'

It stops as we approach the border just after Satuka. Two officers in dust-coloured camo rise from their plastic chairs on the side of the road and trudge to the centre, clutching rusty rifles as we approach. Morocca tells them in Hausa that we're students of Sokoto Polytechnic and are just returning home to Bado in Niger, where our families live. They don't give a damn about his story. 'Anything for the boys?' they say. Morocca digs into his back pocket and pulls out two fifty-naira notes. One takes the money with a yawn and rolls it into a ball, while the other opens the low rusty gate in front.

'Motherfuckers,' Morocca says after we pass.

'Fools,' Slim says.

Patience hisses, raising her phone. 'No network.'

We speed on. It's strange: we're in a different country, but it still feels like home. The only difference is the sparseness of things around here; the few trees sprinkled about are thorny with thin leaves. We keep racing, raising dust, people on the roadside looking sweaty and grimy in rag kaftans and chadors. I finger the platinum in my pocket once more.

I try to picture our future, five years after leaving Nigeria and Africa. I'm twenty-one, my droogs and Patience a year older. They and Serena are now Spanish citizens. We're meeting this evening for dinner in a deluxe restaurant in Madrid. Morocca has finally gotten his record deal, and after our dinner he'll perform some of his hits in a club near the restaurant. Slim and his Spanish boyfriend have finished art school and they've just concluded their first major exhibition. Patience works at an insurance company; Serena is in primary school getting excellent grades. Eileen and I have just flown from the UK to see them. We're holding hands, heading to our rendezvous. I'm studying for a master's at Oxford, and we've just come to tell them of our engagement.

I sigh. Look outside. At the mud huts. The refuse dumps. The scanty dusty trees.

Just as we arrive in Dosso, the car breaks down again. I check my phone. Eileen leaves in three hours, and it's supposed to take two and a quarter hours to reach Niamey. We'll definitely not make it. Maybe this is the end of Everything, of Eileen and me.

'Fuck,' I say. 'Fuck fuck fuck!'

Serena turns to me, her eyes sad. I look away. Like maggots, shame eats my insides.

I shut my eyes. And the harder I shut them, the clearer I begin to see. All over us, around the car, on the road ahead, I see a hundred tentacles of HXVX. Trying to frustrate us. Pushing us back home, back to our cages.

+

After managing to find a Samaritan mechanic and fixing the car, we hit the road again. Fly like never before. Drivers honk and curse us. People on the roadside scream we're going too fast. I drum and drum my fingers, tap and tap the floor with my feet.

In Niamey, Eileen messages to say she'll be boarding in thirty minutes, that things are so slow here. Morocca stops to ask for directions to the airport.

+

I run into the departures wing, my white shirt brown with dust and soot, my blue jeans red with mud from the rain, my reflection in the glass pure shit. But I don't stop. I scan my phone for directions, run left, run right.

And there she is. In a red dress and heels. Platinum long and full behind her back. Scanning through her phone. She dials my number. My phone vibrates but she doesn't hear. About ten yards away from her are a middle-aged white couple. Her parents. They're reading a flyer. Her father is the blonde, but his shade is much darker than Eileen's, more like dark gold. He's really handsome, though, in fact better-looking than his wife. She's a brunette, as tall as her husband.

I'm suddenly afraid. How could I dare walk to this flawless seraph before me, looking like the pig and ape that I am? She'll scream. Deny knowing me. Security will appear, whisk me away, throw me into another cell.

I move closer to her.

'Eileen,' I say.

She turns. Looks at me up and down. Covers her mouth in shock. Runs to me and hugs me.

I sniff her. She sniffs me.

Her parents are looking at us, at me, wondering who the hell this dirty nigga is, hugging and staining their seraphic love-of-their-life.

'Andy,' she says.

'So happy to see you.'

'Me too,' she says. 'You smell great.'

Is she lying? Is she trying to be nice?

'What happened?'

We slowly break off.

'Long story,' I say. 'Very long story, Eileen.'

I want to call her babe, my pretty baby, but dare not. Her meadows and perfect skin and expensive dress are beyond my league, beyond the league of this whole land.

'You'll tell me everything when I get onto my flight, then.'

Her parents come to us. Her father is wearing a blazer and jeans, her mother a cream dress. They smile at me. They look at her and back at me, expecting her to introduce me. Eileen just blushes. She scans her phone, opens an app, presses the power button, pockets the phone.

'Hello,' her father says to me. He stares at me from head to toe, focuses on a patch of mud and soot on my jeans. Is he looking at my zip area? Have I peed on myself?

'Hi,' I say to him.

Still Eileen doesn't say a word.

Say his name is Andy, Eileen. Say he's your new boyfriend. Say he's not always shabby like this, that it's the fault of this Cursed land, of HXVX.

Are her parents super-strict? Will they ground her if they know she's dating me?

Her mother looks at me again, this time uninterestedly, assuming I'm a porter or something who loves hugging white chicks. She tells her daughter it's time to board.

'Okay, Mum,' Eileen says, and starts walking away with the two of them. On her fifth step Eileen turns, waves at me, blows me a kiss. Her parents don't see any of this. I raise my hand to wave, but it just hangs in the air.

They go through a glass door. She turns and waves again. But my hand is motionless in the air.

I realise my hand has been hanging in the air when an officer comes to me and asks in Hausa why I'm raising my hand, and, in fact, what the hell am I doing here? 'Are you a cleaner or something? Is this how you do your job?'

He escorts me out of the glass doors, out of the air conditioning, into red-hot earth. 'Don't you ever come to this airport again. You hear me?'

Eileen is ashamed of me. She couldn't even introduce me to her parents. Perhaps all she feels for me is pity. The pity one shows for an abandoned dog or cat. The pity that they are a dog, that they are a cat.

I walk like a lamb down the dusty road, sun roasting my neck, people in suits and kaftans staring at me. I want to take out the platinum and throw it away, but I am weak. So I try to summon Ydna. But there's just emptiness on the other end. I think of Mama. Call up her mustiness. She'd probably be alive if Eileen hadn't come to holiday, if Father McMahon hadn't thrown her a party.

Every moment on this land is a curse. Mama died of the Curse. I'll die of the Curse. Unless I leave.

+

My droogs and I are talking to The Man. We're standing in a motor park under a mango tree debating the price. The amount he mentioned is so steep we can't afford it. There are dirty old buses around us, sweaty passengers leaning on them, waiting for other passengers to arrive. Girls in chadors are hawking bananas and Cokes on their heads, calling customers in Hausa and Zabarma. There are peanut shells and date seeds and banana peels everywhere on the dusty ground. Above: clear skies, sunset approaching.

The Man's maroon kaftan is faded, its buttons undone, his hairy chest contrasting with his bald skull. He must be an alhaji because he's got a gold tooth.

He tells us that he's ready to move in two hours, that he only has room for four in his pickup, but that he could find a way to fit us in if we pay what he asks. He nods at Serena holding Patience's hand. 'There are a dozen people on the way that I need to pay off, na rantse,' he says, his eyes red and dilating, swallowing us. 'The land of the white man is very, very far. In the end it's only a quarter of the money that will be mine, na rantse da Allah.'

We call him mai gida, beg him to reconsider. Tell him that even if we gave him all our savings, we'd still be unable to raise the amount he mentioned.

He suddenly becomes annoyed. 'You boys don't know what you're talking about, do you? Do you even know where you want to go to? Do you know it will take at least two weeks to get there? You're not serious – you're only wasting my time. Many people are fighting for this opportunity, for this special route. When I go, you'll never hear from me again.' And he begins to walk to his pickup. We follow him, beg him. He starts his engine, begins to drive away. Morocca calls after him, offers to add the car. The Man stops, asks to see it. He walks around it, kicks the tyres, opens the bonnet, checks the dashboard. Morocca hands him the key. He tests-drives by the side of the road.

'Okay,' he says, coming out to us, handing Morocca the key. 'Okay. This might work.'

He tells us to go to the ATM down the street and withdraw the money and wait for him here. He'll come pick us up at eight.

'Mun gode, alhaji,' we say, almost bowing. 'Mun gode. Allah ya bada lada.'

'Ameen,' he says, walking to his dusty pickup.

He enters the pickup, starts the engine, looks out of the window at us. 'Nigerians,' he says, shaking his head, flashing his gold tooth. 'These Nigerians.'

19

This is the Sahara: Emptiness. Endlessness. Everywhere you turn. Far into the distance. Miles and miles. No plants. No cars. No markets.

Just sand. Sand and sand. Yellow. Or is it brown? Or is it amber, flaming amber?

There is sand everywhere. In your nose. Your hair. Your pores. Your dick.

Sand.

A tree every mile. Leafless.

Far, far in the distance, there are mountains. Of sand. Of rocks. The air is an oven. Smells of nothing. Just dust. Dust!

This is the third day of our journey. We've been driving and driving. We only stopped to sleep last night and only for a couple hours. We're twenty-four in the back of the pickup. We the ten boys and men sit on benches on the edges of the truck, our legs dangling outside, our hands gripping sticks nailed to the benches so that we don't fall off. The fourteen girls and women are in the middle, all wearing chadors. The driver and his mate in the passenger seat insisted they all wear chadors so that they don't 'draw attention'. Most of the women are Nigerians. My droogs and I are the only Nigerian guys. Three of the men are from Ghana, the others speak Hausa or French or Arabic or languages I don't know. We men have beanies on and handkerchiefs tied round our noses and mouths. The tyres and wind hurl dust at us. We struggle to breathe.

'My ass is kicking the bucket, man,' Morocca says from my left.

'You know nothing,' Slim says from my right. 'My legs are hurting like shit. They feel like they'll fall off any moment.'

Their eyes are insanely red. They look like monsters. I'm sure I look like a monster too.

We shake our heads. I'm also hurting like mad, especially my neck and lower back. The woman behind me has been resting her body on me since yesterday. The one beside her has been stabbing my sides with her elbow. I've pushed away the elbow many times to indicate my discomfort, but she keeps hitting me. I'll have to tell her to stop asap.

Since we set off, my droogs and I have been mostly silent. When we do speak, we talk about the life ahead. The food we'll eat, the places we'll visit, the jobs awaiting us. Morocca talks about how he'll become a superstar rapper there; I talk about the libraries and books and schools I'll be able to access; Slim Whispers about Freedom, how he'll finally date freely without being beaten or stoned. The night before we left we called Okey to update him on our plans. Okey woohooed and wawued, said it was the perfect choice, promised to meet us at the camp in Spain. 'I'm so happy for you guys o,' he said. 'Your lives will be changed forever. Seriously. See my own life here, eh? See as I dey ball here. Dat our country na shit, I dey tell you. Na shit.'

I check my watch. It's nine. Two and half hours since we set out today. The sun is already like noon, like three times the noon in Kontagora.

'When will this journey ever end?' Slim says.

'Hmm,' Morocca and I say, our new catchphrase, our last resort to all conversations.

'Guys, look at that.' Slim points at something we've just passed.

'What's that? Is that a skeleton?'

'That's a human skeleton, damn.'

The Ghanaian man beside Morocca hisses. 'Is that the first one you've seen?'

'Yeah.'

He shakes his head. 'That's the fourth one I've seen now.'

It's a skeleton, a real human skeleton. Grey and sharp and screaming. Trapped in the sands. This is the first time I've ever seen one.

+

We drive.
And drive.
And drive.

sun like a stove
wind like witches

We drive.
And drive.
And drive.

it is
new sand
we meet

+

I think of you, Mama.
I think of you every day.
I think of all the jokes you told me.
I think of all the lies I told you.
I think of your laughter.
I think of your frowns, your smell.
I think of your box at home, full of your photos.
Under the photos, there are funeral programmes you gathered.
Every burial you attended, you kept the programme safe in your box.
Why did you do that? How long had you been thinking of leaving?
I think of your silences when I asked you questions.
I think of your mysteries.

I think of you, The Unnamed.
I do not need to think much.

Because I am Ydna.
And you are Andy.

I try to think of you, Eileen.
I try to find what to think.

+

We pass three sand dunes, each the height of a grown person. We pass a crop of massive rocks which reminds us of Ososo. The tallest of them has incisions like lettering on its side.

The driver slows down, then increases speed. He and his mate are having a laugh in the cab. Ahead of us, hard stony earth. The truck jerks left and right. The little water in my belly jerks too.

Morocca the Sand Lord leans back, asks chador Patience how chador Serena is. Patience is silent for a while, and then she says that Serena the Sand Lady is sleeping.

In the distance are huge twin sand dunes. As we approach, we see a dead tree several yards away from it, and dots of people under it.

The driver stops before them, pokes his turbaned head out the window. There are two men in dusty shirts and trousers and three women in sweaty chadors. The driver speaks to them in Arabic, smiles, laughs. They talk for some time, then appear to argue. The driver comes out, walks to us, scans our faces, scratching his nose.

He smiles, flashing his gold tooth. He tells my droogs and me in Hausa to come down, and Patience and Serena too.

'There's been a mix-up somewhere,' he says. 'It appears that your names are not on the list.'

'What list?' I say.

'What list?' Slim and Morocca say.

'It's a list we use on the route to prevent people from cheating us and prevent the officers from spoiling our business. I tried getting your names on the list, but my bosses removed them. That's why these people are here,' he says, pointing at them. 'You know, I'm just a driver. I follow orders.'

A long silence.

He smiles again, shows off his gold tooth. 'Please just come down let's resolve this, don Allah.'

'We are not coming down,' I say, pulling off my hat, my face itchy. 'We paid for our journey on this truck. You will deliver on your promise.'

I gave him all my prize money to help pay for our fare.

'No, mai gida,' Morocca says. 'You cannot treat us this way. How can you tell us to come down? Where do you want us to go in this place?'

'That is exactly what I am saying,' the driver says. 'These people here paid for the places you've been occupying even before you did. In fact, they paid much more. That's why their names are on the list. In truth, everybody here paid more than you did. Out of kindness, after you kept begging me, I decided to give you a discount and try getting your names on the list. I did my very best, I swear. But my bosses were not convinced, and now they have put your names on another list. Your car is coming for you, in sha Allah. We operate a large network, can't you see? We're God-fearing people, na rantse. We keep our promise. I'm sure your names are on the next list, na rantse da Allah.'

We know he's trying to get rid of us because we're the young-est and the most disposable of the passengers.

We tell him we won't come down. That he must take us to Algeria and help us cross.

He folds his arms, grinds his teeth. He turns to the other passengers. 'I swear by almighty Allah,' he says, dipping his fore-finger onto his tongue, 'if these people don't come down I won't move one inch.'

He walks away to the tree. Sits in the tiny shade by the trunk amidst the two men and three women. He splays his legs, brings out a kolanut from his pocket and begins to munch, whistling a tune.

The other passengers in the truck beg us to come down.

'Please come down,' they say.

'Ku sauka, don Allah.'

'You people should come down abeg,' a middle-aged Nigerian woman says to us. 'The driver says another car is coming for you people. Why don't you just come down and let us go?'

We don't.

'You want us to die?' Patience screams, her voice breaking. 'Look around here. Does this look like a place where cars pass?'

Serena begins to cry.

'Then how did those people get here?' the woman responds.

'None of our business,' I say. 'Why are you people so wicked? Can't you see that the driver is lying?'

'Just come down first, joor,' another Nigerian woman says.

'You guys should obey before complain,' a Ghanaian man says.

'Just obey the driver,' another says. 'He has promised you another car.'

The other men speak French and Arabic to us, indicating with their fingers that we should get out.

'I don't even know why you little children want to go to abroad sef. What are you looking for? What do you want?'

'Shut your mouth!' Morocca shouts. 'We ain't coming down. We paid for this ride.'

'How dare you tell my sister to shut up.'

'When did she become your sister?' Morocca says to the Ghanaian.

He hisses, jumps down from the truck. He's quite tall and muscular. 'Is it because we're trying to reason with you?' he says.

The Ghanaians and the other men jump down. The men under the tree join them. In a flash, the tall Ghanaian drags Serena off Patience's arms and throws her onto the sands. This prompts Patience to jump out. Two men hurl Morocca off his seat; the lanky Ghanaian pulls Slim by his collar and throws him out. The driver is laughing under the tree, flashing us his gold tooth, the incisor of HXVX. I cling tightly to the stick between my thighs.

A punch strikes me on the back of my head. A slap. Then another. I find myself on the ground.

The sand is madly hot. It scorches my hands, my neck. I sit up quickly.

Slim and Morocca are writhing and moaning beside me. Patience is screaming. Serena is shrieking and shrieking.

The passengers get onto the truck with the new ones taking our place.

'Just wait here,' the driver says to us. 'A car will come for you, in sha Allah. Believe me.'

He starts the engine and the pickup begins to move. I get up, run after it. I run and run.

The truck gets further and further. Smaller and smaller. Shooting spirals of dust.

I walk back to my droogs, crash onto the sands between them, panting. Once I land, I jerk up again. The heat of the sands barks at me. Curses me. Tells me to flee from it.

+

I tell my droogs and Patience that our best chance of survival is to sit here and wait. That the driver might be right, a pickup might pass soon and take us to Algeria and help us cross. 'Look, we're so far from everywhere. Look!'

We stand gazing around us, round and round. Nothing. Emptiness. Just sand. Yellow sand. And the sand dunes before us, and the dead tree. There are no tracks to follow. We're nowhere. Even God cannot find us.

'We can't give up now,' I say. 'We're so close! If we leave here, a truck might pass soon and we'll miss it. And we can't afford to miss it!'

For several minutes, we keep gazing around us, undecided.

'Let's just wait here,' I say.

A gust blows from the north, spitting dust in our faces. We rub the dust out of our eyes. We cough and cough.

The sky is stark and still. No feather of cloud, no wing of bird. Just emptiness.

Serena cries aloud, says she's thirsty, very thirsty.

We realise we don't have water. We left our backpacks in the truck. We have nothing. Just sand. Sand that we can't eat or drink.

'Fuck,' I say. 'Fuck!'

'We're fucked,' I add. 'We're so fucked!'

307

'This can't be happening. This really can't be happening!'

'Shut up!' Morocca says.

He hugs Serena, pats her head. He hoists her onto his neck, then takes Patience's hand.

'We're leaving,' he says. 'We're going back home.' He points at the distance. 'There's a village near where we came from. We'll go down there. We'll get water, and then head home.'

The last time we passed a village was early this morning. We'd slept at the village, drunk water from a well.

'It's too far,' I say.

'No, it's not,' Morocca says.

'There's no way you can reach it.'

'We'll stay in the shade of those rocks we passed.'

'And then what?'

'There might be water there. I even saw some cacti around the rocks.'

'I didn't see any cacti shit.'

'If we don't find water, we'll stay there till the sun goes down. Then we'll walk to the village.'

'Why are you so sure you can find the way?'

'I'm a driver, remember? And a former Boy Scout too.'

'Let's just stay here and wait.'

'Stay here, then. We're leaving.' He turns to Slim. 'You coming with us?'

I watch my droogs and Patience walk away back south. They begin to grow smaller. Smaller, smaller, smaller. And with each passing moment, I begin to miss them, to feel more alone.

I pace around. What kind of a person am I? Why would I part from my droogs? What if they need me?

What if it's all a lie? What if I stay here for hours and hours and black out and nothing comes?

Minutes pass. Suddenly, I turn and run after them. I run and run, each breath scalding my nostrils. If they're walking to their deaths, then I'd rather join them.

+

We walk and walk and walk.
Serena whimpering.
Our pores leaking.
Sun flaring.
World expanding before our eyes.
We walk and walk and walk.

> And again I think of you, Mama.
> I think of you, The Unnamed.
> I try not to think of you, ———.

We walk and walk and walk.
Walk and walk and walk.
Come into a sea of sand.
Our feet burning in our sneakers.
Our tongues dry as the bark of a tree.
Our breaths scorching like blowtorches.

Morocca trips on the sand, falls. Serena is flung from his neck. She cries out.

We decide to take a break. We sit on the ground. Morocca cradles Serena in his arms. He kisses her. They look so pitiful I want to cry.

I want to tell them that I'm sorry. That I should've known better. That I'm not a good person, not a good leader. I open my mouth. Nothing comes out.

And as I watch Serena, too thirsty to shed a tear, I begin to see how stupid and blinded I've been all along. Blinded by the dreams of blue oceans, of green eyes, of blonde strands. The trucks will never come. Everything has been a long con: My entrance into this black world. The Hollywood flicks. The Man, his smile, his gold tooth.

Maybe it's not too late. Maybe there's something left that I could do, a switch I could flip to make Everything well again. I reach into my pocket. The platinum has to be the switch. It definitely is. All I'll have to do is take it out, flip it.

But I am weak.

I try and try.

Ydna?

. . .

You there, bro?

. . .

I want to do it.

. . .

I really want to do it.

. . .

I get it now.

. . .

I really do.

. . .

Help me.

. . .

Help me, man.

. . .

Help me, Ydna.

. . .

'Ydna.'

. . .

'Ydna!' I scream.

No one even twitches, despite my scream.

I take out the platinum. Stare at it. Hold it out. Let it go.

A breeze takes it. The strands untangle. They flutter up and down, left and right. Disappear into the dust.

I instantly feel better.

I rub the sweat from my face. My droogs and Patience are looking droopy, heads bent, breathing slowly.

I clear my throat.

'All will be well,' I say.

My droogs say nothing.

'Let's just be patient,' I add.

'This feels like a dream I had years ago.

'We'll reach the rocks soon.

'You'll see.

'Let's rest and then keep walking.

'We'll get there soon.

'Thirty minutes or so.

'We'll reach the village tomorrow morning.'

'Yeah, Andy,' Slim says. 'We'll make it. All will be well.'

Serena cries again, says she's thirsty.

'Don't cry, baby girl,' Patience says. 'We'll get water soon.'

'Yes, Serena,' I say. 'We'll soon get water. All will be fine.'

As I reach forward to touch her face, Morocca glares at me. Still I don't stop. I touch her cheek and he yells at me. He hands Serena to Patience, pounces on me. He punches my face and mouth and chest and belly. I don't fight back. 'It's your fault,' he keeps saying. 'It's your fault. Your fault. You brought us here. You caused everything. You and your love of Eileen. Your fault. Your fault. Who the fuck do you think you are? Who do you think you are?'

i am andy africa
greatest of all superheroes
suffering servant
conqueror of the sands
i'm fly!

Acknowledgements

I'd like to thank the following people and organisations:

The Library at St. Michael's International School, Kontagora; every Irish kid/family who donated those books; the SMA fathers and Notre Dame sisters; Bishop Bulus Dauwa Yohanna.

Joseph Kaufman: for those long, long emails; for those aha moments he helped me to see myself in the mirror (i.e. my text editor); my very own Dumbledore (or is it Morpheus?).

The 'Gamma-One Non-Deranged Permutations' research group, especially Dr Kazeem Olalekan Aremu, Dr Abdulkarim Hassan Ibrahim, and Fatima Abdulwaheed Akinola: for those boiling afternoons in the tiny office where we dyed white boards green with equations.

Nick Herbert for 'quantum animism' in 'Holistic Physics – or – an Introduction to Quantum Tantra'; Anthony Burgess for *A Clockwork Orange*; Arwa Damon and CNN for the 4 December 2017 report on the plight of female migrants travelling through the Sahara; the many, many works that nurtured me.

The Booker Prize Foundation: for raising the Lazarus in me.

The UEA Development Office; the UEA Faculty of Arts and Humanities (for the dope studentship).

UEA LDC, especially my supervisors Prof. Andrew Cowan and Prof. Anshuman Mondal; also: Prof. Giles Foden, Prof. Jean McNeil, Dr Julianne Pachico.

The Deborah Rogers Foundation.

Bloomsbury Publishing (UK and US), especially my editors Alexis Kirschbaum and Daniel Loedel; Ros Ellis, Maud Davies, Lauren Whybrow, Amanda Dissinger.

Silvia Crompton, for copyediting; Saba Ahmed, for proofreading.

Nicola Chang, my agent, my very own Zahrah. Also: David Evans, the David Higham Associates.

Troy Onyango and Jekwu Anyaegbuna: for those super-long world-spanning conversations, for those circumnavigations of Norwich.

My mother, my siblings: for those endless, endless sacrifices.

And especially, Tina.

A Note on the Author

Stephen Buoro was born in Nigeria in 1993. He has an MA in Creative Writing from the University of East Anglia as well as a first-class degree in Mathematics, and is a recipient of the Booker Prize Foundation Scholarship. He was awarded second place in the 2020 Deborah Rogers Foundation Writers Award, and is currently studying for a fully funded PhD in Creative & Critical Writing at UEA. *The Five Sorrowful Mysteries of Andy Africa* is his first novel.

A Note on the Type

The text of this book is set in Bembo, which was first used in 1495 by the Venetian printer Aldus Manutius for Cardinal Bembo's *De Aetna*. The original types were cut for Manutius by Francesco Griffo. Bembo was one of the types used by Claude Garamond (1480–1561) as a model for his Romain de l'Université, and so it was a forerunner of what became the standard European type for the following two centuries. Its modern form follows the original types and was designed for Monotype in 1929.